GONE

Lisa Gardner

First published in Great Britain in 2006 by
Orion Books
an imprint of The Orion Publishing Group
Orion House, 5 Upper St Martin's Lane,
London WC2H 9EA

All characters in this publication are fictitious
and any resemblance to real persons, living or dead,
is purely coincidental.

A CIP catalogue record for this book is
available from the British Library

ISBN-13 (hardback) 978-0-75287-306-0
(trade paperback) 978-0-75287-360-2
ISBN-10 (hardback) 0-75287-306-7
(trade paperback) 0-75287-360-1

Printed and bound in Great Britain by
Clays Ltd, St Ives plc

The Orion Publishing Group's policy is to use papers that are natural,
renewable and recyclable products and made from wood grown in sustainable
forests. The logging and manufacturing processes are expected to
conform to the environmental regulations of the country of origin.

www.orionbooks.co.uk

GONE

GONE

1

SHE IS DREAMING AGAIN. *She doesn't want to. She wrestles with the sheets, tosses her head, tries to keep the dream version of herself from walking up those stairs, from opening that door, from entering the gloom.*

She wakes up stuffing the scream back into her throat, eyes bulging and still seeing things she doesn't want to see. Reality returns in slow degrees, as she registers the gray-washed walls, the dark-eyed windows, the empty side of the bed.

She heads for the bathroom, sticking her head under the faucet and gulping mouthfuls of lukewarm water. She can still hear the rain thundering outside. It seems like it has been raining forever this November, but maybe that's only her state of mind.

She goes into the kitchen. Note's still on the table. Seven days later, she doesn't read it anymore, but can't quite bring herself to throw it away.

Refrigerator inventory time: yogurt, tuna fish, pineapple, eggs. She grabs the eggs, then realizes they expired two weeks ago.

Screw it, she goes back to bed.

Same dream, same images, same visceral scream.

One a.m., she gets up for good. She showers, scrounges for clean clothes, then stares at her gaunt reflection in the mirror.

"How do you spell fuckup? R-A-I-N-I-E."
She goes for a drive.

"BABY'S CRYING," he mumbled.

"Wake up."

"Mmmm, honey, it's your turn to get the kid."

"Carl, for God's sake. It's the phone, not the baby, and it's for you. Snap out of it."

Carlton Kincaid's wife, Tina, elbowed him in the ribs. Then she tossed him the phone and burrowed back under the covers, pulling the down comforter over her mocha-colored head. Tina wasn't a middle-of-the-night sort of person.

Unfortunately, neither was Kincaid. Sergeant Detective, Major Crimes, Portland office of the Oregon State Police, he was supposed to be prepared for these sort of calls. Sound intelligent. Commanding even. Kincaid hadn't gotten a good night's sleep in nearly eight months now, however, and was feeling it. He stared sulkily at the phone, and thought it had better be damn good.

Kincaid sat up straight and attempted to sound chipper. "Hell-oh."

A trooper was on the other end of the line. Had gotten called out by a local deputy to the scene of an abandoned vehicle on the side of a rural road in Tillamook County. So far no sign of the owner at the vehicle's site or at the owner's legal address.

Kincaid had one question. "Is the vehicle on public or private property?"

"Dunno."

"Well, figure it out, 'cause if it's private, we're gonna need consent to search the grounds. You'll also need to contact the local DA for a warrant to search the vehicle. So get the DA rolling, buckle up the scene, and I'll be there in"—Kincaid glanced at his watch—"fifty-five minutes."

"Yes, sir."

The trooper hung up; Kincaid got moving. Kincaid had been with the OSP for the past twelve years. He'd started as a trooper, spent some time on a gang task force, then transferred to Major

Crimes. Along the way, he'd acquired a beautiful wife, a big black mutt, and as of eight months ago, a bouncing baby boy. Life was going according to plan, if you included in that plan that neither he nor his wife had slept or chewed their food in over half a year.

Kids kept you hopping. So did Major Crimes.

He could hear the rain coming down in sheets off the roof. What a bitch of a night to be pulled out of bed. He kept two changes of clothes in the trunk of his take-home car. Night like this, that'd get him through the first half hour. Shit. He looked back at the bed with a pang and wished it'd been the baby crying after all.

Moving on autopilot, he dug through the dresser and started pulling on clothes. He was just buttoning up his shirt when his wife sighed and sat up.

"Bad one?" she whispered softly.

"Don't know. Abandoned vehicle over in Bakersville."

"Baby, what's that got to do with you?"

"Driver's-side door's open, engine's still running, and purse is sitting in the passenger's seat."

She frowned. "That's weird."

"Yeah."

"Baby, I hate the weird cases."

Kincaid pulled on his sports coat, crossed to his wife and planted a big one on her cheek. "Go back to sleep, honey. Love you."

Tuesday, 1:14 a.m. PST

SHE CAN'T SEE A DAMN THING. *Her wipers are on high speed, flailing violently across her windshield. It makes no difference. The rain comes and comes and comes. Bend in the road. She takes the turn a little too late and promptly hydroplanes.*

She is breathing hard now. Hiccupping. Is she crying? It's hard to tell, but she's grateful to be alone in the dark.

Easing off the gas, she steers carefully back into the proper lane. There are advantages to being out this late at night. No one else on the road to be punished by her mistakes.

She knows where she is going without ever telling herself. If she thought about it, then it would be a conscious decision, which would underline the fact she has a problem. Far easier to simply discover herself pulling into the parking lot of the Toasted Lab Tavern. Half a dozen other vehicles are sprinkled across the graveled lot, mostly wide-cab pickup trucks.

The hard-core drinkers, she thinks. You have to be hard-core to be out on a night like this.

What is she doing here?

She sits in her car, gripping the steering wheel hard. She can feel herself starting to shake. Her mouth is filling with saliva. She is already anticipating that first long, cold sip of beer.

For one moment, she hangs on the precipice.

Go home, Rainie. Go to bed, watch TV, read a book. Do something, do anything but this.

She is shaking harder, her entire body convulsing as she hunches over the wheel.

If she goes home, she will fall asleep. And if she falls asleep . . .

DO NOT *climb those stairs.* DO NOT *open that door.* DO NOT *peer into the gloom.*

There is so much darkness inside of her. She wants to be a real person. She wants to be strong, resolute, and sane. But mostly she feels the darkness move inside her head. It started four months ago, the first few tendrils fingering the corners of her mind. Now it consumes her. She has fallen into an abyss and she can no longer see the light.

Rainie hears a noise.

Her head comes up.

She sees a large figure loom ahead suddenly in the pouring rain. She doesn't scream. She grabs her gun.

The drunken cowboy lurches past, never knowing how close he came to losing his ass.

Rainie sets her Glock back down in the passenger seat. She is no longer trembling. She's wide-eyed. Grim-faced. A stone-cold sort of crazy, which is far, far worse.

She puts her car into gear and heads back into the night.

Tuesday, 3:35 a.m. PST

BAKERSVILLE, OREGON, was a small coastal town smack dab in the middle of Tillamook County. Nestled in the shadows of the towering coastal range inside Tillamook County. It featured endless acres of verdant dairy farms, miles of rocky beach, and from a detective's point of view, a growing methamphetamine problem. Pretty place to live if you were into honky-tonks and cheese. Not much else to do if you weren't, and didn't the local kids know it.

It should've taken Kincaid fifty minutes to hit Bakersville. On a night like this, with zero visibility, slick mountain passes, and driving sheets of rain, it took Kincaid an hour fifteen. He pulled onto the lit-up site, breathing hard and already feeling behind the eight ball.

In the good-news department, the first responders had done their job. Three strategically placed spotlights glared into the night, high-powered beams slicing through the ribbons of rain. Yellow crime scene tape roped off a decent-sized perimeter, outside of which the vehicles were starting to pile up.

Kincaid noted a deputy's truck, then the sheriff's, then a slick black SUV with all the bells and whistles, which he figured belonged to the Tillamook County DA. They would need more bodies if they decided to launch a full-scale search, and they would need the forensic lab and Latent Prints to process the scene, but those would be his calls to make.

An hour and forty minutes after the first call out, they were still covering the basics: Did they, or did they not, have a crime? Most taxpayers probably liked to think the police went into these situations full bore. Notify the crime lab, bring in the National Guard, call in the choppers. Yeah, well, those same taxpayers kept hacking away at the OSP's budget, until Kincaid now had three and a half detectives working for him instead of the original fourteen. Real-world policing meant all decisions came attached to dollar signs. For better or for worse, these days he was operating on the cheap.

Kincaid pulled in behind the monstrous black Chevy Tahoe and cut his engine. No way around it. He opened his door and stepped out into the deluge.

The rain nailed him square on the forehead. For a moment, he paused, steeling himself against the onslaught. Then, his hair was soaked, the water trickled beneath the collar of his Columbia raincoat, and the worst of it was over. He no longer had to worry about getting muddy and wet; he was already there.

Kincaid trudged around to the trunk of his Chevy Impala, pulled out the giant plastic bin containing his crime scene kit, and ducked beneath the tape.

Trooper Blaney trotted over, black Danner boots splashing through the muck. A good doobie, he was wearing full department-issued rain gear, including a black-and-blue OSP jacket that looked like a biker coat gone bad. No one really liked the jacket. Kincaid kept his stashed in the trunk for the rare occasions the press was around—or a superior officer.

Blaney had obviously been standing outside awhile; his coat looked slick as glass beneath the high-powered lights, while beneath the cover of his wide-brim hat, the water ran in rivulets down his square-jawed face and dripped off the end of his nose. Blaney stuck out his hand; Kincaid returned the favor.

"Trooper."

"Sergeant."

The Tillamook County sheriff and a deputy had followed in the trooper's wake. Blaney made the introductions as they all stood in a rain-soaked huddle, teeth chattering, arms tight against their sides for warmth.

Deputy Dan Mitchell had been the first responder. Kid was young, farming stock, but trying hard. He didn't like the look of things—the open door, headlights on, engine running. Seemed kind of Hollywood to him. So he'd called Sheriff Atkins, who hadn't been wild to be pulled out of bed on such a night, but had headed down.

The sheriff was a bit of a surprise. For one thing, he was a she—that would be Sheriff Shelly Atkins to you. For another, she had a firm handshake, a no-nonsense stare, and apparently didn't feel like beating around the bush.

"Look," she interjected halfway through her deputy's energetic spiel, "Tom's waiting"—she jerked her head toward the DA, who Kincaid now saw was tucked back inside his SUV. "We got a search warrant for the car and, per your trooper's instructions, we've confirmed this is public land. Now, I don't know what the hell happened here, but someone left that car in a hurry, and that's a source of concern for me. So let's get this ball rolling, or there won't be anything left to find but a bunch of soggy police reports."

No one could argue with that logic, so their little scrum moved toward the car, edging carefully toward the open door.

Vehicle was a late-model Toyota Camry, white exterior, blue cloth interior. Nice, but nothing fancy. The driver had pulled well over, conscientiously trying to get off the road. To the left of the driver's door was the winding backwoods lane. To the right was a steep embankment leading up into a heavily shrouded forest.

As the trooper had reported by phone, the driver's-side door was slung wide open, tip of the door scraping the edge of the asphalt. Kincaid's first thought was that most people didn't open their doors that far. Maybe if they had really long legs. Or maybe if they were loading something in and out of the car.

Something to think about.

From this angle, Kincaid could make out the shape of a brown leather handbag sitting in the passenger's seat.

"Did you check the purse?" he asked no one in particular.

"I picked it up," Deputy Mitchell reported, already sounding defensive. "To check for ID, you know. I mean, it just seemed strange to find the car, lights on, engine running, door open wide as day. I had to start somewhere."

"Did you find a wallet?"

"No, sir. But then I opened the glove compartment and found the vehicle registration. I pulled the name off that."

"Purse was empty?"

"No, sir. Lots of stuff in the purse—cosmetics, pens, PDA, etc. But I didn't see anything that looked like a wallet. I placed the purse back just how I found it. Swear to God I touched nothing else."

"Except the glove compartment," Kincaid said mildly, but he wasn't really angry. The deputy was right—you had to start somewhere.

The car's engine had been turned off; the trooper had done it to preserve the tank of gas. Always useful when you found an abandoned vehicle, to see how much gas was left in the tank. But the engine had been running fine when Deputy Mitchell had arrived, and at a glance, there was nothing wrong with the tires. Seemed to rule out pulling over due to mechanical problems.

Kincaid walked to the rear of the Camry, eyeing the fender. No sign of dents or scrapes, though it was hard to tell with everything so wet. He made a halfhearted attempt to look for other tire tracks or footprints. The driving rain had destroyed the ground, leaving nothing but shallow pools of muddy water. Sheriff Atkins's warning had been on the money, but a dime too late.

He moved to the interior of the vehicle, careful not to touch.

"Owner a woman?" he asked.

"According to the registration," Trooper Blaney supplied, "name is Lorraine Conner from Bakersville. Sheriff Atkins sent a deputy to the address. No one answered."

"Do we have a physical description?"

"According to DMV records, she's five six, 120 pounds, brown hair, blue eyes."

Kincaid eyed Sheriff Atkins.

"Five five," she supplied. "I didn't want to touch anything just yet, but at a glance, the seat looks about right."

That's what Kincaid thought, too. Seat was fairly close, about what he'd expect. He needed to check the mirrors, of course, steering column, too, but that'd have to wait until after the lab rats and Latent Prints were done. According to Blaney, the gas tank had registered half full before he'd shut down the engine, so while they'd canvass the local gas stations just to be safe, Lorraine probably hadn't fueled up recently.

He straightened, blinking his eyes against the rain while the wheels of his mind started to turn.

Kincaid had spent his first three years as a trooper working along the coast. It amazed him how many of his reports had started with the discovery of an abandoned vehicle. The ocean seemed to draw people, speak to them one last time. So they'd drive out to the coast, catch that final glorious sunset. Then they'd lock up their vehicle, head into the woods, and blow out their brains.

But in all of Kincaid's years, he'd never seen anyone walk away from a car like this—engine idling, windshield wipers beating, headlights beaming.

Deputy Mitchell had been right. The scene was too Hollywood. It felt wrong.

"All right," Kincaid said. "Let's pop the trunk."

Tuesday, 1:45 a.m. PST

SHE HAS STOPPED PAYING ATTENTION. *She knows this is a bad thing. Once upon a time, she was a small-town deputy, and God knows she's seen exactly what can happen when, even for a second, a person's eyes stray from the road.*

But she is very tired now. How long has it been since she's slept? Hours, days, months? Fatigue has eroded her motor skills. Her short-term memory is shot. She tries to remember what she did yesterday, but the image that swims in front of her mind could have easily been from last week. She can't track time anymore. Her life exists in a vacuum.

The windshield wipers thump, thump rhythmically. The rain beats against the roof of her car. The headlights sway in the night.

When she was younger, fourteen, fifteen, in the days before her mother was shot, she'd had a boyfriend who loved to go out on nights like this. They would find a back road, cut the headlights, and soar the dark.

"HEEEE-hawwww!" he would roar, before taking a swig of Wild Turkey.

Later, they would screw like minks in the backseat, a blur of whiskey, sweat, and condoms.

Thinking about those days, Rainie feels a pang. It has been so long now since she's felt young and wild and free. It has been too long since she's trusted herself to drive blind in the dark.

And then her thoughts veer, taking her to a place she doesn't want to go.

She thinks of Quincy. She remembers the first time they were together. The way he touched her tenderly. The way he held her afterward.

"Rainie," he assured her softly, "it's all right to enjoy life."

And now she hurts. She hurts beyond pain, she cannot draw a breath. Seven days later, it's still as if she's been punched in the solar plexus, and her lips move, but she can't find any air.

The road bends. She's too distracted to react. Wheels spin, brakes squeal. Her car whips round and round and she releases the steering wheel. She takes her foot off the gas. She finds herself letting go, a solitary version of Thelma

& Louise, *waiting to sail into the Grand Canyon, grateful to just get it over with.*

The car spins to the side, whips back to the middle. Old instincts take place, muscle memory from the days when she was an adept, capable police-woman. She catches the wheel. She turns into the spin. She applies the brakes more carefully and eases over to the side of the road.

Then she has a nervous breakdown. She places her forehead against the steering wheel and bawls like a baby, shoulders heaving, chest hiccupping, nose running.

She cries and cries and cries, and then she thinks of Quincy, the feel of her cheek against his chest, the sound of his heartbeat in her ear, and she starts sob-bing all over again. Except beneath her tears is no longer sadness, but white-hot rage.

She loves him, she hates him. She needs him, she despises him. That seems to be the story of her life. Other people fall in love. Other people are happy.

Why is it so difficult for her? Why can't she just let go?

And then the images appear once more in her mind. The porch steps, the opening door, the beckoning gloom . . .

Rainie reaches reflexively for her gun. To fight back, to lash out, to shoot . . . what? She has met the enemy, and it is herself. Which, in her own crazy way, makes her hate Quincy all over again. Because if he had never loved her, then she'd never have to know what she had lost.

Her fingers caress her Glock. And just for a second, she finds herself tempted . . .

A rap on her window.

Her head jerks up.

The universe explodes in white light.

Tuesday, 3:49 a.m. PST

DEPUTY MITCHELL DIDN'T UNDERSTAND the contents of the trunk at first. Kincaid could see the awareness finally penetrate as the deputy turned various shades of green.

"What the hell . . ." The deputy stumbled back, his arm going up as if to block out the image.

Kincaid reached in a hand and carefully lifted the first page of photos. His gaze shot to Sheriff Atkins. "You don't know the name?"

"No, but I just started the job last month. That's really what I think it is?"

"Oh yeah."

"Sweet Jesus." She stared at the abandoned car. "This isn't gonna end well, is it?"

"Not likely."

Kincaid got out his phone and made the call.

2

THUNDER OUTSIDE.

Quincy woke up too fast. His breath caught, his hands grabbing the mattress, his body steeling for the blow. In the next instant, he rolled fluidly onto his side and was up out of the bed.

His chest was heaving. He had to force himself to look at the heavily floral wallpaper, to remember where he was and how he'd gotten here. The conclusion of those thoughts took the rest of the fight right out of him. His shoulders sagged. His head came down. He leaned heavily against the window and watched the rain slash hard diagonal lines across the glass.

He'd been in the cute country bed-and-breakfast for seven days now, which was about seven days too long. The owner was kind, at least. She didn't comment on a lone man renting a room in an inn obviously intended for lovers. And she didn't pry when each morning he quietly asked to extend his reservation one more day.

Where was this leading? When would it end? He honestly didn't know anymore. And that thought left him tired. It made him feel, for the first time in his life, very, very old.

Quincy was fifty-three, at the stage of his life where his dark brown hair held more salt than pepper, where the crow's-feet at the corners of his eyes had dug in deep, where he felt more and more distinguished and less and less handsome. He still ran twelve miles four times a week. He still trained each month at the firing range. Twice in his lifetime he had dealt with serial predators up close and personal, and he wasn't about to go soft just because he'd passed the half-century mark.

He wasn't an easy man. He understood that. He was too smart, spent too much time living inside his head. His mother had died young and his father hadn't been a talker. There were entire years of his life that had passed in silence. A boy who grew up like that was bound to turn into a particular kind of man.

He'd joined law enforcement on a whim, starting his career with the Chicago PD. Then, when it turned out he had a natural gift for pursuing unnatural minds, he'd joined the FBI as a profiler. He'd logged the miles, working over a hundred cases a year, traveling from motel to motel, always studying death.

While his first wife left him. While his two daughters grew up without him. Until one day, he'd looked around and realized that he'd given so much to the dead, he had nothing left.

He'd transferred to some internal projects within the bureau after that, tried to be home more for his girls. He'd even worked on repairing the fractious relationship with his ex-wife, Bethie.

Maybe he'd made some progress. It was hard to know. It seemed the next time he blinked his eyes, he was receiving a call from Bethie. There had been an automobile accident. Mandy was in the hospital. Please, come quick . . .

His oldest daughter had never regained consciousness. They'd buried her shortly before her twenty-fourth birthday, then Quincy returned to his windowless office at Quantico, once again wading through photos of death.

That had been the hardest year of Quincy's life. Worse had been the horrible realization that someone had killed Mandy, and that that same someone now stalked Bethie and his younger daughter, Kimberly. He had moved quickly then, but still not quite fast enough. The killer had gotten to Bethie first, and maybe would've succeeded in killing Kimberly as well, if not for Rainie.

Rainie had fought that day. She had fought for Kimberly, she had fought for herself, and she'd fought simply for the sake of fighting, because that's what she did and that's who she was and he'd never met anyone quite like her.

He had loved that Rainie. He had loved her big mouth, her wiseass manner, her quick-fire temper. He loved the way she challenged him, provoked him, and infuriated the living daylights out of him.

She was tough, independent, cynical, bright. But she was also the only woman he'd ever met who understood him. Who knew that he remained at heart a secret optimist, trying to see good in a world that delivered so much bad. Who knew that he really couldn't give up his job, because if people like him didn't do what they did, then who would? Who knew that he honestly loved her even when he seemed quiet and withdrawn; it was just that the emotions he felt most strongly were not the kind he could put into words.

When Quincy and Rainie had finally married two years ago, he'd considered himself embarking on a new, healthier chapter in his life. Kimberly had graduated from the FBI Academy and was doing well as an agent in the Atlanta office. They spoke, if not as much as some fathers and daughters, at least enough to satisfy both of their needs.

And he'd done the unthinkable—he'd retired. Or pseudo-retired. Retired as much as a man such as he could.

Now he and Rainie worked only a handful of cases, offering profiling services as private consultants to the law enforcement industry. They'd moved to Oregon, because Rainie had missed the mountains too much to ever call anyplace else home. They had even, God help him, looked into adopting a child.

Imagine, becoming a father at his age. And yet he had.

For a brief three weeks, after the photo had come in the mail, he'd even been excited about it.

And then the phone had rung. They'd gone out on the call.

And the bottom had fallen out of Quincy's life for the second time.

He should probably start finding an apartment.

Maybe tomorrow, he thought, but already knew that he wouldn't. Even a brilliant man could be stupid when it came to love.

A soft rapping sounded at the door. The owner of the B&B stood on the other side, looking frazzled. There was a police officer downstairs, she said. The policeman was asking for Quincy. He was saying it was urgent. That they had to speak right away.

Quincy wasn't surprised.

He had learned a long time ago that life could always get worse.

Tuesday, 4:20 a.m. PST

KINCAID RETIRED to the relative shelter of his car, cranking up the heat and working the cell phone.

First, the Special Agent in Charge of the FBI's Portland office. Waking a feebie in the middle of the night was never a great thing, but Kincaid didn't have a choice. The trunk of the abandoned vehicle had yielded a particularly disturbing find: photos of an eviscerated female body, all stamped "Property of the FBI."

He reached Jack Hughes on the first try. The FBI SAC confirmed that Lorraine Conner was a private-practice investigator, who had worked as a consultant for the Portland field office in the past. To the best of his knowledge, she wasn't handling a case right now, but maybe she was working with another office. Hughes passed along the name of Conner's partner for follow-up, asked to be kept updated, then yawned several times before returning to his nice warm bed.

Kincaid had the same luck with his next two calls. He reached the crime lab supervisor and reported their find. Weather was too bad, conditions too wet to warrant sending out a primary examiner, the supervisor reported back. They'd talk again when the car was in a dry, secure location. And then Mary Senate went back to bed. Ditto Kincaid's call to Latent Prints—you can't print a wet car, so hey, when it dries out, give us a buzz. Good night.

Which left Kincaid alone, soaked to the bone, and wondering why the hell he hadn't become an accountant like his father.

He stepped out of his car long enough to touch base with Sheriff Atkins. The sheriff was organizing her local deputies to do a little bushwhacking. In the bad-news department, the rain continued to pour and visibility was about nil. In the good-news department, the

November night hadn't fallen below the low fifties. Still damn chilly if you were wet, but not immediately life threatening.

Assuming Lorraine Conner was out in those woods, stumbling around.

What would make a woman get out of her car on a night like this? Particularly a trained member of law enforcement, on a road this dark, this remote, this daunting? Kincaid could think of some answers for those questions, but none of them were good.

He called the towing company. If the scientists needed the vehicle safe and dry, then by God, he'd get it someplace safe and dry.

The flatbed tow truck came, driver stepping into the deluge, looking at the muddy swamp surrounding the vehicle, and promptly shaking his head. Car was dug in now. Trying to pull it out would spray mud everywhere and destroy what little trace evidence was left.

Car wasn't going anyplace for at least another few hours.

Kincaid cursed, shook his head in disgust, and finally had a bright idea. He found a local deputy with an easy-up tent and sent him home for the canvas. Thirty minutes later, he'd erected the makeshift shelter over the vehicle and its immediate surroundings. Any impressions evidence was no doubt long gone, but hey, a guy had to try. Besides, beneath the cover of the tent, he could at least get to work.

Kincaid started snapping digital photos, getting halfway around the vehicle before Trooper Blaney returned, followed by a second car.

Kincaid watched as the second vehicle parked behind Blaney's cruiser and a man stepped out into the downpour. He wore a London Fog coat that probably cost half of Kincaid's monthly salary. Expensive shoes. Sharp-pressed slacks. So this was Pierce Quincy. Former FBI profiler. Lorraine Conner's husband. Obvious person of interest. Kincaid took a long, hard look.

Quincy didn't waste any time coming over.

"Sergeant Kincaid." The man stuck out a hand, rain already molding his hair to his skull.

"You must be Quincy." They shook. Kincaid thought the profiler had a strong grip, lean face, and nearly crystalline blue eyes. A hard man. One used to being in control.

"What happened? Where's my wife? I'd like to see Rainie."

Kincaid merely nodded, rocking back on his heels and continuing his assessment. This was his party. Best to make that clear now and save them both a lot of pissing wars.

"Nice coat," he said at last.

"Sergeant—"

"Like the shoes, too. Bit muddy though, don't you think?"

"Mud washes off. Where's my wife?"

"I'll tell you what. You answer my questions, then I'll answer yours. Sound like a plan?"

"Do I have a choice?"

"Actually, since this is my scene, no, you don't."

Quincy thinned his lips but didn't protest. Kincaid allowed himself one moment to puff out his chest. Score one for the state guy.

He still should've stayed in bed.

"Mr. Quincy, when was the last time you saw your wife?"

"Seven days ago."

"Been out of town?"

"No."

"Don't you two work together?"

"Not at the moment."

"Live together?"

A muscle ticked in Quincy's jaw. "Not at the moment."

Kincaid cocked his head to the side. "Care to elaborate?"

"Not at the moment."

"Well, okay, if that's how you wanna play it, but see here, Mr. Quincy—"

"Sergeant, please." Quincy held up a hand. "If you really want to make me dance like a puppet on a string, then by all means, you can spend the next few hours putting me through my paces. But right now, I'm asking you, investigator to investigator, where's my wife?"

"You don't know?"

"Honestly, Sergeant, I don't."

Kincaid considered the man for one more minute, then caved with a faint shrug of his shoulders. "A local deputy found her car shortly after two a.m. No sign of her, however, here or at her residence. I'll be honest—we're concerned."

Kincaid saw the profiler swallow and then, just slightly, sway on his feet.

"Would you like a moment?" Kincaid asked sharply. "Can I get you anything?"

"No. I just . . . No." Quincy took a step. Then another. His face appeared pale in the glow of the searchlights. Kincaid started to notice the details he'd missed earlier. The way the London Fog coat hung on the profiler's gaunt frame. The way the man moved, jerky, tight. A man who hadn't slept well in days.

As grieving husbands went, the former feebie put on a pretty good show.

"Maybe you'd like a cup of coffee," Kincaid stated.

"No. I'd rather . . . May I see the vehicle? I can help you determine . . . maybe some things are missing."

Kincaid considered the request. "You can look, but don't touch. Lab hasn't been here yet."

He led the way to the abandoned Toyota. He'd closed the driver's-side door after photographing and recording its original position. Now he opened it back up.

"You've checked the local establishments?" Quincy asked. He sounded clearer now, an investigator turning to task.

"Not really much around here to check."

"And the woods?"

"Have some deputies going through the surrounding area right now."

"All the vehicles, of course," Quincy murmured. He gestured toward the glove compartment. "May I?"

Kincaid went around to the other side of the Toyota and, with his gloved hand, opened it. He already knew the contents from checking it before: half a dozen McDonald's napkins, four maps, and the owner's manual for the vehicle, with the vehicle registration tucked inside. Now he watched Quincy intently study the contents.

"The purse?" Quincy requested.

Kincaid obediently held it open. Quincy peered inside.

"Her gun," Quincy said at last. "A Glock forty, semiautomatic. Rainie generally kept it in her glove compartment, if not on her."

"She always travel armed?"

"Always."

"Where were you tonight, Mr. Quincy?"

"I turned in after ten. You can ask Mrs. Thompson, who runs the B&B. She was downstairs when I first came in."

"She man the door?"

"No."

"So you could have gone out later without her knowing it?"

"I have no alibi, Sergeant. Just my word."

Kincaid changed tactics. "Your wife often go driving in the middle of the night, Mr. Quincy?"

"Sometimes, when she couldn't sleep."

"Along this road?"

"It heads to the beach. Rainie likes to listen to the ocean at night."

"Is that what she was doing September 10, when she got the DUI?"

Quincy didn't seem surprised Kincaid knew of the arrest. He said simply, "I would check the local bars."

"Your wife have a drinking problem, Mr. Quincy?"

"I think you'd have to ask her that."

"Things don't sound like they're going too well."

It wasn't a question and the profiler didn't answer.

"What are we going to find in the woods, Mr. Quincy?"

"I don't know."

"What'd you think happened here, on this road in the middle of the night?"

"I don't know."

"You don't know? Come on, Mr. Quincy. Aren't you the hotshot profiler, the supposed expert on human nature?"

Quincy finally smiled. It made his face appear bleaker than Kincaid would've expected. "Obviously, Sergeant," he said quietly, "you've never met my wife."

3

QUINCY WANTED TO MOVE. First instinct: plunge into the dark under-brush, scream frantically for his vanished wife. Second instinct: at-tack Rainie's car, tear it apart, look for . . . anything. A note. Signs of struggle. The magic clue that would say: Rainie is here. Or maybe, Your wife still loves you.

Of course, Sergeant Kincaid held him at bay. Professional cour-tesy only went so far when you were the estranged husband of the missing person. Instead, Quincy was forced back outside the crime scene tape, where he paced for a bit, getting wetter, dirtier, angrier.

Finally, he retreated to his car. He sat on the black leather seat, staring at his state-of-the-art dash, with its beautiful, wood-grained details, and hated everything about his vehicle.

Rainie was missing. How could he be sitting in a luxury sedan?

He tried to follow the efforts through his windshield, but the rain beat too hard, obscuring his view. Best he could make out was the occasional wink of a flashlight as the searchers bobbed and weaved in the neighboring woods. Four deputies. That was it. Local kids, according to Kincaid, experienced in searching for lost hunters, and the best they could deploy given the current conditions. Come daylight, of course, they would summon volunteers, get the full search-and-rescue effort grinding. Set up a command post, bring in the dogs, break up the surrounding woods into an elaborate network of grids.

Assuming Rainie was still missing. Assuming that four deputies, stumbling around blind in the middle of the night, didn't magically find the needle in the haystack.

Rainie was gone. So was her gun.

He should think. That was his forte. No one anticipated the warped human mind quite like Pierce Quincy. No, other people had a talent for, say, juggling. He got this.

He tried to force his scattered thoughts into order. He thought of past abduction cases. He thought of various schemes used to lure unsuspecting women to their deaths. Bundy favored faking an injury, wrapping his arm in a cast in order to entice young college coeds into helping him carry his books. The Virginia Eco-Killer trailed women from bars, planting a nail behind their rear tire. Then it was a simple matter of following their vehicles until the tire went flat. Hey, lady, need some help?

Others went the blitzkrieg-style approach. Ambush the victim, catch her unaware. So many methods, so many ways it could be done. Middle of the night, middle of a deserted, heavily wooded road. It wouldn't be hard.

But Rainie was armed. Rainie knew better. Rainie had seen the crime scene photos, too.

His train of thought broke down again. He tried to develop a theory, tried to picture what had happened here sometime after two a.m. His mind simply refused. He didn't know how to be the trained death investigator just yet. He was too busy being the shocked, overwhelmed husband.

Rainie was missing. So was her gun. F 140.279

And in those two sentences, Quincy discovered his real, genuine fear. The one he couldn't put into words yet. The one he really, truly couldn't face.

Rainie was missing. So was her gun.

Quincy closed his eyes. He rested his forehead against the steering wheel. And he wished, as he had wished too often in life, that he didn't know all the things that a man like him knew best.

Thursday, three weeks ago, 5:45 p.m. PST

"YOU'RE QUIET THIS EVENING."

He could tell the sound of his voice startled her. She looked up abruptly, blinking as she roused herself from her reverie. Then his words must have finally penetrated; she smiled wanly.

"Isn't that my line?"

He attempted to smile back, entering the great room, but still giving her plenty of space. There had been a time when he would've thought nothing of crossing to her on the sofa. He would've kissed her cheek, maybe tucked a wayward strand of dark chestnut hair back behind her ear. Or maybe nothing even that intrusive. Maybe he would've taken his favorite spot in the wingback chair by the gas fireplace, opening a book, sharing the silence.

But not this time.

"Penny for your thoughts." There was a hitch in his voice; he hated that.

"Just work," she said. She flipped her hair over her shoulder, then uncurled from the loveseat. October was normally a warm, balmy month in Oregon. This month, however, had seen record rainfall, and the endless gray days of drizzle created a chill that seeped deep within the bones. Rainie had already dug out her winter clothes. She wore an oversized, cable-knit cream-colored sweater with her favorite pair of broken-down jeans. The jeans emphasized her long, slim legs. The sweater set off the red highlights in her tumbling chestnut hair.

Quincy thought that she looked beautiful.

"I should get going," Rainie said.

"You're heading out?"

"I'm meeting Dougie. Thought I told you that last night."

"You just met with Dougie."

"That was Tuesday, this is Thursday. Come on, Quince, I told you when this started that it was going to demand a lot of my time."

"Rainie . . ." He didn't know how to say it.

"What?" She finally crossed to him, hands on her hips, voice impatient.

He could see her feet now. Bare, no socks. A row of ten unpainted toes. He was a doomed man, Quincy thought. He even loved his wife's toes.

"I don't think you should go out."

Her blue eyes widened. She stared at him incredulously. "You don't think I should go out? What the hell is this? Surely you're not jealous of Dougie."

"Actually, I have a lot of issues with Dougie."

She started to protest again; he raised a silencing hand. "However, I know Dougie's not the real problem." And just like that, it was as if he'd struck a match.

Rainie stalked away from him, movements jerky, agitated. She found her socks and lace-up boots beside the sofa, sat down defiantly, and started pulling them on.

"Let it go," she said firmly.

"I can't."

"Sure you can. It's pretty easy. Just admit once and for all that you can't fix me."

"I love you, Rainie."

"Bullshit! Love is accepting, Quincy. And you've never accepted me."

"I think we should talk."

She finished pulling up her socks, then grabbed a boot. She was so mad though—or maybe she was sad, he didn't know anymore, which was half the problem—that her fingers struggled with the laces. "There's nothing to discuss. We went to the scene, we saw what we saw, and now we'll work it like we work it. They were just two more murders, for God's sake. It's not like we haven't seen worse."

She couldn't get the boot on. Her fingers were too thick, too shaky. She finally jammed her left foot in, left the laces undone, and crammed on the right boot.

"Rainie, please, I'm not trying to pretend to understand how you feel—"

"There you go again! Another line straight out of the shrink's handbook. Are you my husband, or are you my therapist? Face it, Quincy—you don't know the difference."

"I know you need to talk about what happened."

"No I don't!"

"Yes, Rainie, you do."

"For the last time, let it go!"

She moved to barge by him, laces flapping against the rug. He caught her arm. For a moment, her eyes darkened. He could see her contemplating violence. Rainie, backed into a corner, knew only how to fight. Part of him was encouraged to see her cheeks finally flush with color. The other part of him played the only card he had left.

"Rainie, I know you've been drinking."

"That's a lie—"

"Luke told me about the ticket."

"Luke is an idiot."

Quincy just stared at her.

"Okay, look, so I had one drink."

"You're an alcoholic. You don't get to have one drink."

"Well, forgive me for being human. I stumbled, I caught myself. Surely two beers in fifteen years is no reason to call the police."

"Where are you going tonight, Rainie?"

"To see Dougie. I already told you that."

"I spoke with him this afternoon. He didn't know anything about tonight."

"He's a boy, he's confused—"

"He also didn't know about Tuesday night."

She stalled out. Caught, trapped. The look on her face broke Quincy's heart.

"Rainie," he whispered, "when did it become so easy to lie?"

The fire finally left her cheeks. She looked at him for a long time, stared at him so hard, he started to have hope. Then her eyes cooled to a soft gray he knew too well. Her lips settled, her jaw set.

"You can't fix me, Quincy," she told him quietly, then she pulled her arm from his and headed out the door.

Tuesday, 5:01 a.m. PST

QUINCY SAT IN HIS CAR, peering out into the gloom.

"Oh, Rainie," he murmured. "What have you done?"

4

SPECIAL AGENT KIMBERLY QUINCY liked to hit the ground running. Five a.m. she was rolling out of bed, years of habit waking her the instant before her alarm. Five forty-five she was completing her six-mile run. Six a.m. she was out of the shower, pulling on sleek black pants and a body-skimming cream-colored silk top. Into the kitchen for OJ, toast, and coffee, then she grabbed her jacket and hit the road.

By six thirty a.m., the morning commute was already starting to thicken. Traffic was slow but not stalled. Kimberly liked to use the forty-five-minute drive to compose her mental list for the day. This morning she had some research she wanted to get done, which meant filling out forms for the research analysts. The bureau provided the most powerful firearms in the world for its agents, but heaven help you if you needed access to a computer.

After filling out the research paperwork, she had stacks of boxes to sort through for her latest case: A bunch of high-class art forgeries had turned up in the Atlanta market. Kimberly's case team was trying to identify a connection between the pieces by tracing them back through the various art galleries and dealers.

As someone who already had experience working two serial

killer cases, Kimberly had once envisioned working in the bureau's violent crimes task force or, better yet, counterterrorism/counterintelligence unit. But the fact remained that she was a woman, and white-collar crimes remained the launching point of choice for females in the bureau.

In the good-news department, it looked like one of the task forces was serving a felony warrant this afternoon, and Kimberly had been asked to tag along. Extra bodies always came in handy for these operations, and as her supervisor liked to remind her, it was good exposure for a young agent. So that would add a little spice to the day.

Two years after joining the bureau, Kimberly felt she was finally settling into things. She liked Atlanta; the city was younger, hipper, than she would've imagined, while still retaining its old-fashioned Southern charm. She loved the warm weather; she loved the outdoor culture of hiking, biking, jogging, swimming. And just possibly, she was madly in love with Mac.

They'd been together two years now. Who woulda thunk? A young, ambitious feebie and a slightly arrogant but very cute state detective. It wasn't exactly a traditional relationship. She couldn't even count anymore the number of canceled Friday nights or botched getaway weekends. His cell phone, her cell phone. Seemed like one of them was always being called away.

But it worked for them. They both loved what they did, and they both appreciated the small moments they were able to snatch in between. Speaking of which, they were currently planning on meeting up in Savannah for the weekend. Which meant one of them was bound to be pulled onto a major case at any second.

It kind of made Kimberly curious about the rest of the week.

Now, she parked, entered the office, poured herself a second cup of coffee, and headed for her desk. She had to sashay around the stack of boxes surrounding her chair, then she was ensconced in her little piece of paradise, sipping bad coffee and wielding an FBI agent's most commonly used weapon—the ballpoint pen.

She made it all the way until eight a.m. without her cell phone ringing. Even then, seeing a familiar number light up the digital display, she wasn't worried.

"Hey, Dad."

Connection was bad. First she heard a lot of fuzz, then a crackle, followed by her name. "... Kimberly."

"Dad, I can't hear you."

"Rainie. ... Two o'clock this morning. ... State police ..."

"Dad?"

"Kimberly?"

"You have to switch locations. You're fading out." More crackle and fuzz. Followed by two clicks. Call was dropped. Kimberly sat there glaring at the phone in annoyance. The phone chimed again. She answered it instantly.

"Hey, Dad."

No sound. Nothing.

But that wasn't quite right. She could hear background noises. Something muffled and rhythmic. Crunching sounds. Sputtering. Almost like an automobile.

"Dad?" she asked with a frown.

Heavy breathing. A grunt. A thud.

Then she could hear the breathing again. Closer. Fast. Almost ... distressed.

"Hello?" she tried again.

More white noise. Kimberly strained her ears but couldn't identify an individual sound. She finally thought to check the caller ID again. But this time, it wasn't her father's number.

"Rainie?" she asked with surprise.

Call was breaking up now. She heard more static, a dead spot, then the heavy breathing.

"Rainie, you're going to have to speak up," Kimberly said loudly. "I'm losing you."

Crackle, fuzz, nothing.

"Rainie? Rainie? Are you there?"

Kimberly stared with frustration at her phone but, according to the display, the call wasn't dropped. At the last moment, the hazy white noise returned. Then a strange metallic ping. Bang, bang, bang. Pause. Bang, bang, bang. Pause. Bang, bang, bang.

Then the call was gone for good.

Kimberly closed her phone in disgust. It promptly rang again. This time, it was her father.

"Where are you guys?" she asked Quincy. "The reception is terrible."

"Back roads," her father said. "Outside of Bakersville."

"Well, whatever is going on, you're going to have to start at the beginning. I didn't understand anything you said, let alone Rainie."

There was a long stretch of silence.

"You heard from Rainie?" Her father's voice sounded funny, strained.

"A few seconds ago, she called from her cell—"

"Her cell phone," Quincy interjected harshly. "Why didn't we think of the damn phone?"

Kimberly heard lots of noises now. A car door opening, slamming shut. Her father shouting for a sergeant named Kincaid.

"Dad, you're scaring me."

"She's missing."

"Who's missing?"

"Rainie." He was talking fast, curt, obviously on the move. "They found her car. Two o'clock this morning. The engine was still running, lights on. Purse in the passenger's seat. But there's no sign of her gun. Or, of course, her cell phone. Now tell me, Kimberly. Tell me every single word she said."

And then finally, Kimberly understood. The sound of a moving car, the heavy breathing, the metal pings. "She didn't say anything, Dad. But she was signaling. I think . . . I think she signaled SOS."

Quincy didn't say anything more. He didn't have to. In the silence, Kimberly could picture the thoughts running through her father's head. Her sister's funeral. Her mother's funeral. All the people he had loved who had left him much too soon.

"Mac and I are on the next plane," she said tightly.

"You don't have to—"

"We're on the next plane." Then Kimberly was out of her chair and running for her supervisor's office.

5

"LET ME GET THIS STRAIGHT—your daughter received a call from Lorraine's cell phone."

"Exactly."

"But not from Rainie. Just her phone."

"She never heard Rainie's voice," Quincy reiterated, "but she did hear the sound of someone breathing heavily in what seemed to be a moving car. Then she heard a distinct sequence of metal pings, which Kimberly believes may have been an attempt at signaling SOS."

Sergeant Kincaid sighed. He was standing beneath a white awning covering Rainie's Toyota. He'd been photographing it for the past twenty minutes. Now he was sketching out the position of the seat and mirrors, as well as documenting each dial—how many miles on the odometer, how much fuel in the tank. The sergeant's hair was soaked, his smooth black face was wet; he looked exactly like what he was, a man who'd been pulled out of his snug bed in the middle of the night, to stand in the middle of a rainstorm.

"Mr. Quincy—"

"My daughter is an FBI agent. She's been with the Atlanta field office for the past two years. Surely, Sergeant Kincaid, you are not going to discount the instincts of a fellow law enforcement officer."

"Mr. Quincy, I would 'discount the instincts' of my captain if he came to me with a story like this. All you know is that your daughter received a call from a specific phone; you've given me no proof of who the caller might be."

"It's Rainie's phone!"

"It's a cell phone! People lose them, drop them, share them with friends. For God's sake, my eight-month-old son has already placed a call on my cell phone by holding down one of the speed-dial buttons. It's not so hard."

"Pull the records," Quincy said stubbornly.

"As part of my investigation, I most certainly will. And I'm gonna look at her landline phone, too. As well as her credit card statements and a detailed reconstruction of her past twenty-four hours. You know, I've done this kind of thing before!"

Kincaid seemed to realize how strident his voice had become. He took a deep breath, then exhaled slowly. "Mr. Quincy—"

"I've done this kind of thing before, too," Quincy said.

"Yeah, I know you're the expert—"

"I lost my oldest daughter to a madman, Sergeant Kincaid. He killed my ex-wife, he almost got my youngest daughter. Maybe in your world these kinds of crimes don't happen, but in my world, they do."

Kincaid inhaled deeply again. Quincy could tell the sergeant didn't want to believe him. And in his own way, he understood. Detective work was inherently about playing the odds. And the statistics said that of the 200,000 adults who went missing each year, only 11,000 stayed missing, and of those, only 3,400 were deemed abducted against their will. If Rainie had been a small child, or maybe a college coed, things might be different. But she was a middle-aged woman and an armed member of law enforcement.

Kincaid was here because of two possibilities: one, that the missing driver of this vehicle, possibly under the influence, had wandered into the woods and gotten lost, or two, that the missing driver of this vehicle, possibly under the influence, had gone into those woods and killed herself.

He would investigate all options, of course. But police work inherently started with a theory. Kincaid had his theory, Quincy now had his.

"Okay," Kincaid said abruptly, surprising Quincy. "Just for a moment, let's have it your way. Your wife was abducted from this car; that's what you think."

"I would like to pursue that possibility."

"How? According to you, she carried a piece at all times. Plus she's trained in self-defense. Seems to me, a woman like that doesn't disappear without a fight. Look around, Mr. Quincy. What fight?"

"One: I don't know for certain that she had her Glock. As a general rule, she did keep it on her person, but we would need to conduct a thorough search of the residence to confirm that assumption. Two: we can't, at this point, discount the fact that she may have been drinking, and that may have diminished her capacity to protect herself. Three: look around, Sergeant Kincaid. It's a giant mud puddle, what evidence either way?"

Kincaid frowned, regarded the mud, then gave Quincy a speculative stare. The sergeant, at least, was digging this game.

"All right. Who would do such a thing? Who would have a motive to abduct Lorraine Conner?"

"You mean other than her estranged husband?" Quincy asked dryly.

"Exactly."

"Rainie handled a variety of cases, as a deputy with the Bakersville Sheriff's Department, then as a private investigator, and then as my partner. That put her in contact with a certain segment of the population right there."

"Can you provide us with a list of names?"

"I can try. I'd also contact Luke Hayes, the former sheriff in Bakersville—"

"Sheriff Atkins's predecessor?" Kincaid's voice implied another question.

"Luke decided to step down from the office for personal reasons," Quincy supplied. "I haven't met Sheriff Atkins just yet, but I've heard good things."

"Okay, so Mr. Hayes should be willing to talk about the good old days. What about current cases? Working anything sensitive right now?"

Quincy shook his head. "We've been assisting with a double homicide out of Astoria, but our activities are behind the scenes. If the suspect in question was nervous, maybe he'd target the officer in charge, but not us."

"Wait a minute—you're talking *the* double homicide out of Astoria?"

"We don't get that many around here."

"Beginning of August, wasn't it?" And then, Sergeant Kincaid proved he really was bright. "The September tenth DUI," he murmured.

"The September tenth DUI," Quincy acknowledged.

Kincaid's gaze shot back to the woods, to the thick blackness just beyond the reach of the powerful spotlights. Once again Quincy knew what the sergeant was thinking, but he still couldn't go there. Then again, Quincy had never thought Rainie would take a drink again, so maybe the husband was really the last to know.

"I didn't think there was a suspect in that case," Kincaid said curtly.

"Our analysis revealed one very clear suspect. Last I heard, however, there was no evidence for making the case. The detectives are continuing to work it, of course. As of this time, however, I am not optimistic."

"Shit," Kincaid murmured.

"Shit," Quincy agreed, quietly.

"What about the photos in her trunk?" Kincaid probed. "That looked like a helluva case. Poor Deputy Mitchell is still puking his guts out."

"Nineteen eighty-five. Most of the work we do now is seeing if we can shed new light on an old crime. Sometimes it works, sometimes it doesn't."

"Old crimes lead to new time," Kincaid murmured. "Any murderers out there still have incentive not to get caught."

"True, but how would they know about our work? We're consultants, Rainie and I. For the most part, we operate under the radar screen."

Quincy had flipped open his cell phone. He was trying Rainie's number again. Still no luck. It was ringing though, which told him it was turned on. So maybe the phone was out of range, or in a place where she could no longer reach it.

Maybe she was in no condition to reach it.

He didn't want to have that thought. Rainie had never believed him, but the Astoria case had disturbed him, too.

"So where does that leave us?" Kincaid was asking. "By your own admission, there really isn't anyone out to get your wife."

"Maybe. Well, wait a minute." Quincy held up a hand, frowning. "One, we can't yet rule out a stranger-to-stranger crime. But two, there is an avenue to pursue. Rainie had started some recent volunteer work—"

"Volunteer work?"

"She wanted to become an advocate for foster children. Represent them in the courts; there's an organization you can join . . ."

Kincaid waved away Quincy's explanation. "Yeah, yeah, I've heard of it. So she was going to help kids." Kincaid nodded, showing once again he could read between the lines. "That makes some sense."

"She already had her first charge. A young boy, Douglas Jones. Douglas—Dougie, actually—claims his foster father is beating him. According to the foster family, however, Dougie is making it all up because he's finally met his match in their 'tough love' parenting style. I should add that Dougie already has a long history of theft, animal cruelty, and petty arson."

"How old?"

"Dougie's seven."

"Seven?" Kincaid's brows shot up. "You want me to suspect a seven-year-old?"

"No, no," Quincy said, then added dryly, "though it won't be too long before you may wonder about that statement. Rainie has been assigned to work with Dougie, to basically determine if he's telling the truth, in which case she'll be his voice in court, or determine once and for all that he's lying, in which case she'll try to mediate some sort of resolution between him and his foster family. The father in the case is Stanley Carpenter. Who's thirty-six years old, works the loading docks for the cheese factory, and is rather famous for being able to lift half a pallet of cheese on his own."

"Big guy."

"Very big guy. Interestingly enough, that's his defense in the case. A man his size hitting a boy Dougie's size . . . You wouldn't have to wonder about the abuse. The ME would be documenting it at the morgue."

Kincaid laughed. "That's the craziest damn defense I've ever heard. And yet . . ."

"It makes sense."

"Yeah, it makes sense." Kincaid turned back to the car, more thoughtful now. Quincy had his phone back out. He was compulsively hitting Send. Rainie still didn't answer, but nor did the sound of ringing come from the woods. It gave him the slightest bit of hope.

"She think he did it?" Kincaid asked. "This Stanley guy was beating his kid?"

"She had her doubts. And those doubts could lead to her filing police charges, which for Stanley . . ."

"Would be a very bad thing."

"Yes."

"And a guy that big," Kincaid filled in, "could probably abduct a woman against her will, even someone with training. Assuming, of course, she didn't have a gun."

"Assuming she didn't have her gun."

"All right," Kincaid said abruptly. "That's it. Not like we can do jackshit here anyway until the rain dries out. We're off."

"I get to come, too?"

"As long as you stay in my line of sight, and promise not to touch."

"I'll be a good boy," Quincy assured him. "Where are we going?"

"To find the gun, of course. With your permission, we're gonna search your house."

6

As QUINCY AND KINCAID PILED into Kincaid's vehicle, the sun was struggling to break through a cloud cover so thick, day was only a paler version of night. It felt as if the entire month of November had been this way, one endlessly long day of drizzle, interrupted by periods of torrential downpour.

Quincy hadn't quite gotten used to the Oregon climate yet. He was a New Englander, a man who could take the bracing cold as long as it was partnered with a bright winter sun. Frankly, he didn't know how Oregonians could go so long with rain clouds pressed against the tops of their heads. Rainie always said the gray days made her feel cozy, snuggled up in the refuge of their home. Lately, they had been making him feel like beating his head against a brick wall.

"So when did you and Rainie split?" Kincaid asked from the driver's seat. Apparently, he wasn't one for small talk.

"I moved out a week ago," Quincy said tersely.

"You or her?"

"Officially speaking, I'm the one who left."

"File for divorce?"

"I'm hoping it won't come to that."

Kincaid grunted, already sounding skeptical. "Counseling?"

"Not at the moment."

"Mmm-hmmm. Federal pension, right?"

"I have one, yes." Quincy already knew where Kincaid's thoughts were going. As an FBI agent who'd served the required twenty years, Quincy had retired with full base pay. Not many pension programs like that around anymore. Particularly since most of the FBI retirees were still young enough to keep working in the private sector, garnering an additional revenue stream while building a second retirement program. Double-dipping it was called. And yes, it had worked out well for Quincy. Hence the car, his clothes, his house.

"Divorce would be expensive," Quincy agreed.

"Mmm-hmmm," Kincaid said again.

"You're still not asking the right question, Sergeant."

"And what's that?"

"Do I love her?"

"Love her? You left her."

"Of course I left her, Sergeant. It was the only way I could think of to get her to stop drinking."

They'd arrived at the graveled drive. Kincaid made the hard right turn, tires crunching on the ground stone as they fought for purchase. The driveway was impractical. An absolute bitch during bad weather. Last winter, Rainie and Quincy swore they'd do something about it as soon as it got warm. Have it regraded, have it paved.

They never did. They loved their little wooden castle perched at its top. And without ever saying as much in words, they appreciated the driveway as their own version of a rampart. Not just any vehicle could make it up. And absolutely no one approached their house without being heard.

Kincaid dropped his car into a lower gear and gunned the engine. The Chevy crested the hill just in time to startle a deer feeding on a salt lick Rainie had placed in the garden. The deer crashed back into the forest. Kincaid parked next to a bank of drenched ferns.

He climbed out, already giving Quincy an arched stare.

Quincy and Rainie had found the house just a year ago. It wasn't large, but the custom-built Craftsman-style home presented the best of everything. A towering picture window that offered a panoramic view of the mountains. A crested roofline of alternating peaks and valleys. A sweeping front porch, complete with matching Adirondack rockers.

Rainie had loved the open floor plan, exposed beams, and enormous stone fireplace. Quincy had appreciated the large windows and multitude of skylights, which maximized what little light one could eke out of such gray days. The house was expensive, more than they probably should've spent. But they'd taken one look and seen their future. Rainie curled up in front of the fireplace with a book. Quincy sequestered in the den writing his memoirs. And a child, nationality still unknown, sitting in the middle of the great room, stacking toys.

They had purchased this home with hope in their hearts.

Quincy didn't know what Rainie thought when she looked at their home now.

He led the way up the steps, then stopped in front of the door. He let Kincaid tug at the knob. The door was locked; Rainie never would've left the house any other way.

Wordlessly, Quincy produced his key. Kincaid worked the bolt lock.

The heavy door swept open to a shadowed foyer, light slowly seeping across the stone-inlaid floor. The wooden staircase, with its rough-hewn railing, was immediately to the left. The great room swept open to the right. At a glance, both men could see the vaulted family room with its massive stone fireplace, then, deeper in, the dining area and kitchen.

Quincy processed many things at once: the plaid flannel blanket tossed in a puddle in front of the fireplace; the half-read paperback, lying print-side-down on the ottoman. He saw an empty water glass, Rainie's running shoes, a gray cardigan slung over the back of the hunter green sofa.

The room was disturbed, but nothing that suggested violence. It was more like a scene interrupted—Quincy half expected to spy Rainie walking in from the kitchen with a cup of coffee in her hand and a perplexed look on her face.

"What are you doing here?" she would ask.

"Missing you," he would answer.

Except maybe Rainie wasn't carrying a cup of coffee. Maybe it was a beer instead.

Kincaid finally walked into the room. Quincy drifted in his wake, glad the sergeant was studying the room and not registering the raw look that had to be on Quincy's face.

Kincaid made quick work of the family room. He seemed to register the book, the glass, the running shoes. Then he was in the breakfast nook. The note was still on the table.

Kincaid read it, glanced at Quincy, then read the note again. The investigator didn't say anything, just walked into the kitchen. Quincy wasn't sure if that made the invasion of privacy better or worse.

The OSP sergeant opened the fridge. He caught Quincy's eye, then opened the door wider, until Quincy could see the six-pack. Quincy nodded, and the other man moved on. Not much food in the fridge, but the kitchen was neat. A mug and bowl in the sink. Counters wiped down.

Rainie had never been the best housekeeper in the world, but she was clearly keeping up with things. Not the kitchen of a woman totally lost to despondency. Then again, Quincy had once worked a case of a forty-year-old mom who'd cleaned the house from top to bottom before hanging herself in the bathroom. In her suicide note, she'd included instructions to her husband on how to reheat all the meals she'd left for him and their three kids. The woman—who'd gone off her antidepressants—didn't want to inconvenience anyone. She just hadn't wanted to live.

Kincaid traveled down the back hallway to the study. This was one of the few rooms with carpeting, a thick wool pile that Quincy liked to pace when trying to come up with the right turn of phrase. This was his domain, and walking into it a week later, he caught the faint smell of his own aftershave. He wondered if Rainie had entered this room in the past week. If she had caught that fragrance and thought of him.

The desk was cleared off, the black leather chair neatly pushed in. The room already had a slightly abandoned feel about it. Maybe not a room for remembrance at all, but an omen of things to come.

Kincaid wandered back out and hit the last room of the downstairs: the master bedroom.

This room was more chaotic. The down comforter, covered in a duvet of greens, gold, and burgundy, had been kicked to the foot of the bed. The cream-colored sheets were twisted into a pile, the corner of the room lost to a mound of clothes. The room carried the musty odors of stale linens and recent sweat.

And because Quincy knew Rainie better than he knew his own heart, he could look at each item in the room and see clearly what must have transpired in the middle of the night. The tossed covers from another bad dream. The skewed lampshade from when she'd fumbled for the light.

Her trek to the bathroom, kicking aside socks and jeans along the way. The mess around the sink as she tried to clear the dream from her mind with water on her face.

The water hadn't worked, though. At least it hadn't when Quincy had still been around. She'd scrub her face while he watched her from the open doorway.

"Would you like to talk?"

"No."

"It must have been a bad one."

"All nightmares are bad, Quincy. At least they are for us mere mortals."

"I used to have bad dreams after Mandy died."

"And now?"

"Now it's not so bad. Now I wake up and reach for you."

He wondered if that's when she grew to hate him. Because her love gave him comfort, and his love, apparently, gave her nothing at all.

Kincaid was finished in the bathroom. He moved around the dresser, opening each drawer, then checking the nightstands.

"When Rainie was at home, where did she keep her weapon?"

"We have a gun safe."

"Where?"

"The study."

Quincy led Kincaid back to the wood-paneled room. He gestured to a print on the wall, a black-and-white portrait of a little girl peering out from behind a white shower curtain. Most people thought the picture was mere art, purchased, perhaps, for the whimsical quality of the girl's gap-toothed smile. In fact, it was a photo of

Mandy taken when she was six years old. He used to carry it in his wallet. Years ago, Rainie had had it enlarged and framed for him.

And sometimes, when a case was particularly bad, say the Astoria case, Quincy would sit in here and simply stare at the photo of his daughter. He would think of the wedding she never got to have, the children she never got to bear. He would think of all the life she never got to lead and he would feel the sorrow press down upon him.

Some people believed there was a special home for children in heaven. A place where they never felt sickness, or pain, or hunger. Quincy didn't know; his relentlessly analytical mind didn't do well with matters of faith. Did the children who had loving parents or grandparents get to be reunited with them? What about the new-born who starved to death while her mother went on a weeklong drinking binge? What about the five-year-old thrown down the stairs by his father? Were there foster parents in heaven?

Or did these children spend eternity all alone?

Quincy didn't have these answers. He just got up and went to work each day. It was what he did.

Kincaid took Mandy's photo down from the wall. The safe was mounted behind it.

Quincy gave the combo. Kincaid turned the dial. The door opened and they both eyed the contents.

"I count three handguns," Kincaid said with a trace of triumph, while Quincy said:

"It's not there."

"But look—"

"All backups. That's a twenty-two, a nine-millimeter, and my old service revolver. I don't see her Glock."

"Would she have left it anyplace else?"

"No. The rule is when at home, the gun is locked in the safe. We wanted to make sure we were in the habit. You know." For the first time, Quincy's voice cracked. He caught it, soldiered on. "For when we adopted our child."

"You're adopting a child?" Kincaid sounded honestly flabber-gasted.

"Were. Past tense. It fell through."

"Why?"

"The DUI. That event, coupled with a few things from Rainie's past, made her look emotionally unstable."

"No shit," Kincaid murmured.

"The system isn't meant to be easy."

"But you thought you were adopting? Right up into September?"

"For a while, Sergeant, we had a picture of the child."

"Damn," Kincaid said. He looked back at the safe, mental wheels obviously churning: Burnt-out investigator, overwhelmed by failed marriage, failed adoption, takes her own life. In policing, once again, you had to play the odds.

"Well," Kincaid said philosophically, "morning's here, conditions are improving. I think the thing to do now is get some dogs in the woods. Do you have any family?"

"My daughter's coming."

"Good, good. That's probably best."

"Don't give up on her," Quincy said tightly. "My wife is a former member of law enforcement. She deserves better than to become just one more neglected case piled on the desk of an overworked Major Crimes sergeant—"

"Whoa—"

"I have resources, too, Sergeant. Hasn't that occurred to you yet? Say the word, I can call in old favors. There are people in this town who know and love Rainie. They believe in her. They'll plow through those woods, they'll slog through the mud and the rain—"

"Hey, I'm not giving up on this case!"

"You're already jumping to conclusions!"

"As an objective outsider—"

"You didn't know my wife!"

"Exactly!"

Kincaid was breathing hard. Quincy, too. For a long time, the men stared at each other, each one waiting for the other to back down.

Then Quincy's phone rang.

He glanced at the screen and immediately held up a silencing hand.

"Is it—?"

"Shhh. It's Rainie."

7

"HELLO?"

Static. A beeping sound. Then a click as if the call had been disconnected.

"Hello?" Quincy tried again, voice more urgent, hand white-knuckled on the phone.

The call was lost. He cursed, tempted to hurl the tiny phone across the room, then it rang again. He flipped open the phone before the ring completed its first musical chime.

" . . . morning paper."

"Rainie? Where are you?"

"She can't come to the phone right now." The voice sounded distorted, mechanized.

"Who is this?"

"You must read the morning paper," the voice intoned.

"This is Investigator Pierce Quincy. I'm looking for Rainie Conner. Can you tell me where she is?"

"You must read the morning paper."

"Do you have her? What is it that you want?"

"What everyone wants—fame, fortune, and a finely baked apple pie. Goodbye."

"Hello? Who is this? Where are you?"

But the caller was gone. Quincy knew it before the first syllable left his mouth. He immediately returned the call, but on the other end, Rainie's phone just rang and rang and rang.

"Who was it? What'd she say?" Kincaid was standing over him, looking as agitated and impatient as Quincy felt.

"It was a man, I think. Using some kind of voice-distortion machine. He kept saying I must read the morning paper. Word for word. *'You must read the morning paper.'* Quick—pen, paper. While it's fresh, we need to write this down."

Quincy fumbled around his desk, jerking open drawers, scattering a tray of pens.

Kincaid was behind him, rifling a second drawer in search of a notepad. "Why read the paper?"

"I don't know."

"Which paper?"

"I don't know. *'Read the morning paper.'* That's what he said. *'Read the morning paper.'*" Quincy finally got a pen. His hand was trembling so badly, he could barely grip it between his fingers. Too many thoughts were in his head. Rainie kidnapped. Rainie hurt. Rainie . . . So many things that were far, far worse.

Nine years ago, Bethie on the other end of the line. *"Pierce, something's happened to Mandy. You'd better come quick."*

Kincaid had found a spiral notepad. He thrust it across the desk, where it slid to a stop in front of Quincy.

But Quincy couldn't write. His fingers wouldn't hold the pen, his hand wouldn't scrawl across the page. He was shaking. He'd never seen his hand tremble so much, not in all of these years. And then he suffered a surreal moment, where he stood outside his body, staring back down at this scene, and what he saw was a hand, old, thickened, soon to be age-spotted, grasping ineffectively at a pen.

He felt powerless. His wife was kidnapped, and for a heart-stopping moment, he didn't know what to do.

Kincaid took the notepad away from Quincy. There was more sympathy in the sergeant's eyes than Quincy was prepared to accept.

"You talk," Kincaid said. "I'll write."

Quincy started from the beginning. There wasn't much to document after all. A disguised voice on Rainie's phone, ordering Quincy to read the morning paper and claiming to desire fame, fortune, and apple pie. Four lines spoken, a total of thirty-two words.

They started with the first instruction: *You must read the morning paper.*

"Local," Kincaid declared.

"What? The call? It wasn't a good signal, but that would put the caller anywhere in the coastal range. And pulling the records won't help—it'll just list a call placed to my phone."

"No, no, not the call, the paper. Otherwise he'd say 'morning *papers*,' plural. But he kept saying '*paper*.' That's specific. I'm guessing the *Bakersville Daily Sun*."

"Ah, the Daily Oxymoron," Quincy muttered. "We don't get it delivered. But . . ." He thought about it. "We should be able to find something online."

"Screw that, we're going straight to the source."

"You have a contact?"

"Better. I have a public information officer. He can get straight through to the owner if we have to." Kincaid pulled out his cell phone and punched two buttons. Seconds later he was talking to a Lieutenant Mosley, and a few seconds after that, he was gesturing frantically for the return of the spiral notepad.

"Is there a return address? When was it postmarked? No, no, no, I don't want it handled! Listen, I'm sending over two scientists from the Portland lab right away, along with Latent Prints. Anyone who's touched that letter needs to be sequestered now; I don't care if they own the damn paper. We're on our way."

Kincaid flipped his phone shut and headed immediately for the door. The sergeant was already at a half-jog; Quincy quickly picked up the pace.

"What is it? What did he say?"

"Ransom note. Op-ed editor of the *Bakersville Daily Sun* just notified our PIO twenty minutes ago. They found a note in this morning's mail. Says a woman has been kidnapped, and if anyone wants to see her alive again, it will cost ten thousand dollars cash."

"Who sent it?"

"Not clear."

"When?"

"Postmarked yesterday."

"But that's not possible." They were at the car. Kincaid jumped in on the driver's side, Quincy rounded the front.

"It is and isn't," Kincaid said, already firing up the Chevy. "It's not possible that the man had kidnapped your wife yesterday afternoon. But then the ransom note didn't mention a specific name, or provide a description."

"Stranger to stranger," Quincy filled in. "The guy didn't know who he was taking. He just knew he was taking someone."

"Exactly. Crime of opportunity."

"Against a trained member of law enforcement?"

"Maybe he got lucky. Or maybe . . . We don't know how he chose his target yet. Maybe," Kincaid's voice was quiet, "he started at a bar."

Quincy didn't say anything. Kincaid headed down the steep driveway at an unhealthy pace. Quincy grabbed the dash.

"Listen," Kincaid was saying. "A letter's a good sign. Guy's making contact and every contact provides an opportunity. We started with the phone call to you. Now we've got an envelope, a letter, and a postmark all worth analyzing. All we need is a little saliva to seal the envelope, and we got DNA. A postmark close to home, and we have geography. Add the handwriting sample and we've nailed a suspect. This is a good thing."

"I want the letter sent to the FBI lab."

"Don't piss me off."

"Sergeant, with all due respect—"

"Our Questioned Documents unit is very good, thanks."

"The bureau's is better."

"The bureau's lab is all the way across country. We'd lose a day just in transport. My guys can handle the letter just fine, and they can get started this afternoon. You do understand the need for speed."

"It's always a matter of minutes," Quincy said curtly. His gaze had gone out the window. "Always."

"You ever work with a local you thought had brains?"

"Only the one I married."

Kincaid arched a brow. He was still driving too fast, cutting S-curves and swinging around traffic. It was obvious to Quincy that the sergeant had once been a big fan of *Starsky and Hutch.*

"Give me thirty minutes," Kincaid said abruptly, "and I think you'll change your tune."

"You can find my wife in half an hour?"

"No, but I can find out if the author of the note actually took her."

"How?"

"The letter included a map. Follow the directions to the scavenger hunt and discover proof of life. Guy's reaching out, Mr. Profiler Man, and we're going to nail him for it."

"I'm going with you," Quincy said immediately.

Kincaid finally flashed him a grin. "Somehow, I never doubted that."

8

DOWNTOWN BAKERSVILLE, OREGON, wasn't much—a four-block Main Street that housed a variety of family businesses, most of them struggling now that Wal-Mart had built on the outskirts. The Elks still maintained a lodge, which was actually an old bowling alley, painted bright blue. Then there was the corner florist, the Ham 'n Eggs diner three doors down from that, an office supply store, an undersized JC Penney's. The businesses existed to serve the locals; most of the summer tourists passed straight through from the beaches in the south to the Tillamook Cheese Factory in the north.

Quincy couldn't remember the last time he'd come into the town, but Kincaid seemed to know his way around. The sergeant swerved around one corner, made a hard right on the next. All the while he was working his cell phone. Calls for a detective to head straight for the *Daily Sun* and secure that note. Calls to his lieutenant, requesting more manpower. Calls for the crime lab and Latent Prints to get their butts to the coast. Then a call in to Sheriff Atkins, still conducting the search.

Finally, Kincaid had the public information officer back on the phone, getting the lowdown on people and titles at the *Daily Sun*.

Policing was management. It was throwing a million balls into the air, and keeping them all going without ever stepping out of bounds or disobeying the rules. It had been a long time since Quincy had been in the thick of it, working a fast-breaking case. He could feel the adrenaline rush whooshing up his spine, the unmistakable tingle of excitement, and it left him feeling vaguely guilty. His wife had been abducted. Surely it shouldn't feel like the good old days.

Kincaid slapped shut his phone. A two-story cement structure had just appeared on their left, a seventies-issue office building, all flat roof and boxy angles. Kincaid careened into the parking lot and wedged the Chevy between two SUVs. Welcome to the *Daily Sun*.

"I talk," Kincaid said as he bounded out of the car. "You listen."

"How many kidnapping cases have you worked before?" Quincy asked.

"Oh, shut up." Kincaid headed into the building.

Inside, the hoopla was immediately obvious. Reporters, copy editors, and assistant gophers who should've been bustling around with the endless number of tasks that went into creating a daily paper instead hovered on their tiptoes inside the foyer. Some clutched manila file folders to their chests. Most, however, didn't bother with pretense. Everyone knew something important had occurred, and all waited anxiously to see what would happen next.

Kincaid didn't disappoint. The sergeant squared his shoulders, approached the receptionist, and flashed his badge, his expression pure TV-cool. "Sergeant Detective Carlton Kincaid, here to see Owen Van Wie, *immediately.*"

Van Wie was the publisher of the daily rag. He'd been contacted first thing this morning, and much to the PIO's dismay, already had a lawyer on site. Thus far, at least, Van Wie was promising the paper's complete cooperation. They'd see how long that lasted.

The receptionist led the way, Kincaid tipping his head in acknowledgment at the gathered masses.

"Carlton?" Quincy murmured behind him.

"Oh, shut up."

The *Daily Sun* was a small-town paper, and the publisher's office looked it. Cramped windowless space, one bank of strictly utilitarian gray metal filing cabinets, and one completely overwhelmed desk. Van Wie sat behind the desk. Across from him sat another man in a suit and tie. Lawyer, Quincy guessed.

The men already occupied the only seats in the room, leaving Kincaid and Quincy to stand shoulder to shoulder in the narrow doorway. Kincaid flashed his badge, providing quick, perfunctory introductions.

Quincy shook Van Wie's hand, then met the publisher's attorney, Hank Obrest. Suit was off-the-rack, tie a cheap polyester blend. Local lawyer for the local paper, Quincy thought. The two had probably gone to high school together and remained best buds ever since.

"You have the note?" Kincaid asked. The sergeant clearly wasn't a fan of small talk.

"Right here." Van Wie gestured to two sheets of paper lying in the middle of the desk. Both men were eyeing the letter warily, as if it were a bomb that might go off at any instant.

"Did you save the envelope?"

"Right next to it. Cynthia, that's our Opinions Editor, she opened it first. She likes to use a letter opener, so it's a nice clean slice along the top. Don't know if that kind of thing helps you or not."

Kincaid whipped out a handkerchief and used it to move the two pages closer to him. Quincy tried to scan the document first, but Kincaid's shoulder blocked him.

"Who else touched it?" Kincaid asked.

"Mail department," Van Wie answered, ticking off fingers. "Jessica, who sorts the letters. And probably Gary, Cynthia's assistant."

"We'll need to print them for comparison."

"I'm sure that won't be a problem," the publisher said.

"I'm sure it won't," Kincaid agreed firmly.

Quincy leaned to the left and, using a capped pen from his breast pocket, tugged the note into his field of view.

The letter was typed, cheap white copier stock, standard business format. No header, no footer. Only address listed was the one for the newspaper.

Dear Editor:

You don't know me. I don't live here. But I know this town.
Last night, I kidnapped a woman who lives here. Do not be
horrified. I am not a pervert.

I want money. $10,000 cash. I will return the woman alive. I
am serious. I am professional. Follow the rules, and all will be
well. Ignore me, and the woman will die.

I have included a map showing where to find proof of life. Find
the X by noon or the woman will die.

Ignore this letter, and the woman will die. Remember, I am a
man of my word.

Sincerely,
The Fox

Quincy read the note three times. Then he carefully pushed it
aside. The second page, also cheap white office paper, revealed a
crude drawing done in thick black pen. As the note implied, X literally marked the spot.

Quincy was already forming impressions in his mind, and his
first instinct had been that the map would be complicated.
Something that would clearly prove that the unidentified subject—
UNSUB—was the one in control, and the police must obey his
every command.

Instead, the map was nearly cartoonish in its simplicity. One
walked out of the *Daily Sun,* headed south on 101, took a left, took a
right, and ended up near the Tillamook Air Museum in a cemetery.
Amateurish. Adolescent. And yet brilliant. A location remote enough
that the chance of someone noticing a man there in the middle of the
night was small. And distinct enough that it wouldn't be hard for the
police to find the "clue."

Quincy read the note again. Then again.

He didn't like the icy feeling beginning to settle in at his gut.

Kincaid was now examining the envelope. "Return address," the
sergeant murmured to Quincy. "Gives the initials W.E.H. and a

street address in L.A. Trying to prove his point that he's not from around here?"

"Maybe."

"Postmark is Bakersville, however, so he mailed it in town."

A knock at the door. A detective, Ron Spector, from OSP's Tillamook County office had arrived. Kincaid stepped back into the hallway, where he and Spector huddled together, speaking in low tones.

Quincy reviewed the map again. Part of him wanted to bolt out the door, head to the air museum, and race through the cemetery in an ironic search for proof of life. But the cooler, analytic side of him understood an investigator should never rush. The ransom note itself was a treasure trove of information, not to be ignored. So much could be found in the small play of words. Let alone paper type, ink choice, fingerprints on the page, saliva on the seal. A detective should be assigned to chase down the return address. Quincy himself wanted to run a search of the initials, W.E.H., which were already niggling at the corners of his brain.

Something he'd seen before? Someone he knew?

There were so many pieces of the puzzle they hadn't even begun to put into place. They had yet to canvass the local hotels and motels, to interview twenty- to forty-year-old males traveling alone. They had yet to retrace Rainie's last steps, determine who might have seen her. Had she been drinking somewhere? Did she still have her gun?

That last thought gave Quincy pause. If the abduction had been random, maybe the UNSUB didn't yet realize he'd taken a member of law enforcement. . . . At one point, Rainie had been able to reach her cell phone. What about her weapon?

The idea made Quincy feel curiously seasick. On the one hand, if Rainie stood up to her attacker, she might get away. On the other hand, how many killers had he interviewed over the years who claimed their bloodlust was initially triggered by a woman's resistance? *She fought me, so I killed her.* For some men, it was really that simple.

Kincaid was back. He informed Van Wie that Detective Spector would now be handling things at the *Daily Sun*. Then Kincaid carefully picked up the two-page ransom note, still using the handkerchief. Detective Spector would enter the original pages into evidence and start the process of preserving chain of custody. Kincaid and Quincy, however, would need a copy of the note and the map for their own efforts.

At the last moment, Kincaid gestured for Quincy to follow him down the hall.

"What do you think?" Kincaid asked as they approached the copy machine.

"Simple," Quincy said. "But clever."

"Simple but clever? Come on, Mr. Profiler Man. Surely you earn those big bucks coming up with more than that."

"I want a raunchy ruling analysis of the note," Quincy said abruptly, "testing the paper for signs of indentation. Can your QD people do that?"

"They've been known to be competent."

"You'll ask for the test?"

"I've been known to be competent, too."

"All right." Quincy ignored the other man's sarcasm. "I think the author of the note is lying. I think he's telling us what he wants us to believe, but not what's necessarily true."

"Ah, so your first instinct is rampant paranoia. Do tell."

"He claims he's a professional. He claims it's about money. But have you ever heard of a ransom case where the victim was random? Around here, given the demographics, you'd stand a decent chance of kidnapping someone who didn't have the kind of resources necessary to meet the ransom demand."

"Ten grand isn't that much," Kincaid protested.

"Exactly," Quincy said. "Why ten thousand dollars? That's not a lot of money for holding a person hostage."

"He has to make the amount accessible. You said it yourself, this isn't the richest part of the state. Plus, don't get me wrong, but for some of us, a quick ten grand isn't doing so badly."

Quincy merely shrugged. "Why invite in the police? Don't most ransom notes specifically state *not* to contact the authorities? For someone trying to score a quick ten grand, in your own words, he's just bought himself a bigger headache."

"Ah, but see, given this guy's system, he has no choice. Without us affirming that it's a ransom note and verifying proof of life, the family of the missing person wouldn't know to take the letter seriously. And if the family of the victim doesn't take things seriously, Señor Fox doesn't get paid." Kincaid had finished copying the two pages. Now he laid the envelope across the glass.

"Now let me tell you what I think. Point one—I actually agree with you. I think the note is a big ball o' lies. But here's where we differ. You think if the guy is lying, he must be devious. I think the guy is lying because he's a rank amateur."

"Ah, so *your* first instinct is basic stupidity." Quincy spread his hands. "Do tell."

"Okay, get this. Our guy—"

"The UNSUB."

"Yeah, that's right. In the feebie world, gotta have an acronym for everything. Okay, so our *UNSUB*. He needs to make some money. Now, I'm assuming this guy isn't so bright and isn't so together in this world. For that kind of mutt, ten grand can be a lot of dough. Maybe pay off a gambling debt." Kincaid's look was pointed; there were a number of casinos along the coast, and they brought with them the requisite casino issues, including gambling, loan-sharking, alcoholism. "Or maybe just pay off his new ATV. I don't know. Thing is, for this guy, ten grand is enough, especially for a day's work."

"Day's work?"

"Yeah, which brings me to point two: our UNSUB, he's not sophisticated enough for a big operation. He needs something quick and easy. So instead of, say, identifying a target, tailing her for days, and then trying to figure out how to kidnap her from her home or at work, he goes with a crime of opportunity. Something easy. Say, a woman, who may have been drinking, pulled over in her car in the middle of the night.

"Of course, not knowing who this woman is or anything about her background, how can he make contact? Simple, use the local paper. And maybe in this case, we weren't moving fast enough—I don't know—so he decides to make direct contact as well. We're still not talking anything that complicated. He has the victim's cell phone, he uses a voice distorter any idiot can buy from Radio Shack. Boom, done.

"Now, if he's watched any movies at all, he knows the first thing that's required in these cases is proof of life. Well, he's making this all up on the fly, so again, how to communicate? Hey, I know, bury it in the middle of a cemetery. That'll get the job done, plus he can have a good chuckle, picturing a fine, handsome state detective trying desperately not to dig up any bones. God knows I'm gonna have to laugh about it.

"Then the UNSUB introduces a few deadlines, 'cause this yokel can't afford for things to get drawn out. He sends the note before five p.m. the day before to ensure we're called first thing in the morning. Gives us a deadline to find proof of life, to make sure we're moving. I bet you now, we get to the cemetery, and we'll find the drop details for the money, along with another deadline, in probably one, two hours. Hell, it'll probably include another map. Stick money beneath tombstone A, find a map to tree B, where we'll find the girl.

"Quick, clean, and not a bad way to make ten grand." Kincaid whipped the envelope off the glass, picked up the duplicates, and closed up the copy machine. "Now let me ask *you* something: Do you have ten grand?"

"Yes."

"Would you pay it to ransom your estranged wife?"

Quincy didn't bat an eye. "Yes."

"There you go. It's gonna be a good day. Let's go hunt a fox."

"I don't think it's about money," Quincy insisted quietly.

"More rampant paranoia?"

"Maybe. But I know something you don't know."

"And what's that, Mr. Profiler Man?"

"I know who the Fox is."

9

DOUGIE WAS OUT IN THE WOODS. Dougie was always out in the woods. He didn't mind the rain, the wind, the cold. Outside was good. Outside meant trees and pine needles and green moss that felt nice to the touch, but didn't always taste so good. This morning, he'd tried three different shades of moss. One had tasted like dirt. One had tasted like tree bark. The third had made his mouth tingle curiously.

He hadn't eaten any more of the third.

Now, Dougie was excavating the remains of a dead tree. The thick trunk had fallen probably ages ago, at least before Dougie had been born. Now it was a great, big rotted-out log, sprouting interesting fungus and housing loads of bugs. Dougie had a stick. He was digging, digging, digging. The more he dug, the more interesting bugs ran out.

Dougie was seven. At least that's what people told him. He didn't remember his birthday. Maybe sometime in February. His first "second family" had made up a date for him, his "homecoming day." That had been in February, and they'd fed him cake and ice cream.

His first second family had been okay. At least he couldn't remember anything bad. But one day the lady in the purple suit had arrived and told him to pack his bag. He was going to a new second family, but don't worry, they would love him lots, too.

"Dougie," the lady in the purple suit had told him quietly when they were out the front door, "you can't play with matches like that; it makes people nervous. Promise me, no more matches."

Dougie had shrugged. Dougie had promised. While behind them, the garage of his first second family's home lay in smoldering ruins.

The second second family hadn't celebrated birthdays or "homecoming days." They hadn't celebrated much of anything. His new mom had a thin, stern face. "Idle hands are the devil's playmate," she'd tell him, right before ordering him to scrub the floor or scour the dishes.

Dougie didn't like doing chores. That meant being in a house and Dougie didn't like being inside. He wanted to be outside. In the trees. Where he could smell the dirt and leaves. Where there was no one around to look at him funny or whisper about him behind his back.

He'd made it three weeks with his second second family. Then he'd simply waited until they went to sleep, went out to the fireplace, and had a ball with the great big long matches. Those suckers could burn.

He still remembered the shocked look on his new mama's face when she came tearing out of her bedroom. "Do I smell smoke? Oh my God, is that a fire? *Dougie! What have you done, you evil devil's spawn!*"

His second second mom slept in the nude. So did his second second dad. The fire people had giggled about that when they'd arrived at the scene. Then they'd seen him, sitting up in the branches of the giant oak tree, listening to the house snap, crackle, pop. They'd stopped, pointed, and stared.

He'd gone to a boys' home after that. A center for "troubled youths," they'd told him. But the lady in the purple suit had appeared again. Dougie was too young for such a facility, he'd heard her say. Dougie still had a chance.

Dougie didn't know what that meant. He simply packed his bag and trotted along to the next home. This house had been near the town. No woods, no park, not even a decent yard. Dougie had discovered only one perk in this tiny house, overrun by all sorts of new brothers and sisters, who weren't brothers and sisters at all, but just other kids who hated one another: The house was only a block from the convenience store.

Dougie learned to steal. If they were going to keep all the matches out of his reach, stealing was second best. He started out small. Twinkies, doughnuts, the little penny candies they kept down near the floor. The kind of stuff no one really noticed. The first time, he brought his loot home, and one of his "sisters" took it from him. When he complained, she socked him in the eye. Then she sat there and ate all his candy while his eye swelled shut.

Dougie learned his lesson. He found a loose brick in the back of the gas station, and that's where he stashed his loot. It was good to have your own supply of food, you know. Sometimes, just looking at all the stuff, he would feel his tummy rumble. There was hunger and there was *hunger,* and already Dougie understood that he was hungrier than most.

The store owner caught him one day, his pockets bulging with Ho Hos and apple pies. The owner had twisted his ear. Dougie had cried and surrendered the goods. "I'll never do it again," he promised, wiping his nose with the back of his hand. More candy fell out of his coat sleeve.

And that was it for home number three.

The lady in the purple suit decided Dougie needed more attention. A home with that many kids hadn't been the right kind of home for Dougie. He needed a hands-on approach. Maybe with a Positive Male Role Model.

Dougie went to home number four, where he was excitedly introduced to his ten-year-old "big brother," Derek. Derek was in Boy Scouts, Derek played Pop Warner football, Derek was a "great kid" and he'd be a good influence on Dougie.

Derek had waited until the lights were out, then he'd taken Dougie all over the house.

"See that chair, little boy? That's my chair." Derek belted him in the stomach.

"See that ball, little boy? That's my ball." Three fingers to a kidney.

"See that Xbox? That's my Xbox." A karate chop across the neck.

Dougie had lasted longer at this house. Mostly because he was scared to leave his bed at night. But one day, Derek went to spend a weekend at his grandma's house. Dougie got up promptly at one a.m. He started in the bedroom. Peeling the sheets off Derek's bed, pulling the clothes from Derek's drawers, dragging the toys out of Derek's closet. He took the chair. The ball. The Xbox.

He built one helluva pile in the front yard. And then, being more experienced now, he found the gas can and started spraying. One little light and *whoosh*!

Dougie lost both eyebrows and most of his bangs. He was also summarily whisked off the premises by the lady in the purple suit, who was having a hard time yelling at a child who looked perpetually surprised with all the hair seared from his face.

Dougie had been in BIG TROUBLE.

This was going in his FILE. No one would touch him now. Didn't he want a FAMILY? Didn't he want a CHANCE? How COULD he?

He could because he did and he would again. He knew that. The lady in purple knew that. Dougie liked fire. He liked the fiery spark of a match. He liked the way the flame gobbled up the little paper stick, then licked at his fingertips. It hurt. He'd seared his fingertips countless times, even blistered the palm of his hand. Fire hurt. But it wasn't a bad sort of pain. It was real. It was honest. It was fire.

Dougie liked it.

And now, here he was. Living with the Carpenters. Good people, the lady in the purple suit had told him. Honest, hardworking. They'd specifically asked for a problem child ("Heaven help them," the woman in the purple suit had murmured), so maybe they would know what to do with him. His new second father, Stanley, was reported to be very good with boys. Assistant football coach at the high school. Grew up with four brothers himself.

Maybe he would be the one to finally take Dougie in hand.

Dougie's new bedroom in his fifth second home contained only a mattress. If he wanted sheets, Dougie was informed, he had to earn them. If he wanted blankets, he had to earn them. If he wanted toys, ditto.

The wall in the kitchen contained an elaborate chart. Perform a chore, score a point. Ask for something politely, score a point. Do as he was told, score a point.

Curse, lose a point. Talk back, lose a point. Break a rule, lose a point. So on and so forth.

His new parents weren't taking any chances either. No matches, no gasoline, no lighter fluid anywhere on the property. 'Least, not that Dougie had been able to find. 'Course, his searching time was limited. Every evening, come seven p.m., he was escorted to his room and locked in.

First night, he got up at three a.m. and peed in the closet. In the morning, Stanley had simply handed him a sponge and escorted him back to his room.

"You can use the sponge, or you can use your tongue, but you will clean that up, Dougie. Now get busy."

Stanley had stood there the entire time, big, muscley arms crossed over a big, muscley chest. Dougie had cleaned. At least the next night they left him a bucket.

Dougie waited till midnight, then flipped over the bucket and used it to climb up to the window. His new "role model" dad had already nailed it shut.

Stanley was a thinker. So, however, was Dougie.

Dougie invested a whole three days into his next project. Yes, ma'am, I'll do the dishes. Yes, ma'am, I'll eat carrots. Yes, ma'am, I'll brush my teeth. In return, he gained a sheet and the small art kit that he'd specifically requested.

Night five, he was standing on his bucket, using a pen cap from the art kit to slowly and methodically wiggle out each nail. Took him until four a.m., but he got it. And then, for two whole weeks he could come and go as he pleased. They locked Dougie in his room, and quick as a wink, he was gone again, heading for the woods, or slogging into town in search of matches. Third week, however, Stanley caught him.

Turned out his new second dad knew a lot more about punishment than Dougie did.

The lady in the purple suit had visited shortly thereafter.

"Dougie," she'd said, "don't you realize this is your last chance?"

She had looked like she was going to cry. Her eyes had welled up.

Her lower lip had trembled. It brought back a hazy memory to Dougie. Of a time and place he didn't really remember. It was just a sensation in his mind, like a smell, or the feel of the wind on his face.

He had wanted to go to the lady. He had wanted to curl up against her, press his face against her neck, the way he had seen other children do. He had wanted her to hug him, to tell him that everything would be all right. He had wanted her to love him.

And that had made him stare at the purple suit and wonder how it would burn.

"Stanley beats me," Dougie said.

And that changed everything.

The lady in the purple suit brought him another lady, who wore jeans. Her name was Rainie and she was his advocate. That meant she worked for him, she told him. It was her job to assess what was going on, to determine if there really were issues in the household. If so, she would help him defend his rights. If not, she was supposed to help mediate a solution between him and his new foster parents, who, according to her, weren't ready to give up on him just yet, even though Dougie needed, in the words of Stanley, a "massive attitude adjustment."

At least Rainie wasn't so bad. She liked to be outside, too, and she didn't make him talk a lot, particularly about his feelings, which was nice. Dougie didn't have many feelings that didn't involve fire, and deep down inside, even he understood that made him a freak.

Now he ripped back more bark. A big, hairy beetle came racing out, and Dougie chased it with his stick. It was fast. He was faster.

"Dougie."

The voice came from behind him. Dougie turned. His second mom was standing a careful distance away. She wore a faded gray sweatshirt, her arms folded around her for warmth. She looked tired and unhappy. She always looked tired and unhappy.

"Come inside for breakfast, Dougie."

"I already ate." He opened his mouth, revealing a feast of three beetles.

"Dougie . . ."

She stared at him, he stared at her. One of the beetle's legs moved between his lips. He used his index finger to shove it back in.

"Have you seen Rainie today?" his second mom asked abruptly.

"What?"

Her voice grew impatient. She was already moving away from him and his beetle-churning cheeks.

"Have you seen your advocate, Rainie Conner, today? Did she stop by, maybe call?"

"No."

"All right. That's all I needed to know."

"Are they looking for her?"

His second mom stopped. "What do you mean, Dougie?"

"Are they looking for her? Is she missing?"

"Do you know something, Dougie? Is there something you need to tell me?"

"I hope she's dead," he said simply, then turned back to the log and prodded another beetle from its rotten depths. "She lied to me. And liars get what they deserve."

10

THE RAIN WAS FINALLY RELENTING. Driving down Highway 101, Quincy watched the misty clouds ease their grip on the coastal range, allowing dark green peaks to appear here and there amid the gloom.

Rainie loved these mountains. She had grown up here, in the shadow of the towering Douglas firs, within whisper distance of the rocky coast. She believed the outdoors should be awe inspiring, a presence grand enough to make mere mortals shake in their boots. When Rainie was happy, she went outside. When she was nervous, she went outside. When she was excited, fearful, stressed, or content, she always went outside.

When Rainie was depressed, Quincy had learned the hard way, she stayed curled up inside her darkened bedroom.

Kincaid put his right blinker on. The detective was finally driving at less than the speed of light, lost in his own thoughts.

With the arrival of the note, the case had finally taken shape and Kincaid appeared to be settling in. He had an adversary. He had claim of a crime. He also had a note, which generated a slew of tangible leads and logical tasks. Kincaid could now work his phone like a general marshaling his troops for war.

In contrast, Quincy could feel himself slowly start to disintegrate. He was an investigator well versed in crime. He was also a man who knew, better than most, that bad things could happen to you. And yet still, up until this point, the night had contained a surreal feel. Rainie was tough. Rainie was capable. He worried about her drinking and he worried about her state of mind. But he'd never honestly worried that an outsider might cause her physical harm.

And now, this was one of those times when Quincy wished he'd never become a profiler. He wished he might be an engineer, or a high school math teacher, or even a dairy farmer. Because then he could be just a man, an anxious husband. And he could console himself with the fact that he did have ten thousand dollars and he would gladly pay ten times that amount to have Rainie safe in his arms.

He could tell himself everything was going to be all right. He could assure himself this was just a small, strange interlude, and in only a matter of hours, he would see his wife again.

He wouldn't have to know so many statistics, such as that the majority of ransom cases ending with the kidnapped victim being discovered dead.

Kincaid made the turn. In front of them, the Tillamook Air Museum finally loomed into view.

Under normal conditions, it would be hard to miss the air museum. Housed in an old World War II blimp hangar, it had the distinction of being the largest wooden structure in the entire world. It soared over fifteen stories high and engulfed a whopping seven acres. The museum's collection of thirty different warplanes barely made a dent in the dark, cavernous space.

He and Rainie had toured it once. At the end, Rainie had turned, regarded him thoughtfully, and said, "You know, this would be a great place to hide a body."

The blimp hangar was part of a Naval Air Station. Though NAS Tillamook was decommissioned in '48, it still had the look and feel of a Navy space. Low, sprawling buildings to house officers, men. Vast tracts of land for various training exercises. A maze of roads looping in and around the compound.

In addition to the air museum, a plane charter company had

taken up residence. Then there was the neighboring prison, its walls topped by guard towers and rolls of barbed wire.

It was a busy area, but not too busy. Given the tourist traffic to the museum, a stranger wouldn't be out of place. Even after hours, Quincy would bet any man could travel the grounds unquestioned as long as he looked like he knew what he was doing. In other words, it was the perfect place for an illicit rendezvous.

Following the map, they took a hard right before hitting the museum. That took them straight to a small cemetery, plopped in the middle of open pastureland.

"It's the Catholic cemetery," Kincaid remarked as he parked the car and they both climbed out. "Maybe your UNSUB's got issues."

"Don't we all?" Quincy murmured, and crossed to study the map.

It took a moment to orient the crude drawing to the space. A road had been sketched into the left side of the map, a small bush toward the back. It was a rough system. Nothing appeared to scale, and given the lack of trees or shrubs on the grounds, none of the landmarks appeared particularly distinct.

"Well, I can tell you one thing," Kincaid said after a moment. "The UNSUB clearly failed art class."

"I think the trick is not to try too hard. Treat the landmarks like points on a compass. We want the bushes to be south of us, the trees to the left. If we stand that way . . ."

"X doesn't mark the spot," Kincaid filled in. "But a cross does."

"Let's go."

The five-foot gray granite cross was pockmarked with age and green-tinged from decades of rain. Moss had sprung up on the edges. Ferns sprouted along the base. The tombstone maintained a certain timeless dignity, however. The last sentinel of an entire family, it maintained its watch over four generations.

Ashes to ashes, Quincy thought, dust to dust.

"I don't see anything," Kincaid said. "Do you?"

Quincy shook his head, still circling. The family plot was old and appeared undisturbed. No fresh flowers, no churned earth. He frowned, backed up, frowned again.

The cemetery was active. Dark mounds of fresh-turned earth indicated new additions. Bright-colored flags adorned many monuments, leftovers no doubt from Veterans Day. Here and there, vases boasted fresh bouquets of carnations, daisies, roses. He took the map from Kincaid, studied it, and decided he hated this whole game.

"Time check," Kincaid said.

"Ten fifty-eight."

"So we have an hour until deadline." The sergeant eyed the cemetery. "If we got a whole hour, how hard can this be?"

"Let me ask you something," Quincy said abruptly. "This deadline . . . how will he know if we *don't* meet it?"

Kincaid had the sense not to whip around. Instead, his body went perfectly still. "You think he's watching?" he whispered.

"Or has a lookout. Or . . . electronic surveillance?"

"Not easy out here."

"If he's set up a wireless surveillance system, I think you would have to categorize him one step up from a 'dumb mutt,'" Quincy agreed.

"Shit. That's all we need, a little felonious MacGyver."

"I don't think I'd care for it much myself."

Quincy expanded his walking path, moving more carefully now, trying to get a broader sense of his surroundings. The neighboring buildings could conceal someone quite easily. The tall surrounding grass as well. And as for cameras . . . behind a flag, peering out from a basket of flowers, nestled within the ferns. The possibilities were endless. They would need a full team of trained investigators to cover such a broad complex. No way two men could do it in an hour.

"Maybe you should tell me about this Fox guy," Kincaid said tightly, staring hard at the surrounding buildings, the overgrown roads, any tombstone over five feet tall.

"He kidnapped a twelve-year-old daughter of a prominent banker in L.A.," Quincy supplied. He started working his way toward the lone bush, still acting casual. He noticed Kincaid had his hand inside his jacket, near where an officer might holster a gun. "Her father received a series of ransom notes, all demanding fifteen hundred dollars in cash and signed 'The Fox.'"

"Fifteen hundred dollars isn't much money."

"It was in 1927."

"Say what?"

"Perry Parker, the father, gathered the money. As per the instructions, he handed over the bag to a young man who was waiting for him in a car. In the passenger seat of the vehicle, he could see his daughter. As soon as Perry handed over the money, however, the suspect drove off with Marion Parker still in the car. At the end of the street, he dumped her corpse onto the pavement."

Quincy had reached the rhododendron now. He was just about to take another step when the bush suddenly shook.

"Duck," Kincaid roared.

Quincy ducked. The black raven took flight. And Kincaid nearly blew off its fool head.

"Holy mother of—"

"It's a bird, it's a bird! Cease fire, for God's sake."

Kincaid drew up short, body still shaking, eyes wide and white-rimmed in his dark skull. He had his finger off the trigger, but remained in a shooter's stance, every muscle tense. Quincy felt it as well.

His gaze was ping-ponging all over the place. Trying to see everything, focusing on nothing. He was losing it, Kincaid was losing it. They had started out as professionals, and now were two schoolboys, spooked out in the local cemetery.

"I don't see anything," Kincaid said brusquely.

"Me neither."

"But I'm pretty sure if he was around, he'd know we'd followed his stupid map."

"Seems like a safe bet."

Kincaid inhaled. Exhaled. He finally eased up, his Glock .40 disappearing once more inside his jacket. He took a few steps, then shook out his arms. "I'm going to have to report discharging my weapon thanks to that damn bird," he muttered, still sounding royally pissed off, but at least in a healthier sort of way.

"The bird that got away," Quincy observed.

"Ahh shit. I shoulda become an accountant. You ever think that? My father, he's a CPA. Maybe it's not the most exciting job in the world, but he's off most of the summer, and better yet, I don't think he's ever had to run around a cemetery hunting for masked men. He sits at a desk and adds numbers. I could do that."

"I've always wanted to be a teacher myself. It would still involve spending large periods of time with violent offenders, but at least it would be at the beginning of their careers, and not later when they'd already killed half a dozen people."

Kincaid stared at him. "You got a really interesting way of looking at things, Mr. Profiler Man."

"I'm an absolute hit at cocktail parties," Quincy assured him.

Kincaid sighed and resumed inspecting the grounds for signs of an X. "So you were saying? About this Fox guy?"

"Oh. Mr. Parker paid the ransom, and in return, the Fox dumped out his twelve-year-old daughter's body. Marion's legs had been chopped off, her innards cut out, and her eyes wired open to make it appear as if she were alive. Later, the police found her internal organs strewn all over sections of L.A."

Kincaid looked faintly ill. "Jesus. This really happened?"

"It's a fairly infamous case."

"In 1927? Well, you can't really blame that one on violent video games, can you? I don't get it though. You're talking nearly eighty years ago. I kinda doubt that's the same cat we're dealing with now."

"Oh, I'm sure it's a different 'cat.' The Fox is dead. Mr. Parker recognized him immediately as a former employee, the police picked him up, and he was hanged in '28."

"So in other words, it's got nothing to do with us," Kincaid said with a frown. "One guy signed notes The Fox, another guy signed his note The Fox. Probably just thought it sounded cool."

"In real life," Quincy said quietly, "the Fox's name was William Edward Hickman."

Kincaid stopped, looked faintly ill again. "W.E.H."

"Return address L.A."

"Ah jeez . . . Can't a criminal just be *normal* anymore? I swear even the felons have watched too much TV."

"The nom de plume, the map, the cemetery." Quincy gestured around the gray-gloomed space. "Whatever we're dealing with here, I doubt it's just about money. Frankly, if the criminally inclined wanted money, they could knock over a 7-Eleven. These, ransom cases, are always about something more."

Kincaid narrowed his eyes. "All right. I'll bite: How many of these cases *have* you worked?"

"Six."

"And the success rate for happy family reunions?"

"Thirty-three percent. Two of the six abductees were returned alive."

"Did the other four families pay up?"

"Yes. But it didn't matter. In the other four cases, the victims were killed within an hour of abduction. There was never any intent to return them alive. It's difficult to have a hostage, you know. One, if they've seen your face, they'll identify you later. Two, there's the sheer logistics of housing them, feeding them, dealing with them. It's much cleaner to simply kill them from the start.

"Three of them were children," Quincy added. "One was a girl who was only two years old. We caught the man later. He was a former business partner of the parents, who felt they owed him more money than they'd given him in the original buyout. So he killed their child in an effort to extract fifty thousand dollars. These kinds of predators . . . It's never just about money, Sergeant Kincaid. It's almost always a little bit personal."

"I do not like the things you know."

"Most of the time, neither do I."

Kincaid glanced at his watch. "We have forty minutes."

"I think we'll only need another ten. Assuming, of course, you brought a shovel." Quincy pointed to the ground. Kincaid made a small "o" with his mouth, then headed for the trunk of his car.

11

QUINCY HADN'T NOTICED IT AT FIRST. Neither had Kincaid. But upon further inspection, not all the ferns around the base of the cross-shaped monument were created equal. Four of them were common woodland ferns, short, a bit yellowed from too much sun, and spotted around the edges. The fifth, however, was greener, richer, and unblemished. A household fern, Quincy determined upon closer inspection. Probably purchased from any florist or greenhouse and plopped next to the grave marker to cover signs of recent digging.

He felt around its edges with his fingers, but couldn't come up with any sign of a plastic pot. The soil was looser, however, loamy, a commercial potting-soil mix.

Quincy used his hands to start digging. The fern came up easily, its roots still molded into the shape of a flower pot. As he'd feared, however, the loose muddy soil promptly rolled back into the hole, obscuring its depth.

Kincaid returned with a midsize shovel, like that a small child might have. He saw Quincy's questioning glance and shrugged.

"Sometimes you gotta dig out around here, and this size fits nicely in the trunk."

"We're going to need a plastic sheet," Quincy told him. "Two of them. Do you have an evidence kit in your trunk?"

"Hey, I'm a state cop. I got *everything* in my trunk."

Kincaid disappeared again. Quincy used the opportunity to stick his fingers back into the hole. He felt around fast, furtive, feeling a little guilty. He wasn't sure yet what they were looking for, and as the lead detective in the case, Kincaid owned the evidence. But Quincy needed it more. It was his only link to Rainie.

His fingers finally touched something, solid, hard, like a rock. His fingers moved along the edges until the shape became unmistakable.

He leaned back on his heels then, plopped down on the wet grass. He had mud on his hands, streaks of moss across his pants. For the first time, he could really feel it—his damp clothes, his wet hair, the endless string of sleepless nights.

His eyes stung. He tried to swipe at them, tried to pull himself together before Kincaid returned, but only succeeded in smearing more dirt across his face.

Kincaid was back, armed with a box, and staring at him with an expression that was hard to read. Quincy cleared his throat. His eyes still smarted; his voice came out gravelly and rough.

"Have you excavated evidence before?"

"Yeah."

"The trick is to take the whole side of the hole, one spadeful at a time. Then dump the dirt on the plastic, hole side facing up. We'll cover it with another sheet of plastic, and that will preserve it for the evidence technicians to process. You never know what the UNSUB may have transferred to the site. Soil samples from his own spade, bits of hair, carpet fiber from the trunk of his car—"

"I know."

"It's important to do it right," Quincy whispered.

"I know, man. I know."

Kincaid took over. Quincy sat there like a lump. He should stand up. He couldn't summon the energy. Instead, he listened to the rhythmic scrape of spade against dirt while watching the rain clouds gather in the north. He could see the angry gray line forming on the horizon, the wall of rain looking like a dense fog about to sweep across the valley. A rainy day after a rainy night.

He felt the moisture on his face and told himself it was only the clouds that were weeping.

"I got it," Kincaid said.

Quincy turned. The sergeant stood in front of an arc of plastic sheets piled with dirt. In front of him lay two objects. One was a plastic container. The other was a gun.

Kincaid was pulling on a pair of latex gloves. He pointed to the gun first.

"Hers?"

"Yes."

"You're sure?"

"I'd have to check the serial number to be certain, but that's a Glock forty, slightly older model . . ."

"Yeah, okay." Kincaid worked the container. "GladWare," he reported. "Watertight, but disposable, cheap. He's a thoughtful one."

Quincy merely nodded. He hadn't realized how much he'd been hoping that Rainie still had her gun until this moment. If it had been a random abduction, if the kidnapper really had been Joe Schmo amateur, unaware of who he'd grabbed . . .

Maybe she'd been tipsy, Quincy had been thinking in the back of his mind. But once she figured out what was going on, got her wits about her . . .

He had been holding fast to his memory of his wife the fighter, his wife the survivor. Of course, since the Astoria case, he wasn't sure that woman existed anymore.

"It's another note," Kincaid said. "Little shit."

Quincy stood up. He shook the raindrops from his coat and forced himself to cross to Kincaid. "What does it say?"

"Another rendezvous, four p.m. Follow the instructions for the ransom drop."

"This is how he ensures we've taken his first note seriously," Quincy said quietly. "Without it, we wouldn't know where to go for the drop."

"Gets the job done."

"It's also getting to be a bit of work for ten thousand dollars."

"It's in our favor, though." Kincaid held up the note triumphantly. "Look—this one's handwritten. We just got ourselves more evidence."

Quincy, however, was already shaking his head. "Don't bother. I can already tell you who wrote the note. It's his proof of life, after all; the handwriting is Rainie's."

12

SHE IS DREAMING. *She is walking up the steps, through the door, into the gloom. Water drips from her hood onto the threadbare carpet.*

"Stop right there," a young-faced uniformed officer instructs. "Orders are no shoes, no hair." The female deputy points to a corner of the small breezeway. There is a long, low shelf that probably holds the homeowner's boots and sandals and all that dirty outdoor stuff, now covered in tarp. On top of the tarp rests a pile of crime scene smocks, disposable feet booties, and hairnets.

Quincy and Rainie exchange glances. Hazmat gear is generally only worn when there is a high risk of cross-contaminating bodily fluids. It's their first clue that this scene is going to be a really bad one.

Wordlessly, they fold up the umbrella, strip off their raincoats and shoes. They put on the smocks, the footies, the hairnets. Quincy is done first; Rainie has to work to get the full mass of her long, heavy hair contained beneath the net.

Outside it is still pouring. It's eleven in the morning, but the summer thunderstorm has rendered the inside of the old duplex nearly pitch black.

Quincy holds the door for Rainie. A habit so ingrained, he never thinks not *to do it at a crime scene. She finds it both charming and a little heart-breaking. Kindness doesn't seem to belong in a place like this.*

She walks through the door and the smell hits her first. The rusty scent of blood, underlaid with the foul odor of loose bowels, exposed intestines. Rainie has visited so many crime scenes, her nose can tell her nearly as much as her eyes. So she immediately understands, still standing just one foot inside the door, that this one's a slasher. Knife, big blade, extensive postmortem mutilation.

The shoe booties, she deduces. The UNSUB made a big mess, then stepped in it, leaving behind bloody footprints. It's the kind of evidence even the locals know better than to fuck up.

They enter an enlarged space, open kitchen to the right, family room to the left. Still no sign of the body, but now the blood is everywhere. Dark streaks, looking almost like paint, spray across the walls, drip upon the floor. There are stains on the sofa, handprints on the chair.

Rainie has only ever seen one other scene this bad, and memory of that time makes her reach back and squeeze Quincy's latex-covered hand. His grip is cool and strong within hers. He's doing okay.

They turn toward the kitchen, where they can now see two detectives huddled in front of the stove.

"Starts here," one was saying to the other. "She reaches in to get something in the fridge, and bam!"

"But how'd he get in?"

"Slider was forced. It's a pretty cheap model, so it wasn't too hard."

"Breaks in, attacks the woman."

"Breaks in and waits," the first detective corrects. "No way she didn't hear someone forcing that slider. My guess is he did it hours before. When, of course, is the million-dollar question. But the guy saw the place was empty and made his move. Maybe she arrived while he was still in the house, and that forced him to take cover, or maybe an ambush was his plan all along. Don't know that one yet. But he broke in, then he took cover. That's the only way you can explain her taking the time to tuck in the child."

Child? Rainie stops in her tracks without even being aware she has done so. Now she can feel Quincy's fingers grip her own.

"Okay, so he takes cover, waits for the kid to go to bed, and then . . ."

"Finds her in the kitchen."

"Rams her head into the refrigerator."

"And the carnage begins."

"Probably, she never saw it coming," said the first detective.

And the second detective said, "It's more than you can say for the kid."

Tuesday, 12:08 p.m. PST

JOLT. HARD SEARING PAIN to her hip. Rainie's eyes flew open, saw only darkness, and she thought, finally, I'm dead.

New jolt. Harder. She could feel the entire vehicle buck beneath her, tires straining for footing. More sensations trickling in now, a jumble of impressions for her sightless eyes. Metal, hard against her cheek. Gasoline, astringent in her nostrils. Cotton, wadded into her mouth.

She tried to move her hands, couldn't. The bindings were too tight. Her fingers tingled with the final death throes of sensation before her hands went totally numb. She checked her feet, found the same results.

The vehicle heaved again, throwing her bound body up toward the hatch. Her head came down first, pounding against something even harder and less giving. Tire jack, tool kit. The possibilities were endless. She didn't even groan anymore. Just squeezed her eyes shut against the pain.

She was confused, more confused than she ought to be. In the clearer part of her brain she suspected drugs, but even that thought was hard to hold. She'd been in her car. White light. Then black. A sense of movement. A desire to kick her feet, struggle. Gun, she'd thought. Gun. Her hands had been too heavy. Couldn't lift her arms.

Then for a while, she hadn't thought of anything at all.

Now, mind straining toward consciousness, eyes frantic to see, the absolute darkness panicked her. She could feel the closed door of the trunk just inches from her face, hear the rain pounding on its lid. She was in a vehicle, being driven to God knows where, bound, gagged, helpless.

She tried to move her hands again. Tried to move her feet. And then all at once, she went a little nuts.

She beat at her steel tomb, whacking her head, smashing her nose. Still she writhed wildly. Carjackers didn't truss people up like

Thanksgiving turkeys. Mere purse snatchers wouldn't bother drugging a woman unconscious. But she knew the kind of people who did. Rapists, killers, men who fed off a woman's terror and agony.

Too many thoughts rushed into her head. Photos of women with hacked-off limbs. Audiotapes of poor girls who had accepted the ride with the wrong man, now begging for mercy while he did unspeakable things with pliers.

She needed her gun. She needed her hands. She did not want to die feeling so helpless.

She flailed again, flipping herself over, lashing out with her feet. Her thoughts came faster, clearer: Find the taillights and disable them, maybe get the attention of a nearby patrol officer. Or find the trunk latch and force it open, definitely shocking the driver behind her. There were options, there were always options, she just had to find them.

She could feel moisture trickling down her chin. Blood from her smashed nose. The gas fumes were making her nauseous, the darkness gathering once more on the fringes of her mind.

If she could just find the latch, just wiggle her fingers.

She heard a scraping from her waist. Her cell phone. She had her phone!

One quick twist, her cell phone rattled free. She wriggled after it, her fingers scampering around the tiny space. She could feel it slowing now, hear the squeal of brakes as the vehicle made a hard left.

Her fingers found a button. She held it down, and finally, after an eternity seemed to pass, she was rewarded with a voice. Kimberly.

Help, she tried to say. *Help,* she tried to scream.

But not a single sound emerged from her throat.

Even when she won, she lost. The connection broke. The car stopped. And Rainie slipped back into the abyss.

Saturday, four months ago, 9:58 a.m. PST

THEY WERE STANDING *at the funeral, trying to blend in with the other mourners while their gazes worked the crowd. It was a long shot, but one any trained investigator had to take. Some killers hit and run, but others liked to return to the scene of the crime. So they had detectives working the funeral and a surveillance system set up for the night.*

In a case this public, this shocking, all budget requests were receiving green lights.

An older woman stood weeping in the front. The grandmother, flown in from Idaho. Her husband stood beside her, arms crossed in front, face impassive. He was being strong for his wife. Or maybe he was still stunned to realize that coffins came in sizes that small.

Rainie was supposed to work the crowd. Sort through the sea of hundreds of faces, an entire community, standing in a cemetery, shocked into unity and chilled to the bone.

She kept hearing the grandma's keening wails. She kept seeing that small pair of pink-flowered panties, tossed aside on the floor.

"Urine," Quincy had said quietly, inspecting the underpants. Because that's what happened when a four-year-old girl woke up at night and saw a strange man standing in her doorway. That's what happened when a four-year-old girl watched that man walk into her room.

"Mommy," had she cried? Or had she never said anything at all?

The grandparents had chosen a tombstone with a baby angel carved on top, curled up in eternal sleep. Rainie stood at the monument long after the proceedings ended and the mourners departed.

"Do you believe in Heaven?" she asked Quincy softly.

"Sometimes."

"Surely you must think about it? You've buried half your family, Quincy. If there's no heaven, what do you have to look forward to?"

"I'm sorry you hurt," he said quietly. It was really all he could say.

"God sucks. He's fickle, He's savage, like any child deserves such a thing—"

"Rainie—"

"The grandparents said she went to church. Shouldn't that kind of thing help? This wasn't a nonbeliever. This was a four-year-old girl who loved her mommy and believed in Christ. How can that not help?"

"Rainie—"

"I mean it, Quincy. Heaven's just our futile attempt to pretend we're better than animals. But we're not. We're born into this world like animals, and we die like animals. Some of us take a long time to get there, and some of us are slaughtered in our sleep. It's stupid and senseless and this poor little girl,

Quincy. Her mother fought for her so hard and yet . . . Oh God, Quincy. Oh God . . ."

"We'll find who did this. We'll make sure it doesn't happen again—"

"She was a four-year-old child, Quincy! She didn't want justice. She wanted to live."

He tried to take her hand, but Rainie pulled away.

Tuesday, 12:17 p.m. PST

A DOOR OPENED, SLAMMED SHUT. The noise woke her, jerked her out of one dark place and into another. A second creak of metal and the trunk must have been opened, because suddenly, she could feel the rain on her blindfolded face.

Fight, she thought dimly, struggling to regain her earlier clarity. Kick legs, punch hands. She couldn't pull herself together. The gas fumes had permeated her brain, leaving her in a dense fog where the only thing she wanted to do was throw up.

She lay curled in the car, passive deadweight.

"I'm going to loosen your bindings," a male voice said calmly. "If you do what I say, everything will be fine. Struggle, and I'll kill you. Understand?"

Her assent was implied; with the gag in her mouth, they both knew she couldn't answer.

She felt hands move in front of her. The man's fingers were rough and not particularly nimble; he struggled with his own knots.

Kick him, she thought again. But still her body wouldn't respond to her brain.

He slapped her hands. A sharp pain raged up her forearms, blood-starved nerve endings protesting their abrupt return to life. He shook out her fingers and they struggled to obey. He already controlled more of her body than she did.

"This is a pen. Take it." He folded her right fingers around the cool metal cylinder. "This is a pad of paper. Take it." He thrust the paper into her left hand and again, her fingers found life in his orders.

"Now write. Exactly what I tell you. Word for word. Obey, and you can have some water. Disobey, and I will kill you. Understand?"

This time, she managed to nod. The motion pleased her some-how; it was the first one she'd managed on her own.

He dictated. She wrote. Not too many words, in the end. The date. The time. Where to go, what instructions to receive.

She was abducted. He wanted ransom. For some reason, that made her giggle, and that made him mad.

"What's so funny?" he demanded. "What's wrong with you?" When he got angry, his voice got higher, sounded younger.

"Are you making fun of me?"

And that made her laugh harder. Laugh as tears leaked from her eyes and soaked into the blindfold. Which made her aware of a few more things. Such as it was still raining and that if she strained her ears, she could hear the sound of the ocean, breaking against the shore.

He whipped the pen and paper away from her now. Jerked her wrists together at her waist, wrapped them this time with a zip tie.

"I hold your life in my hands, you stupid bitch. Make fun of me, and I'll throw you outta the car right now and let your body roll right down the cliff. Now whaddaya think of that?"

She thought it didn't matter. He'd managed to kidnap the one woman in the world who didn't care if she lived or died. And now what was he going to do? Ransom her back to the only family she had—a husband who had left her? When the lucky tree had come calling, this man had clearly been out to lunch.

"Poor stupid bastard," she murmured around the wad of cotton in her mouth.

The man's demeanor suddenly changed. He leaned down, his face mere inches from hers. She could practically feel his smile by her ear. "Oh, don't worry about me, Rainie Conner. Think I'm young, think I'm stupid? Think I have no idea who I'm holding in my hands? This is just the beginning of our relationship. You're going to do every single thing I ask. Or someone quite close to you is dead."

He shoved her back into the trunk. The metal door clanged down, the scent of gasoline filled her nostrils.

Rainie lay in the dark. She didn't think of Astoria anymore. She didn't think of her situation. She didn't even think of Quincy. She just wished she had a beer.

13

THE MINUTE THE JET'S WHEELS hit the ground at Portland International Airport, Kimberly was digging for her cell phone. The flight attendant caught the motion, took a disapproving step forward, then saw Kimberly's expression and did an abrupt about-face. Mac chuckled. Kimberly hit speed dial for her father.

Quincy answered on the first chime.

"We're at PDX," Kimberly reported. "You?"

"Oregon Department of Fish and Wildlife."

"You're going fishing?"

"Setting up central command in their conference room. Apparently, they have more space."

Kimberly absorbed that news — that the situation had evolved to setting up headquarters for a task force — and asked more quietly, "Rainie?"

"Appears to be an abduction-for-ransom situation, possibly a crime of opportunity." Her father's voice was eerily calm. "The local paper received a note this morning. Following its instructions, we discovered proof of life, as well as further instructions for the money drop."

"Proof of life?" Kimberly wasn't sure she wanted to know. The plane had just arrived at its gate. Mac sprang up, grabbing their bags from the overhead bins. He muscled his way down the aisle, Kimberly hot on his heels.

"Her gun," Quincy reported on the other end of the phone.

"Okay." No fingers or other extremities, which was what Kimberly feared. Her father had probably thought the same. "How are you doing?"

"Busy."

"And the officer in charge?"

"Sergeant Detective Carlton Kincaid, OSP. Seems competent."

"Wow." Kimberly turned to Mac. "My father just rated a member of the state police competent."

"Must be the grief talking," Mac said. "Or that detective's a rocket scientist."

The plane's door finally pushed open; Kimberly and Mac stepped out onto the jetway.

"So where's Oregon Fish and Wildlife?" Kimberly needed to know.

"Third Street, by the fairgrounds."

"We'll be there in an hour."

"Good. Next contact is two hours twenty."

Tuesday, 1:52 p.m. PST

THE OREGON FISH AND WILDLIFE DEPARTMENT in Bakersville seemed to be a fairly new building. Very outdoorsy. Big open lobby with giant exposed beams. An entire wall of windows, looking over verdant pastureland, framed by the coastal range. Quincy's first thought was that Rainie would like the place. His second was that he'd work a lot better if he didn't have a giant elk head watching his every move. Then there was the otter. Stuffed, mounted on a log, peering at him through dark, marble eyes.

Roadkill, one of the wildlife officers had proudly proclaimed. Real nice specimen. Amazing to find the otter in such great shape.

That simply made Quincy wonder what else the man had in his freezer, and given Quincy's line of work, that thought wasn't very comforting.

The front doors of the building swung open. An older, solidly built woman marched in, wearing the tan uniform of the Bakersville Sheriff's Department. Wide-brimmed hat pulled low over her eyes, black utility belt slung around her waist. She moved toward Quincy without hesitation and grabbed his hand in a startlingly firm hand-shake.

"Sheriff Shelly Atkins. Good to meet you. Sorry about the cir-cumstances."

Shelly Atkins had deep brown eyes set in a no-nonsense face. Quincy pegged her age close to his, with the lines crinkling her eyes to prove it. No one would call her a looker, and yet, her features were compelling. Strong. Frank. Direct. The kind of woman a man would feel comfortable buying a beer.

"Pierce," Quincy murmured, returning the handshake. Prelimin-aries done, the sheriff released his hand and moved to the oak con-ference table. Quincy remained watching her. He was still wondering why he had said Pierce, when he had always gone by Quincy.

"Where are we?" the sheriff asked.

At the head of the table, Kincaid finally looked up from the stack of paperwork he was sorting. The room already contained numerous state and local officers. With Sheriff Atkins's arrival, however, their party could apparently get started. Kincaid picked up the first pile of papers and started passing.

"All right, everyone," Kincaid's voice boomed around the room. "Let's have a seat."

Since no one had said otherwise, Quincy took the empty chair closest to Kincaid and did his best to blend in.

The handouts included copies of the first two notes from the UNSUB, as well as a typed transcript of the caller's conversation with Quincy. In addition, Kincaid had worked up a rough time line of events and a pitifully small list of what they currently knew about "UNSUB W.E.H."

Nothing in the handouts was new to Quincy. He skimmed the four pages briefly, then turned his attention to the task force instead.

With the operation ramping up, Kincaid had been busily sum-moning his troops. In addition to him, Detective Ron Spector, OSP Portland Office, had arrived, along with a young female, Alane

Grove, who operated out of Tillamook County. Detective Grove appeared barely a day over eighteen in Quincy's opinion, but he probably appeared just a shade younger than dirt in her eyes, so he supposed the bias was mutual.

The PIO—public information officer—Lieutenant Allen Mosley, was also at the table. Older, solidly built with short-cropped silver-blond hair, the lieutenant wore the uniform of the OSP and would serve as the official mouthpiece of the investigation. Quincy already understood that kidnappings were rare enough and sexy enough to spark the public's appetite for coverage. Given that this kidnapping involved a former FBI profiler's wife, the case would be nothing short of sensational. Forget the investigation; Quincy should hire an agent and start negotiating book and movie deals.

Quincy wished he didn't feel quite so angry. He didn't want to be sitting here, discussing insignificant details of a thus-far insufficient investigation. Mostly, he wanted to plant both hands on the wooden table and scream at Kincaid, "Stop fucking around and *find my wife!*"

He reshuffled the papers and worked hard on taking deep breaths.

Kincaid took up position in front of a whiteboard. More uniforms were arriving—OSP troopers, county officers, Bakersville deputies—and the sergeant seemed genuinely jazzed.

"So this is what we got," he was explaining. "At approximately two this morning..."

Had Rainie gone to a bar? That's the thing Quincy didn't understand. Given the storm, the conditions. Had she been that desperate for a drink? He had hoped his absence would shock her into sobriety. He hadn't fully contemplated that it might simply push her over the edge.

Maybe it wasn't an ambush. Maybe she'd never had to fight. Maybe it was merely a case of a lonely woman, sitting in a lonely bar, then seeing the right/wrong kind of man.

Quincy pinched the bridge of his nose with his forefinger and thumb. He didn't want to think these things. He didn't want to have these pictures in his head.

"So upon finding proof of life," Kincaid was intoning, "we also discovered a second note enclosed in a GladWare container. This second note includes instructions for an upcoming money drop. If you will please take a moment to read."

Quincy obediently shuffled Exhibit B to the top of the pile. The note said:

Dear Police:

If you have made it this far, then you know how to follow instructions. Good. Keep following instructions, and you will find the woman alive. I am not a monster. Do as I say, and everything will be all right.

The contact must be a female. She will bring $10,000 to the fairgrounds. Cash. Nothing larger than a twenty.

She must carry Pierce Quincy's cell phone. I will make contact. The moment I get the money, you get the hostage. 4 p.m. Don't be late. Failure to follow orders will be fatal.

Remember, I am a man of my word.

Sincerely,
Bruno Richard Hauptmann

Detective Grove was the first to finish the note. She looked up with a frown. "He signed his name?"

Quincy was about to open his mouth, but Sheriff Atkins surprised him by beating him to the punch. "Not unless you believe in reincarnation. Hauptmann was executed in '36. After being found guilty of kidnapping and killing Charles Lindbergh's son."

"Hauptmann was the one who stole the Lindbergh baby?" Lieutenant Mosley this time, sounding equally shocked.

Sheriff Atkins nodded, looking at the first note again, then pinning Quincy with her stare. "This first note—the Fox. Was that somebody, too?"

"Yes. William E. Hickman. Also a fairly notorious kidnapper."

"From the thirties?" Detective Grove queried.

"The twenties. There were a series of high-profile ransom cases during the twenties and thirties. All involving wealthy families. All ending in tragedy."

Everyone absorbed that news.

"Maybe he thinks by using other names, it will throw us off track," Grove speculated, the young detective sounding tentative. "We'll waste time chasing ghosts."

"Maybe he's obsessed with the past," Mosley offered. "Misses the good old days."

"It's gamesmanship," Quincy said abruptly. He was aware of Sheriff Atkins, still regarding him frankly. "He's taunting us, trying to show off what he knows. On the one hand, he does things that make him appear amateurish—handwritten notes, crude maps. On the other hand, he wants us to know that he's done his homework."

"He knows your name," the sheriff said.

"I gave it to him. First time he called, I introduced myself." Quincy faltered, realizing too late how much information he had needlessly given away to the kidnapper. Rookie mistake; he was ashamed.

"Is he experienced?" Sheriff Atkins asked steadily.

"I don't know."

"Leaving a handwritten note isn't so bright. Gives us something to trace."

"It's not his handwriting. It's the victim's." Quincy's voice cracked on the word. He said more softly, "It's Rainie's."

At the front of the room, Kincaid cleared his throat. All attention returned to him, and Quincy was grateful for the distraction. Kincaid flipped to the last page of the handouts, Exhibit D, holding it up for all of them to see.

"We've already started compiling information about the perpetrator. As you can tell, not much is known. We're talking a male, probably twenty to thirty years of age. He claims to not be from around here, but the postmark is local, so I don't think we can make any assumptions just yet. Given the crudeness of his approach, I would guess a limited educational background, certainly nothing beyond high school. And given the relatively low ransom demand, I'd speculate that he's someone living at below-average income. In terms of bulletins, we need people to keep an eye out for a lone male, particularly a stranger, driving an older-model pickup truck . . ." He paused, glanced at Quincy.

"Cargo van," Quincy provided. "A subject such as this needs a cheap mode of transportation that also has room to transport a victim, and double as lodging for when the UNSUB is on the hunt. In these cases, we see a lot of used cargo vans. Nothing fancy. Say a vehicle someone could pick up for a grand or two." His gaze switched to Sheriff Atkins. "I would have your people check camping grounds. This time of year, that would be a particularly inexpensive and relatively private place to stay."

"We can do that," the sheriff said. "'Course, you're missing the obvious."

Kincaid arched a brow. "Which is?"

Atkins shrugged. "A roundup of the usual suspects. The guys we already know are money-grubbing hustlers who wouldn't think twice about selling out their own mama, let alone snatching a woman off the streets. You said yourself you can't be sure this boy isn't from around here. Sounds to me like we should shake some local trees, see what falls out."

"What are you going to do?" Kincaid said dryly. "Go door to door and ask the good old boys if they've kidnapped someone recently?"

Sheriff Atkins didn't blink an eye. "Personally, I think I'd take a little tour of their property, see if I happen to notice any brand-new pickup trucks or ATVs that might put someone in the hole ten grand. Then maybe I'd make myself known, ask for a little tour of the home. Check out the rooms, the outbuildings, see if I can make 'em sweat. Who knows, I might even rustle up a few more meth labs for you fine folks to process."

The last comment was a dig at the state police's current efforts— or lack thereof—to contain the growing methamphetamine problem in the county. Kincaid took the barb in the spirit in which it was intended.

"Sounds like a plan to me," the sergeant said tightly. "I'd recommend that your people travel in pairs and exercise due caution on your tours, though. Surprise someone with a hostage and things can get very dicey, very quick."

"Well, thanks, Sergeant. We'll try to remember how to do our jobs."

"Fine." Kincaid cleared his throat again, rustled his papers. "That leaves a canvass of the local hotels and motels, plus retracing the victim's last steps. I want a detailed profile of every person Lorraine Conner has seen in the past twenty-four hours, plus every place she's been. Detective Grove, why don't you handle that? Determine how many troopers you need, I'll make it happen."

"Yes, sir." Alane Grove sat up smartly. Assigned a meaningful task, she was glowing.

"That leaves Detective Spector to coordinate the scientists. Both Latent Prints and two primary examiners from the Portland lab should be here at any time now. We have the car still to process, not to mention two notes, an envelope, a plastic container, and the gun. Should be a wealth of information right there. Which brings us to the final immediate task—managing the *Daily Sun*. In the good-news department, the owner, Owen Van Wie, has promised us complete cooperation. He also assigned his best news reporter, Adam Danicic, to work with us on coverage of the case."

Lieutenant Mosley nodded, picking up his pen. "We'll need to hold a press briefing ASAP. Better that the media hear the details from us than from wildly speculative rumors. Of course, the first question will be, *Are* we calling in the FBI?"

Kincaid didn't miss a beat. "No. There's no indication the victim has crossed state lines, and nothing here our own crime lab can't handle. Naturally, we appreciate the assistance of local and county investigators with our efforts."

"Aw, shucks," Sheriff Atkins said.

Kincaid flashed her an equally gracious smile.

Quincy, however, had had enough.

"Final immediate task?" he asked incredulously. "What about securing the fairgrounds? What about procuring the ransom money? What about wiring a female officer? The tasks you just outlined will take days to complete. We have two hours."

Kincaid wouldn't look at him. Neither would Mosley. The room took on a sudden, expectant hush. And in that silence, Quincy finally understood. He slammed his fist on the table.

"I'm going to pay the money," he said harshly. "Goddammit, you cannot stop me from paying that money."

"Mr. Quincy—"

"She is my wife! She is a fellow member of law enforcement, how dare you—"

"We are going to make every effort in our power to find your wife."

"Except follow his instructions!"

"We're not going to disregard them either. Lieutenant Mosley and I were discussing it earlier; I think it's highly appropriate to open a two-way dialogue—"

"No! It's too big a risk. We don't know enough, I won't allow it."

Kincaid fell silent again. Lieutenant Mosley, too.

And then Quincy got the rest of it. He had been so pleased Kincaid had let him participate in the investigation. He had never stopped to wonder about Kincaid's motives. For example, did he really value Quincy's help, or did he just want to keep the former investigator busy?

When Quincy spoke again, his voice wasn't angry anymore. It was deceptively quiet. "When?"

Kincaid glanced at his watch. "The special edition of the *Daily Sun* is probably rolling off the presses as we speak."

"Who crafted the message?"

Kincaid didn't flinch. "I did."

"You're not qualified. Call the FBI. Get a profiler. Do things right."

"I would never heedlessly endanger the life of the hostage," Kincaid said firmly. "Our message is simple and clear. We will absolutely pay the ransom, we just need more time. That works in all of our favors, Mr. Quincy, including Rainie's."

"You don't understand yet. It's not about the money, Sergeant Detective Kincaid. It's about power: his desire to have it and hold it over our heads—"

"Thank you, Mr. Quincy."

"One wrong word from you and he'll kill her out of spite."

"Thank you, Mr. Quincy."

"You need to bring in a professional—"

"It's *done,* Mr. Quincy. It's done."

In the silence that followed, Quincy felt those words like a blow to the chest. The breath caught in his lungs. He could feel his heart race, adrenaline, anger, anguish. Thirty years. Thirty years of building a knowledge base, of honing an instinct, of earning a reputation for being the best of the best. And now, when it mattered most, when Rainie was out there, helpless, vulnerable, needing him . . .

He gathered up his things. He made it out the front doors just as the skies opened up and it once more started to rain.

14

SHELLY ATKINS CAUGHT UP with him in the parking lot. She ran up behind him. Quincy turned at the last minute, shoulders hunched, lips thinned. He wasn't in the mood and felt no need to disguise it.

The sheriff came to a halt several feet back. She didn't speak right away. The rain pelted between them, running in rivulets off Shelly's hat and forming puddles at their feet.

"Long night," she said at last.

Quincy shrugged. They'd all been up since the early hours of morning; it wasn't worth discussing to him.

"State likes to run their own show," the sheriff tried again.

"They always do."

"I talked to Luke Hayes this morning. He had a lot of nice things to say about your wife. As a person, as an investigator. He was real surprised to find out she'd gone missing. He said he'd do some asking around on his own."

"I appreciate that."

"He also said you used to work with the bureau, that you're pretty good at these things."

Quincy merely shrugged again.

"Do you think he's local?" she asked abruptly. There was no need to define who.

"I think the UNSUB knows this area," Quincy stated carefully. "I think he's either lived here in the past, or at least visited enough to be very familiar with the terrain. Kidnappings entail complicated logistics; an UNSUB would want to be somewhere he feels comfortable."

"I read somewhere," Shelly said, "that most ransom cases have a personal connection. A business partner, a family member, or hell, even a loan shark, looking to get back something owed to them."

"Rainie didn't gamble, I'm her business partner, and the only debt we have is our mortgage. Though with banks these days . . . maybe I shouldn't put anything past them."

The rain was picking up, starting to come down in sheets. The sheriff didn't seem to notice. Quincy had already spent so much of the day being wet and tired, he didn't care that much himself. Maybe they never should've moved to Oregon, he found himself thinking. Maybe if he'd demanded that they remain in New York, Rainie would still be safe.

"Kincaid's not so bad," Shelly offered up at last.

"He has his moments."

"And all of us, we're going to work real hard on this."

"I appreciate that."

"Of course, if I were you, I wouldn't want to take anyone at their word."

Quincy cocked his head, finally eyeing the sheriff with interest.

"I'd want to do my own asking around," Shelly was saying. "I'd want some good ideas of where to start."

"Yes," Quincy agreed quietly. "I would like that."

"I had a deputy making some calls this morning, routine checks of places Rainie was known to frequent. You know, in case she magically showed up. One of those calls was to Dougie Jones's foster mom, Laura Carpenter. According to her, the minute she mentioned Rainie's name, Dougie asked if she was missing. Dougie seemed to think that Rainie was a liar, and liars get what they deserve."

"What else did Dougie say?"

"Mrs. Carpenter didn't have anything else to report. 'Course,

Dougie's statement does seem to warrant some kind of follow-up. Then again, Dougie doesn't do so well with uniforms. Or for that matter, men."

"Then it's a good thing my daughter's coming to town," Quincy said.

"Why, yes, it would be." Shelly Atkins finally cracked a smile. It took ten years off her age and made him notice her eyes once again. She had soft brown eyes. It was hard to imagine a woman with eyes like that ever telling a lie.

"What brought you to Bakersville, Sheriff Atkins?" he heard himself ask.

"The job. Used to work in La Grande. In comparison, this is a big step up."

"Miss the quiet old days yet?"

She grinned at him. "Never in a million years."

Shelly trotted back toward the Fish and Wildlife building just as a car turned into the parking lot. Quincy caught a glimpse of Kimberly behind the wheel, Mac in the passenger's seat.

Quincy had a plan. Now he had his own crew. He also had one last item Kincaid had neglected to grab when Quincy had bolted from the room—his cell phone. The kidnapper had already called it once. Quincy was willing to bet money he'd call it again soon.

Tuesday, 3:01 p.m. PST

"WELL, TO GIVE THE OSP CREDIT, the statement's not half bad," Kimberly said fifteen minutes later. They were seated in Martha's Diner, on the outskirts of town. It had always been a favorite spot of Rainie's; she was addicted to Martha's homemade blueberry pie. Quincy had ordered a piece. It sat, uneaten at the table, like a memorial.

Kimberly pushed the *Daily Sun* across the table toward Quincy. Rainie's kidnapping was front-page news, except that her name and occupation were never revealed. Quincy could read signs of the OSP's influence everywhere. Key facts had been withheld to keep from informing the abductor of things he may not yet know. Other leading statements had been deliberately included—victim may have last been seen at a bar—in an attempt to elicit information from the public.

The article concluded with a formal statement from the PIO. "'We are eager to work with the abductor in this matter,' said Lt. Mosley, 'to do everything in our power to ensure the return of the victim, safe and sound. Unfortunately, new federal banking requirements do not allow us to meet the abductor's current demands in the time frame given. We encourage the abductor to call us immediately, at a number set up just for his use, so that we may discuss this matter with him and work out an agreeable payment plan. Again, we understand the abductor's demands and we want to be of help, we just need a little more time.'"

The number was at the end of the article, a hotline that probably led straight to the op center, where an entire task force and a tape recorder were standing by. Quincy thought that was too obvious. He had his own ideas about what number the UNSUB would call, and it wasn't some police-controlled hotline.

"So the abductor calls in," Kimberly said, "and they have an expert ready to negotiate."

"I believe they have Kincaid ready to negotiate. I don't know yet if I would call the sergeant an expert."

"But you don't think he's a dumb bunny."

"I will grant him one step above bunny level of intelligence."

"I see the bloom is off the rose," Mac murmured. He was working his way through an enormous piece of chicken-fried steak with apparent gusto.

On the other hand, Kimberly had inherited her father's lack of appetite. Her tuna salad remained largely ignored; same with his cup of soup.

"OSP's strategy?" Kimberly asked her father.

"Kincaid didn't feel it necessary to share the details with me, but I would assume they're going with the classic approach: buy time to allow the police to further their investigation and get their ducks in a row. If all goes as planned, they'll find Rainie before it ever gets to a ransom drop."

"New federal banking requirements." Mac finished the last bite of steak, pushed away his plate. "Nice touch, but only if the guy hasn't done his homework."

"Kincaid's current assumption is that the kidnapper is of limited educational background. The local yokel, if you will."

Mac grinned at that. "And you?"

"The means of communication has been simple but clever. The notes, while short, are properly spelled and adequately articulated. Some aspects of behavior have been crude, but then again, very effective."

"Simple does not necessarily equal dumb," Kimberly murmured.

"Exactly."

"Well, the guy had to have something going for him to abduct a woman like Rainie. I can't imagine her falling for just any ruse, or going down without a fight."

Quincy didn't say anything. The silence grew long, and in that silence he heard months' worth of fighting and arguing and worrying. He had never said anything to Kimberly about it. He hadn't wanted to violate Rainie's privacy. Or maybe he just hadn't wanted to admit to anyone, not even his daughter, that his second marriage was failing.

Kimberly and Mac exchanged a look. Quincy saw it, but still couldn't bring himself to speak.

"Was she really at a bar?" Kimberly finally asked, voice gentle.

"I don't know. We have yet to retrace her last steps."

"Dad, you should know her last steps."

"You assume I was still living at the house."

"Oh, Dad." Kimberly reached across the table, squeezed his hand. She and Mac exchanged another look, with Mac suddenly declaring, "I think I'll go to the bathroom."

"No, no." Quincy removed his hand, shaking aside his daughter's concern and Mac's obvious ploy. He forced himself to sound firm, matter-of-fact. For a man who'd spent most of his life dissembling, it wasn't so hard after all. "It's not a secret, certainly nothing the Oregon State Police don't already know. Rainie and I have separated. It happened last week. I had hopes that it would be temporary. I thought if I left, it might shock her into finally stopping drinking."

"Oh, Dad." Kimberly sounded dismayed again. In contrast, Mac was to the point.

"When?"

"It started several months ago. At least that's the best I can tell. We were called in for a double homicide in August. The scene involved a mother and her small child. Rainie's been struggling ever since."

"You've both been to bad scenes before," Mac said.

"Define bad," Quincy challenged with a shrug. "As a professional, I can give you theories. That the combined weight of so many cases finally caught up with her—the tipping point, if you will. That actively preparing to adopt a child made her more vulnerable to this particular case—lack of compartmentalization, if you will. None of it really matters. At the end of the day, it seems that each and every member of law enforcement has that one case that hits too close to home. You had your case several years ago, Mac. In August, Rainie found hers."

Mac looked away. He wasn't going to comment on that, and they knew it.

"What about the upcoming adoption?" Kimberly asked. "That must have given Rainie something to look forward to."

"It fell through."

"Oh, Dad," Kimberly murmured again.

"Naturally, the separation puts me in a slightly different light in the OSP's eyes," Quincy said briskly. "Sergeant Kincaid has opted to share some details of the investigation with me, but has obviously kept many more to himself."

"Lovely," Mac muttered. "As if you don't have enough things to worry about."

"In the good-news department," Quincy continued, "I seem to have found an ally in Sheriff Shelly Atkins, Luke Hayes's successor. She gave me a lead: Apparently the boy Rainie has been working with, Dougie Jones, commented first thing this morning that Rainie might be missing. He called Rainie a liar and said liars get what they deserve."

"You think a child did it?" Kimberly asked with a frown.

"Dougie's seven, which makes that doubtful. But then again . . ." Quincy shrugged. "He's a troubled, mixed-up boy who's led a troubled, mixed-up life. It's quite possible he knows something about what happened."

"So when do we go talk to him?" Mac spoke up, pushing away from the table and gesturing for the bill.

"I was thinking Kimberly would interview him. Soon as possible."

"Me?" Kimberly looked around the table.

"Dougie doesn't like cops or men."

Kimberly narrowed her eyes. "And while I'm following up with this charming young boy, what are you two going to be doing?"

"Going to the fairgrounds, of course. Kincaid spent a lot of time and energy preparing the newspaper article, but he also made one very big assumption: that the UNSUB would read it before four p.m."

"Oooh, fun," Mac murmured, already reading between those lines.

Quincy said, "My thought exactly."

15

"Do you believe in true love?"

The voice came from far away, accompanied by the rattle of pots and pans. She was dreaming again, Rainie thought. Dreaming of a dark void filled with a booming voice. Maybe this was heaven.

Heaven smelled like bacon, she realized without a trace of irony. Then the voice boomed again.

"My mom believed in true love. Believed it when she fell in bed with my father. Believed it when she scrubbed his clothes, bought his whiskey, and bruised from the impact of his fist. Yeah, my mom was a real romantic. Probably loved my father right until the moment he beat her to death. My mother called it love, my father called it obedience. Frankly, I think they were both full of shit."

A hand touched her shoulder. Rainie flinched, discovered that she was propped precariously on the edge of a hard wooden chair and nearly fell off.

"Relax," the voice said impatiently. "It's time you pulled yourself together. You have work to do."

More sounds, the person—lone male, probably early twenties to early thirties, based upon the voice—was moving around the room.

A refrigerator door sucked open, slammed shut. A crack, sizzle, then a new smell filled the air. Eggs frying. Bacon and eggs. Breakfast.

It must be morning, she thought, but that estimation didn't feel quite right. Still blindfolded, hands bound, it was hard to get her bearings. She'd been drugged, fading in and out. She could remember white light, movement, writing a note. Surely those things took time. But how much time?

She should sit up, clear her head. It was easier to remain in her dark, bound cocoon, slouched in the middle of God knows where. Captives didn't have to think. Captives didn't have to feel.

She realized faintly that the gag was gone, though her mouth was so dried out, it was no more capable of forming words without the gag than it had been with it. After another moment, she determined she could move her feet. So he'd removed the gag and unbound her feet. Why? Because she had work to do?

It couldn't be morning, she decided. She had left her house shortly after one a.m. It felt as if that had been at least twelve hours ago. Her abductor must have gone back to bed. That made sense to her. After rampaging around in the middle of the night, he'd gone back to bed and was now eating a late breakfast/early lunch. Midday. That felt better to her.

He was scraping a pan now. The air in the room tasted smoky, laced with grease. She had a mental image of a small room without being sure why. Tiny kitchen in a shut-up house. Beneath the grease, she thought she could smell moldy linens and stale, uncirculated air.

The squeaking sound of something—a chair—being dragged across linoleum. The man sat down heavily and Rainie suddenly felt a forkful of eggs pressed against her lips.

"Eat, but slowly. The drugs can leave you feeling queasy. Throw up and you're on your own. No way I'm dealing with that kind of mess."

Just the smell of the eggs made her stomach roll. Rainie licked her lips, tried to form a word, had to try again. "Water," she croaked. Then, slightly louder, "Water."

Her voice sounded foreign to her. Harsh, guttural, raw. The voice of a victim.

The chair screeched again. The man was up, moving. She could sense his impatience in the hard slam of a plastic cup against a counter, the jerk of a water faucet being snapped on.

A moment later, the cup was thrust against her lips. "Four sips, then some eggs, then more water. Come on, start drinking. I don't have all day."

She did as she was told. On some level this surprised her. But maybe it didn't. How long had she been feeling helpless now? It had started way before Abductor A had discovered her at Point B. She had felt overwhelmed and powerless since first walking through that house in Astoria, since gazing down at that small lifeless body. Since feeling the terror that still pervaded that room, since knowing what that little girl had been forced to know. No one to help her anymore. No one to save her. And that man would have loomed so large and powerful, as he ripped off her pajamas, as he prepared to do what he was going to do.

No happy ending here. The man had done what he'd wanted, then he'd placed a pillow over four-year-old Aurora Johnson's face and smothered her to death. Where was the justice in that? Where was God?

And Rainie had been feeling herself slip away ever since. Time spent on the Internet, searching for stories she knew she shouldn't read. A twelve-year-old boy who raped and murdered a three-year-old toddler. A mudslide killing a mother and three small children after the husband popped out the door to buy them all ice cream. Then there was the tsunami. Over two hundred thousand people gone in the blink of an eye, a third of them children who never stood a chance. Not that the survivors were much luckier. According to news reports, slave traffickers promptly took advantage of the chaos to pick off orphans and turn them into sex slaves.

All of these children born into the world simply to lead lives of terror, misery, and suffering.

What was one person to do? For every murder she helped investigate, millions more were happening. And the perpetrators were no longer hard-bitten criminals, with yellowed crooked teeth and small beady eyes. They were charming suburban husbands. They were soccer moms. They were children themselves, ten, eleven, twelve years old.

Rainie's head was filled with too many things she didn't want to know. Pictures that tormented her. Questions that haunted her. Had little Aurora died knowing how much her mother had loved her, how hard her mother had fought to the bitter end? Or had she died hating her own mom for failing her so completely?

"Another bite," her captor demanded.

She opened her mouth, obediently swallowed, then much to the surprise of them both, projectile-vomited across the table.

"Ah, Jesus Christ!" The man sprang back, his chair clattering to the floor. "That's disgusting. Oh, man . . ."

He didn't seem to know what to do. Rainie continued to sit, an impassive lump, letting him sort it out. She could taste bile in her mouth. Water would be nice. Maybe orange juice. Anything to soothe her throat.

And then she thought of Quincy. She saw him, standing in front of her so clearly she tried to reach out her bound hands. She was in the study. It was late at night. He stood in the doorway, his dark green bathrobe belted around his waist.

"Come to bed," he said.

But she couldn't. She was reading another horrible story and couldn't possibly tear her eyes away. She was a sponge, soaking up the sorrows of the world and feeling the last of herself silently erode away.

"Rainie, what are you looking for?" he had asked her quietly.

She didn't have an answer for him and when she looked up again, he was gone. So she reached down into the filing cabinet, and pulled out her beer.

"Shit, shit, shit," her captor was grumbling now. "I mean, really. Ah jeez." Water running in the sink. The sound of a sponge being squeezed. So he was cleaning it up after all. His only other choice was to untie her hands and he couldn't do that.

The thought amused her. So her captive was helpless, too, a victim of his own making. She started to smile.

The next instant, the man slapped her across the face and she slammed to the floor.

"Get that goddamn smirk off your face," he roared. "Don't you smile at me!"

She could feel him towering above her, his rage a physical presence that suddenly filled the room. In her mind, she could see him clearly. Hands fisted. Jaw clenched. He wanted to do it: pound her, smack her again and again. Beat her like his father had beaten his mother. Beat her, like her own mother had been beaten by an endless slew of faceless boyfriends.

What comes around goes around. The children who suffer today will be the monsters who inflict suffering tomorrow.

And then, even with the blindfold on, Rainie knew exactly who her abductor was. She had known him most of her life. He was a piece of herself, her past coming back to get her. The minute she'd opened that first beer three months ago, she had plummeted into the abyss, and he was simply the devil who'd been waiting her whole life to find her.

The man grabbed the collar of her shirt. He jerked her to her feet, dragging her shoulder through the vomit and smearing the unbearable stench upon her clothes. She reeled, off balance. He pushed her again and the back of her legs connected with something low and hard. A coffee table, a chair. It didn't matter. No place to go. No room to retreat. She stood there, breathing hard and feeling his advance.

"Your husband left you, Lorraine," the man jeered.

She didn't say anything, didn't quite understand. How could he know that?

"What'd you do? Whore around? Sleep with his best friend?"

"N-n-no," she finally whispered. Her heart was pounding. Funny how his physical advance did little to intimidate her, but his questions left her terrified.

"Are you a slut, Lorraine?"

Her chin came up. She didn't answer.

"Yeah, I can see it. Probably screwed around all over town. Left your husband no choice but to run out with his tail between his legs."

Rainie surprised herself. She drew together what little moisture she could find in her mouth and spit in the man's direction.

In response, her captor grabbed her hair and jerked back her head. She couldn't quite stop the cry that escaped from her throat.

"Does he hate you?"

"N-n-no." At least she didn't think Quincy hated her. Not yet.

"You wrote the note, you know what I want. Will he pay it, Lorraine? Will your husband cough up ten grand for his lousy, whoring wife?"

"Yes." She said the word with more confidence. Quincy would pay. He would pay ten times that amount, a hundred times that amount. And not just because he was a responsible man or a former FBI agent, but because he did love her, had always loved her. Those had been the words in his note. Not "goodbye," not "get your head out of your ass," not "stop drinking, you stupid bitch." He had written, her man of few words, "I love you." And that had been it.

"I hope for your sake you're telling the truth," her captor said now. "I hope for your sake your old man coughs up the dough. Because I'm not looking for a roommate, Lorraine. In the next hour, I get the cash, or you get an early grave. So don't play any games. Don't you try messing with me."

The man's hand was still wrapped around her hair. He used her mane like a rope, jerking her toward the door.

"There is no such thing as true love," the man said again. "There's just the beauty of cold hard cash. And now, it's time for Quincy to pay."

16

KIMBERLY PARKED HER CAR, looked around, then sighed heavily. The rain had finally subsided to a light mist but there was no getting around it; she was about to ruin her favorite pair of shoes.

Kimberly's slim-fitting black slacks and tailored silk top had made perfect sense for a seventy-degree day in Atlanta, Georgia. Bad news about dashing to the airport, however, was there'd been no time to stop by her house. Instead, she'd grabbed her emergency duffel bag from the trunk of her car. It contained one FBI-issue navy blue windbreaker, one change of underwear, toothbrush, toothpaste, hairbrush, and deodorant. That was it.

In other words, no boots appropriate for slogging through a fifty-foot stretch of mud. No casual clothes more suited for approaching a small child. No sweater to protect her arms from the raw chill. She could try the windbreaker, but given the subject's reported dislike of law enforcement, it probably wasn't best to arrive in a jacket emblazoned *FBI*.

Nope, she was overdressed in nice slacks, nice shirt, and a positively killer pair of heels. And now she was going to suffer. God, you had to love this job.

She opened the door of her rental car and stepped out into the muddy driveway. Her heel promptly sank down two inches. She pulled it out, and the mud made a giant sucking sound.

She tried a second step, hell-bent on her efforts, and nearly jumped out of her skin when a voice suddenly spoke from the woods.

"Those shoes are pretty."

Kimberly turned toward the sound, precariously balanced with one foot sunken forward, one foot sunken back. She saw a young boy peering at her from beneath a towering fir tree. He had large brown eyes, nearly too big for his face. The rest of him was thin and scrawny, his blue sweatshirt and mud-splattered jeans nearly hanging off his frame.

At her look, he shoved his hands into his pockets and hunched his shoulders. He'd obviously been outside awhile. His sweatshirt appeared soaked, his wet hair formed dark spikes against his forehead. He had a smear of mud across one cheek and pine needles stuck to his clothes. He didn't seem to notice, however, just kept staring at her.

"These shoes," Kimberly said at last, "*are* pretty. Pretty worthless." She grimaced, pulled up her front foot a second time, and earned a fresh round of protest from the muck. Screw it. She slid off both shoes, dangling them from her hand, and proceeded toward the boy barefoot. The mud oozed between her toes, kind of reminding her of this one time in Virginia . . . Best not to think of it.

She slogged forward and the boy started to giggle.

"Don't tell me you never walked barefoot in the mud," Kimberly said. "And splashed in puddles? Oh, you haven't lived until you've marched barefoot in the rain."

Dougie Jones, she presumed, took her bait. He knelt down, working eagerly on the laces of his filthy tennis shoes. He had thin, fast-moving fingers. They struggled, however, with the rain-soaked knots, giving Kimberly time to approach.

"Would you like some help?" she asked him.

Wordlessly, Dougie stuck out a foot.

With her outfit well beyond ruined already, Kimberly squatted down in the dirt and went to work on the boy's laces. "Other foot."

He complied. She got both shoes off, then Dougie eagerly stripped off his socks. They were cheap white athletic socks, the kind with colored bands around the top. The heels were threadbare, the toes stained the color of nicotine. Something about their pitiful state made Kimberly sad. It didn't seem like it should be too much to buy a boy a new pair of socks.

"You're Dougie Jones, aren't you?"

The boy nodded distractedly.

"Hi," she said softly. "My name is Kimberly."

Dougie didn't seem to care. He planted his feet in the mire. He wiggled his toes, watching the muck ooze around each little piggy.

"I like beetles," Dougie said. "Want to see one?"

He reached into his pocket. Being a trained FBI agent, Kimberly managed not to scream as the boy pulled a giant black bug out of his pants and plopped it down on her arm. The bug was huge. And fast. It scurried right up her shoulder to her wet, streaming hair.

"That's a fine bug," Kimberly said faintly, holding perfectly still. Dougie remained staring at her, watching, waiting, testing.

The beetle arrived at her neck. Before she gave in to impulse and opened fire on the insect, Kimberly grabbed it in her left hand. Sticky legs promptly flailed frantically against her fist. She dropped the beetle back to earth.

"It's a beautiful beetle, Dougie," Kimberly said. "But it doesn't belong in your pocket. Beetles belong outside in the woods. It'll die in captivity."

Dougie looked her in the eye. Then he raised his bare foot and squashed his pet into the mud. He stood on top of the beetle for a long time, staring at Kimberly with big, emotionless eyes.

Kimberly had a sudden insight into why Rainie might have started to drink.

"Why are you standing on the beetle, Dougie?" Kimberly asked quietly.

"Because I want to."

"The beetle might die."

The boy shrugged.

"If you don't care about that beetle, Dougie, who will?"

Dougie frowned, seeming caught off guard by that question. He raised his foot, almost curiously. The beetle churned around in the empty footprint, still seeking some means of escape.

Dougie watched the beetle for a long time. Kimberly remained squatting beside the boy, shoulder to shoulder, in the mud.

"The agency sent you," Dougie told her.

"No."

Dougie frowned. "The agency sent you," he repeated, more firmly now. "Are you taking me away? Because I don't mind. We can go. Just go. Where is the lady in the purple suit?"

"Dougie, I'm a friend of Rainie's. I came here looking for Rainie."

Dougie scowled. His shoulders hunched, he turned away from Kimberly. "I don't want to talk to you anymore."

"I'm sorry to hear that."

"She drinks, you know."

"Rainie drinks?"

"Yes."

"You saw her drinking?"

"No." He sounded matter-of-fact. "But I know. She says she wants to help me. She says she's my friend. But she's a drunk. I know these things."

"I see. Did you know, Dougie, that Rainie is missing?"

He shrugged.

"That's sad for me. I'm Rainie's friend and I would like to find her."

Dougie looked at her. "You're stupid."

The vehemence in his words caught her off guard. Kimberly leaned back, almost lost her balance, and had to catch herself with a hand in the mud. "Why do you say that?"

But Dougie wouldn't answer her. His lower lip jutted out, trembling. He grabbed the beetle again, and this time stuck it in his mouth. His right cheek bulged, then his left, as the beetle continued its frantic fight for life.

Kimberly wasn't sure what to do anymore. The interrogation trainers at the Academy had definitely never met the likes of Dougie Jones.

She picked up a stick. She started tracing pictures in the mud; it seemed better than staring at Dougie's plump, churning cheeks.

"When I was younger," she said quietly, "older than you, but still too young, my older sister died. Then, a year later, my mother died. She was murdered actually, in her own home, by the same man who killed my sister. He chased my mother from room to room with a knife. I looked up the story in the news. I saw photos of the crime scene."

Kimberly drew another picture. She wasn't much of an artist. She started out with a square, then turned it into a crude house. The front door was too small, the windows too big. She tried to draw a tree in front, but it quickly overshadowed the tiny house, giving the drawing an ominous flair. She knew children who had been victimized often drew dark, scary pictures. It was her past. Maybe it was Dougie's, too.

"That same man, that killer, he tried to get to me next. I ran. I flew all the way from New York to Portland, Oregon, hoping to get away. But the man chased me, Dougie. He found me. He held a gun to my head. He described to me exactly how he was going to kill me, and in my own mind, I already saw myself dead."

Kimberly finally looked up. Dougie was staring at her, enraptured.

"It's hard to lose your mom," she whispered. "It makes you alone in the world. Alone is scary. Alone is not knowing what's going to happen next. Alone is having no one to help you. Do you know why I'm still alive, Dougie? Do you know why that man didn't kill me?"

Slowly, Dougie shook his head.

"Rainie," Kimberly said simply. "She interceded, she kept him talking, got him distracted. And that bought us time. In the end, he was the one who was shot, not me. Rainie saved my life, Dougie. That's why she's my friend."

Dougie took the stick from her. He scratched out the crude drawing, working on it until nothing was left but waterlogged dirt. Then he opened his mouth and removed the beetle, holding it between his forefinger and thumb. The beetle's legs were still kicking. Dougie watched it squirm.

"Friends aren't perfect," Kimberly said. "Friends make mistakes. I bet you know a lot of people who've made mistakes, Dougie. I bet you know a lot of people who have disappointed you. I wish I could tell you it won't happen again, but mistakes are part of life."

"Stanley beats me," Dougie said abruptly.

"And Stanley is . . . ?"

"My foster dad. He beats me. I told the lady in purple and she told Rainie. Rainie's supposed to stop Stanley, but she didn't."

"I'm sorry to hear that, Dougie. Has Stanley hit you recently?"

"Yes."

"Do you have a bruise?"

Dougie shook his head. "You can hurt little boys without leaving a bruise. Stanley knows that."

In spite of herself, Kimberly felt a chill. She looked at the house, set thirty yards back. The covered porch shadowed the windows. Giant fir trees cast the entire structure into deeper gloom. The house was small and dark, American Gothic. Kimberly certainly wouldn't want to live there.

"Dougie, has Stanley mentioned Rainie's name? Did he tell you she was missing?"

"I don't talk to Stanley."

"Have you ever seen him and Rainie fight?"

Dougie thinned his lips. He finally released the beetle. It went scurrying madly for the nearest rock.

"Maybe they fought recently?" Kimberly pressed. "Did Stanley ever threaten to hit Rainie?"

"Rainie was supposed to see me Thursday," Dougie said. "She never came. She went to a bar."

"Who told you that, Dougie? How do you know Rainie went to a bar?"

The boy refused to answer again, his lips set in a hard line, his chin coming up defiantly. But Kimberly thought she knew the answer this time. The boy had been right; Stanley knew how to hurt without ever leaving a mark.

"Dougie," Kimberly said quietly. "One last time: Is there something you'd like to tell me?"

"I hope Rainie dies," Dougie said, then he ran to a small rock, scooped up the beetle, and went racing back into the woods.

17

QUINCY AND MAC PARKED a block away from the fairgrounds, at the old pink auction house where dairy cattle used to be sold every Tuesday morning and which had now sat abandoned for years. From inside the cover of his car, Quincy eyed the horizon. In theory, several hours of daylight remained. The thick, black rain clouds, however, obscured the sun, casting the afternoon in the deep gray tones of dusk.

He popped open his door, stepping out into a steady mist, and rounding to the trunk of his sedan. Mac followed behind him.

Quincy had spent most of his life being called out at a moment's notice, and old habits were hard to break. The trunk of his luxury sedan still contained the basic tools of any seasoned profiler: a duffel bag with a spare change of clothes; an old pair of hiking boots for accessing deep ravines, favored by so many killers as dumping grounds; two cameras; a box of latex gloves; a thin white hazmat suit; emergency flares, flashlights; a first-aid kit; and, of course, a metal lockbox containing firearms—a shotgun, a rifle, and a backup .22, complete with half a dozen boxes of ammunition.

Wordlessly, the two men prepared. Quincy took the rifle; Mac the shotgun. They each helped themselves to a flashlight. From his own bag, Mac produced a windbreaker, emblazoned *GBI,* topping it with a department-issue baseball cap. Quincy, however, remained a cover model for Brooks Brothers in his tan trench-style raincoat, emblazoned with nothing at all.

"I would wear your ID where it is easily visible," Quincy advised Mac.

"So I don't get shot as a suspected kidnapper?"

"Kimberly would have my hide."

"You know, one of these days, you guys should try having a nice ordinary family reunion. Go hiking, have a picnic lunch, hang out. Get together for a reason other than someone is trying to kill one of you."

"It would never work. In case you haven't noticed, none of us has the gift of gab." Quincy finished belting his raincoat around the rifle. Accessible but not too visible. Extra ammunition went into his pockets. The flashlight he kept in his hand.

Mac was clearly displeased with Quincy's generic outfit. "You don't own anything at all that says FBI? Not even a lousy sweatshirt?"

"The bureau would consider it false advertising. Besides, most of these officers have seen me before. They won't mistake me for a random kidnapper. Much more likely they'll shoot me because they think my presence proves the estranged husband did it after all."

"Wow, you sure know how to show a guy a good time."

The rain picked up speed, pelting Quincy's face. He grinned through the deluge. "That's what they all say."

The Bakersville County fairgrounds were simply enormous. Quincy knew that, had been here before during the hot days of August to enjoy the charming country fair, complete with Ferris wheels, horse races, livestock shows, and booth after booth of fresh, cool ice cream. Now, hunkered down next to an oversized sculpture of Tillamook cheese, he stared at the sprawling compound and felt himself quickly become overwhelmed.

First, there were the fields: endless acres of exposed, flat land, meant for carnival rides, vendors' wares, and cotton candy. Then came the buildings: the main two-story building with its cupola top, flanked on either side by two enormous buildings, each of those split into two distinct areas, auditorium and convention center to the left, youth dairy and open dairy to the right. And that was just at the main entrance. Behind those vaulted structures loomed the grandstands, the racetrack and paddocks, the 4-H livestock barn, the 4-H horse barn.

This time of year, the youth dairy served as indoor tennis courts—not bad once you got used to the overwhelming stench of manure. Another building had been converted to a roller-skating rink, while various organizations rented out the auditorium for banquet functions.

But the effort at granting the fairgrounds a second life during the off-season had always been feeble, and the results were plain to see: four o'clock on a Tuesday afternoon, not a single car in the empty parking lot.

The fairgrounds remained a vast, empty, echoing space. It would take an entire SWAT team to secure the premises. Perhaps two or three. The abductor had chosen well, and for the first time, Quincy felt himself falter.

Was it years that aged a man? Or simply the growing realization of all the things he was powerless to control? That identifying a predator didn't always lead to justice. That even when the courts finally ground out a guilty verdict, it didn't bring a murdered child back from the dead, or help her parents sleep any better at night.

All Quincy wanted was his wife back. He wanted to be in their family room, in front of a roaring fire. Rainie reading a book, snuggled up against his chest. Him, stroking her arm, watching the way the flames reflected in her long chestnut hair. They would both be comfortable, wordless, the way it had been just six months ago.

It seemed so little to want out of life, and yet he honestly didn't know if he would ever have that again. In Quincy's world, happiness had always been a luxury and never a guarantee.

Mac was watching him, waiting for instructions, a plan of attack.

"I don't see signs of other officers," Mac said at last.

"That simply means they're doing their job."

"You're sure this Kincaid guy is here?"

"He would be negligent not to send at least a few bodies. Kincaid might be aggressive in his handling of the case, but he's not stupid."

"So we just march on in?"

"No. If the kidnapper doesn't shoot us, Kincaid's officers probably will. They're doing their job; let's not muck it up now." Quincy took a deep breath, considering the vast space once more. "Main entrance building is too exposed," he murmured. "The upper-level loft supplies a bird's-eye view of the lower floor, rendering it worthless. The barns are also big open spaces with no place to hide. Same with the auditorium, the convention center. These places are meant to allow the maximum exhibit space, not conceal a kidnapper. So where would he go? He chose this space. Why? What does it give him that he needs?"

"Grounds are big, hard to cover."

"But that works both ways. Bigger it is, the more time it's going to take him to get in and out."

Mac was nodding now, picking up the train of thought. "Like us, he's going to want to conceal his vehicle. That means walking in, but he also has a hostage. Maybe she can walk herself, led by him, or maybe . . ." Mac hesitated, not wanting to say the words in front of Quincy, so Quincy said them for him.

"Maybe he's carrying a body."

"Yeah," Mac said softly. "Maybe. So he would want to be near an entry point, someplace readily accessible but that would still offer cover."

"This is the main entrance, but it's no good."

"Too visible," Mac agreed, "being right off Third Street."

"There are fields that serve as extra parking spaces behind these buildings, closer to the racetracks."

"The racetracks," Mac mused, and Quincy knew the GBI detective got it the same moment he did.

"Grandstands," Mac announced. "Plenty of places to hide—"

"But still offers a vantage point of the grounds—"

"And the approaching police task force."

"Right by the back exit," Mac concluded.

And then all of a sudden, Quincy knew the rest. "He's not going to walk off the grounds," he said excitedly. "Even if he enters near the grandstands, he'd still have to cover hundreds of yards of open fields. No way someone wouldn't spot him coming or going. The only way to do it is to drive, but look at the ground around us. He stands a very good chance of getting stuck in the mud; God knows the police will the minute they try to give pursuit."

Mac's eyes got very wide. "ATV."

"Parked in the paddocks where no one can see. Easy in, easy out."

"Throw on a helmet . . ."

"And all any of us can report is the back of a mud-splattered man, driving away."

"Screw the grandstands," Mac declared. "Let's head straight to the paddocks. We find that ATV, and Mr. UNSUB's ten-thousand-dollar dreams are history."

"You sure know how to show a guy a good time," Quincy said.

"Aw," it was Mac's turn to say modestly. "That's what they all say."

Tuesday, 3:58 p.m. PST

THEY WERE ON THE MOVE AGAIN. Not being drugged this time, and sitting in the backseat instead of being stuffed inside a trunk, Rainie was trying to pay more attention.

The roads were rough. Dirt roads, partially washed out by the rain, would be her guess as the vehicle heaved and rolled across the miles. Her stomach moved with it; she could still taste bile in the back of her throat and desperately wanted to vomit.

Not a good idea. Her captor had replaced her cotton gag with duct tape. Vomiting risked aspirating the contents down into her lungs, which would lead to asphyxiation. Basically, she'd choke to death on her own puke. It wasn't a comforting thought.

The vehicle itself smelled vaguely of pine-scented air freshener. She had expected the odor of cigarettes; in her mind's eye, her captor was a smoker. But now that she considered the matter more, she didn't remember the man's clothing or breath reeking of nicotine. Smoking was hard to hide. Drinking, too. Didn't she know.

Last time, she'd assumed she'd been riding in the trunk of a car. But upon further consideration, she felt as if she were riding higher than one would in a car, plus she had a hard time believing any sedan could handle these kinds of roads. So maybe the UNSUB drove a pickup truck or SUV after all. Maybe she'd been stuck in some kind of equipment locker in the back. She'd seen those in the numerous trucks around town. Guys had to have room for their toys.

The truck hit a bump, soared up, flopped down, and her stomach lurched dangerously.

Don't think of food, don't think of the smell. Come on, Rainie, focus. And then: *Yellow-flowered fields. Smooth-flowing streams.* The decades-old mantra returned so easily, it was as if it had never left. She was sixteen years old again, detached and helpless as her mother's boyfriend labored over her body. She was twenty-five, drunk, and being felt up by some guy in the back of a bar. She was thirty, being touched by Quincy for the first time, and realizing how much the promise of love scared her out of her mind.

Yellow-flowered fields. Smooth-flowing streams. Yellow-flowered fields. Smooth-flowing streams.

The vehicle cranked hard to the left. She fell over on her side, helpless to right herself with her hands bound tight at her wrists. Bump, bump, bump. Rhythmic, fast. A gravel road maybe, or hard-weathered asphalt.

The truck came to a sudden halt, and her feet slid off the seat, catching the brunt of her weight hard against the floor. She tried to slither back up into position, hips up first, followed by feet. She heard the driver's door open, then close. He would come around to the back now, fetch his prize.

Kick him, she thought abruptly. Lying on her side, her feet positioned in front of the passenger-side door, all she needed to do was bend her knees for a bit of leverage, then nail him hard in the gut. He'd go down and she could... what? Hop out of the car like a bunny, ankles bound, wrists bound, tape across her mouth? Most likely, she'd fall face first in the mud and drown in a pool of shallow water.

She still wanted to do it. Wanted to feel the satisfaction of her feet sinking into his soft belly, hear his surprised *Oomph*. He made her feel small and helpless; she hated him for that.

The door opened. Belatedly, she lashed out.

He caught her feet with his hands and pushed her legs aside. "Oh, for Christ's sake, I don't have time for this bullshit. Get up. Move."

He used the rope tied around her ankles to drag her like a side of beef out of the back. Her head whacked the running board. Her shoulder drove into the muddy ground, forcing the breath from her lungs. Immediately, her nostrils flared, her back arched. She fought desperately for oxygen, lips straining against the duct tape. She couldn't breathe, she was going to die.

She flailed on the ground, panicked and terrified. Her captor kicked her, the toe of his shoe digging into the small of her back.

"Get up, I tell you. Move!"

Dark spots started to swim before her eyes. At the last minute, her captor seemed to realize her predicament. He bent down, jerked her to her feet, and ripped the duct tape from her mouth.

"Scream, and I will kill you."

She didn't scream, couldn't have if she'd wanted to. She gulped giant, beautiful lungfuls of wet, rainy air and absorbed them into her body. She tasted coastal breezes and fir trees and cow dung. She tasted field grass and dirt. And in that instant, she was pathetically grateful to be alive.

She heard a rasp. It sounded like a knife being drawn from a leather sheath.

She turned toward the noise, still a little dazed, a little confused.

"Lorraine," her captor said in a tone of voice she hadn't heard before. "I'm afraid I have some bad news."

Rainie tried to run, but it was already too late.

18

APPROACHING THE FAIRGROUND PADDOCKS was easier said than done. Mac and Quincy advanced with their backs pressed against the exterior of the livestock barns and their eyes peering out into the gray shrouded fields, looking for signs of movement. The rain drummed hard upon the metal roofs above them, periodically dousing them in walls of water while relentlessly deafening them with the sound.

Quincy slid, was caught by Mac. They made it four more feet, then Mac careened forward in the ankle-deep mud and swamped them both. They picked themselves back up gingerly, breathing hard and soaked to the bone.

"Your entire left side is covered in mud," Mac reported.

"You're assuming it's mud," Quincy replied.

Mac caught the innuendo—they were next to a cow barn, after all—and grimaced.

They reached the end of the second barn, and life got trickier. There was no way to reach the horse paddocks without crossing fifty yards of open ground. Quincy's gaze went to the top of the grandstands, searching for signs of a sniper. The rooftops appeared clear.

They ran for it, dashing across the exposed space, around a

chain-link fence, then wove through a slew of metal bleachers until they finally hit the horse paddocks. Quincy flattened himself against the wooden building, quickly followed by Mac.

The overhang of the roof offered them a temporary respite. Mac could see the water trickling down Quincy's face, disappearing beneath the collar of his shirt. The older man was flecked with specks of mud, the silver of his hair more pronounced, now that it was wet. For a moment, Mac felt a pang of worry. Quincy was in his fifties, and field work was a young man's game. But then Quincy grinned and Mac could see that beneath the stress and fear, the man was jazzed. You could take the man out of law enforcement, but you couldn't take the law enforcement out of the man.

"Ready?" Quincy whispered.

"Let's go."

They entered fast and low, Mac leading with the shotgun, followed by Quincy, who held the rifle nestled in the crook of his forearm. The change in environment was immediate and distorting: from a slippery marsh to hard-packed mud, from a lightly overcast sky to a deep, pervasive gloom, from the smell of wet pine and cut grass to the pungent scent of wood shavings, hay, and old horse manure.

Mac took a split second to glance down the long center aisle, then ducked inside the first stall, adrenaline pounding in his veins, his hands shaky on the shotgun. Hard to see everything in such a long, dark space. And even harder to hear, given the rain beating against the roof in a deafening roar.

He held up his left hand to Quincy and silently counted off one-two-three.

He popped up, flashed a second glance at the interior, then disappeared back down behind the cover of the stall wall.

He indicated his findings to Quincy with a simple shake of his head: nothing. No person standing in the aisle, no ATV magically parked in the middle of the stable. Their search would have to be more methodical now, foot by foot, stall by stall.

Once more, Mac took the lead, creeping into the center aisle. He kept his back hunched to provide a low profile, and his footsteps were small and nimble. His hands steadied on the shotgun. He focused on small even breaths and felt himself sliding into that zone.

Searching to the left, searching to the right.

Inch by inch, row by row, and then. . . .

Movement. Mac caught it first from the corner of his eye. A person, darting out of the end stall, dashing toward the back door.

"Stop! Police!" Mac roared. He unfurled to his full height, pointing the shotgun, finger moving toward the trigger.

Just as another voice spoke up in the gloom behind him. "One move and your friend is dead."

Mac whipped around to find a sharply dressed black man leveling a nine-millimeter at Quincy's head. Mac was still frantically considering his options when Quincy declared wearily, "Kincaid."

And the black man replied just as despondently, "Ahh shit."

Tuesday, 4:38 p.m. PST

"I THINK HE'S A BIT MIFFED," Mac said fifteen minutes later. He and Quincy had been ushered into the roller rink at the front of the fairgrounds. The space was vast, cold, and echoing.

"I was thinking more like irked."

Halfway across the room, Kincaid looked up from his mini-huddle with OSP detective Ron Spector and glowered at them. It was nothing Quincy and Mac hadn't seen before.

Mac was cold. His teeth chattered as he sat on a hard metal folding chair, clothes soaked, face splattered with mud. Quincy was in the same shape. No one had offered them a towel, let alone a hot cup of coffee. Mac wasn't surprised. He'd crossed jurisdictional boundaries once before, investigating a case in Virginia. Interestingly enough, the Virginia State Police hadn't taken it very well either.

The front door swung open. A young guy in a tan police uniform appeared, dragging a disheveled guy in his wake. Mac and Quincy were already on their feet as the deputy thrust the person into the roller rink.

The man, dressed in a khaki trench coat Mac recognized from the horse paddocks, was covered in mud. In fact, he appeared in much the same state as Mac and Quincy, meaning he'd obviously been moving around the grounds for a bit. Now, he stumbled forward, blinked several times fast, then croaked, with both hands in the air, "P-p-press!"

"Ahh shit," Kincaid said again.

He crossed to the intruder and glared down at him. "Who are you?"

"Adam Danicic. *Bakersville Daily Sun.*"

"Credentials." Kincaid held out his hand. A very nervous Danicic reached inside his damp trench coat and gingerly pulled out a bill-fold. He held it out to Kincaid, who snapped it open.

"So Adam *Dan-i-chic,*" Kincaid stressed the reporter's last name, "what the fuck were you doing in the stables?"

The reporter braved a smile. "Getting a scoop?"

"Ah, Jesus Christ. Is anyone in this building a kidnapper? Anyone, anyone? Because there's an awful lot of non-OSP bodies in this room, considering it's an OSP case!"

Not the smoothest thing to have said, and Kincaid seemed to re-alize it the moment the words left his mouth. The Bakersville deputy gave the OSP sergeant a "thanks for nothing" stare, while Kincaid sighed heavily, paced four feet away, then sighed again. Finally, he turned back to the reporter.

"My understanding is that your role is to work in cooperation with us. The prime reason being that you certainly wouldn't want an-other paper hearing from 'confidential sources' inside the Oregon State Police how the inexperienced, self-centered, aggressive re-porter from the *Daily Sun* heedlessly endangered a woman's life."

Danicic didn't say anything. At least he had the good sense to shut up and take his beating like a man.

"Now, I would think that to work in cooperation with our office, you would need to notify our office of your activities," Kincaid con-tinued.

"I investigate on my own, I write on my own," Danicic said lev-elly. "That's what a reporter does. What my editor chooses to print is a matter left up to him."

"Are you serious?"

"Yes, sir."

Kincaid eyed the young reporter again—the clean-shaven cheeks, short-cropped dark hair, conservative trench coat. "You certainly don't look like a left-wing liberal."

"Fox News," the reporter said smartly. "My goal is to be hired by them before I turn thirty. Let's face it: News teams could use some young go-getters like me."

"You have got to be kidding me. You work on a hick paper—"

"Gotta start somewhere."

"You just fucked up a major police investigation."

"Not really. Let's be frank—we all know you're only here as a precaution, and since by all appearances the kidnapper didn't show, no harm, no foul. Now, what I would really like to understand is the presence of those two men right there. Why does his jacket say 'GBI'? Doesn't that stand for Georgia Bureau of Investigation? And does that mean this case now involves multiple policing agencies working together on a cross-jurisdictional task force—"

"Out," Kincaid said tightly.

"Can I quote you on that?"

"*Out!*"

The Bakersville deputy, who'd been loitering inside the door, obviously enjoying Kincaid's discomfort, finally got moving. Payback was a bitch, however, and the deputy took his sweet time escorting the reporter from the room.

"I'll just keep asking around," Danicic threw over his shoulder. "Someone always wants to talk to the press. Hey, maybe I can get an exclusive with the kidnapper himself. Ever think of that?"

"Ah, Jesus H. Christ." The double doors finally clanged shut. Kincaid whirled toward Mac and Quincy. There wasn't much a sergeant could do about an aggressive member of the fourth estate. Them, on the other hand . . .

"You." Kincaid started with Mac. "Who are you, why the hell are you here?"

"Mac McCormack, detective, Georgia Bureau of Investigation."

"Georgia Bureau of Investigation? What, you got out of bed this morning and took a wrong turn?"

"I'm with him," Mac supplied easily, nodding toward Quincy. "Technically speaking, I'm dating his daughter."

"The FBI agent," Kincaid filled in.

"That's the one."

Kincaid's eyes narrowed suspiciously. "And where is *she* right now?"

Mac shrugged. "I don't ask too many questions. She's really good with a gun."

Kincaid looked dangerously close to throttling someone. Mac was used to it by now. Seemed anytime he hung out with Kimberly and her father, someone tried to kill him.

"You look like shit," Kincaid told Quincy.

"Wearing a lot of it, too."

"Whatever you think you're doing, it's not helping."

"True. Actually shooting the reporter would've been much more satisfying."

"I know you consider yourself an expert in these matters, Mr. Quincy, but you're also *family*. Surely a man of your intelligence can realize that there is no way for you to be clearheaded and objective about this investigation."

"She's a number to you," Quincy said softly. "A statistic passing across your desk. Solve it, and your life goes on. Don't solve it, and your life goes on. There's no difference."

Kincaid leaned down. While Mac had expected the OSP sergeant to launch into another tirade, his voice was surprisingly solemn. "All the cases you worked were statistics, too. Did that mean you slept in late, took weekends, went home to have dinner with your family every night? Yeah, I thought as much. I have a wife, Mr. Quincy. I have a beautiful baby boy and there's nothing I would rather do right now than wrap up this case and go home to them. Hey, let's hand over a boatload of cash, get your wife, and call it a day. I can take a hot shower, change into dry clothes, and put my feet up in my favorite recliner with my boy on my chest. Sounds good to me. Let's go."

"You're the one who refused to pay," Quincy said steadily. "You're the one making things difficult."

"Because I'm trying to do it right, dammit! Because I listened to you, the expert, and what you had to say. What was your professional opinion, Mr. Quincy, what did you tell me when we were having a grand ol' time digging up a graveyard?" Kincaid didn't wait for an answer, but counted off the points on the fingers of his right hand. "One, these kinds of cases are almost always personal. Two, the majority end with the victim found dead. You know why I'm dragging this out, Mr. Quincy? You know why I'm busting my balls writing message points to some UNSUB kidnapper when even I know I'm in over my head? Because I'm afraid the minute we agree to pay the ransom, Lorraine is dead. I'm not trying to get home to my wife, Mr. Quincy. I'm trying to save yours."

Quincy didn't reply. His lips, however, were set in a thin, stubborn line.

"If we drag things out," Kincaid said more calmly, "the kidnapper has to keep her alive for proof of life. And maybe, just maybe, we can finally make the link between her and him. I got the scientists working the car and the notes. I got good people retracing your wife's last steps. We got Sheriff Atkins shaking the local felony tree. This case is still in its infancy. We're going to get some leads yet."

"Any calls to the hotline?"

"No."

"But given that he didn't show here, you're assuming he read the paper."

"Maybe he needs a little time to think about things. Form Plan B."

"Do you have a Plan B?"

"Yes, sir, I do. He's going to call, we're going to be as accommodating and cordial as we can be. It's his game, we just want to follow instructions. We would love to give him money, we just need a little time. And then"—Kincaid took a deep breath—"we're going to suggest a show of good faith. He supplies more proof of life, and we respond with a down payment. Not the whole ransom amount, because the bank needs more time, but the first couple thousand, so he'll know we're cooperating."

Mac closed his eyes. He saw through the thinly veiled statement immediately, and so did Quincy. The former profiler was already on his feet.

"You're *not* going to pay him the ransom amount?"

"It's a down payment—"

"You're *shortchanging* him. We see that, he'll see that."

"Not if it's handled right—"

"By whom? An overworked state detective who's never negotiated a damn thing in his life?"

Kincaid flushed, but didn't back down. "As a matter of fact, I made arrangements to bring in a professional negotiator from our tactical unit. Candi, with an 'i.' I'm told she's brilliant."

"Oh my God," Quincy said. He had his hands held to his temples, didn't seem to be able to come to terms with the news.

"This kind of strategy has been done quite successfully before. A case out of Britain—"

"Oh my God," Quincy said again.

Kincaid plowed on as if he hadn't heard him. "They had a perpetrator threatening to poison pet foods if certain manufacturers didn't make hefty payments. Rather than pay up all at once, the task force strung the perpetrator along, making a series of small cash deposits. Naturally, this increased the amount of contact the extortionist had with the companies, as well as the number of times he had to surface to receive payment. Catching him was always only a matter of time."

"This isn't an extortion scheme targeted against nameless, faceless victims."

"Which makes it all the better. The more our guy has to talk to us, the more information he'll give away. I'm not going to drag this out forever. Game plan is a good-faith down payment of a couple thousand, assuming he can show us proof of life. We'll even consider it a bonus, given how patient he's being. Arrange that for late tonight, with a setup for the full ten grand tomorrow afternoon. Meaning that he can walk away with twelve thousand instead of the original ten."

"Play to his greed," Mac commented.

Kincaid flashed him a glance. "Exactly."

Mac looked at Quincy. The profiler appeared ashen. He sat down wearily on the metal chair and Mac wondered once more about the physical toll this must be taking.

"It's a matter of presentation," Kincaid said steadily. "We make him feel like he's maintaining control of the situation while being rewarded for his efforts. We keep him focused on the future payoff, not the change in plans."

"There's only one problem," Quincy said.

"What?" Kincaid asked warily.

A faint chiming sound suddenly emanated from Quincy's pocket. "I doubt the UNSUB is stupid enough to call your hotline."

Quincy pulled out his phone, checked the number, then showed them both the screen. Rainie's name flashed across the display. "Why call you, Sergeant Kincaid, when it's so much easier to call me?"

"Ahh shit." Kincaid motioned furiously to the other detective as Quincy flipped open his phone and prepared to speak.

19

SHERIFF SHELLY ATKINS WAS TIRED. She wanted a steaming cup of hot chocolate, a hot shower, and her bed, though not necessarily in that order. She'd had long nights before; her parents ran a cattle farm out in eastern Oregon. You didn't run a farm without some sleepless nights. But the last sixteen hours had taken their toll. Her boots were soaked, her socks were soaked. Her first shirt, her spare shirt. Every time she ran the heater in the car, she steamed up the windows from all the moisture evaporating off her body.

And her hands were starting to ache now, that bone-deep throbbing that bit into older, long-abused joints. She was trying not to rub her knuckles too much. Not that she thought her deputy, Dan Mitchell, would notice. Dan had been on duty since nine p.m. last night. Sitting in the passenger's seat, he was already slumped down with his eyes at half mast. If she drove much longer, he was going to nod off completely.

A deputy's pay didn't go that far in these parts. Like a few other members of her staff, Dan also worked part-time at a local dairy. He handled the evening milking before showing up for the graveyard shift. Sometimes she wondered how he stayed awake night after night, keeping those kinds of hours. She didn't want to ask. Truth was, Bakersville was mostly a quiet place. If her deputies dozed off every now and then in the early morning hours, no one had ever noticed or complained.

She needed to start thinking about staffing. Thus far, she'd had everyone up and at it since three this morning, not unusual for a critical incident, where a life might be on the line. Now, however, the case felt like it was slowing down, settling in. Kincaid had pushed back the four p.m. ransom drop. She had a feeling come evening, he'd stall again. If the situation entered a second day, or even a third, she couldn't continue to have all her men working 24/7. The combined sleep deprivation would turn them into a bunch of armed zombies.

She'd split them into two twelve-hour shifts, she determined. Send Dan, Marshall, and probably herself home first; they'd been up the longest. 'Course, she had a hard time seeing herself sitting things out for a full twelve hours. Three or four might not be bad. Get enough shut-eye to recharge the gray matter, then get up and at 'em again.

She stifled another yawn and turned left down a long, winding road. Locals liked to say that Tillamook County existed due to three things: cheese, trees, and ocean breeze. The cheese factory kept the dairy farms thriving, the neighboring forests kept the loggers busy, and the beautiful beaches kept the tourists coming back for more. The people tended the land, and the land tended the people, as her father would put it.

But as with any community, even one famous for its quaint, rolling green pastures, the county had its seedy side. Shelly and Dan had left behind the tidy, modernized dairies, with their freshly painted barns, shiny green tractors, and "Dairy of Honor" signs. Now they were looping through skinny back roads, passing trailer parks, crumbling cabins, and the other dairy farms—small, poorly equipped, with barns that looked like they'd disintegrate in the next windstorm.

Shelly knew the kind of folks who lived here. The men were stubble-faced and rangy, with the lean cheeks and soft middles that came from drinking most of their meals out of a beer can. The women were equally thin and hunched, with stringy hair and a propensity to bruise. The kids traveled in packs, generally accompanied by one or two mangy dogs. None of them trusted strangers, and all of them could explain to you why it was not their fault that their farm was failing. The price of milk was down, the price of dairy cattle was down. Too much debt given too readily by greedy banks, looking to squeeze out the little guy. The government didn't do enough to help them, the community wanted to pretend they didn't exist.

Shelly knew all about it. She'd heard all the same stories growing up in La Grande. As her father liked to point out, successful farmers worked more and talked less, whereas some of these farmers never seemed to have much to do, but always had plenty to say.

Visits like these were still the toughest part of Shelly's job. Walking into worn kitchens with peeling linoleum and water-stained ceilings. Trying to explain for the second or third time to some forty-year-old-looking twenty-two-year-old, with her third baby planted on her hip, that she did have options. That she didn't have to stay.

Knowing she'd be back again. Like the sheriff before her had probably done for this girl's mama so many years before. Life was full of cycles, and the older Shelly got, the less she believed she had all the answers. Her parents had certainly never been rich, and God knows there'd been long stretches where their daily supper had contained more potatoes and less meat, but she'd never been forced to see her father bowed and broken. She'd never watched her mother apply makeup to cover a bruise. She'd never heard her parents blame anyone else for their struggles. We just need to work a little harder, her father had always said, so that's what Shelly and her brothers had learned to do.

Now she turned into a dirt driveway. She hit a pothole, her right tire spun shrilly in the muck, and for a second, she thought she was stuck. Then the SUV lurched forward, jostling Dan out of his slumber.

"What the—"

Dan came to his senses just in time to realize he was sitting next to his boss, and bit off the last of that sentence. Shelly grinned at him.

"Good nap?"

"Sorry."

"Don't be. One of us needs to be refreshed. We're here."

She pulled up in front of a small farmhouse with a hole in the front porch the size of a boulder. The property boasted four pickup trucks, three rusted-out Chevys, and what looked like might have been a combine. Not to be outdone, various appliances also competed for real estate—old stoves, ovens, freezer units just waiting for summer to swallow some poor unsuspecting kid.

Hal Jenkins owned this property. It had been a farm in his father's day, and according to what Shelly had heard, a decent one. Small, but well run, tidily equipped. Hal hadn't wanted to be a farmer. He'd decided his calling was in automotive repair, hence the cars. He hadn't been bad at it. No, what had tripped up Hal was stripping car parts off of unsuspecting owners and recycling them into other people's vehicles—while charging them full price for the part, of course. Couple of country boys, not bad with engines themselves, had figured it out.

Calling cops wasn't much appreciated in these parts, so they'd beaten the snot out of Hal instead, then taken a baseball bat to his house. Most of the first-story windows still hadn't been replaced, hence the sheets of MDF nailed over the exterior.

After spending four months in the hospital, Hal decided maybe the automotive industry wasn't for him. He turned his attentions toward oven repair. Not so much money in appliances, however. In this day and age, people bought new instead of repairing old.

Exactly how Hal continued to make a living was subject to much debate. Shelly's best guess was that Hal had finally figured out the true value of a small, backwoods farm with plenty of outbuildings and few neighbors: a meth lab. The state chopper had taken a pass several times, but had yet to detect the heat signature they needed for a warrant. And so far, Hal wasn't big on letting Shelly or her deputies wander the property. Hal would never be a rocket scientist, but he was smart in his own survivalist sort of way.

Shelly stepped out first. Her boots sank deep into the marsh. Shit, they would be lucky to get the truck out. Dan got out a little slower, glancing at his watch. That irked her and she sent him a sharp glance.

"Now's not the time to worry about the evening milking, Deputy."

"Sorry." He was immediately abashed.

Inside the house, they heard a voice. It was the official Hal Jenkins greeting. No open door. Not even a look through a shattered glass window. "What?" he boomed from somewhere in the interior.

"Hey, Hal. It's Sheriff Atkins and Deputy Mitchell. We were wondering if we could have a minute of your time."

"No."

"For crying out loud, Hal. It's pouring down rain and we're covered in mud. Least you could do is offer us a cup of coffee."

"No."

"Well, I got some bad news then. Our truck is stuck—" Dan gave her a startled glance. She shushed him with her hand. "Looks like we're gonna have to dig through that pile of appliances and car parts over there to find something to get us out. Won't take but a minute, though."

The door jerked open. Hal finally appeared, sporting three days' worth of beard, a dark green flannel top, and the sorriest pair of jeans Shelly had ever seen. "Don't you touch nothin'."

"Well, Hal, we don't feel like standing here all day. We're on official police business."

Hal scowled at her. Ironically speaking, he was still a young man, and wouldn't be half bad looking if he ever cleaned up his act. He was tall, with dark wavy hair and the athletic build of an outdoorsman. He had a reputation as a good marksman, a hunter who skinned and hauled his own deer, often pulling the carcass for miles through the woods. And while the local boys had worked him over pretty good, by all accounts he'd put up one helluva fight. They'd arrested all three of his attackers in the emergency room; two were receiving stitches and the third had two broken bones.

Shelly didn't think Hal would have any trouble with a five-foot-six-inch female. And again, when sober and properly motivated, he could be cunning.

Shelly climbed the steps of the front porch. She was trying to peer discreetly into the gloom. She wanted to see if good ol' Hal had the most recent edition of the *Daily Sun*. Couldn't tell. Lighting was too poor, and Hal wasn't exactly a housekeeper; it was hard to pick out anything from the towering piles of trash.

"Got a warrant?" Hal asked.

"Got something to hide?" Shelly replied evenly.

"Yeah. World's greatest Chinese food. Don't want the word to get out. So if you don't mind, Sheriff, I think I'll return to my dinner."

"And to think, you struck me more as a pizza man." Shelly leaned against the doorframe, crowding Hal's space and pushing him back a step. Give her another minute, and she'd have her foot inside the door. Better yet, she'd completely block Hal's view, giving Dan more leeway to walk the grounds.

Hal coughed three times, not bothering to cover his mouth. His own ploy to gain real estate. Shelly didn't budge, though she'd seriously have to consider burning her clothes later today.

"Need cough syrup?" she asked idly. "Bet you have some in the house."

"Bet I do. All this rain, a man's bound to get a cold."

"So that's why you buy it by the case?"

Hal just grinned. Some over-the-counter cough syrups contained the chemical compound pseudoephedrine, needed to make methamphetamine. First sign of increased meth activity in an area was the sudden shortage of cough syrup in the local pharmacies, making drugstores a new and interesting arena in the war against drugs. First, stores were asked to report bulk orders. Budding illegal chemists simply started "cherry-picking" their local markets, buying a bottle here, a bottle there, etc.

At law enforcement urging, stores then stopped carrying the over-the-counter drugs, well, over-the-counter. You wanted children's Sudafed in Oregon, you had to personally request it from a pharmacist. Even this method wasn't foolproof, however, so for the latest round of combat, the giant pharmaceutical companies had promised cough syrups that were pseudoephedrine-free just for these kinds of markets. Would still treat the common cold, without endangering half the teenage population.

Of course, that still left online pharmacies, drug runs to Canada, etc., etc. Criminals were stupid, but never as overwhelmingly stupid as law enforcement would like them to be.

"I heard you owe some money," Shelly said, trying to jump-start things by dangling a little bait.

"Me? No way. Never a borrower or lender be."

"Why, Hal, you're quoting Shakespeare." Shelly batted her eyes.

Hal grinned. Not a good look on him, considering what years of tobacco chewing had done to his teeth. "Shakespeare? Hell, my old man told me he wrote them words himself. Son of a bitch; shoulda known he was lying."

"More like plagiarism. So you ever gonna fix this place up?"

"Why? Guy like me always has a few people who think I've done 'em wrong. New windows will just make new targets."

"Did you do them wrong?"

"Ah, Sheriff, I just want to eat my Chinese food and repair another stove. Can't a guy make a living?"

Shelly nodded, chewing on the inside of her lip. Hal was blocking her view of the house as well as stalling the conversation. Definitely a guy with something to hide, but then again, that's why they'd come here. Hal would always be hiding something, and he was right about not bothering to replace the windows.

"What about some guys who may have done you wrong?"

This was a new tactic. Hal frowned, squirreled an eyebrow, and tried to figure it out. "What'd you hear?"

"I hear some guys are looking to score some quick cash. Doing all sorts of crazy-ass stuff. Kind of activities that bring the state police into the town, and soon, the FBI. That sort of thing fucks it up for everyone, don't you think?"

Hal finally put two and two together—and proved he'd read the most recent edition of the *Daily Sun*. "The kidnapping," he murmured.

"Yes, sir."

For a change, Hal's reply was immediate and forthcoming. "Ah, no way. I do not go there. Abducting some woman, making ransom demands. All for a lousy ten grand? That is crazy-ass. I can barely stand being around some chatty female long enough for sex. Like hell I'm locking one up in my house."

"Well, you do have a barn."

"Ah jeez."

"Just let us take a quick tour. Then we can remove you from the suspect list and save you the same visit from the FBI."

"As long as the FBI is packing the same warrant you are, I got nothing to worry about. Time for my dinner—"

Hal moved to slam the door. Shelly stuck her foot in the way. "We're serious about this," she said quietly. "It's not the same old shit, Hal. One word, one whisper she is anywhere near here, and a judge will grant us permission to tear your place apart board by board. Forget the windows, you won't have a house when we're done with you."

"I don't deal in bodies."

"You know who might?"

Hal stared at her. Shelly stared back. "All I need is a whisper . . ."

"All right," he said abruptly. "You got some paper? I'll write you a goddamn list."

Ten minutes later, Shelly and Dan both climbed back into the department's SUV. The vehicle had sunk down, the tires stuck. Hal cursed them both when he came back out of the house. He grabbed a hammer, yanked the MDF off the windows, and used the boards as giant planks behind each wheel.

They got traction. Hal got covered in mud. Last glimpse Shelly had was of a tall, morose man, plucking wood out of the dirt and preparing to board it once more to his windows.

"What do you think?" she asked Dan.

"Third barn in the back shows a lot of work that's new."

"Good place to stash Rainie Conner?"

"He could, but given the size and location, he'd make a lot more money with a lab."

"My thought, too. Definitely a criminal, but not our criminal."

Dan glanced at his watch again.

"OT pays better than milking, Dan."

"Yeah, but on days like this, I miss the cows."

20

THE VOICE ON THE OTHER END of the phone was once again flat, eerily mechanized. "I don't like crowds."

"I prefer smaller parties myself," Quincy said. His mind was racing. He wished he had notes in front of him, a more thorough analysis of the case. He was supposed to be an outsider, flown in for these situations. Handed a file that contained names and photos of people who meant nothing to him. Then he could coldly dissect the facts and outline key message points, before retiring to a back room to watch others implement his strategy.

A profiler was accustomed to working after the fact, when the damage was already done. He read other people's notes and determined other people's actions. He didn't get involved himself. He didn't, say, speak on the phone with an UNSUB who had kidnapped his wife.

Quincy sat on the edge of the metal chair, his voice containing a quaver he couldn't afford.

"You did not follow my instructions," the voice intoned.

"I want to pay you the money," Quincy said steadily. Mollify, do not challenge. Appease, then coerce. "I'm trying very hard to do as you ordered. The bank, however, could not give me that much cash at once. There are banking laws—"

"You lie."

"I went to the bank—"

"You lie!" The mechanized voice grew shrill.

Quincy broke off his next sentence, already breathing hard. He had erred. The abductor knew something, had access to more information than they had anticipated.

"You did not go to the bank," the abductor accused.

Kincaid started making furious hand gestures, pantomiming holding a phone to his ear. He wanted Quincy to say he called the bank? Quincy shook his head. Too many unknowns. Maybe the kidnapper had staked out Quincy's bank. Or maybe he had an inside connection, or worse, he even worked there. They had not done their homework, and now they were paying for it.

"I have cash," Quincy said abruptly. "In my house. From . . . activities I wouldn't care to discuss."

His innuendo worked. The voice laughed tinnily.

"I thought it would be enough," Quincy continued quickly. "I could pay you, no one would be the wiser. But when I counted the money, it wasn't enough. And I was afraid if I showed up with half the money, you would be mad. I don't want to make you mad."

"You involved the police."

"I did not involve the police. The *Bakersville Daily Sun* involved the police after receiving your note. The police then came to me. I am trying to work with you. I am willing to do as you ask."

"Why?"

The question startled Quincy, broke his concentration. "She's my wife," he heard himself say.

"You left her."

He couldn't summon a reply. How did the UNSUB know that? Had Rainie told him, tried to offer it as a bargaining chip? *You don't want to kidnap me; my only family is my estranged husband and he sure as hell won't pay to have me back.*

Or maybe the kidnapper wasn't a stranger after all. Maybe he was someone they both knew, an associate or even a friend. Quincy had an uncomfortable suspicion then. One he didn't like having at all.

"Do you love your wife?" the mechanized voice intoned.

Quincy closed his eyes. It was not a good question. He could feel the menace behind it, the promise of future pain.

"Rainie has always been a wonderful wife," he said quietly. "We've been looking forward to adopting a child together. She's very active in the community. In fact, she's been working on a memorial for a little girl in Astoria who was murdered this summer. Perhaps you've heard about that?"

The UNSUB didn't take the bait. "She cares," the voice mocked. "She is compassionate. She is a credit to her kind."

"You say you are not a monster. I would think these things matter to you. May I speak to Rainie? Put her on the phone. Prove you are also operating in good faith."

"You did not pay."

"I have money—"

"It is not enough."

"I'll get the full ten thousand—"

"It is not enough. You disobeyed. You will be punished. I am a man of my word."

The caller was hanging up.

"Wait," Quincy said frantically. "Put Rainie on the phone. Let me talk to her. If I know she's all right, I can get you more money. I have assets I can cash in, money in the bank. I love my wife. I am willing to pay!"

"There is no such thing as love," the voice intoned. "Goodbye."

And then the voice was gone. Game over.

"FUCK!" Quincy hurled the phone across the room. It wasn't enough. He snatched the metal folding chair, thrust it high above his head. Mac grabbed for his left arm, Kincaid reached for his right. He fought them both. He was tired and cold, splattered with mud and cow shit. He could hear that horrible voice chiming in his ear. He could feel the tears now streaming down his face.

He had failed. Not asked enough questions, not done enough homework. He should have withdrawn the money, or even part of the money if that was their story. It was a simple precaution, just in case someone was paying attention, but he'd been too busy arguing with Kincaid, too busy promoting his own expertise, too busy telling himself he was still brilliant to take a few basic steps.

He was a fool, and now Rainie would suffer. And she would know that he had failed her. She, of all people, would understand what it meant when her kidnapper approached her with a knife.

They had him on the floor. Dimly he was aware of the cold wood pressed against his cheek, the weight of two men trying to keep him under control.

"Call nine-one-one," Kincaid was yelling. "Get a doctor, quick!"

Stupid ass, Quincy thought. Rainie was the one who needed help.

And then, interestingly enough, the world went black.

Tuesday, 5:43 p.m. PST

KIMBERLY WAS HEADED FOR the command center at Fish and Wildlife when she saw the ambulance pulling out of the fairgrounds parking lot. She hit the brakes, went swinging into the circular drive, and was half out of the car before it even stopped. A crowd of uniforms loitered in front of the large metal doors to the left. She pushed through, searching frantically for signs of Mac, her father, or Rainie.

"What happened, what happened?"

Mac spotted her first. He moved quickly, looping his arms around her waist before ever saying a word.

"Dad? Dad? *Dad?*"

"Whoa, whoa, whoa. Take a deep breath. You gotta pull it together. Easy."

She would not take it easy. Her father was on the floor. He was covered in blankets, his face ghostly pale, his toes pointed straight up, while an older man with a dark funeral suit and a stethoscope gazed down upon him. It was not supposed to be like this. Dear God, she had only left him for a moment.

"What the hell happened?" Her strident voice boomed across the hollow space. Mac covered her mouth with his hand, pressing her hard against his chest, as if his mere presence could make such a scene go away.

"Babe, babe, babe, it's not as bad as it looks. Your father's had an episode. Kincaid called the EMTs, then Sheriff Atkins summoned a doctor. The doctor's with him now."

"But the ambulance just left. If he's had an 'episode,' shouldn't he be in the ambulance? Shouldn't he be going to a hospital? Isn't that what an 'episode' means?"

"He refused to go."

"Son of a . . . I will kill him."

"Easy." Mac rubbed her arms with one hand, the other still wrapped tightly around her waist. She realized now that she was trembling, shaking like a leaf. If Mac hadn't been holding her, she would've fallen.

"He got a call," Mac murmured under his breath, words for only her ears, "from the kidnapper. It didn't go well. The UNSUB implied that since the ransom demands weren't met, he's going to punish Rainie."

"Oh no."

"Your father became . . . emotional. When we tried to calm him, something went. Honest to God, it's like he blew a fuse."

"His heart?" she asked in panic.

"I don't know, babe. I'm not the doctor. But physically, your father could really use some rest."

She nodded against his chest. She held him as tight as he held her, and still she couldn't get over the image of her father lying so still on the floor. "I've never seen him look this old," she whispered.

"I know."

"He and Rainie were going to slow down, adopt a child. I always thought of him as having this whole other life left to live."

"I know, babe."

"Oh, Mac," she sighed. "Poor Dad." And then, a heartbeat later, "Poor Rainie."

Tuesday, 6:04 p.m. PST

THE DOCTOR FINALLY FINISHED UP. At his request, Mac brought around Quincy's vehicle. He and Kincaid helped Quincy out to the car, getting him arranged in the backseat, where he could rest more comfortably. Kimberly tried to peek in on him twice. Both times, Mac had steered her away.

"Not before speaking with the doctor," he instructed her.

"You're just afraid I'm going to yell at him."

"I *know* you're going to yell at him. Not before speaking to the doctor."

Now the doctor was finally available to talk and Kimberly already did feel like yelling.

"Was it a heart attack?" she needed to know.

"His blood pressure is elevated, his pulse is arrhythmic, and his color isn't good," the doctor reported. "That leads me to be concerned about the possibility of a cardiac event. I would need to run some tests, however, before making any determination."

"Then run the tests."

"Your father would have to be admitted to the hospital."

Kimberly narrowed her eyes. "He's still refusing to go?"

"Your father feels it was a simple anxiety attack—which, for the record, is also a possibility."

"So my father is now a medical doctor?"

"Your father is a man of very strong opinions."

"Did someone take his sidearm? Because if he doesn't have his gun, then that makes me the only member of the family who is armed, in which case I think I should get my way."

The doctor took a discreet step back. "One thing to consider would be family history. Do you know if either of your grandparents suffered from heart problems?"

"My father's mother died young. Cancer, I think. And my grandfather . . ." She hesitated. "Alzheimer's," she said at last. It was close enough.

"And their parents, your great-grandparents?"

"I don't know."

The doctor considered the news. "In my professional opinion, the safest course of action would be to proceed immediately to the hospital for a series of tests. If the patient is absolutely unwilling, however"—the doctor rolled his eyes—"I would at least recommend plenty of rest, a hot shower, dry clothes, and no undue exertion for the next forty-eight hours."

"Yeah, right." Kimberly looked around her, sighed heavily. "Do you know why all the police officers are here?"

"I understand this is a very difficult time."

"As long as his wife is missing, there is no way I will get him to relax at home."

"Then at least get him more comfortable. Dry clothes, hot soup, a few hours' rest. If he complains of indigestion, call nine-one-one immediately. And Ms. Quincy—I wouldn't let him out of your sight."

The doctor packed up his things. Kimberly walked over to the car. Her father's eyes were closed, but she didn't believe for a moment he was sleeping. She slid into the backseat, putting his feet up on her lap, rubbing his ankles. She studied his face, relieved to see at least some hint of pink now blooming beneath the ash.

"We're going to keep trying," she said softly. Then, "Rainie knows you love her, Dad."

Quincy finally opened his eyes. "No, honey, that's always been the problem. She's never believed me at all."

Kimberly leaned over and hugged her father. For once in his life, he didn't pull away.

Tuesday, 7:04 p.m. PST

THE NOTE ARRIVED AN HOUR LATER. *Daily Sun* reporter Adam Danicic claimed he'd slogged back the half mile to his parked car only to discover the sealed plastic bag on his windshield.

In the spirit of cooperation, he assured Kincaid by phone, he was bringing the package right over. That he would photocopy the note first, Kincaid figured, was implied.

Once produced, the package appeared to have two parts: a thin, Saran-Wrapped note and a bigger, freezer-sized Ziploc bag, full of something dark and sinister that had a tendency to twitch. Both items were covered in droplets of water, making it difficult to peer inside.

"We'll do the note first," Kincaid spoke up finally. He stood at the head of the conference table in the op center, Sheriff Atkins beside him, Quincy, Kimberly, and Mac over in the corner. Since his "episode," Quincy had been very quiet. Kincaid understood this made his job easier, but he still felt bad for the man. Not that they made Hallmark cards for these kinds of things, but Kincaid was starting to genuinely like the former feebie. And he sure as hell was worried about what would happen with the man's wife.

Now Kincaid pulled on a pair of latex gloves and carefully peeled back the plastic wrapping on the note. The paper inside had been folded twice to form a square. It was damp and ink smudged, despite the protective cover. Kincaid had to work the paper carefully to keep from tearing it.

With the paper unfolded, Kincaid did the honors of reading aloud:

Dear Member of the Press and Assorted Task Force Officers:

I provided you with simple instructions. I promised if you did as I asked, no one would be hurt.

You chose to violate my orders. You chose to challenge my authority. You chose to unleash the monster, and the consequences are on your head.

The ransom is now $20,000. Cash. You will understand why soon enough. Tomorrow. 10 a.m. The officer must be female. Give her Quincy's phone. I will call her with instructions from there.

Disobey me again and things will get worse.

As you can see, I am a man of my word.

Sincerely,
Nathan Leopold

"Leopold?" Kincaid queried.

The sheriff shook her head. Quincy, too.

"I can look up the name on the Internet," Kimberly said, but didn't touch the computer. She was staring at the second item, the Ziploc bag. It was rolling side to side, moving on its own volition.

Kincaid looked up sharply at the reporter, still loitering in the room. "Did you touch this?" He pointed to the rocking bag.

"No," Danicic said.

"I'm not kidding. Did you open it at all, even try to take a peek?"

Danicic flushed. His chin was up, he looked injured at the assault, then ruined it by saying, "Well, I thought about it. But the bag, uh, it kind of twitched in my hand—"

"Twitched?"

"Yeah, twitched. Honest to God. After that, I decided it was a matter best left to the professionals."

Kincaid arched a brow. For the first time, he noted Danicic's stance, closest to the door. Clearly, the *Daily Sun*'s lead investigative reporter wasn't taking any chances.

Kincaid sighed heavily and reached for the bag. Behind him came a distinct snap as Sheriff Atkins unfastened her holster. Kincaid paused.

"Do you know what's moving in there?" she asked.

"No, but I'd like to maintain use of both my thumbs."

"Fine, I'll avoid your thumbs. Now, pinkies on the other hand . . ."

Kincaid picked up the rain-dotted Ziploc bag. He rolled it several times between his fingers. The substance inside was thick, coiled. He didn't like how it felt.

"If it so much as hisses," he murmured to Shelly, "I don't care about my thumbs. Blow its damn head off. Just hit it."

"Roger."

"I shoulda become an accountant."

Kincaid pulled open the bag and dumped its contents on the table. A thick wet rope landed on the table with a small thud, gathered at one end, loose on the other. Kincaid waited almost frantically for something to happen. A hiss, a bite, a snap. Nothing. The dark coil simply laid there.

"It's hair," Sheriff Atkins declared, peering over his shoulder. "Human hair."

Quincy was out of his chair, already coming closer. One look at the rich chestnut color, and Kincaid saw his own guess answered in the older man's face.

"Rainie's hair," Quincy said softly. "He cut it off. Look at the ends. He went after it with a knife."

Quincy prodded the bound end of the wet length with his finger, just as something burst out from beneath.

Kincaid jumped back. The sheriff squeaked. The small black bug raced across the table and promptly buried itself in a stack of papers.

"What the hell is that?" Kincaid demanded to know.

In the corner of the room, Kimberly moaned softly. "Oh, Dougie."

21

THE SOUND OF DRIPPING WATER woke Rainie. Her head snapped back, she startled as if roused from a deep dream, and promptly whacked herself against a wooden beam. She winced, and the pain from her catalogue of injuries assaulted her all at once.

She was someplace new. Same endless black void, of course, but different pungent smell. Wet dirt, fungus, decay. It was not the smell of happily ever after.

Her hands were still bound in front of her, her ankles tied, the blindfold tight around her eyes. In the good-news department, her mouth remained gag and duct-tape free. She could swallow, move her tongue, small luxuries nonkidnapped people never fully appreciated. For a moment, she was tempted to raise her head and scream, but didn't think she had the strength. And then another thought came to her—why hadn't he replaced the gag? Maybe because it didn't matter anymore if she screamed. Maybe she was that alone.

The ground beneath her felt damp. She started shivering, then realized for the first time how cold she was. The wet had seeped into her clothes, penetrating her skin. She was curled up, an unconscious attempt at preserving heat. It wasn't enough. Her teeth were chattering, increasing the throbbing in her head. Her arms were trembling, making the various cuts and bruises sting.

Basement, she thought. Someplace cold, damp, where months of rainfall still seeped down the walls and pooled on the floor. Someplace ripe with the scent of decaying plants and moldy linens. Someplace dank and forgotten, where fat spiders wove huge masterpieces of sticky lace and small animals came to die.

She tried to sit up and failed. Beneath the blindfold she was relatively certain her left eye had swollen shut. Further inventory revealed a split lip, a welted head, and a cascading pattern of cuts, starting at her neck and working their way down, some shallow, some dangerously deep, all too numerous to count. She was light-headed, from loss of blood, lack of food, it didn't really matter. She was officially bruised and battered, with a rib cage that throbbed dangerously anytime she tried to take a deep breath.

And she was freezing, literally freezing. She couldn't stand the feel of her own skin, cold and clammy to the touch, like a body pulled from the morgue refrigerator. She needed to find someplace dry. She needed fresh clothes, heaps of blankets, and a hot crackling fire. She would warm her hands near the flames. She would lean back and remember the days when she could still curl up against Quincy's chest and feel his hands stroking her hair.

It was the memory of her hair that did it. She started sobbing, giant, broken waves of grief that aggravated the ache in her ribs and the emptiness in her stomach. She cried and the inevitable conclusion came to her: She was not doing well. In fact, if something didn't change soon, she was probably going to die.

Funny how it took the little things to see the big picture sometimes. Funny how it took the shearing of her own locks to make her finally feel afraid.

She hadn't realized what her captor was going to do at first. She heard the rasp of the knife. Felt his hand wrap around the rope of her hair. He yanked back her head and her first thought was to protect her throat. Her restrained hands flew frantically to her collarbone, her mind flashing with the visions of crime scene photos where white throats were carved into macabre smiles.

He started sawing away on her hair, and something strange happened: Rainie had gone insane.

She could take the bound hands. She could handle her immobilized feet, the blindfold that obscured her sight, the gag that wicked all the moisture from her mouth. But she couldn't stand the thought of losing her hair. It was her only vanity, her only claim to beauty. How would Quincy ever love her again if she didn't have any hair?

She had lashed out with her elbow. He hadn't been expecting it, so she got lucky and connected hard with his ribs. He made an odd, muffled sound, a man choking on his own breath. Then, savagely, he ripped the last of her hair out of her head.

"What the hell are you doing?" he yelled. "I'm holding a hunting knife, for Christ's sake. Stand still!"

Rainie didn't stand still. She charged with all her might, catching her abductor dead-center. He went down. She went down. Then they were rolling in the muck, her squirming around like a worm with her bound limbs, him thrashing about like a toppled rhino. She was vaguely aware of screaming, some deep primordial cry of rage and grief and hatred. No sound emerged from her throat, however. Even without the duct tape sealing her lips, her rage remained locked tight inside her chest.

He hadn't been lying about the knife. First time he sliced her arm, maybe it had been an accident. The second time, they both knew he meant it, and still she couldn't bring herself to stop.

She hated him. She hated him with a force that was twelve times her size, with a fury that had been stamped into her bones for decades. She hated him for the father she never knew. She hated him for every time one of her mother's boyfriends had split open her cheek. She hated him for Lucas, who had forced himself upon her when she had been too young to defend herself, and too white trash for anyone to believe. She hated him for Aurora Johnson, because children shouldn't have to know that amount of terror and pain.

And she hated him for Quincy, especially for Quincy, because Quincy was supposed to save her. Deep down in her heart, she had always believed that somehow, some way, Quincy would still save her. That's how these things worked. She was intense, angry, self-destructive. But Quincy was her rock. He waited, he held course. He loved her. Even when she was horrible, even when she could barely stand herself, he loved her.

He was the only good thing that had ever happened in her life.

Somehow, she had gotten herself on top of her captor's body. He was on his back, unable to get footing in the slippery mud. If she could keep him down, keep him as mired and immobilized as she felt . . .

He sliced her forearm again. She blindly followed the direction of the pain, beating at him futilely with her bound fists. Then her fingers found his wrist. She dug her thumbs into the soft collection of nerves and tendons at the base of his palm and was immediately rewarded by a low hiss.

"I will fucking kill you!" the man roared.

"Then do it!" she screamed right back at him.

He bucked his hips, dumping her into the mud. She held on to his wrist, thumbs clamped like a pit bull.

"Bitch!"

She could feel him trying to struggle to his feet. She lashed out, catching him in the ankle, and down he went.

Now he was beating her with his left hand, pummeling her head and shoulders with his fist. She didn't care. She was too close to him, inside the kill zone, so he couldn't get any force behind the blows. She just kept working his wrist, visualizing his fingers opening, the knife falling . . .

His fist caught her in the ribs. She gasped. He seemed to realize the advantage and used two fingers to dig into her kidney. A new pain shot up her lower back, accompanied by a warmth between her legs. She'd wet herself. He'd reduced her to the state of an animal, pissing on its legs in its terror to get away.

Fuck it. She let go of his wrist and clamped down hard on his forearm with her teeth.

"Aaaaaaagh!" her captor said. She shook her head from side to side, picturing every feral dog she'd ever seen. She wanted to bite bone, wanted to taste blood. She chewed on his forearm, ground her teeth.

"Son of a—" He still couldn't use the knife in his right hand and couldn't hit her hard enough to dislodge her bite with his left. She was winning, she thought, and in her delirious state, she saw herself chewing off his arm, spitting out his hand. When asked how she managed to get away from her armed captor while being bound and blindfolded, she would reply, "I just pictured him as a nice juicy steak."

He jabbed her kidney again, trying to hit her spleen. Now he had his legs wrapped around hers, was coming up and over, trying to pin her into the muck. She used her hands to fend him off, to keep her precious stance, half on top of his body, her teeth sunk into his forearm.

She fought and she hated and she raged. Her captor, on the other hand, finally got smart.

He pinched her nose shut, and that quickly, it was over. Continue biting and be asphyxiated. Stop biting and be stabbed.

Funny, right up until this moment, Rainie herself had not realized how much she wanted to live.

She thought of Aurora Johnson again. She thought of all the little girls who never had a chance. And she thought, for the first time in a long time, of Quincy's daughter Mandy.

I am sorry, Rainie thought, except she wasn't apologizing to the victims anymore, she was apologizing to Quincy. Because he had already lost so much, she would've liked to have spared him this pain.

She released him. Her captor's arm ripped away. He screeched, half relief and half curse. Then he socked her in the eye.

The force of the blow rocked her back. She tumbled off him, rolling into the mud. Her eye socket exploded. Behind the blindfold, there was a miraculous display of white, shiny lights.

Then she heard him, rising in the rain, pulling himself out of the muck. He stomped toward her. She had the mental image of a large, hulking beast, maybe the Creature from the Black Lagoon.

I love you, Quincy, she thought.

Then her captor raised the knife and smashed the handle across her head.

Now, Rainie forced herself to uncurl from the damp floor and got up. Her bruised muscles spasmed in protest. She could not stand straight; it brought too much pain to her ribs. She huddled over, moving like an old woman as she shuffled with her bound feet across the space.

Her fingers touched the wall, recoiled. Cold, slimy, definitely wet cement. She picked a different direction and used little shuffling steps to map out her domain. Once she hit a hard wooden structure, pain rocketing up her shins. Further inspection revealed a workbench, now devoid of tools. Then she tangled in one spider web, only to recoil into a second. Something big and hairy brushed her cheek; she did her best not to scream.

On the other side of the room, she found wooden stairs. With her hands, she counted over ten steps before they rose up out of her reach. They probably led to a door. She didn't trust herself to climb them in her current state, however, and didn't doubt for a minute that the lone exit would be locked and barred. She returned to the bench. The dusty, wooden surface felt warm compared to the floor. She swung her feet up, curled up in a ball, and told herself she was at Club Med.

Her throat hurt. She coughed and that made her ribs ache. She wondered what Quincy was doing now. Probably driving the case detective crazy, she decided, which at least made her smile.

Her hands moved on the bench. With one finger, she traced the only words he needed to know: *I love you, too.*

Then a sound came from overhead. Door opening. Footsteps on the stairs.

She stiffened, tried to swing herself off the bench, tried to prepare herself to defend.

There was a soft thud, followed by an immediate moan.

"Brought you something," the man said, then his footsteps retreated back up the stairs. The door slammed shut, she heard a lock click shut. Then, silence.

"Hello?" Rainie tried.

Slowly she crossed to the stairs, her hands groping out in front of her, her fingers feeling in the dark. She found the body at the bottom, curled up against the floor as she had been not that long ago. Smaller frame than she expected, encased in wet jeans and an even wetter sweatshirt.

Her fingers moved, determining the welt at the back of the head, then discovering the face.

"Oh no. Oh no."

She rocked the boy up onto her lap. She cradled his still form against her, stroking his chilled cheek and willing some heat from her own cold frame into his body.

"It'll be okay, it'll be okay," she murmured over and over again. But she didn't know who she was trying to convince anymore, herself or Dougie Jones.

22

QUINCY SAT ALONE IN A CORNER of the command center. He had a blanket on his lap, a mug of black coffee in his hands. In front of him, officers buzzed around the conference table with the brisk steps of people who had serious work to do and not nearly enough time to do it. Kincaid and Sheriff Atkins were in the middle of a heated debate, both looking tired and strained. Mac was talking on his cell phone, glancing from time to time in Quincy's direction like the diligent baby-sitter he'd promised to be. Kimberly had been sent out on an errand at Quincy's personal request; his daughter had departed only after wringing a blood oath from Mac that he wouldn't let Quincy out of his sight.

When Mac glanced over for the third time, Quincy couldn't resist raising a hand in acknowledgment. *Haven't managed to croak yet. Please, carry on.*

So this, he thought, was how it was going to feel one day when his workaholic daughter stuck him in an old folks' home. He took another long sip of coffee and pretended his hand didn't shake.

In contrast to his daughter's opinion, he did not think he was going to drop dead just yet. No tightening of the chest, no tingling in the extremities, no cramping in his stomach. He was just tired. Bone-deep weary, hitting the stage that was officially beyond stress.

He didn't only miss Rainie anymore. He didn't just worry and wonder and ache. He could feel himself slowly but surely letting her go. Shutting down the small details—the flannel-gray color of her eyes, the quick, lithe way she crossed the room, a woman who made no effort at all to be sexy and thus captivated the attention of every male around.

First time he'd met Rainie, it had been professional. She'd been a deputy in Bakersville, serving as the primary officer on her first big case—a shooting at Bakersville's K–8. The number one suspect was the sheriff's son, which put the whole department, of course, under enormous pressure.

Quincy had come waltzing in—federal agent, expert on mass murderers, doing a special research project on school shootings—expecting to be welcomed with open arms. It was possible that he'd had an ego, even been quite full of himself.

Rainie had mocked his title, derided his credentials, and then said some pretty uncomplimentary things about his tie. And that had been it for SupSpAg Quincy. Other people fell in love over candle-light dinners or walks on the beach. Quincy fell in love sitting across the desk from a small-town deputy who liked to splinter number two pencils when feeling enraged.

He still gave her a box of pencils every Valentine's Day. And she would laugh and spill them out on the table like a happy child.

"I don't have to break pencils anymore," she would tease him. "I'm married to the perfect man."

The pencils would go atop her desk. Sooner or later, he'd find them in shattered bits all over the floor. Because that was marriage, a collection of all the little things outsiders would never understand. Number two pencils for her, Republican ties for him. She still had a weakness for Bon Jovi; he much preferred jazz.

They had their system. It wasn't for everyone, but until recently, it had always worked for them.

Would she hate him when the end came? Would she blame him for failing his last case? Or would she understand? Everyone has to lose sometime, even Quantico's former best of the best.

It was not the past that broke you, Quincy thought. It was the empty future, the endless string of days filled with none of the people who mattered most.

Mac came over. He hunched down in front of Quincy, hands clasped across his knees.

"Tell me about Astoria," Mac commanded.

And much to his surprise, Quincy did.

Tuesday, 8:41 p.m. PST

THE HOSTAGE NEGOTIATOR arrived twenty minutes later. The conference room doors blew open. A strikingly gorgeous woman strode in. Kincaid looked up. Mac turned. So did most of the men in the room.

Candi with an "i" turned out to be a six-foot Hispanic woman with a wild mane of curly jet-black hair that added another two inches to her height. She wore slim-fitting jeans, a tight-fitting red shirt, and a short-cropped black leather jacket. Forget police work; she looked like she ought to be on a runway in Paris.

"Candi Rodriguez," she announced by way of introduction. Then, without waiting for a reply, "Is this the phone? Have you tested the system, because let me tell you, these recorders never work as well as promised. I'm going to need an outline of everything we know about the subject at this time. Age, occupation, interests, ethnicity. If we know it—or suspect it—I want it in front of me in bullet-point form. I'm also going to require plenty of water and enough space to move around. I like to pace while I talk. It helps me think."

She was pacing now. The rest of the room remained staring, mouths agape.

Quincy took another sip of coffee. He wondered what Kimberly would do if she were here right now. Shoot first, question later? Or maybe simply tackle the larger, more exotic alpha female to the floor? Men could always arrange for a quick game of hoops, or perhaps a drinking contest in the local bar. With women, it was always much more complicated.

"What?" Candi with an "i" demanded in clear exasperation. "I was told to hustle, clock ticking, yada, yada, yada. Why the hell do you think I just blew through the mountains at ninety miles per hour? I'm here. Let's move."

Kincaid finally cleared his throat. "Sergeant Detective Kincaid," he introduced himself. "There's been some new developments."

"Got a handout?"

"We haven't had time to write a report."

"Well then, you'd better start talking, Sergeant Kincaid, because I sure as hell can't read your mind."

Quincy took another sip of coffee, mostly to hide his grin.

Kincaid ran through the wrap-up. The botched attempt to delay the ransom drop via an article in the newspaper. The subsequent note left by the abductor on the windshield of a local reporter's car.

Officers had immediately followed up with Laura and Stanley Carpenter, Dougie Jones's foster parents. Laura had last seen the boy at four thirty, when he came inside demanding a soda. No one had seen Dougie since. Local deputies were now combing the woods. It was their second search operation in fifteen hours, and they were pretty sure the results would be the same.

"So he now has custody of a woman and a child?" Candi summarized.

"That's our current assumption."

"And what's the relationship between Lorraine Conner and Douglas Jones?"

"Rainie," Quincy spoke up. "Rainie and Dougie. If you use their full names, he'll know you're an outsider."

Candi shot him a look. "And you are?"

"The estranged husband."

Kincaid's turn to receive an arched brow. "You're letting him hang out in the command center?" the negotiator asked.

"Hell, half the time I let him run the case. He's a profiler, retired FBI."

"Well damn, this really is a party. What else don't I know yet?"

"Rainie was serving as Dougie's advocate," Quincy spoke up. "She's been working with the boy for the past two months, visiting with him at least once or twice a week."

"And who would know this?" Candi with an "i" was no dumb bunny.

"Anyone involved in the situation—the local court officers, so-cial services, friends and family of the Carpenters. Then again, given how people like to talk, that probably means most of the town."

"So he's a local?"

Kincaid opened his mouth, already frowning, but at the last minute, seemed to change his mind. He still didn't agree with Quincy on this point, but perhaps was coming around.

"Yes," Quincy said firmly. "I believe he is a local."

"So it's personal?"

"The abductor has a relationship with Rainie and/or Dougie," Quincy replied. "It remains a possibility, however, that the relation-ship is one-sided."

Candi frowned. "Stalker?"

"That's my guess. Rainie is private. Her circle of friends is small and loyal. I doubt one of them would turn on her. It's quite possible, however, that someone on the outer fringes, a face that for her is only part of the visual landscape of her day, has taken a greater interest."

Kincaid made a noise in the back of his throat. The sergeant was more hesitant to fully abandon the theory of a stranger-to-stranger crime. Quincy, however, had no doubt in his mind. The subject had taken Rainie's gun. Then he had cut off her hair. Finally, he had ab-ducted Dougie Jones. A total stranger would never have known three such perfect ways to hurt her.

He glanced discreetly at his watch. Kimberly should be at her destination now. Good.

"So we're talking someone local who knows the victims," Candi said. "That brings us down to what, three, four thousand suspects?"

Shelly Atkins finally spoke up. "Hey, I can do you better than that. I got a list."

"Really?"

"Prepared by one aspiring felon to rat out the others," the sheriff admitted. "But I think we can use it."

"Absolutely. I need to know something unique about every name on that list. Something personal, that's not common knowledge. In official negotiationspeak, we call that bait."

"If the caller reacts—"

"Then your list might be better than you think, Sheriff."

Shelly appeared genuinely impressed. She gave a small grunt of acknowledgment; maybe there was more to Candi with an "i" than big hair after all.

"You're assuming you get to speak with the subject," Quincy said mildly. "He's not due to call until ten tomorrow morning, and then it's time for immediate lights, camera, action. He calls this phone, and directs a female officer to the ransom drop. I don't think that would be the time to renegotiate the deal."

"You don't think I can do the ransom drop?"

"I think my daughter's doing the ransom drop."

"Your daughter?" A fresh look to Kincaid.

The sergeant shrugged. "Current FBI."

"She a negotiator?"

"She's quick on her feet," Quincy said.

"But is she a negotiator?"

"She's taken classes."

Candi with an "i" rolled her eyes. "I tell you what, proud papa. Your daughter can be the body, but I'm still the mouthpiece. You people have had all day to do it your way, and may I be the first to say 'Wow, what a fuckup.'"

Kincaid started to protest; Quincy, too. Candi simply raised her hand and silenced them both. "In less than twenty-four hours, you have not only failed to negotiate the release of the first hostage, but you have provoked the kidnapping of a second. Now, maybe you guys didn't go to the same police academy I did, but we consider that a real bad day. But hey, at least you got one thing right."

"We called you?" Kincaid said dryly.

She flashed him a stunning smile. "Absolutely right, Sergeant. Now, if you'll excuse me, I'm gonna get some water."

Candi with an "i" sauntered from the room, leaving a sea of dazed silence in her wake. Mac was the first to recover.

"Twenty bucks says Kimberly kicks her ass by five p.m. to-morrow."

The officers gathered round. No one could pass up that kind of action.

23

HE WAS ALREADY OUT on the covered porch when she pulled up; he'd probably heard her rental car whining furiously as it climbed the drive. The rain poured off the pitched roof of the porch, cutting a deep trench into the sodden ground. Luke Hayes didn't seem to notice. He stood at the top of the steps in a short-sleeved polo shirt, toned arms crossed over a toned chest, seemingly impervious to the elements. After all these years, Kimberly thought, the former Bakersville sheriff still knew how to make an impression.

She took her time getting out of the car. She was already cold, wet, and muddy. Slogging through five more feet of washed-out driveway hardly mattered. She didn't know how to handle this conversation, however, and picking her way precariously through the muck bought her precious minutes to collect herself.

No doubt about it, her heels were ruined. Probably her pants, too. After this, she'd have to go to Wal-Mart for new clothes. Given her penchant for Ann Taylor, Mac would die laughing. She didn't care. At this point, warm and dry were her only requirements for apparel. Please just let her find something that was warm and dry.

"Hey," Luke called out as a greeting.

"Hey yourself." Kimberly had known Luke for nearly a decade. He was an old friend of Rainie's and had once helped save Quincy's life. Under the heading of things she'd never tell her father, Kimberly used to have the biggest schoolgirl crush on the man. Oh, the nights she'd gone to sleep dreaming about those cool blue eyes, that hard muscled body, those rough callused hands. No doubt about it, Luke Hayes had a way with women.

She really did not want to have this conversation.

He pushed away from the railing. "Come in, hon. I just put on a pot of coffee."

"Sure you don't mind? I'm soaked to the bone and covered in mud..."

"And here I thought you'd jump at the chance to inspect my home." Luke held the door open, his expression somber. "Come inside, Kimberly. Have some coffee."

Her face flushed. She followed Luke into his house. It was a small, two-bedroom ranch, featuring a large common room and a tiny kitchen. Good house for a single guy. Surprisingly clean, but also filled with the signs of someone recently divorced—the ratty furniture picked up from a buddy's garage. A kitchen stocked primarily with paper products. No pictures on the wall, no personality in the room.

This was merely a way station, a place for a guy to catch his breath and wonder what to do next.

Luke poured her some coffee. The paper cup was hot to the touch, so he layered it inside another cup before deciding it would do. "Cream or sugar, or are you like your old man?"

"I prefer it black," she admitted with a smile.

Luke smiled back. Closing in on forty, he was still a handsome guy. Startlingly bright blue eyes bracketed by laugh lines. Trim muscular build. Hard chiseled face.

Rainie had once described Luke as the anchor of the Bakersville Sheriff's Department. She could be intense and moody, prone to small fits of rage. Luke, on the other hand, could stare down the devil himself. It was something in the way he moved, something about the quiet calm of his gaze. He always seemed in control, even when, they all realized now, he wasn't.

"Nice place," she said at last.

"I hate it."

"Well, a can of paint certainly wouldn't hurt."

"I'm a log cabin guy. I spent four years building our home. She always told me it was too manly. 'Course she kept it in the divorce."

"She" was Deanna Winters, a former dispatch worker for the sheriff's department. She and Luke had wed two years ago, finally ending Luke's reign as the town's most eligible bachelor. Ten months ago, Luke had caught Deanna *in flagrante delicto* with one of his deputies. He'd thrown them both out of the house. Literally. Tossed them out of the front door stark naked. The theatrics had only grown uglier from there.

Luke sued for divorce. Deanna slapped him with allegations of spousal abuse. He claimed she'd been unfaithful from the very beginning. She countered he had, "with knowledge and foresight," withheld the information that he was sterile, thereby deliberately denying her children.

Given the amount of public attention, Luke had stepped down from his position as sheriff. Deanna promptly went crying to a judge that he was trying to reduce his income to cheat her out of her rightful amount of alimony.

Kimberly didn't know all the details, but in a battle of spite and wills, Luke seemed to cave first. He got his divorce. Deanna got everything he ever owned. At least, people liked to murmur behind their backs, there hadn't been any children.

"We could go into the family room," Luke offered now, "but I should warn you up front, the sofa has no springs and the recliner cripples grown men."

"So what, you sit on the floor?"

"I pace. I find as long as I keep moving, I'm less likely to break things."

Kimberly arched a brow. Luke shrugged, took his coffee and walked into the family room.

"You're here about Rainie," he said, his back to her.

"Yes."

"Quincy wants to know if I'm involved."

"He wondered if you had heard anything—"

"Bullshit. Quincy's a suspicious bastard. Always has been, always will be. Given his line of work, I can't really blame him." Luke took a seat on the edge of the coffee table. "But he's wrong about Rainie and me."

"Why is he wrong, Luke?"

"We were never involved, never even thought about it. We're close, of course, but not in that kind of way. She's more like the sister I never had."

"The divorce has been hard," Kimberly murmured.

"Tell me about it."

"Deanna wiped you out."

"I see the gossips are as busy as ever. What? I hit a little financial hardship so I decided to kidnap a fellow cop? Tell your father that's paranoid thinking even from him. I married the wrong kind of woman. That doesn't mean I'm the wrong kind of man."

Kimberly finally crossed to him. She squatted down so she could study Luke eye to eye. Up close, she could see the fresh lines creasing his face, the unhealthy pallor that came from too many sleepless nights. He was a man who was hurting. But his head was up, his shoulders square.

"I'm very sorry," she said quietly.

He shrugged. "Aren't we all."

"Luke, did you know Rainie had been drinking?"

"Yeah, yeah I did." Luke sighed, sipped coffee. "I called Quincy about the DUI. What I didn't tell him was that it was her second. I buried the first, hoping she'd clean up her act. Then, when she proved me wrong . . . I did what I always knew I should've done the first time around. She hasn't spoken to me since."

"Oh, Luke."

"Rainie's strong. She'll find her way back. 'Least that's what I like to tell myself."

"Do you have any idea what might have happened last night? Who might have grabbed her?"

He shook his head. "I've been thinking about it ever since Shelly Atkins called. Sure, we have some boys around here who aren't adverse to underhanded ways of earning a buck. But kidnapping and ransom . . . That's a serious crime. Involves planning, logistics, face time with the victim. Frankly, most of our boys are too lazy. They'd rather plant a few 'medicinal herbs' in the woods or start a lab on the farm. And as for the violent ones, I hate to say it, but that's why they have wives." Luke grimaced. Kimberly could read his thoughts. The world was filled with sons of bitches, and here he was, basically a good man, only to find himself dumped on by his wife. "Do you know where she was last seen?" he asked.

"Not yet. We're working on it, of course."

"If it was a bar . . ."

"No telling who she might have met, including someone from out of town," Kimberly filled in for him.

"Exactly. Of course, Rainie liked to drive, especially when she was upset. Maybe she didn't go anyplace at all. In which case . . ."

"We're back to it could be anyone." Kimberly stood, stretching out her legs. "I'll be honest, Luke, we don't think it was a stranger-to-stranger crime."

Luke frowned, rising off the coffee table, staring at her curiously. "But I thought, when Shelly called . . . She said the note had been mailed before the actual abduction, that the man basically committed to grabbing a female before he ever snagged Rainie."

"That was how things looked in the beginning. But we've had some new developments since then. The UNSUB has grabbed a second person—"

"Who?"

"Dougie Jones."

"Dougie Jones?"

"Now how many out-of-towners could make that connection? And he delivered a particularly personal token with the news."

Kimberly watched Luke steel himself, stomach muscles tightening, jaw clenching, as if preparing for a blow. If he was acting, then he was very, very good.

She said, "The UNSUB cut off Rainie's hair."

"No!"

Kimberly nodded thoughtfully. "If this guy's watched too many movies, you'd think he'd go for a finger, or maybe an ear. Hair is almost too innocuous. Except . . ."

"Rainie has the most beautiful hair," Luke filled in softly.

"Her one vanity. It seems like a particularly intimate thing to do."

"Ah, Jesus." Luke sat down again, hard, on the edge of the table. Coffee sloshed over the edge of his cup, splattering his jeans. He didn't seem to notice. "So you're searching for a man, probably local. Somebody who's looking to make a quick buck—"

"Not necessarily. Quincy thinks the ransom may be incidental. The UNSUB's goal isn't a conclusion—receiving money—but the process itself and the feeling of control it gives him over Rainie and the task force."

Luke closed his eyes. He sighed heavily, and when he opened his eyes again, he looked to Kimberly as if he'd aged years. "Then Quincy is missing the obvious."

"The obvious?"

"You're looking for a man who knows Rainie. Someone with a personal reason to hurt her and the Bakersville Sheriff's Department."

"The sheriff's department?"

"Oh yeah, most definitely. You've been looking at recent changes in Rainie's life, the most obvious being that she's resumed drinking. And that's diverted your attention, had you looking at seedy bars and drunken strangers. But what's the other major change? Rainie and Quincy returned to Bakersville. Rainie came home and now she's in trouble."

Kimberly shook her head. "I still don't get it."

"Didn't she ever tell you she killed a man?" Luke's tone was even.

"Oh no . . ."

"Lucas Bensen was listed as missing for nearly fifteen years. It was only eight years ago that Rainie confessed to killing him when she was sixteen and burying his body. The case officially went to trial, and Rainie was found innocent due to the mitigating circumstances— Lucas had raped Rainie, then shot her mother when she tried to intervene. Naturally, next time Rainie saw Lucas looming outside her door, she shot first and questioned later."

"I've heard the story. It's still not something that's easy for her to talk about."

"Point is, Rainie confessed, Rainie produced the body, then Rainie left town."

"You think now that she's returned, Lucas has risen from his grave?"

He looked at her curiously. "Not Lucas, of course. But didn't Rainie ever tell you? The man had a son."

24

SHELLY ATKINS HATED COFFEE. This was not something one admitted in law enforcement. Stakeouts, long nights, early mornings, bitter, foul coffee was always the brew of choice. Frankly, it didn't look the same when you whipped out your box of herbal tea.

Shelly couldn't afford to look different. She was a woman commanding in a male-dominated world. In the good-news/bad-news department, at least she wasn't pretty. She had broad shoulders, muscled arms, and stocky legs. She could plow a field, churn a vat of butter, and heft a calf. Around these parts, men respected that sort of thing.

She still wasn't wife material, however. Or maybe she hadn't met the right man. Who knew? But Shelly had given her youth to farming. Her adulthood, she was keeping for herself.

Now, she left the command center in the conference room, walking out into the main lobby. This time of night, the building was deserted, doors closed to the public, Fish and Wildlife officers done for the day. She moved into a corner dominated by a slab of tree trunk and a beautifully mounted rack of antlers. There, she fished around in her chest pocket for her packet of chamomile tea, then plunked it into her cup of hot water. She put the lid back on, ripped off the dangling tag from the tea bag, and no one was the wiser.

Everyone had their little secrets, Shelly thought wryly, then was somewhat saddened that this was as good as hers got. She was nearly fifty years old, for God's sake. Sometime soon, she was going to have to run off to Paris and sleep with a painter, just to keep herself from being totally boring in old age. Maybe in Paris, she would be considered exotic. Their own women were so pale, wraithlike. Surely there was a painter somewhere on the Left Bank who would enjoy the challenge of painting the last of a dying breed—the quintessential American farm wife. She would strap a plow to her back. She would pose nude.

It would give her something to remember during all the sleepless nights to come. I, Shelly Atkins, once sipped from the cup of life. I, Shelly Atkins, for at least one moment, felt beautiful.

"Penny for your thoughts."

Quincy's voice came out of nowhere.

"Holy shit!" Shelly exclaimed. She jerked the cup of hot tea away from her body, so at least she only sprayed it on the floor. Her heart thundered in her chest. She had to take several deep breaths before her hands would stop shaking.

"Sorry," Quincy said contritely. He moved into view and she realized he had followed her from the conference room. He looked better now than he had an hour ago. Composed again, some color infusing his cheeks, his posture erect. Hell, he looked downright handsome, which was not a thought Shelly wanted to be having right now.

Shelly knew more about Quincy than he'd want her to know. She was a bit of a true-crime junkie, and when she'd heard through the grapevine there was a genuine retired profiler in her community, naturally she'd dug up everything she could find on the man. Gruesome cases, fascinating stories. She'd spent the past few weeks trying to work up the courage to approach him. She would love to hear about his work, pick his brain on major cases. She didn't know how to introduce herself, however, without coming off as some kind of FBI groupie. Which maybe she was.

Truthfully, Shelly didn't really want to travel to Paris. But she'd sell her soul to attend the National Academy for police officers at Quantico. If only the Bakersville Sheriff's Department had those kinds of resources . . .

Shelly sighed heavily. She was hopeless, and there would be no good stories for the old folks' home after all.

"How are you feeling?" she asked roughly. Quincy was standing beside her now. Tall, lean, distinguished, with the silver streaking through his dark hair. He smelled of rain, mud, and fir trees, a walking advertisement for the great outdoors. She wished she'd stop noticing these things.

"Apparently not well enough for people to stop asking me that question," Quincy answered dryly.

"You gave us a good scare. I've never seen a man collapse like that."

"When did you arrive?"

"Just as you picked up the metal folding chair and simultaneously tried to rip Kincaid limb from limb."

"It was sublimation. I've secretly been plotting to maim Sergeant Kincaid ever since he decided not to meet the first ransom demand. Going insane about my missing wife simply gave me the chance."

"That young guy moves quick."

"Mac? He's a good man."

"How long has he been with your daughter?"

"Couple of years."

"Think this is the real thing?"

"I don't know. Kimberly rarely talks of matters of the heart." Quincy nodded thoughtfully. "But I wouldn't object. Not that any father feels that any man is good enough for his daughter, but in this case . . ."

"Seems like he can handle her," Shelly filled in for him.

"Something like that."

"She's beautiful," Shelly said. "You must be very proud."

"She's beautiful, intelligent, and stubborn to a fault. I'm enormously proud. And yourself?"

"Never done it. No husband, no kids." Shelly jerked her head toward the conference room. "I gotta keep all those yokels in line. That's enough mothering for me."

"Well said."

Shelly took a sip of her tea. The steam wafted out and Quincy inhaled the fragrance.

"Chamomile," he commented.

"I'll pay you fifty bucks not to tell."

"Your deputies are morally opposed to herbal tea?"

She scowled. "Men. You know what it's like."

Quincy smiled. It lightened his face, bracketed his eyes. She felt his grin in her chest, which only made her twenty times a fool.

"Indeed I do," he said.

Shelly turned away from him. She studied the antlers, the tree stump, the dust that was collecting around the edges of the displays. Hell, she was no good at these things, had never been any good at these things. This was the real reason Shelly was still single: honest to God, she only knew how to talk shop.

"I looked up Nathan Leopold," she said.

"And?"

"Same as the others. Famous abduction case from the twenties. Leopold was a rich kid who saw himself as some sort of criminal mastermind. He convinced his friend Richard Loeb, also rich and spoiled, to kidnap and murder a fourteen-year-old young boy 'for the experience.' The two drafted a ransom note but, like the other cases, never planned on returning the boy alive. After the police discovered the body, Leopold inserted himself into the investigation. Didn't take long for the cops to figure things out, however. For one thing, brilliant Nathan dropped his spectacles near the body. Turned out there were only three frames like them made in the whole United States. Ah, the good old days before everything was mass-produced from LensCrafters."

"A partner crime," Quincy mused softly, "with elements of a thrill kill."

"Yeah, but Leopold was clearly the instigator, the alpha partner, no doubt about it. Similarities I see between the names given by our guy are that all are from infamous cases and none of the abductors ever planned on returning the hostage alive." At the last minute, Shelly realized how blunt she sounded. "Sorry," she murmured awkwardly, and hastily sipped more tea.

"You don't have to apologize."

"It's just . . . She is your wife. I can't even begin to imagine how hard this must be."

"I doubt it's ever easy."

"You could go home, you know, get some sleep. We can handle this."

"If you went home, Sheriff Atkins—"

"Shelly, call me Shelly."

"If you went home, Shelly, would you sleep?"

"Probably not."

"It's easier to be here. It's even easier to discuss theories on what kind of psychopath took my wife. At least that's doing something. And maybe, if I keep busy now, I won't go insane thinking of all the things I should have done earlier. The signs I ignored, the conversations I didn't have, the symptoms I didn't recognize. You know—all of the ways in which I probably failed my wife."

"Coulda, woulda, shoulda," murmured Shelly.

"Rainie's an alcoholic," Quincy said abruptly. "Yet in all the time I've known her, she's never attended AA. If you asked her about it, she would say, 'I was an alcoholic.' It sounds very forthcoming, honest, and yet . . ."

"She's using the past tense."

"As if she's magically cured, as if it's no longer an issue in her life. Which of course—"

"Is denial of its own kind."

"I never pushed her. I never asked her about it. Rainie always accused me of wanting to fix her. I disagreed, of course, but maybe that was my own version of denial. Because how else could I accept her statement so readily, as if she had been broken but was now repaired? The human psyche is not that simple. Addictions are not that kind."

Shelly didn't know what to say. She drank more tea.

"I'm sorry," Quincy said abruptly.

"For what?" Shelly looked around, honestly confused.

"For talking so much. I didn't intend to come out here to run off at the mouth. I'm sorry. You're . . . you're a very good listener."

Shelly shrugged, sipped more tea. Yeah, that was her lot in life. To be a good listener.

"I'm supposed to be informing you that Sergeant Kincaid will be holding a briefing at nine p.m.," Quincy said. "Please be prepared."

"Briefing on what?" Shelly snorted. "That my deputies still haven't found Dougie Jones? That we still don't know who abducted your wife? Hell, I only wish I *had* something to prepare."

"I don't think the sergeant is planning on using the meeting to recap what we haven't done."

"Well, praise be and hallelujah."

"I believe he's going to use the meeting to discuss what will happen next."

"And that would be?"

"The ten a.m. ransom drop. No more fooling around. We tried things Kincaid's way. Now we'll let the UNSUB call the shots."

"Ahh shit," Shelly said tiredly.

"Quote of the day."

Shelly pulled herself together, belatedly trying to remember that this was the husband of the victim and he could use more from the local sheriff than profanity. "We're working hard," she rallied. "We're going to find her. It'll work out."

Quincy merely smiled again.

"First rule of thumb in this business, Shelly," he murmured quietly. "Don't make promises you can't keep."

25

KIMBERLY HAD ONE LAST STOP to make before she headed back to the command center. Luke did her the kindness of looking up the name and address. She took it from there.

Bakersville didn't have a lot of apartment complexes, and those that existed weren't in the best state of repair. This building in particular appeared to sag on its foundation, the second story tilting dangerously over the first. The establishment looked like it might have been a cheap motel once—the cracked asphalt parking lot, the dismal attempt at a playground where a swing set still remained, though devoid of swings, a pool that had been hastily filled with dirt. As Kimberly pulled in, her headlights picked up peeling white paint and cockeyed red shutters. There was very little about the property to call home.

She checked the numbers on the doors until she found 16. Light knock. The curtain over the window next to the door was drawn back, and a young woman peered out at her.

Kimberly flashed her creds. "My name is Kimberly Quincy, FBI. I have some questions about Dougie Jones."

That did the trick. The curtain fell back into place. The door swung open.

Peggy Ann Boyd appeared to be about Kimberly's age, with long dark hair pulled back into a ponytail. This time of night, her face was scrubbed free of makeup. Her suit had been traded in for a pair of gray sweatpants and a black and orange sweatshirt that proudly proclaimed *Go Beavs!* That meant she'd either attended Oregon State University or was a fan of its football program. Without a pro team to call their own, most Oregonians took college ball very seriously.

"I'm sorry to bother you after hours," Kimberly said as she entered the apartment. The one-room studio confirmed her earlier assumption of a motel that had been converted into rental units. Same drab brown carpet and gold floral drapes. A back wall that boasted a one-counter kitchenette, adjacent to the bathroom. Kimberly couldn't help thinking that if anyone could benefit from ten grand, it would be Peggy Ann Boyd.

"What did Dougie do this time?" the social worker asked tiredly.

"It's not what he's done. It's where he may be."

"He's run off?"

"He's missing."

Peggy Ann sat down heavily on the edge of the double bed. That left one chair in the room. The young woman gestured toward the old wingback and Kimberly took a seat.

"At least he didn't burn anything down this time," Peggy Ann said wryly. "In its own way, that's progress."

"How well do you know Dougie?"

Peggy Ann smiled; it did not diminish the strain on her face. "I'm not sure anyone knows Dougie. I've tried. Others have tried. But if there was ever a resistant subject. Oh, that poor boy. I honestly don't know what to do with him next."

"I understand that he's been through four different homes already, even had a stay in juvie. I'll confess, given his history of theft and arson, I'm surprised you were able to place him again. I'm surprised you tried."

Peggy Ann didn't answer right away. She was twisting her hands in her lap, this way and that, as if trying on her own fingers for size. "As a federal agent, you must work a lot of cases," she said abruptly.

"Yes."

"Some are just the job, I'm sure. You do what you're supposed to do, go through the paces."

"Sure."

"Dougie wasn't just the job for me. He wasn't just a case file. I wanted . . . I *still* want, to get this case right. Yes, he has problems. Yes, he has issues. But . . . But you had to see Dougie Jones four years ago. Dougie Jones four years ago was a truly great, very well loved, little boy."

Kimberly frowned, now confused. She hadn't seen Dougie's official case file; she'd have to wait until morning to subpoena those records. But according to what she'd been able to piece together, Dougie hadn't even entered the system until three years ago.

"How did you first meet Dougie?" she asked carefully.

"I've known Dougie since the day he was born."

Kimberly's eyes widened. "You're not . . . That wouldn't be appropriate—"

Peggy Ann laughed. "I'm not his mother, not even his relative. I'm his neighbor. Dougie was born in this apartment complex right here. Unit number twenty-two. That's where Dougie started his life."

"You knew his parents?"

"Yes and no." Peggy Ann shrugged. "My path would cross with his mother's from time to time. We'd both be picking up mail, or maybe I'd pull in while she was unloading groceries, that sort of thing. First you smile, then you say hi, and by the third or fourth time, it's not so strange to have a conversation or two.

"She was young, unwed-mother material. Had fallen madly in love with Dougie's father. Unfortunately, he hadn't fallen madly in love with her. The usual story. Best I could tell, she didn't have any family in the area. The state provided resources, and she had enrolled in a local program we have to help single moms earn their GEDs. It's run through the Episcopal church. The women provide day care for the kids and tutoring for the moms. The state kicks in a small stipend for each day the girls attend. It's not much, but the program has had success. Gaby—Dougie's mom—looked like she might be one of the better stories."

"No drugs, no alcohol, no other men?"

"No, no, from what I could tell, she lived a very quiet life. I'd stop by every now and then, never as part of my job, but as a neighbor. I grew up with a single mom, I know how hard it is. Sometimes I'd even watch Dougie for an hour or two while Gaby ran to the grocery store, that kind of thing. He was precocious. Apartment living isn't easy for a toddler, especially in units this small. I won't tell you he was magically an angel while his mother was alive. He was a master break-out artist from the time he was two. I think all of us discovered him out of the apartment at one time or another and returned him home.

"But he was loved, well cared for. Clean clothes, well fed. She'd pick him up all kinds of toys at garage sales. Even found him a tricy-cle for when he turned three. Gaby really went all out for her son. She wanted to make a better life for both of them."

"So what happened?"

"She died. Hit and run, one night when she was walking back from the convenience store. Dougie had gone to bed and she'd gone out for milk. No family ever stepped forward to claim him. He be-came a ward of the state and I got his file."

"Did you ever think of adopting him?"

"Me?" Peggy Ann raised a brow. "I'm single, working a govern-ment job that barely covers my rent and will probably cause me to burn out before I'm thirty-five. What could I offer Dougie Jones? He deserved a family. So that's what I found him."

"The first set of foster parents."

"The Donaldsons are good people. In social-services-speak, we consider them the Mercedes-Benz of foster parents. Good marriage, nice home, comfortable middle-class lifestyle. I told them Dougie's story, and Mrs. Donaldson couldn't file the paperwork fast enough to get him into her house. Here was a kid who had a good start. He was loved, he had bonded, he had more potential than ninety percent of the kids who cross my desk. And here were people ready to take up where his mother left off. This should have been a happy ending, Ms.—"

"Kimberly, call me Kimberly."

"Well, it should've been a happy ending. To this day, I can't tell you why it wasn't."

"He burned down their garage."

"Only after breaking apart most of their furniture, shredding his bedding, and punching holes the size of basketballs in his room. The garage was the final straw. They didn't feel they could handle him anymore. Mrs. Donaldson told me that she was honestly afraid."

"Of Dougie?"

"Of Dougie."

"But you found him another home."

Peggy Ann smiled wanly. "There's money in foster kids, Kimberly. As long as there's money, I can always find them another home."

"Oh."

"Yeah. Not as good a situation, with predictable results. For the record, I pulled some strings to get mental health resources available to Dougie after he burned down his second home. The state ponied up the money and I lined up a local psychologist who specializes in children. Unfortunately, Dougie's third foster mother never took him to the appointments. She had five kids to manage; thrice-weekly appointments were simply too much. And yes, Dougie imploded, and yes, she kicked him out, and yes, we started the cycle all over again. And again, and again.

"Dougie's an angry little boy. I wish I could tell you why. I wish I could tell you how to fix him. All I know for sure is that Dougie is very, very mad. At the world, at the foster system, and even at me. And right now, according to the experts, he would rather be angry than be loved."

"I met him this afternoon," Kimberly said.

Peggy Ann arched a brow. "Well, at least you look like you're in one piece."

"He was playing with a beetle, out in the rain, enjoying the mud. I thought I could talk to him about Rainie Conner. The minute I mentioned her name, however, he became furious."

"Really? Last I'd heard, she was one of the only people he tolerated."

Kimberly tilted her head to the side. "You don't know?"

"What?"

"Rainie has been kidnapped."

"Oh no."

"We're concerned that Dougie may know something about it."

"A *kidnapping*? He's only seven. I mean, if he'd burned down her house, I'd understand. But kidnapping?"

"According to Laura Carpenter, he knew Rainie was missing before anyone told him."

"That doesn't make any sense."

"Which is why I went to see him."

"And did he give you an explanation?"

"No. But I got the impression . . . The way he said some things didn't sound like a seven-year-old boy talking. It sounded like a boy repeating something an adult had told him."

Peggy Ann's turn to frown. "You think maybe he knows the person who kidnapped Rainie?"

"I'm not sure yet. But I think he does know something. Can you think of other close friends he might have? Anyone in which he would confide?"

"I don't get involved in the day-to-day. You'd have to ask Laura—"

"Nothing personal, but I don't think Laura Carpenter is that close to Dougie."

"Maybe Stanley?"

"I haven't met him yet." Kimberly was silent for a moment. "What about the abuse charges Dougie made?"

Peggy Ann sighed. "Off the record?"

"Off the record."

"If I thought Dougie was in any real danger, I'd pull him out of that house in a heartbeat. I have noplace to take him, of course, but I'd figure something out. I've followed up with both Stanley and Laura Carpenter; I can't find anyone who has an unkind word to say about them, and I did find about half a dozen boys from the high school football team who swore Mr. Carpenter helped them turn their lives around. And I've visited Dougie multiple times; I've never seen any sign of bruising on him, nothing to suggest violence. Given his troubled past . . ."

"You think he's lying."

"I think Stanley Carpenter's 'tough love' approach feels like war to Dougie. But it may also be the only hope Dougie has left."

"Do you know if Rainie had made any conclusions?"

"I haven't seen any report."

"Rumors?"

Peggy Ann frowned, shook her head. "I haven't heard any rumors, either. Last I knew, she was still investigating."

Kimberly nodded, sat back. Quincy had hinted that Rainie was beginning to think Dougie's case had merit. When she'd talked to Laura Carpenter, however, she didn't seem to know anything on the subject, and neither did Peggy Ann. The real question in Kimberly's mind wasn't what Rainie had concluded, but what others *thought* she had concluded. By all appearances, however, Rainie had played things close to her chest.

Kimberly sighed now, frowning, trying to think of what to pursue next. "Was Dougie in school?"

"First grade."

"Can you give me the name of his teacher? Maybe he or she will know something."

Peggy Ann got up and moved toward the table, which Kimberly could see also doubled as a desk. "Mrs. Karen Gibbons is her name. I'm sure she won't mind you giving her a call. For the record, however, Dougie isn't exactly the teacher's pet."

"That's what I figured. What about a psychologist? Now that he's at the Carpenters', is he going to appointments?"

"Not that I know of, but again, Laura could tell you more."

Kimberly had talked to Laura briefly after her run-in with Dougie. From what she could tell, Laura didn't know anything. Really, honestly, didn't know anything, which Kimberly had thought was an interesting trait in a foster mom. It was as if Stanley had wanted to take in a foster child and Stanley had designed a program for a foster child and Stanley now had a foster child. Laura was simply along for the ride.

Kimberly hadn't seen any outward signs of bruising, but in her personal opinion, Laura fit the profile of an abused wife. She wondered if Rainie had thought the same.

Peggy Ann finished copying a name and phone number down on a sheet of notebook paper. She handed it over to Kimberly.

"Is it still raining outside?" Peggy Ann asked.

"Drizzling, yeah."

"Did you look? Maybe he took a coat with him, or umbrella, hat and gloves." The woman's tone was wistful. She was worrying about Dougie again, and Kimberly understood that Peggy Ann would not be sleeping tonight.

"He was last seen in sweatshirt and jeans," she said quietly. "We have the sheriff's office out searching for him now."

"I see," Peggy Ann said, but still she frowned. "Wait a minute. If the sheriff's office is looking for him . . . Didn't you say you were FBI?"

"We don't really think he's lost," Kimberly said as kindly as she could. "We believe he may have been kidnapped."

Peggy Ann stuffed her hand into her mouth. "Oh no."

Kimberly rose out of the chair. "If there's anyone else you can think of for me to speak with . . ."

"I will let you know immediately."

"And if for some reason you should hear from Dougie—"

"I will let you know immediately."

Kimberly was at the door. Peggy Ann remained standing in the middle of the room. She looked forlorn now, shoulders slumped in her oversized sweatshirt, a few strands of dark hair tangled around her pale face.

"Peggy Ann, if we do make contact with Dougie," Kimberly asked abruptly, "can you think of anything we can say to him, anything or anyone that might get his attention? Does he have a favorite toy or an invisible friend? Maybe a memento from his mother?"

Peggy Ann gave her a sad smile. "What do you think he used to start the fire in the Donaldsons' garage? He gathered together all his personal possessions—his clothes, his toys, his pictures of his mom—and he set them aflame. Every last item. There's not even a portrait of his own mother left."

Kimberly honestly didn't know what to say.

Peggy Ann smiled forlornly. "I hope for his own sake Dougie has a matchbook tonight."

"Why?"

"Have you checked the thermostat? It's dropping into the low forties. And if he's already cold and wet . . ."

The rest didn't need to be said. "We're doing everything we can," Kimberly reiterated.

Peggy Ann wasn't fooled. "And yet when it comes to Dougie Jones, all that we can do is never nearly enough."

26

KINCAID KICKED OFF THE TASK force debriefing by having Shelly Atkins go first. It was a subtle but effective dig at the Bakersville Sheriff's Department, as Shelly had already admitted she had nothing to report.

"We'll go round the table," Kincaid announced at promptly nine p.m. "Catch everyone up on where we're at with our individual efforts. Then we'll discuss protocol for tomorrow's exchange. Shelly, what do you have?"

Shelly, sitting across the table from Kincaid, blinked in surprise. She stared at Detective Spector, sitting to Kincaid's right, then at the hostage negotiator, Candi Rodriguez, sitting on Kincaid's left. Finally, she sighed, knowing an ambush when she saw one, and got on with it.

Kimberly walked into the conference room just as Shelly stood to make her report. Quickly, she slid into the chair Quincy had saved between him and Mac, using her hand to wipe the rain from her face. Only one other seat remained empty, for OSP Detective Alane Grove. Apparently, Kincaid wasn't in the mood to wait for even his own people. He made a motion with his hand, and Shelly started talking.

As discreetly as she could, Kimberly nudged her father's elbow and sketched a quick update on the yellow legal pad in front of him. She wrote: *Luke Hayes = no. Lucas Bensen's son???*

Quincy stared at that notation for a long time.

"So, as per the last meeting," Shelly was saying roughly, "the sheriff's department has had two primary tasks. One, we've been checking local offenders' alibis, as well as rattling some cages. Two, we've been involved in the search for seven-year-old Douglas Jones. As for our first mission, we drew up a list of twenty-seven 'people of interest.' As of this time, we have personally visited twelve of these individuals. Eight have been definitely ruled out as having alibis. Three we have moved to the 'unlikely' category. One remains a 'person of interest,' as well as the other fifteen, whom we hope to visit shortly.

"Now, during one of these visits, the individual in question volunteered a list of names he thought might be willing to kidnap a woman for ransom. Several of these names were already on our list. But three more emerged that I have added to the 'people of interest' column, bringing that total to nineteen local males."

She glanced over the table at Kincaid, cleared her throat. "I'll be honest. Given the late hour, and all of the other responsibilities my people have, it is doubtful we can clear nineteen names by ten a.m. tomorrow. We'll keep at it until midnight, then I'm going to start sending my officers home in five-hour shifts, so that everyone can grab at least a little shut-eye by morning. What names we don't have cleared—I'm guessing it'll be a good dozen—I'll flesh out into mini-profiles for Ms. Candi. Yes, I'll use bullet points."

Shelly gave the hostage negotiator a droll look. Candi responded with a sickeningly sweet smile of her own.

"Now, in regard to Dougie. I got three deputies coordinating efforts with the local search-and-rescue team, as well as the fire department, and about two dozen volunteers. They'll keep at it for another few hours, but the woods around the Carpenter residence have been pretty thoroughly searched. Either Dougie is hiding and doesn't want to be found, or the boy is gone, kidnapped as we suspect."

"Have you spoken to the foster parents?" Kincaid asked.

"I haven't, but one of my deputies has."

"And?"

Shelly shrugged. "And what? Stanley Carpenter personally thinks Dougie has run away—according to him, Dougie remains a hellion, willing to do anything to avoid taking responsibility for his actions. 'Course, last we knew, Dougie was alleging that Stanley's abusive. The person in charge of sorting all that out is Rainie Conner, who is our first kidnap victim and can't exactly be reached for comment. Do I think Stanley's telling the truth? Hell if I know. Do I think Dougie has been kidnapped or willfully ran away? Hell if I know. I only slept four hours out of the past forty. I'm just happy I'm standing up straight."

Kincaid blinked his eyes. "Fair enough," the sergeant said. "Did you go inside the home?"

"No, Deputy Mitchell paid the visit. The Carpenters are cooperating. Stanley's alibis—working all day, football practice at night—both checked out. Laura spent the day home alone, so it's a bit harder to account for her time. They allowed Deputy Mitchell to walk through the house and tour the kid's room. It's pretty bare, just a mattress and a sheet. The window is nailed shut and the door locks from the outside, which made Mitchell uncomfortable. But again, according to Stanley, Dougie has a history of breaking out of foster homes and committing arson, which is consistent with what we've heard."

"I'd like to send the crime lab there, see what they might be able to turn up."

Shelly shrugged. "We can try it. I think Mitchell would tell you there's just not much to search in Dougie's room. No desk, no books, no dresser, no toy chest. In his cursory inspection, he couldn't even discover a trash can. I don't know. Maybe turning a kid's room into a jail cell is the only way. Now see, this is why I stick to horses."

"Did Deputy Mitchell speak with Laura Carpenter?" Kimberly spoke up.

Shelly turned toward her. "She was present when he entered the home, but it sounded like Stanley did most of the talking."

"And did this strike Deputy Mitchell as odd?"

"You're asking does Stanley rule the household with an iron fist?"

"I met Laura Carpenter earlier today. I was . . . concerned by her seeming lack of interest or involvement with her foster child."

Shelly considered it. "Mitchell didn't say anything, but I could follow up with him."

"Do you have a deputy you consider an expert in domestic abuse cases? Or maybe an officer you consider better at speaking with battered women?"

"I do."

"I would send that person for the follow-up visit, see if he or she could get Laura alone. Stanley is never going to tell you anything. But maybe, if we reached out to Laura . . ."

Shelly was nodding. "That makes sense. Consider it done."

Kincaid cleared his throat, and ruffled the papers in front of him. It was his meeting, after all. "So, Kimberly. Sounds like you've had a busy evening. Anything you'd care to share with the task force?"

"I simply did some follow-up on Dougie Jones," Kimberly said casually. She had no intention of mentioning her visit to Luke Hayes, nor, she knew, would her father want her to. "I paid a visit to his social worker, Peggy Ann Boyd, who was actually Dougie's neighbor when he was born. According to her, Dougie's always been very precocious, but at least for the first four years of his life, he was very well loved. Unfortunately, his mother was killed in a hit-and-run accident. When no family claimed him, he became a ward of the state, and his adventures with his various foster parents began. She insists that deep down inside, he's still a good kid. He's very angry right now, however, and in her own words, he needs that rage more than he needs to be loved."

"In other words, nothing we didn't already know."

"I asked if there was any good way to reach out to Dougie. A special memento he might hold dear, a stuffed animal, blanket, whatever. According to her, he destroyed all of his personal possessions during the first fire he set in his foster parents' garage, including each and every photograph of his mom."

"Ah jeez," Shelly murmured from her end of the table, while the other officers shifted uncomfortably.

"I think Dougie still loves his mother very much," Kimberly said softly. "I think if someone exploited that information the right way, they could manipulate even a tough, suspicious boy like him. Say, lure him closer to their vehicle, or even convince him to go for a ride."

"Meaning, you're thinking he has been kidnapped," Kincaid stated bluntly.

"Before, even with the ransom note and the beetle . . . Maybe Dougie is only seven years old, but by all accounts he's quick, strong, and deeply distrustful of strangers, not the kind of boy who's going to go without a fight. So how did our guy grab this kid without anyone noticing? In the beginning, that thought troubled me. But now . . . I can see how it might be done."

"Do you think Dougie is a second kidnap victim," Kincaid asked steadily, "or have you considered that he might be an accomplice?"

"Seven is a bit young to be considered an accomplice."

"You know what I mean."

Kimberly hesitated. She did know what he meant and it wasn't a pleasant thought, but one that bore considering. "It's possible Dougie's aiding whoever took Rainie," she said, after a moment. "He's angry, isolated, young. Clearly, that would make him a target for coercion."

"I'd like us all to keep our minds open when it comes to Dougie Jones," Kincaid said briskly. "There are two pieces of this puzzle that continue to trouble me. One, that Dougie Jones seemed to know Rainie was missing before anyone else did. Now maybe it was purely coincidence, maybe he asked if she was missing because he wanted her to disappear. As Sheriff Atkins so eloquently put it, who the hell really knows when it comes to kids. However, that brings me to the second point: It appears more and more that Rainie was a targeted victim. Furthermore, that whoever took her knew a great deal about her and her life. Now, according to Mr. Quincy, Rainie was a private person with a very small inner circle. So who could have learned so much about her without getting on her radar screen? I'm beginning to wonder if these two pieces don't fit together. Someone knew all about Rainie, because Dougie Jones told him. And Dougie Jones knew Rainie had disappeared because . . ."

"He helped set her up," Quincy filled in quietly.

Kincaid nodded. "At this stage, it's just a theory, of course, but one we can't rule out. Hence my desire to search Dougie's room."

"Not his room," Kimberly said abruptly, eyes narrowing. "In Dougie's world, that house is clearly controlled by Stanley, it's enemy domain. The outdoors, in the woods, that's where Dougie feels most comfortable. If he wanted a place to stash his treasures—say, a special rock, or his beetle collection, or who knows, notes from a new 'friend'—that's where they would be. In a tin can stuck in a tree or buried under a boulder. You know, someplace secretive, but accessible to a seven-year-old."

"More quality time outdoors," Shelly deadpanned.

"Maybe your deputies, as long as they're there, searching the grounds . . ." Kincaid suggested.

"Getting soaked to the bone." Shelly rolled her eyes. "I'll get to work on the warrant. Chances are something like that isn't going to be lying around in plain sight."

She sighed, made a note on the pad in front of her, and the debriefing moved on.

Detective Ron Spector from the OSP had an update from the two primary examiners who'd arrived from the Portland Crime Lab—which, interestingly enough, was located in Clackamas.

"It's good news, bad news," Spector reported. "Car is in the process of being towed to the lab to be worked overnight. At the scene, they did a cursory exam of the interior with high-intensity lights. In the good-news department, no sign of blood, plus they discovered an imprint of a shoe tread pattern on the brake pedal, as well as a variety of fiber, trace, etc. So they anticipate plenty of evidence to process—whether any of it is helpful remains to be seen. Bad news is—this rain is killing us. Nothing is conclusive until the car dries out, but the scientists aren't optimistic about recovering anything from the exterior of the vehicle. Needless to say, recovering trace evidence from around the vehicle is also considered hopeless.

"Latent Prints also plans on spending more quality time with the vehicle tonight. In the interest of speed, they printed the rearview mirror, interior door handle, and gearshift, which are the most likely places to get results. The mirror yielded a full thumbprint. They're running a comparison of it now against the victim and her family." The detective glanced at Quincy, cleared his throat, then continued.

"The first note has already arrived at the lab. It's taking a quick spin through Latent Prints and DNA, before QD—Questioned Documents—does their thing. Bad news here is that DNA in particular is going to take some time, plus we happen to have a big load in-house at the moment. We're looking at weeks, if not months, for the finished report, not tomorrow at ten a.m."

Spector glanced at Kincaid. The lead detective shrugged. It wasn't even worth arguing this was a high-priority case. They were all high-priority cases.

"Finally, the victim's gun has also been printed and sent to the lab. One of the primary examiners, Beth, is already on her way back. She'll test it for trace evidence tonight, then get it to Ballistics. They have a report they're going to need you to fill out"—Spector nodded toward Quincy—"about your wife's gun habits. Does she always clean it after firing, etc., etc.? It'll help them determine if the gun had been fired recently."

"She does always clean it," Quincy answered. "And it hasn't been fired recently. We would've been able to tell from the smell."

Spector shrugged. The lab needed to do what it needed to do, and it was not the detective's place to argue. "In conclusion, there's plenty to process. Unfortunately, a great deal of it is periphery evidence. The primary crime scene—the roadside where the victim was most likely abducted—has been destroyed by the elements. And sure, we can send the scientists to the woods where Dougie Jones lives, but I think they'll tell you the same thing. Trace evidence simply can't survive these conditions. It's a fact of life."

Kincaid nodded glumly, the detective's report not telling any of them anything they didn't already know. In a case such as this one, with no suspect and a thirteen-hour window before the next contact, it was assumed that any evidence report would arrive too late to be of use to them. Instead, the information would be leveraged later, by a DA building a case to go to trial. What remained to be determined by Kincaid and the task force was what kind of trial it would be: one for kidnapping, or one for murder?

Kincaid cleared his throat, turning toward Mac for an update on procuring the ransom money, when the conference room door burst open. Alane Grove pushed into the room, still shaking out her umbrella and looking positively wired.

"Sorry I'm late," she announced breathlessly, "but I have news."

Kincaid arched a brow at his young detective. "Well, by all means."

She barely waited for the invitation, tossing down her wet umbrella and now working furiously on her raincoat. "I've been retracing Lorraine Conner's past twenty-four hours. No bars, from what I can tell, which I guess is good, but I discovered something else: She had a doctor's appointment at three p.m. yesterday."

She looked squarely at Quincy. Kimberly did, too. He slowly shook his head. He obviously had no idea where this was going.

"It was a follow-up appointment. Naturally, the doctor didn't want to talk about it—doctor-patient confidentiality and all that. But the moment I said she was missing, he became very concerned. Apparently, he prescribed a drug for Rainie starting three months ago. The appointment today was to adjust the dosage. It's an antianxiety medication—"

"Oh no," Quincy whispered.

"Paxil," Detective Grove volunteered brightly. "You've heard of it?"

"Oh no."

"Exactly. According to the doctor, this isn't a drug that can be quit cold turkey—you have to be weaned off of it. As of yesterday, Rainie was up to sixty-two milligrams a day, which is the highest dosage. According to the doctor, she's gotta keep taking it or the withdrawal symptoms will be pretty horrible—confusion, headache, nausea, hypomania, sensory disturbances. Some people have reported being unable to stand up, feeling like there were constant electric shocks going off in their brain. It's really not good."

Kimberly was looking at her father again. Quincy was still shaking his head, ambushed, stunned. Rainie had found a new way to hurt her husband after all. She had sought help—she just hadn't reached out to him.

"I got the listing of the contents of the victim's purse found in her vehicle," Detective Grove was saying now. "No report of any prescription medication. But then I got to thinking: What if the victim didn't want anyone to know she was taking an antidepressant? People are pretty touchy about these things, you know. So I thought, where's a logical place to hide some pills where she would always have them with her, but no one would suspect a thing? And I found them. Inside the Pamprin bottle she carried in her purse."

The detective's tone was triumphant. "I counted them all out. The number matches the prescription given by the doctor. So best I can determine, the victim took her dose yesterday morning, but hasn't had one since. Meaning . . ."

"We have to find her," Quincy said tightly.

"Yep. Or apparently, she'll lose her mind."

27

SHE COULD NOT FALL ASLEEP. Would not fall asleep. Absolutely, positively should not fall asleep.

Rainie forced herself to remain vigilant, hyperaware. She focused on the sound of water, dripping down the cellar walls, the feel of Dougie's small body, pressed against her side, the smell of mildew filling her nostrils. She was freezing, shivering in periodic spasms that wrenched through her aching body and rattled her teeth. She used the discomfort to keep herself alert. It gave her something to feel, lost in a black world devoid of sight.

She had wanted to get Dougie up off the damp floor. With her bound hands and feet, however, it had been impossible to manipulate the boy's unconscious body onto the dry table. Instead, she'd done the best she could to drag them both up the first few steps. The hard wooden edge of the staircase dug into her bruised ribs, cutting off circulation to various parts of her body. She developed a routine, shifting first left, then right, then stomping her bound feet. Movement brought warmth, warmth brought hope. So she kept moving.

Rainie had once been involved in a case where a young girl had been abandoned in an underground cave. She knew from that experience a person could die of exposure at fifty-five degrees. All it took was wet clothes and the constant chill.

She and Dougie were both soaked to the bone.

She had a feeling the basement was a good deal cooler than fifty-five degrees.

Funny, how many long nights she had spent the past four months, her mind racing with thoughts she didn't know how to control. She'd fallen asleep to horrible nightmares. She'd awakened to a displaced anxiety that often felt far worse than her dreams.

She had watched herself erode from the outside. From a relatively happily married woman with a challenging job, to a jumpy, hunch-shouldered bundle of nerves, who couldn't concentrate, couldn't sleep, couldn't hope. She developed a hair-trigger temper that frightened even her.

Any time she thought of Astoria, of Aurora Johnson's final moments of terror, she went nearly out of her mind with rage, felt the anger claw at her skull like a feral beast, desperate for escape. Even when they completed their profile, even when the lead detective read it, and said, "Hey, I know this guy," nothing changed. The maintenance man had a built-in alibi: Of course his prints were in the apartment—he maintained the unit. Of course there was blood on his shoes—he had called in the bodies.

Quincy devised a strategy for interrogation. The stringy-haired twenty-one-year-old high school dropout shrugged for four consecutive hours, stating, "I don't know nothin' 'bout that."

And so it went. They worked, they churned, they dug frantically for details. And Aurora Johnson's cries for help once again went unanswered.

Professionals were supposed to be able to handle that sort of thing. They were supposed to shrug it off, dig deep, as Quincy seemed able to do. *You can't win them all. The subject will screw up sooner or later.* Which implied another slaughtered mother, of course, another terrified little girl.

Rainie couldn't find that level of acceptance inside herself. She dreamed of the bloody apartment, night after night. Sometimes she even fantasized about visiting the maintenance man herself.

She knew how forensic science worked. Like any law enforcement officer, she had spent her fair share of time contemplating the perfect crime. She would take care of matters up close and personal. She would make sure that what happened to little Aurora Johnson never happened again.

Except, of course, the maintenance man was only the tip of the iceberg. Obsessively, she started following other news cases: kidnapped children, abuse cases, stories from the Iraq war. She would wait until Quincy was out of the house, and then she would sneak to the computer like a thief. Google search: three starved children. Google search: house of horrors. Google search: rape of infant.

It was amazing the amount of horror that would appear on her screen. She would sit there, hours at a time, reading, reading, reading, while the tears poured down her face. So much pain and suffering. So much injustice. The world was a miserable, cruel place, and there was nothing one woman could do that would ever make a difference. How could so many children be screaming, and nobody answer their cries?

Then she would hear the crunch of Quincy's tires on the drive. Quickly, she would close out the windows, scrub at her cheeks.

"I was just checking e-mail," she would tell her husband when he appeared in the hallway, smelling of rain and fir trees. And he would nod at her, and he would continue on to their bedroom, while she sat there, hands folded, head down, wondering how she could lie to someone she genuinely loved.

And she would feel the darkness grow in her, a living, breathing beast, cutting her off from the rest of civilization, isolating her from her own husband. She continued her horrible research and she didn't tell Quincy about any of it. He wouldn't understand. No one would understand.

It had been a relief when she had finally taken that first drink.

She was an idiot, she knew. It was her lot in life to live both inside and outside her body. She moved, she functioned, she felt. She was also an objective party, quick to criticize her own actions.

Aurora Johnson was dead. How did Rainie drinking, Rainie lying, Rainie self-imploding, change anything about that? On her better days, when the fog receded from her mind, when her hands shook less and her thoughts grew clearer, she understood she was doing all the wrong things. On one of those days, when Quincy was shut in his office working on his memoirs, she even called and made a doctor's appointment.

Much to her amazement, she kept the appointment two weeks later, though she'd actually managed to sleep the night before and down some eggs for breakfast, so maybe the worst was behind her and she was starting to be sane after all. These things came and went, right? She'd been strong once, she'd be strong again. Hey, she was Rainie. Nothing got her down.

She went to the doctor, a kind elderly gentleman who looked like he was straight out of a TV show. He told her she had an anxiety disorder and gave her a prescription. She carried the prescription in her purse for two more weeks, before one day having it filled. Then she went into the ladies' room, and for reasons she couldn't even explain to herself, she poured the pills into a Pamprin bottle, keeping one in the palm of her hand. She stared at it for a long time.

She probably should've told the doctor about the number of beers she consumed in a day. The whole drinking thing probably made a difference.

She took the pill. She waited to sleep like a baby. And when she bolted awake at three a.m., her head filled with Aurora Johnson's soundless scream, she went straight into the shower so Quincy would not see her curl up into a tiny ball and weep from pure frustration.

She took more pills. She drank more beer. She let the darkness swell inside her, turning herself over to it, resigned and accepting.

While her best friend pulled her over for driving under the influence. While her husband asked her again and again if she was okay. While her young charge realized that she'd lied to him and ran away from her to hide in the woods.

It was amazing the things one could do to one's own self. How much you could lie to yourself. How much you could hurt yourself. How you could have everything you ever wanted—a loving husband, a good job, a beautiful home—and still not find it enough.

Rainie tortured herself. And then she stood back from the outside and watched herself fall.

Until here she was, bound and gagged in a basement, hair hacked off and a seven-year-old child unconscious at her feet. Her inner demon should be roaring with approval. *See, the world really is a bad place and there's nothing you can do.*

Instead, for the first time in months, her mind felt quiet.

Yes, she was nauseous. Her head pounded. She had a strange tingling sensation shooting up and down her left leg. But overall, she felt focused, resolute. Somewhere above her in the dark was a man. He had kidnapped her, he had hurt Dougie.

And for that, Rainie was going to make him pay.

In the dark, Rainie's lips curled into a smile. The old Rainie was back, and finally, ruefully, she understood. Quincy only gave her someone to love. Apparently, what she needed more was someone to hate.

Tuesday, 10:15 p.m. PST

"YOU'RE TOUCHING ME."

Dougie's voice roused Rainie from her reverie. She swore she hadn't dozed off. Well, maybe just for a second.

"You're a pervert. I'm going to tell."

Rainie straightened in the dark. A cold, stabbing pain shot up her left hip, like an electric shock. She winced, uncurling from Dougie's body, and tried to stretch out her legs.

"How do you feel? Does your head hurt?" she asked.

"Where are we? I can't see. I don't like this game!"

"It's not a game, Dougie. Someone kidnapped me. The same person also kidnapped you."

"You're a liar," Dougie said angrily. "Lie, lie, lie. I'm going to tell Miss Boyd! You're nothing but a drunk. I want to go home!"

"Yeah, Dougie. Me, too."

With consciousness came the chill. Rainie reached up instinctively to rub her arms, only to be thwarted again by her bound hands. She wished she could see. She wished she could feel her fingers. It occurred to her that Dougie's voice sounded normal, unencumbered, meaning that he wasn't gagged. She dared to be optimistic.

"Dougie, there's a blindfold over my eyes. Is there a blindfold over your eyes?"

"Yes." He still sounded sullen.

"What about your wrists and ankles? Are you tied up?"

"Y-yes." More of a hiccup now. Dougie was starting to become more aware of his surroundings, and with that awareness came fear.

Rainie forced her voice to sound calm. "Dougie, did you see the person who took you? Do you know who did this?"

The boy was quiet for a while. "White light," he said at last.

"Me, too. I think he's using some kind of blinding flash, followed by a drug, maybe chloroform. You might feel sick to your stomach. It's okay if you need to throw up. Just let me know, and we'll get you off the stairs."

"I don't like you," Dougie said.

Rainie didn't bother to respond to that statement anymore; Dougie had been saying it for weeks, ever since she was supposed to meet him one Wednesday night and wound up at a bar instead. It had taken her months to gain the boy's trust. She lost it all in less than four hours. *This is your life,* Rainie thought not for the first time, *and this is your life on booze.*

"Dougie," she said carefully now, "I'm going to reach forward and see if I can untie your wrists. I can't see anything either, so just hold still for a sec while I figure it out."

The boy didn't reply, nor did he move away. Progress, she supposed. Leaning over him, she could feel him shiver, then stiffen his body against the tremors. His sweatshirt was still damp, stealing precious heat from him. Rainie swore if she ever got out of this basement, she was never going out in the rain again.

Her fingers finally found his bound arms. She explored his wrists, then swore softly. The man had used hard plastic ties. The only way to get them off would be with something sharp, such as scissors. Son of a bitch.

"I can't do it," she said at last. "I'm sorry, Dougie. We need a special tool."

Dougie just sniffed.

"Let me check out the blindfold. Maybe I can do that."

Dougie turned his head; Rainie found the knot. The blindfold had more potential; it was a simple strip of cotton fabric. The knot was tight, however, and Rainie's fingers stiff. She had to pick at it again and again, occasionally pulling Dougie's hair and making him yelp.

In the end, she never mastered the knot. But her constant pulling stretched the worn fabric. Dougie surprised them both by sliding the blindfold off his head.

"It's still dark!" he said with surprise.

"I think we're in a basement. Can you see any windows?"

The boy was silent a moment. "Up," he said at last. "Two of them. I'm not that tall."

Rainie thought she knew what he meant. Two high portals, probably set above the foundation. At least that allowed in some natural light. Anything had to be better than the endless dark. "Dougie, do you think you could work on my blindfold now?"

The boy didn't answer right away. Resentful, angry? Still thinking of all the ways Rainie failed him? She couldn't turn back time. That much she knew to be true.

Finally, she felt his fingers. They moved up her arm to her neck, then the boy stilled.

"Where's your hair?"

Rainie didn't want to scare a young child, but at the same time, she needed him as an ally, which meant she needed his hatred of their abductor to be greater than his anger with her.

She answered truthfully. "He cut it off. Sawed it off, actually, with a knife."

The boy hesitated. She wondered if he was now processing the rest of the information his fingers must have given him. The sticky feeling of her skin, where crisscrossing cuts still bled and oozed. The warm swollen area around her elbow where something had gone dreadfully askew.

"Work on the blindfold, Dougie," she ordered quietly. "We'll start by gaining our eyes, then see what we can do about our feet."

He went to work on her blindfold. His fingers were smaller, nimbler. Even with his bound wrists, he had her blindfold off in no time at all. Dutifully, they both checked out their ankles. Thankfully, not a zip tie, but old-fashioned strips of cotton. As Dougie had already proved himself more adept, he went first.

The minute the ties came off and Rainie's legs sprang apart, she felt an explosion of electrical impulses up and down her legs. Her toes shook, her left leg quivered. For thirty seconds, she gritted her teeth in agony as nerve ending after nerve ending filled with blood and fired to life. She wanted to scream, bang her hand in open-fisted frustration. Mostly, she wanted to kill the son of a bitch upstairs.

Then the worst of it passed, leaving her shaky and rubber-limbed, as if she'd just climbed Mount Everest instead of enduring a round of muscle spasms.

She tried for a deep, steadying breath, realizing for the first time how much her head hurt, the low ringing filling her ears. She had missed at least one dose of medication. She had no illusions about what would happen next.

She went to work on Dougie's bindings, moving to the bottom step. Her eyes were still adjusting to the gloom; the two high portals let in a distant glow, probably from an overhead patio light. It was enough to allow their prison landscape to transform from pitch black to shades of gray. Dougie's shoes became a darker silhouette against a lighter backdrop. She fumbled around with her heavy fingers until she found the knot, picking and tugging away.

"You're not very good at this," Dougie said.

"I know."

"I'm hungry."

"Did you bring any food?" she asked him.

She could feel him scowl in the dark. "No."

"Then we have nothing to eat."

"He took my beetle," Dougie said, and for the first time, sounded angry. "He stole my pet!"

"Dougie, you know how adults are always telling you not to hit? No biting, no scratching, you have to play nice?"

"Yeah."

"This man is the exception. You get the chance, go after him with everything you've got." The knot finally loosened. The cloth fell down and Dougie kicked his legs in triumph.

They had use of their feet, their eyes, their mouths. Not bad for a day's work.

Rainie picked up the loose strips of cloth. She didn't know how she would use them yet, but waste not, want not.

Now, in the dark, she could see Dougie bring his wrists to his mouth and start chewing at the zip ties. Theoretically speaking, it should be difficult to chew through the tough, plastic strap, but she didn't want to dampen his enthusiasm. She got up on her own, trying to walk off the strange sensations still ping-ponging up and down her side.

It felt good to take a real solid step. She felt strong, almost human. Aching head, ribs, and arms aside. Then her teeth started chattering again, reminding her of the numbing cold.

She gazed up the flight of stairs. She could see a glow of light underneath the door. So he was still awake, still moving, still doing whatever it was abductors did.

"Hey, buddy," she told Dougie, "I have a plan."

28

SHORTLY AFTER TEN, the task force dispersed. Shelly Atkins met separately with her deputies to coordinate sleeping shifts. The OSP detectives went in search of hotel rooms for themselves. People were tired and edgy, exhausted but wired. Everyone would try to grab at least a little shut-eye. Maybe half would succeed.

Quincy felt nearly giddy, in that strange euphoric state that preceded a body's total physical collapse. In the good-news department, he didn't have any tightness in his chest or fluttering in his stomach.

In the bad-news department, however, his mind was racing wildly, thoughts ricocheting between Dougie Jones's troubled childhood, Luke Hayes's suspicions, and the wisdom of involving his own daughter in the ransom drop. He thought of Astoria, and the way the entire task force worked so quietly, so seriously, and yet never saw anything that yielded results. He remembered walking into his house just last month, spotting Rainie reading in front of the fireplace, and stopping to admire the curve of her neck as she bent over her novel.

There were moments when Quincy wished he could stop time. He would like to reach out his hand like some great cosmic conductor, and say, *Freeze. Let this moment linger. Please, for just a little while, let this moment last.*

He would like to extend first thing in the morning, when he could watch Rainie sleep, her hair spilling across the pillows, the smudge of her eyelashes against her cheeks. Once awake, Rainie was all hard angles, fast steps, and jerky motions. She moved as she talked, moved as she ate, just moved, moved, moved. Of course, he admired her energy, her attitude, her lithe, catlike grace. But he preferred her in the morning. He liked knowing he was the only person who saw this Rainie, soft, still, vulnerable.

He felt ashamed now. As if all along he'd been sleeping with a woman, but never really seeing her. How much she hurt, how desperately she needed, how terribly their work was eroding her little by little, until she needed a pill to get through the day, and a drink to get through the night.

Underneath his shame, however, was a growing sense of fury. Because she was broken, and he couldn't fix her, and that left him feeling so damn helpless, and so damn weak, which made him mad at Rainie all over again. Why couldn't she be tougher, he—the trained professional—found himself thinking. Why the hell couldn't she pull herself up by her own bootstraps?

He'd been at the crime scene, too. He'd had to look at the body of that little girl. And he'd seen Amanda and Kimberly and he'd felt what any father feels when he realizes he's too late, that he can't protect his little girl anymore, that no parent is as omnipotent as their child believes.

The world was filled with shit. And the only way Quincy knew how to deal with it was just keep shoveling. It's what he did, and once upon a time, that's what Rainie had done, too. They had been a team. They were supposed to make each other feel strong.

But his strength wasn't enough for her. His love hadn't been enough for her. He had held her every night, and she had broken anyway.

He could feel an unbearable pressure building in his head. And just for an instant, he wanted to open his mouth and scream.

Instead, he caught Kincaid's gaze from across the table. Quincy got out his notes, straightened his tie, and prepared for what they had to do next.

"LET ME BE THE FIRST TO SAY, I know this is highly irregular," Kincaid began. "Given the tight time constraints, however, Mr. Quincy and I both agreed it was most expedient to have him serve as a profiler for this case. Naturally, any good defense attorney will have issues with documents generated by the husband of the victim, but that doesn't change the fact that we need an expert psychologist to devise strategy for tomorrow morning's chat. Given his past experience with ransom cases, Mr. Quincy is qualified for that role, and better yet, he's available."

Kincaid gestured toward Quincy, who acknowledged the OSP detective's underwhelming introduction with a slight nod of his head. "I'm touched."

"You should be. Any minute now, the Tillamook County DA is going to catch wind of this meeting and come charging in here to chew off my head. Let's enjoy the honeymoon while it lasts."

Quincy nodded again and picked up his yellow legal pad. Sitting across from him were Kincaid, Candi, and Kimberly. Mac had moved out to the lobby, where he was using Kimberly's laptop to research Lucas Bensen's family—not that Quincy felt like volunteering that particular tidbit of information just yet.

Otherwise, there were no OSP detectives present, no members of the Bakersville Sheriff's Department. The meeting was strictly for those who needed to know—Kincaid as the leader of the task force, Quincy as the psychological expert, Candi Rodriguez as the negotiator, and Kimberly as the officer who would be making the ransom drop. Kimberly and Kincaid each appeared suitably intent. Candi, on the other hand, looked like she might yawn at any moment.

"Profiling in ransom situations is a slightly different beast," Quincy said by way of introduction. "In a traditional murder case, much of the psychological information is derived from the murder itself—key data points include how the victim was killed, condition of the body, placement of the body, probable method of abduction, profile of the victim, etc., etc. And generally, by the time someone such as myself has been called in, there are several crime scenes for analysis, meaning we have a lot of data for consideration. This case, on the other hand, provides only a limited amount of information. We have identified the victim, but not the means of abduction. We have a geographic location for the kidnapping, but no idea where the victim is being held, the condition she might be in. We don't even have forensic evidence to help us understand the means of abduction, given the extreme weather conditions. What we do have is five separate communications from the subject, and that's what I have used as the basis of my analysis."

Quincy pulled out photocopies of the three ransom letters plus transcripts from the two phone calls. He fanned the five sheets out in front of him. They were labeled Communication 1 through 5 and presented in the order in which they occurred. All these years later, Quincy remained bureau to the core.

"There are several important things to consider when analyzing these types of communication. First, the method of communication. In this case, the subject is using both written correspondence and phone calls to initiate contact. The fact that he is reaching out indicates he clearly wants to be heard. Indeed, on both occasions when we failed to respond to his letters fast enough, he followed up by phone. Dialogue is extremely important to this person. He wants to feel connected to the investigation; more to the point, he wants to feel in control of the investigation. Control is the primary motivation of the subject, as we will see over and over again.

"The second key consideration when analyzing these communications is that the subject initiated contact through the press. His first letter is addressed 'Dear Editor,' his third letter, delivered directly to a senior reporter, is addressed to both 'member of the press and assorted task force officers.' Clearly, the subject wants attention. In his first conversation with me, he went so far as to identify fame as one of his goals."

"'Fame, fortune, and a finely baked apple pie,'" Kincaid murmured.

"Exactly. I believe the apple pie is a reference to the American

Dream, and the sentence as a whole—'What everyone wants: fame, fortune, and a finely baked apple pie'—is a rather wry observation about America's obsession with celebrity. So now we know two things about this individual: He wants to feel in control and he craves recognition.

"Both of these character traits are further substantiated when we look at the contents of the letters. On numerous occasions he refers to rules. We, the police, must follow his rules. Do as he says, the victim will be fine. Dismiss him, and the victim will be punished. Obviously, when we deviated from the orders in his second letter, he retaliated by snatching a second victim and upping the ransom demand. It's important to note that he 'punished' the task force by taking a second victim, not by killing the first. Why? Because killing the first victim would render the subject out of control. Without a hostage to dangle over our heads, he has no bargaining chip. I'm not saying the subject will not kill—in fact, I think there's a very high probability he will turn violent, as we will soon discuss. For the short term, however, his desire to manipulate the police outweighs his bloodlust. If he begins to feel out of control, however"—Quincy's gaze went hard to Candi—"that equation could change instantly."

Quincy continued. "The control element is further evidenced by his demand for a female officer to deliver the money—most men find females to be less threatening. And finally, by his choice of victims themselves. Our subject didn't kidnap the mayor or a key business leader—logical targets if his primary objective was money. He kidnapped a lone woman, then a seven-year-old child. Our subject needs to be the master of this game, so logically, he's chosen victims he perceives to be much weaker than himself.

"The other key pieces of data from the letters are the names chosen as signatures. As we've discussed, all three aliases are kidnappers whose crimes garnered them instant and widespread notoriety. In short, these men have received the recognition our subject craves and thus he has chosen them as his role models.

"Third set of considerations when reviewing the content of these letters: the letters are well articulated, showing proper business format and grammar. The salutations also reveal a keen grasp of policing procedure. While the first letter is addressed to the editor, the second is addressed only to the police; our subject obviously anticipated detectives being called in to work the case. More tellingly, the third letter is addressed to both the press and members of the task force. Again, this is someone who's done his homework: He's anticipated an entire team will be formed to work this case, and that the press will cooperate with that investigative body.

"Finally—and this is a bit more theoretical here—I think there are ample signs that the subject has at least a basic understanding of forensic science. The only handwriting used has belonged to the first victim. All letters have been printed out on plain white paper. The first letter, the only one mailed, was put inside a self-sealing envelope with a self-adhesive stamp, eliminating the need for saliva and, of course, traces of DNA. I think it's not a coincidence the abduction happened during a severe rainstorm. I believe the subject is actively using the weather to cover his tracks—certainly, he anticipates the weather in all of his communications, protecting them in plastic, etc., etc. And the last detail to note: on both phone calls to me, the subject has used a voice-distortion machine. Again, he's clearly put some thought into this."

"Research?" Kimberly asked. "Or experience?"

"Research," Quincy stated. "If it was experience, we'd see even more details in the notes and the phone calls. There is enough roughness around the edges to reveal someone in the infancy of his crime spree. But don't mistake inexperience for stupidity. The subject has gone out of his way to be prepared. And, as someone who views himself as the master of the game, he's doing everything in his power to remain one step ahead of the police."

Quincy took a deep breath. "All of this leads me to the following profile: We are looking for a white male in his mid-twenties to midthirties—the average age we see for predators beginning their crime sprees. Of above-average intelligence, he attended college, but did not graduate. He is very articulate and it's quite possible that he's in a stable relationship with a woman who is beautiful but submissive—this is not a man who would tolerate being challenged by a mate. The subject is of lower socioeconomic means, but holds himself above his neighbors; he may live in a trailer park, for example, but he does not consider himself trailer trash. The subject also has some connection with Rainie Conner, but I caution against using that as an investigative tool, as that connection may only exist in his head."

"Stalker," Kincaid stated.

"Exactly. The subject is very neat and well groomed. Appearances are extremely important to him. At face value, neighbors will claim him to be very smart, handsome, and upwardly mobile. Closer digging, however, will reveal a pattern of 'never quite succeeding.' For example, he got into college, but something happened—say, a parent died—forcing him to drop out. He had a great job, but something happened—say, the company declared bankruptcy—and he was laid off. Our brilliant subject was doing brilliantly, until something not under his control caused him to fail. The past is never his fault and the future is always an opportunity waiting to happen. Recently, there has been another one of these major life changes. Given the financial element of a ransom case, I would theorize that he lost his job. Statistically speaking, however, pregnancy, childbirth, and the end of a long-term relationship are also common predicators of criminal behavior."

"Sounds a little like Stanley Carpenter," Kincaid said. "High-school educated, blue-collar job, subservient wife. Physically controlling, and maybe just a tad stressed out by the addition of his new foster child."

"I wouldn't mind digging a little deeper into Stanley's alibi," Quincy agreed. "He's older than I would like, however, with a steadier lifestyle—he's held the same job, had the same wife, and lived in the same house for a long time now. The subject we're looking for is less emotionally mature. He aspires to a lifestyle much more dazzling than Stanley Carpenter's, while not possessing the follow-through to be able to deliver on that dream.

"People around this man will like him, but they may not trust him. The more streetwise ones will sense in him the soul of a con man. In fact, he probably has committed a string of shady financial dealings, if not outright cons. But what this man is really about isn't scamming money—he's selling himself, an image of himself. He's working very, very hard so that no one will recognize the monster he harbors inside."

"The notes," Kincaid said. "He keeps claiming he's not a monster."

"Exactly. Which is the most important clue in these letters. From the very beginning, the subject has gone out of his way to assert that he's not a pervert, not a monster. He claims it's about money. But where is money in these messages? Most kidnappers include long, detailed instructions about the ransom drop. What kind of denominations, how the bills must be packaged. They're fantasizing about the payoff and that anticipation is conveyed in everything they do.

"Not this subject. His communications revolve around two things—I'm not a monster, but you must obey me, or *I will become a monster. I will do bad things. It will be your fault.*"

"He's looking for a scapegoat," Kimberly breathed.

"He's a psychopath," Quincy said steadily. "He recognizes it in himself. He's drawn to murderers such as the Fox and Nathan Leopold. I don't think he's killed yet—if he has, it was probably accidental. But he fantasizes about killing. He wants to feel powerful, and what is more omnipotent than taking another person's life?"

"Granting another person life," Candi muttered.

Quincy smiled faintly. "Touché. But that's not what drives our subject. His impulses are already dark and violent. Kidnapping a woman, holding her bound and gagged, is the first step in his fantasy. Maybe he told himself it was about money. Maybe he convinced himself it really was a ransom case. But there are a lot of ways to make money. From a psychological perspective, why abduct a human being? Furthermore, why a woman? He's going someplace else with this, even if he can't admit it yet."

"You think she's dead!" Kincaid said, stunned.

"No. Not yet." Quincy's voice had dropped. He took a steadying breath. If he kept this objective, about an unnamed victim, he could function. If he at any point in time remembered she was his wife, he would collapse.

"The subject wants us to make this easy for him," he said quietly. "He wants us to give him an excuse, any excuse, so he can do what he really wants to do, while blaming someone else. That's how he works. He's always in control, but nothing is ever his fault.

"When he calls tomorrow"—Quincy looked at Kimberly—"he's

going to give you a long list of instructions. They will be logistically complicated, nearly impossible to follow. You"—his gaze switched to Candi—"will be put in the awkward position of trying to clarify his demands while buying us more time. He will get angry very quickly. He will accuse us of breaking the rules for failing to do what he says. He will become openly hostile and threaten to kill both victims: We give him no choice."

Candi was no longer looking bored. "Shit."

"Whatever happens, you must make him believe that Kimberly is doing as he's instructed. You must never imply that his orders are too hard, or too fast, or too inconvenient. Of course, at the same time, you will need to have him repeat things again and again, because Kimberly probably will be lost and/or confused."

"Can I offer him more money? You know, a reward for his patience?"

Quincy thought about it. "No, money isn't what he wants. It's fame, recognition. Headlines, that's what we need."

"Adam Danicic?" Kincaid asked with a frown.

"No, the subject has already reached out to Danicic—we're not giving him anything he can't get on his own. We need someone bigger, maybe an investigative journalist or popular columnist for *The Oregonian*. Someone whose name is immediately recognizable and yet can be successfully impersonated by Lieutenant Mosley."

"What, you don't want the real journalist present?" Kincaid deadpanned.

"That will be our bait. We have a very important journalist in the room who came all the way to Bakersville to talk to the subject himself. This is the UNSUB's big chance to get on the record. To tell everyone his story. And of course, to prove he's not a monster by letting the journalist speak directly to both victims."

Kimberly started to nod. "That might work. It gives Rainie and Dougie fresh value as hostages. He's getting to manipulate the police, as well as garner more attention."

"It's not a guarantee, of course. Remember, our subject just craves attention. He doesn't care if it's positive or negative."

"You think he would harm them with a journalist on the line?" Kincaid asked sharply.

Quincy could only shrug. "There are serial killers out there mailing trophies from their victims to local papers. Welcome to the media age. It really *is* about fame, fortune, and apple pie."

"Coming to a reality TV show near you," Kincaid muttered.

"Let's not give the TV execs any ideas."

Quincy gathered up his notes, sliding them all back into his legal pad. He saw the name Lucas Bensen again, but still didn't say a word.

"So what do we do now?" Candi asked.

Kincaid slapped his binder shut. "Now," the lead investigator replied, "we get some sleep."

29

MAC AND KIMBERLY SWUNG BY the local Wal-Mart in search of dry clothes. Unfortunately, the superstore had already closed for the day. They toured the dark streets of Bakersville one last time before finally giving up and heading for the B&B where Quincy had reserved them a room. Kimberly had wanted her father to come with them. Naturally, he'd refused.

After their meeting with Kincaid, they had walked out to the rental car for a task force meeting of their own. The rain had slowed, becoming a dense mist none of them even noticed anymore.

Mac had made some headway on Lucas Bensen. He found articles from Rainie's trial, listing the victim as being survived by a son, Andrew Bensen, who was being raised by his maternal grandmother, Eleanor Chastain. Accounts of Andrew's mother were hard to come by, but it appeared that Sandy Bensen had died before Lucas had disappeared, meaning Andrew had spent most of his life with his grandmother. Interestingly enough, neither Eleanor nor Andrew had appeared at Rainie's trial.

Typing *Eleanor Chastain* into the Google search engine had produced several phone numbers from different states, as well as maps to all of their homes, courtesy of MapQuest. The Internet remained the investigator's favorite friend. Of course, all the perverts loved it, too.

Mac had chosen two phone numbers, one in Eugene, Oregon, the other in Seattle, Washington. He nailed it, however, the first time out, in Eugene. Eleanor seemed pleasantly surprised to hear from an old friend of her grandson's, trying to locate Andrew. No, she couldn't help him. Last time she'd seen Andrew, he'd been tearing out of the driveway after stealing her stereo.

She'd heard rumors he'd enlisted in the Army, and could only hope he was now in Baghdad. Maybe military service would finally do the boy some good. In the meantime, if Mac did find him, could he please remind Andrew that he still owed his grandma five hundred bucks? Thanks. And that had been it from Eleanor Chastain.

Best Mac could tell, Andrew Bensen would be nearly twenty-eight years old, making him the right age for the profile. Petty theft also fit, but it didn't sound like Bensen had bothered with college. The real question remained, was the man even in the country?

Mac had left messages with the local recruiting offices in Portland. Chances were, however, he wouldn't hear back until morning.

And that was it for the family meeting. The hour was late, sleep as good an idea as any. They'd all be up with the crack of dawn, and tomorrow would be a big day.

Kimberly tried one more time to get her father to come with them. And one more time, he declined.

He was exhausted, Quincy said, just needed some time alone. He was going back to the house and going straight to bed.

Kimberly didn't believe him for a moment. Sleep? Her father? Even now, he was probably roaming from room to room, torturing himself with might-have-beens.

Similar to what she might do, she supposed, if she didn't have Mac beside her, his hand folded around her own as they drove to the B&B in companionable silence.

Once inside the room—beautiful cherry furniture, hideous floral wallpaper—Kimberly went to work draping her wet clothes over the towel racks. Mac produced an old T-shirt out of his bag, and she gratefully slipped into the oversized jersey while taking a hair dryer to her dry-clean-only wardrobe. She put the blower on high, closed the bathroom door, and heated the tiny space to approximately five hundred degrees. It felt marvelous. Sweat dotting her upper lip, arms loosening into rhythmic cadence.

She walked out of the bathroom to discover Mac sprawled on top of the queen-size bed, wearing nothing but a pair of plaid boxers and a heavy-lidded look she knew too well. In spite of the late hour and the day's events, she felt the familiar answering tingle low in her belly. Here was the upside of a relationship where they never saw each other nearly enough; Mac merely had to walk into a room, and she was ready to take him then and there. He had yet to complain.

Now, she crossed to the bed, aware of how his eyes were following her, lingering on her pale neck, her broad shoulders, her small rounded breasts. "Nice room," she said.

"If you like chintz."

"If memory serves, chintz has been very good to us."

"True."

She crawled on the bed, the top of the oversized T-shirt gaping low enough to reveal that she wore nothing underneath.

"It's been a long day," Mac murmured.

"It has."

"Upsetting."

"Yep."

"I would understand if you needed to talk."

"Talk? Don't you remember? I'm my father's daughter." And then Kimberly was climbing on top of him.

His chest was warm and broad. She liked the way his skin felt against the palm of her hand, the brush of her cheek. She nuzzled his neck, reveling in the scent of him. Soap, aftershave, sweat. She should shower; he should shower. They had always taken such considerations for each other; again, weekend lovers who could afford to be on their best behavior. Now, however, she didn't want to let him go. She needed the hard planes of his body pressed against her own. She wanted to hear his heartbeat thundering against her ear. She wanted to taste the salt of his skin and feel the sharp intake of his quickly drawn breath.

She was tired. She was sad in a place way down deep, difficult to decipher, hard to touch. So much of her life had been spent in the company of death. First sharing her father with a caseload that seemed to need him more than his own children could. Then her first forays into his office, sneaking down his homicide textbooks, looking at all the pictures. Realizing at the age of thirteen, when her own body was starting to bud and ripen, what a pair of pliers could do to the human breast. Reading at fifteen all the ways deviant sexual behavior could turn violent, sadistic, cruel.

She inundated herself with case studies, stories of depravity, summaries of the worst horrors committed against women and children. She did not know how to bring her father into her world, so she threw herself into his. If these victims were her father's taskmasters, then she would learn to fight for them, too.

In time for her sister to die, for her mother to be murdered, for herself to stand in a hotel room with a madman's gun stroking her temple. As a child, violence had taken her father from her. As an adult, that same violence gave him back.

Now she followed in his footsteps, a fellow FBI agent, counting the days until she was qualified to do profiling, so that what? She could squander her marriage, abandon her children, become an island lost inside herself?

She kissed Mac harder. His hands were tangled in her hair, his erection hot against her thighs. She ground herself against him. He caught her hips with his hands.

"Shhh," he whispered against her lips. "Shhh."

It took her that long to realize she was crying, that the hot warmth she felt was her own tears sliding down her cheeks, splashing across his chest. She kissed them, too, following the rain across his collarbone, catching the salt upon her tongue.

Then she was on her back and he was leaning over her, his weight upon his knees, his large hands impossibly gentle as they gathered up the T-shirt, slid it over her head.

"Now," she commanded urgently. "Now!"

But he wouldn't do it. No matter how hard she tried to grab his shoulders, to twine her legs around his waist. He was the model of control, nuzzling her earlobe, whispering across her neck until her entire body bloomed with the most delicious goose bumps and she was so acutely aware of her own skin she would scream if he didn't touch her again.

His head was at her breast, his whiskered cheeks rasping lightly across her nipple to be followed by the soothing pressure of his lips. She had an athlete's body, slim, narrow-hipped, flat-chested. But he made her feel voluptuous, his broad, dark hands splayed across her pale white breast, the silk of his hair tickling her belly.

Finally he took pity on her, his hips settling between her legs, his large body rocking against her own.

She opened her eyes at the last minute. She watched her lover, head thrown back, teeth gritted as he lost himself in the pleasure of her body. And she felt, through her ecstasy, through her sadness, a moment of unbearable tenderness. She splayed her hands across his face. She willed him to come, wanted to see the moment crashing across his features. She needed him to find release. She needed to know that she made this one person happy.

The dam broke. The unbearable pressure building inside her spiked and shattered. She was falling down, down, down, her arms and legs still wrapped around Mac and, for a moment at least, it was enough.

Tuesday, 11:28 p.m. PST

"YOU KNOW, I'D TIE YOU UP if I thought it would work," Mac said sometime later. "I'd beat my chest, engage in some quality male posturing, and count on you, as the weaker, subservient female, to do as you were told."

She slugged him in the shoulder.

"Ow."

"That was for saying 'weaker.' I'm still thinking of the punishment for 'subservient.'"

He rolled on top of her, pinning her against the mattress, and surprising her with the sudden moves. "I am bigger," he said quietly. "I am stronger. But I know when I've met my match, Kimberly. And I respect your need to help your father. I understand that you need to do what you need to do, even if it puts you in harm's way."

She didn't know how to respond. The room was dark, shuttered.

It saved her from being too exposed, but offered him the same protection. She could see just the glitter of his eyes in the dark. Mostly, she felt the weight of the words he didn't say, of all the fears neither one of them would ever discuss. Like all the things that could go wrong tomorrow, or maybe the next day, or the day after that.

Neither one of them feared for themselves, but they did not know how not to fear for the other.

Mac got up off the bed. She watched the silhouette of his body, shadow against shadow as he rifled through his duffel bag.

A moment later, he was back.

"Round two?" she asked, slightly surprised. But what he slipped into her palm wasn't a condom. It was a small square box. A jeweler's box.

At first, she didn't understand.

"I'd planned this whole thing out," he said roughly. "Booked us a special restaurant in Savannah. Even bought a dress for you to wear. We'd go out, the waiter would bring over champagne, and in front of the orchestra, the staff, and the other diners, I would drop down on one knee and do it proper-like.

"Of course, we're not going to make it to Savannah. Frankly, the more I hang out with you, the more I'm beginning to think I'm lucky to get a B&B in the middle of dairyland. Whatever lucky stars are out there, your family wasn't born under them."

He ran a hand through his hair, sounded more nervous than she'd ever heard him. "So what I'm trying to say, of course, what I mean is . . . Oh hell." He was back off the bed, this time dropping down to one knee and grabbing her hand. "Kimberly Quincy, will you marry me?"

"But I'm naked," she said rather stupidly.

"I know. It's part of my strategy. Naked, you can't run away."

"Somehow, when this moment came, I always thought I'd be wearing clothes."

"True, but if it's any consolation, I don't mind."

"I'm also tired and cranky."

"I don't mind that, either."

"You really don't, do you?"

"Ah babe, I love you cranky, hostile, armed, dangerous, and any other way I can have you. I already even started a pool about how fast before you kick Candi Rodriguez's butt."

"I really don't like her," Kimberly said instantly.

"That's my girl."

Mac reached over and turned on the bedside lamp. Then, with hands that were shaking nearly as badly as hers, he slowly opened the box still nestled in the palm of her hand.

The ring was old, a vintage setting of small diamonds and platinum. Nothing bold, nothing flashy. Kimberly thought it was the most beautiful ring she had ever seen.

"It was my grandmother's," Mac said quietly. "If you don't like it, we could always rework it—"

"No!"

"No, you won't marry me?" He sounded a little panicked.

"No! I mean yes. Yes, I will marry you; no, don't you dare touch that ring! Well, actually, yes, touch that ring, but slide it on my hand, silly man. Put it on."

He did. Then they both sat there, stark naked, admiring the ring for a long while.

"It's beautiful," Kimberly whispered.

"You're the most beautiful thing in the world to me, Kimberly. Hell, I love you so much, it scares me half out of my mind."

"I'm scared, too."

"Then we'll take it slow. I just . . . I wanted you to have the ring tonight."

"I love you, Mac," she said solemnly, then leaned forward and hugged him till it hurt. Then they both looked at the ring, still glittering on her finger, and they both understood.

"I can't wear this tomorrow," she whispered.

"I know."

She looked up, understanding again the words that weren't said. "Hold me, Mac."

He took her in his arms. Then she removed the ring and wordlessly returned it to its box.

30

QUINCY COULDN'T SLEEP. He roamed the house, trying on the different rooms, as if he could recapture the feel of his wife, sitting in this chair, drinking out of this cup, using this desk. It didn't work. The space loomed too large, shadowed and empty. Everyplace he went, he was only reminded that Rainie was no longer there.

He went to his study. Perused the notes Mac had made regarding Andrew Bensen. If the man was approximately twenty-eight years old now, then he would've been a mere toddler at the time of his father's disappearance. It was hard to say how that kind of thing would've affected a boy. On the one hand, he'd been forced to grow up without parents. On the other hand, given Lucas Bensen's lifestyle, no one had filed a missing persons report. Apparently, not even his friends had missed him.

Of course, twenty-odd years later Andrew had learned the whole story: How Lucas had raped the sixteen-year-old daughter of his girlfriend. How he killed his girlfriend when she confronted him with the knowledge. How he then returned to the house—presumably to attack Rainie again—except that she shot him, then buried the body under the back deck so no one would know what she'd done.

Rainie's story had been convincing enough for a jury of her peers. But how would Andrew have taken the news? He and his grandmother had never even attended the trial. Maybe Lucas Bensen meant exactly that much to them.

Quincy couldn't decide.

He left a message of his own with an old friend at Quantico. Mac's military officers wouldn't call him back until nine a.m. PST. In contrast, Glenda Rodman liked to be in her office by eight a.m. sharp Eastern Standard Time, meaning Quincy could plan on a call around five. Given the situation, the four-hour lead time would come in handy.

His last call was local. The hour was well beyond being socially appropriate. Quincy didn't care.

Former OSP detective Abe Sanders picked up on the first ring. Quincy had a feeling Sanders wasn't sleeping well these days. It was ironic, given that Sanders had quit the state police in pursuit of a quieter life.

"What the hell ever happens in Astoria?" Sanders had said to Rainie and Quincy over dinner two years back, when announcing he was taking the position in the scenic coastal town. "A few B&E's, some minor drug trafficking, and various tourism mischiefs. Why, I couldn't do any better if I moved to Bakersville."

They had toasted him and his lovely wife that night. Back in the days when life had been happier for all of them.

"What?" Sanders said now, voice alert, demanding.

"Sleeping with the phone in your hand, or not even bothering to go to bed?"

"Just catching the news." Hearing Quincy's voice, Sanders seemed to relax. Quincy didn't bother to mention that the evening news had ended fifteen minutes ago.

"I wanted to follow up on our favorite maintenance man," Quincy said.

"Funny, you're the second call I've gotten about Duncan today. The first was from an old OSP buddy, Kincaid. Don't suppose you know him?"

"As a matter of fact, we're working together."

"Kidnapping case, right? He already called in you and Rainie?

Wow, the lottery business must be booming if the state can afford to hire consultants that fast. In my day, we were cheap, cheap, cheap, all the way home."

Sanders was referring to the fact that for the first time in the agency's history, the state police finally had designated revenue— from the Oregon State Lottery. The legislation was good news for the state police, and even more fun for the general public. Everyone joked that the troopers would now start handing out scratch tickets with each speeding citation. Whatever worked.

What Quincy considered more relevant was that Kincaid had followed up with Sanders, but refused to provide any details about the case. How like a law enforcement officer to reach across jurisdictional boundaries, but still give nothing away. For a moment, Quincy hated all of them.

"I thought I'd call you myself," he told Sanders at last.

"Well, I'll tell you what I told him: We still got nothin'. Best we can tell, good old Duncan sits around his house most of the day scratching his balls, then shows up at his mom's for dinner at night. She still calls him her baby. The neighbors hate his guts."

"He's under surveillance?"

"Not formally, but I got enough manpower to keep the guys swinging by. We can't account for every second of his day, but we know large segments."

"And today?"

"Just another day in the Duncan household."

"And tonight?"

"I don't have eyes on him tonight." Sanders's voice grew cautious. "Should I?"

"We have a situation developing," Quincy said crisply. "Next communication with the subject is scheduled for ten a.m. If Duncan really is involved, that means he'd have some business to take care of tonight, or first thing in the morning. Meaning, it would be helpful to account for Duncan's activities in the next twenty-four hours. Even if that meant only eliminating him as a suspect."

"I could arrange it."

"I would consider that a personal favor."

"Well now, no getting mushy on me. But I gotta say, Quincy, I don't get it. You think Duncan kidnapped a woman for money? Come on, you saw the crime scene. If Duncan can get a woman alone, it's not money he has on his mind."

Quincy should just say it. He didn't know why he didn't say it. But at that moment, sitting in the dark space of his study, his eyes on his daughter's photo, he couldn't form the sentence: *Rainie is missing.* He just didn't have the strength anymore to hear those words out loud.

"Thank you," Quincy said simply. He hung up the phone and sat alone in the dark.

Later, he made it to the bedroom, with the rumpled linens, the pile of Rainie's cast-off clothes. He started in the corner and methodically tossed everything onto the bed. Old jeans, dirty underwear, used socks, he didn't care. He covered the bed in Rainie's laundry.

Then he stood in the doorway and started to strip. His damp jacket, his wrinkled shirt, his limp tie. He shed his investigator's uniform piece by piece, until finally only the man remained. It was Quincy's custom to throw his clothes into the hamper or return them to their hangers. Tonight, he left all the pieces as a chaotic pile, a lump of shed skin.

Then he crossed the room and crawled stark naked into the pile of Rainie's clothes.

He rolled among the sheets. He felt the softness of cotton sweatshirts, flannel pajamas, satin underwear. His hand found the duvet, then he rolled himself up in a cocoon of fabric, desperate for the scent of his wife, for the feel of her pressed against his skin.

She was gone. Kidnapped, bound, disarmed, her hair hacked off and God knows what else. Alone in the silence of the room they once shared, Quincy could feel the enormity of it finally catch up with him. His mind was a jumbled collection of images—Rainie the first time she smiled for him, Rainie with a contented cat's purr in the seconds after they'd made love. Rainie crying when he dropped down on one knee to propose to her. Rainie and the soft, mesmerized look in her eyes the day the photo came of their soon-to-be-adopted daughter.

Rainie happy, Rainie sad. Rainie furiously denying his accusation that she'd started drinking. Rainie looking so desolate as she stood by the window after one of her nightmares and he honored her privacy by pretending to sleep.

He was sorry for all of it now. He was sorry he gave her space. He was sorry he gave her time. He was sorry he didn't lock her in this damn room with him and force her to tell every single thing that was on her mind.

He had loved her, he had worshipped her, and he had trusted her.

Now, in hindsight, he could see that it still hadn't been enough.

Love did not fix all things. Love didn't heal all wounds. Love did not guarantee that you would never feel alone.

He had her sweatshirt in his hands, the old blue FBI one she had commandeered from him to wear around the house. He held it up to his face. He inhaled deeply, still searching for her scent.

Then he marshaled all his strength. He channeled his focus, and he sent out, with all the willpower one man could muster: *Rainie, please be safe.*

But when he opened his eyes, the room was still dark, the air was still cold. And nothing on the bed could bring the feel of his wife back to him.

31

"SEE THAT LIGHT UP THERE?" Rainie said to Dougie. "Let's break it."

"Break it?"

"Bust it to bits."

"Okay," Dougie said.

The light in question was two long fluorescent bulbs encased behind an open metal cage. It was mounted just above the basement door, dimly visible in the door's glowing halo. Best Rainie could tell, it was the only light in the basement. Break it, and their abductor would have no choice but to join them in the gloom.

Rainie liked that idea. She wanted the man to descend those darkened stairs. She wanted to watch him bump around their damp, fetid prison, banging against the workbench, slipping on the wet cement floor. She wanted to reduce him to their level with a feral rage that made her impervious to the throbbing in her temples, the strange, painful currents running up and down her left side, and the pangs of hunger now cramping her belly.

One problem: They couldn't reach the high-mounted light. One solution: Any old rock or piece of debris chucked through the metal grate would do. She and Dougie had skipped some stones in their day. She thought they could do it.

So she and Dougie started scouring the shallow puddles covering the floor. In Dougie's world, looking for rocks was always a good idea.

Dougie had given up on his tied wrists. Chewing didn't work and neither did sawing the plastic band ties against the corner of the wooden workbench. Instead, he worked like Rainie, back bent, hands dangling in front of him.

She could feel him shivering from the cold, and her own body responded with a teeth-rattling tremor. She couldn't feel her fingers or toes anymore. Her nose had gone numb, and bit by bit, she was losing the rest of her face. Her core body temperature continued to drop. Dougie's, too. Soon their legs would feel sluggish, their eyes heavy. It would be easy to just sit on the stairs, maybe curl up on the workbench.

Their overworked hearts would slow. Their systems would shut down, circulating less blood, pumping less oxygen, and that would be that. They would close their eyes and never have to worry about anything again.

It would be peaceful, Rainie found herself thinking, which only made her disgusted with herself. If she was going to die, she wanted a shot at taking Super Jerk with her. She stomped her feet, wiggled her fingers, then, purely on impulse, curled her arms in front of her and trumpeted like an elephant.

Dougie giggled.

So Rainie trumpeted again.

"I'm the elephant king!" Dougie shouted. He stampeded across the basement floor, splashing water and emitting a ferocious elephant roar. Rainie followed in his wake. They hit the wall, trumpeted together this time, then turned and ran the other way. Rainie's lungs heaved. Her heart pounded. She felt the best she had in days.

They slowed, gasping for breath. Being an elephant was much harder than it looked, and it didn't provide them with any ammunition. So they resumed running their fingers through the shallow pool covering the basement floor, searching for rocks.

"How's your head?" Rainie asked, now that the moment felt right and Dougie seemed to hate her a little less.

Dougie merely shrugged. That was his answer to most things. On one of their outings, he'd fallen five feet while scrambling up a tree. Rainie had immediately run to him, expecting tears, or at least a bravely contained hiccup. Dougie had merely brushed himself off, the mud, the leaves, the blood, then returned to the tree. She'd watched him do the same thing on numerous other occasions.

Dougie seemed indifferent to the physical realm. Pain, cold, heat, hunger. Nothing bothered him. When Rainie mentioned it to Quincy, he'd dug up a research study on how some children, in situations of chronic abuse, learned to disconnect themselves from their own bodies. It was a form of coping, he told her: Their abusers hit them, and the children literally didn't feel a thing.

That was the first time Rainie had begun to wonder about Stanley Carpenter, to think that perhaps Dougie really was telling the truth. The lack of physical evidence remained puzzling, however. If Stanley was beating his foster son, shouldn't Dougie have bruises?

A few weeks ago, however, she'd had a startling insight into that riddle. It was shortly thereafter that Dougie had started to hate her in earnest.

"I can't find any rocks," she said now. "You?"

"Nope." Dougie started splashing around the wet floor instead. It kept him distracted and, hopefully, warm.

"Seems odd," Rainie murmured. "In a basement, you'd think you'd find all sorts of stuff. Discarded tools, old toys, forgotten debris. Guess our friend did his housekeeping."

Dougie stopped splashing. Across the dim space, she could see him scowl.

"Dougie," Rainie said quietly, "you know I used to be a police officer, right? I'm trained for these kinds of situations. I'm going to get us out."

"You're hurt."

"You don't need hair to escape from a basement," Rainie said lightly.

Dougie's gaze dropped to her arms. He had felt the cuts, then, and he had understood.

"This is what we're going to do," Rainie declared briskly. "We're going to break those lightbulbs. Then, we're going to bang real hard on that door and demand food and water and some warm clothes. We're going to make such a fuss, he'll have no choice but to open the door. And then, we're going to play a little game of hide-and-seek."

"I don't like hide-and-seek."

"But this is a good game, Dougie. The man is going to come looking for us, and we're going to run away from him. We'll be ghosts, flitting back and forth, quicker than the eye. Before he knows it, you'll go dashing up the stairs, boom, boom, boom. Once you're at the top, I want you to run as fast as you can. Out of this house, to the closest neighbor you can find. Then all you have to do is ask them to call the police, and they'll take it from there."

Dougie was not an idiot. "If I were the man, I'd bring a gun," he declared. "Definitely, I'd have at least one gun. And maybe a snake."

"The man and his gun—and his snake—are my problem, Dougie. You, I just want focused on running up the stairs."

"I like snakes."

"All right, here's the deal: If he brings a snake, you can tackle the snake. But if he brings a gun, then you run for the stairs. Swear it?"

Dougie considered her offer. Finally, he nodded. He spit on his palms, rubbed them together. Rainie spit on her palms, rubbed them together. They shook, Dougie's version of a solemn vow. They had done it once before, when Dougie had offered to show her his stash of secret treasures and she had sworn never to tell anyone its location.

She still remembered that afternoon. The gray mist shrouding the moss-covered trees. The gnarled old oak with a hollowed-out knot just the right size for a metal lunch box. The impassive look on Dougie's face as he took out his mother's charred photo, her soot-covered rosary.

"My mom's dead," Dougie had said, the only time he'd ever spoken of her in Rainie's presence. "So I live with other families. Until I burn things. People don't like that."

"Why did you set fire to your mother's photo, Dougie? I think that would make her very sad."

"My mother's dead," Dougie repeated, as if Rainie didn't understand. "Dead people don't feel anything. Dead people aren't sad."

Then he looked Rainie right in the eye and tore his mother's picture in half. Rainie got the message: In Dougie's world, dead people were the lucky ones. But she was willing to bet that if she snuck back to his treasure trove later in the week, she'd find the battered photo taped back together. Because Dougie still belonged to the land of the living, and he still felt things, no matter how much he hated it.

Now, she and Dougie retreated to the staircase. With no ammunition to throw at the light, there was only one other thing she could think to do.

"Dougie, if you sat on my shoulders, do you think you could reach those bulbs?"

Dougie's eyes lit up in the dark. "Yes!"

"We'll take the cotton strips," Rainie decided, "and wrap them around your hands. You get on my shoulders, and then with your fists, see if you can either break the bulbs or wiggle them out of there."

"Yes!"

Of course, without use of their hands, getting Dougie on her shoulders was easier said than done. Dougie balanced on the top step. She stood three steps beneath him. He spread his legs. She leaned down and eased him back onto her shoulders.

Very slowly, she straightened. With her arms bent at the elbow, she could just grab his ankles. Her bound wrists, however, limited her movement, making it impossible to counter every motion he made. She had an image of Dougie leaning back too far and both of them crashing down the flight of stairs.

She almost said something, but at the last minute held her tongue. Dougie was unpredictable during the best of times; she didn't want to give him any ideas.

He shimmied a bit from side to side on her shoulders, trying to get comfortable.

"Okay," he called down.

Very carefully, she climbed to the top. "Well?" she asked breathlessly, neck aching, legs wobbling.

"I can touch them!" Dougie reported triumphantly.

"Then let's do it."

She could feel him stretching up, his body reaching into the black void above them. For a moment, the weight eased off her shoulders and she realized he must be half hanging from the metal grill. She heard creaking, then a load of dust wafted down. Rainie bit her bottom lip to fight the sneeze.

"It's . . . stuck," Dougie gasped.

"Then break the bulbs. Just smash them with your fingers. It doesn't have to be pretty. But, Dougie . . . hurry up."

The strange, painful sensation was returning to her left side, as if electrical currents were ping-ponging madly down her leg. Her left knee spasmed, and for a moment, she feared it would buckle, her entire leg collapsing. She gritted her teeth, fought through the pain. Just this once, for God's sake. Just this once . . .

She could feel moisture on her arms. The knife wounds had opened; she'd started to bleed.

Then, the light tinkle of shattering glass.

"I got 'em!" Dougie punched through the first bulb, then the second.

"Oh, thank God." She eased down one step, then another, collapsing forward and depositing the boy above her. "Good work! Now we just need to—"

The basement door opened. Rainie had an instant impression of dazzling light, haloing a figure in black. She squinted reflexively, throwing up her arms to shield her eyes.

"Holy shit!" the man said.

And Rainie heard herself scream, "Dougie, run!"

She threw herself up the stairs, shoulder connecting with the door just as the man came to his senses and moved to slam it shut. For an agonizing moment, she was suspended on the top step, leaning precariously forward as the door weighed against her. Her eyes were shut, retinas burning from the sudden brightness after living for so long in the dark. She could feel movement against her legs, Dougie scrambling forward.

The weight behind the door suddenly disappeared. She crashed, staggering forward.

As swiftly as it came, the light was gone. The man flipped off the switch and fled down the hall.

"Dougie," Rainie called out urgently. But there was no answer.

She groped her way to the wall, trying to get her bearings. When she opened her eyes, her vision was studded with white dots.

No lights, she thought. At this stage of the game, light was not her friend.

Instead, she once more embraced the dark, starting to pick out the rectangular shape of a window, two box appliances. A washer and dryer, she determined. She was in a tiny laundry room, with a door that led down to the basement. And Dougie?

She strained her ears, but still didn't hear a sound. All she could do was pray that he remembered their game plan, that he was bolting out the front door. He was young, fast, resourceful. If he could get out of the house, he would be okay.

She moved around the room, finding another door. Locked. She searched for the deadbolt, but couldn't find one. She didn't know what that meant.

Only one way out then, and that was down the hall.

She got down on her knees and crawled.

Galley kitchen, she determined. Narrow, with one long window above the sink. No moonlight. Instead, she could hear the steady drum of more rain. Slinking by the stove, she caught a digital display of the time and was momentarily startled. 12:30 a.m. Had she been gone one day? Or two?

She needed to call Quincy. To tell him she was all right. She would get out of this.

And then it came to her. What she needed was a knife.

She wrenched open the nearest cabinet, hands scurrying through the glass contents, and was immediately pinned by a beam of light.

"Well, well, well. Would you look at this?"

Rainie turned slowly, her hands already curling around the only weapon she could find. She was staring straight into the beam of a flashlight. Behind it, she could just make out the dark silhouette of the man. At his side, he held a squirming Dougie in place.

"It's like I told you, boy," the man drawled softly. "Woman's nothing but a drunk."

Belatedly, Rainie followed the light, only to discover that she'd stumbled upon the liquor cabinet, and right at this moment, her hand was curled around a bottle of Jim Beam.

Rainie swallowed hard. She didn't know what to say. It had been purely accidental. Except, in some small part of her brain, she was terrified that it wasn't.

She took a better grip on the bottle. "Let him go," she said roughly.

"I don't think you're in a position to negotiate."

"Sure I am." Rainie raised the bottle and flung it. The bottle shattered against the flashlight. She heard the man's enraged roar. She tasted whiskey sprayed across her lips, and it really was sweet and she really did want more.

She sprang forward, grabbed Dougie's startled form, and bolted for the door. She made it two steps, and the man's foot connected with her left knee. She went down hard, feeling something twist, then tear. Frantically her hands swept across the floor, searching for a weapon, a handhold, anything. She found only shattered glass.

"Dougie, run!"

But once again, it was over before it began. The man grabbed Dougie's arms and jerked him up short. Dougie protested savagely, beating at their attacker. He was only fifty pounds, however, no match for an adult.

"Let me go!" Dougie howled.

The man belted Dougie in the side of the face. The boy crumpled. Then it was just the man, smiling down at Rainie.

She dragged herself up to all fours. She didn't know why. Her knee was wrecked, her running days were over. But she could still crawl. She got her head up. She lurched forward.

The man kicked her in the chin.

And Rainie dropped like a rock, tasting the blood and booze. Get up, get up, she thought frantically. Do something.

But her head felt too heavy. Her leg throbbed. She had nothing left.

The man dropped to one knee beside her.

"Rainie," he whispered in her ear, "I'm really, really going to enjoy this."

He yanked her to her feet. Pain tore through her leg. She had one final thought and it made her smile—she was going to have the last laugh after all.

Then she passed out cold, leaving the man furious and all alone.

32

Wednesday, 4:28 a.m. PST

QUINCY HAD SET HIS ALARM FOR FIVE. He rose at four thirty instead, threw on nylon shorts, a runner's shirt, and lightweight jacket, then hit the road. He ran for three miles down the twisty back road where he and Rainie lived. Rain pelted his face, rolled down his cheeks, splashed his legs.

His sides ached. His stomach rumbled. He ran down the empty road, around the winding corners. He startled two deer, who responded to his bright yellow coat by crashing into the woods.

He hit the three-mile marker, swung around and headed back, jogging uphill now and making his legs burn.

Five fifteen a.m., he was back home and in the shower.

Five thirty, Supervisory Special Agent Glenda Rodman returned his call. An experienced agent as reserved and overworked as Quincy, she didn't bother with pleasantries:

Andrew Bensen had enlisted in the Army three years ago and served one year in Iraq. His unit had been recalled six months ago, but he had failed to show, and was now considered AWOL. She had already spoken to a contact in the Pentagon; they had no leads.

Andrew was six foot two, brown hair, brown eyes. On his upper left shoulder, he sported an *American Chopper* tattoo. He liked his Harley and was known to frequent biker bars. His military record had been clean, if unimpressive, before he'd gone AWOL. His fellow grunts liked him, his officers found him to be quick and cooperative. The tour in Iraq had not been great for him. At least one officer noted that Bensen exhibited signs of post-traumatic stress disorder. Bensen, however, had never followed up with his local VA.

And that's all she could tell him about Private Andrew Bensen.

Quincy thanked Glenda for her time, hung up the phone, and got dressed. Navy blue suit, starched white shirt, a Jerry Garcia red, orange, and turquoise tie. Rainie had given him the tie one Christmas as a joke. He wore it anytime he felt he needed luck.

Five forty-five a.m., he headed for the task force room.

Kincaid was already there.

Kimberly was up at five. She showered for what felt like an hour but was probably only five minutes. Her shoulders were already tight, her body pumping with unfocused adrenaline. She felt like going for a run. She harnessed the energy for later, when she would need it most.

Five twenty, she rolled Mac out of bed. He landed on the floor with an "Oomph" and still refused to open his eyes. She went with the time-honored approach and tickled him. Who knew a grown man could be so ticklish under his chin?

That, of course, led to some earnest groping on Mac's part. She swatted his hands away and sent him to shower.

Alone in the room, she sat on the edge of the bed and once again studied the engagement ring. She put it on, she admired it in the light. She thought of her mother, who hadn't lived to see this day. And of her older sister, Mandy.

Then she closed the ring box, hid it in her duffel bag, and packed up her clothes.

Five fifty, she and Mac were checked out and loading up the car. He wasn't a morning person, so she did the driving. They had just closed the doors when he started to speak.

*   *   *

"I've been thinking about the Astoria case," Mac said. "The double murder in August."

"The case that upset Rainie."

"Exactly. I was wondering if it was purely coincidental that Rainie should be kidnapped after working such a disturbing case."

"Unless the fact she's been so upset made her a more vulnerable target."

"It's possible. I asked your father some questions yesterday."

"And?"

"And they think they know who did it. The victims lived in a duplex maintained by a local kid named Charlie Duncan. Duncan's a twenty-one-year-old high school dropout. Known for being good with his hands, but not so into bodily hygiene. Lives on his own in a studio apartment in another unit owned by the same landlord. Neighbors consider him to be quiet, if perhaps a little creepy. He has a tendency to show up at female tenants' units unannounced and let himself in with his master key. The landlord said he's been working with Duncan on his 'communication skills.'"

Kimberly rolled her eyes.

"Here's the deal," Mac said. "Duncan's fingerprints were all over that crime scene. Same with his bloody shoe prints. But he had a built-in alibi—he's the maintenance man. Of course his fingerprints are in the unit, and he's the one who called in the bodies—claimed he discovered them when he went over to change a lightbulb."

"Change a lightbulb? Because a young, single mom is so helpless she calls the maintenance man to fix a broken bulb?"

"The guy's not brilliant," Mac conceded, "but he gets the job done. Which makes me wonder, of course, if he hasn't moved on with his crime spree."

"He doesn't fit the profile," Kimberly said immediately.

"He's lower socioeconomic class, has a connection with Rainie."

"You're assuming he knows she's involved with the investigation."

"Duncan likes to drop by the duplex, remember? Including showing up one day when Rainie and Quincy were reviewing the crime scene. He asked all sorts of questions about the investigation, including their role."

"Like they told him anything."

"They didn't have to. Their job is implicit in their presence at the unit. Plus, Rainie is beautiful, which gets any man to pay attention."

Kimberly shot him a look.

"You're prettier," he said immediately.

"Nice save."

"Look, Duncan's not a perfect fit. According to Quincy, we're looking for a white-trash anal-retentive. Duncan's clearly not anal-retentive, and way too socially stunted to snag a girlfriend. But still. The guy is smart. Sounds like he's already getting away with two murders. Maybe we shouldn't underestimate him."

"The murder of the little girl bothers you," Kimberly said softly.

"The mom fought hard. She had to know what he'd do next."

"It's a sucky world," Kimberly murmured.

"Quincy devised an interview strategy. Tried to trick Duncan into saying what he'd done. Didn't work. They installed cameras at the grave sites. Nothing. Only hope they have now is if the guy confesses to someone. Unfortunately, the only person Duncan hangs out with is his mom, and apparently, she thinks he walks on water."

"It's only been a few months," Kimberly said more philosophically. "They're still processing evidence at this stage. You never know what might turn up."

"What would it matter?" Mac grunted. "Hair, fiber? His job still explains it away. Only thing that would help now is if he was caught cold turkey on film. If the unit had a security camera, or hell, even a nanny cam stuck in a toy bear."

"No such luck?"

"No such luck."

They were turning into the parking lot of Fish and Wildlife, Kimberly's mind already moving to the day ahead.

"Unless," Mac said abruptly.

"Unless what?"

The other officers were also turning into the parking lot. They saw the PIO, Lieutenant Mosley, as well as Sheriff Atkins, both heading briskly for the conference room.

"Showtime," Mac muttered.

They got out of the car and prepared for the day ahead.

Wednesday, 7:02 a.m. PST

KINCAID'S DEBRIEF WAS SHORT AND SWEET. They reviewed the twenty thousand dollars, procured by Mac, now inventoried and neatly stacked inside a duffel bag. They reviewed the electronic equipment, including the GPS device Kimberly would be wearing, as well as the surveillance equipment that would be used to follow her. Sheriff Atkins and Mac would be inside the unmarked white van that would be in charge of tailing Kimberly's footsteps. Their job would be to keep Kimberly in sight at all times. Kincaid, Lieutenant Mosley, and Quincy would be back in the op center, working with Candi on the phone call. Their job would be to keep the UNSUB calm and talking at all times.

The sheriff confirmed that Dougie Jones had not been magically found overnight. Her deputies had also narrowed the persons of interest down to an even dozen.

Candi accepted a profile of each person, complete with bullet points. Lieutenant Mosley supplied her with a tray filled with bottled water. He looked the most alert of all of them, with his buzz-cut hair, crisply pressed state trooper uniform, and camera-ready face. He had arrived with a dozen copies of the *Bakersville Daily Sun,* the morning edition blaring news of the kidnapping across the front page: "LOCAL BOY FEARED KIDNAPPED; *Police still searching for missing woman.*" Next to the banner headline were two photos, a head-and-shoulders shot of Rainie and a school portrait of Dougie.

It gave Quincy an eerie feeling to see the grainy mug shot of his wife, blown up to huge proportions on the newspaper's front page. To have her eyes peering back at him.

Adam Danicic's story ran three pages. He included Rainie's name, description, and details concerning the discovery of her car. He mentioned the task force, their desire to work with the kidnapper, and their fear that a local boy had also been kidnapped. Then, much to Quincy's dismay, Danicic included bits and pieces from Rainie's past, including her former position with the Bakersville

Sheriff's Department, and that she'd "recently" been found innocent of killing Lucas Bensen when she was sixteen years of age.

"Which pieces of this story did we control?" Quincy asked wryly, after skimming the article.

"No mention of the maps nor proof of life," Mosley replied seriously, ticking off his fingers. "Oh, and Danicic was kind enough not to mention that Dougie Jones was probably kidnapped because we fucked up. I give him some credit for that."

"He sold out Rainie easily enough."

"We couldn't stop him from using her name. And once he's included her full name . . ."

"Everything about her is just an Internet search away," Quincy murmured.

"Danicic isn't an idiot. The fact that the victim is former law enforcement with a troubled past makes for a great story. On the other hand, he left out that she was serving as Dougie's advocate, which did us a slight favor."

"Give with one hand, take away with another."

"It's a game," Mosley said with a shrug. "The media are the biggest players around. Speaking of which . . ." The beeper on the public information officer's waist was going off for the sixth time in the past thirty minutes. Mosley glanced at the screen, grimaced. "We're gonna have to talk about a morning briefing. The AP wire has picked up the story, and if my beeper is anything to go by, everyone wants a piece of the action."

"Not till after the ransom drop," Kincaid said immediately.

"We could use them," Mosley pushed. "Deliver the profile Mr. Quincy's developed. Get the public looking for our man."

"And scare the UNSUB into thinking he's going to be caught at any minute, so he might as well kill both victims to cover his tracks."

"The longer we go without a briefing, the more the press will dig on their own. And the more they discover on their own, the less I have to bargain with."

"Not till after the ransom drop," Kincaid repeated. And that was the end of the discussion.

Eight a.m. They fidgeted, reread the UNSUB's past communications, and in general, worked themselves into a state.

At nine, Mac took a call on his cell phone. The Portland recruiting branch of the Army confirmed that they had record of Private Andrew Bensen, currently listed as AWOL.

Quincy offered the information to Kincaid. Kincaid ranted for twenty minutes about Quincy daring to impede an official police investigation by deliberately withholding a vital lead, not to mention the importance of trust in a multijurisdictional investigation. Sheriff Atkins issued an all-points bulletin for a man fitting Bensen's description. Lieutenant Mosley muttered about the number of press agents who monitored police radios and that they had just added fuel to the fire.

Then, for the most part, everyone retired to their separate corners and fumed.

Quincy's phone sat in the middle of the conference room table. It was hooked to a speakerphone, all incoming calls being recorded and traced—not that anyone held out much hope for locating the origin of the caller. Cell signals bounced off towers in random patterns, making it virtually impossible to trace back a signal. But they went through the motions, because sometimes, that's all a task force has left.

Nine fifty-nine a.m.

The phone rang.

Candi put on the headset.

Lieutenant Mosley hit the Record button.

It began.

33

"This is Officer Candi. Can I help you, sir?"

The sound of mechanical laughter filled the room. "You sound like a Time-Life operator. What's next, a free subscription with my twenty grand?"

"You requested a female officer, and as you can see, we aim to please." Candi's voice was easygoing, just a neighborhood girl shooting the breeze. The approach was exactly what they had discussed and immediately it made Quincy nervous. He rose, pacing a small circle, as Candi continued, "Now, personally, I always like to know with whom I'm speaking. As I said, my name is Candi. And yours?"

"You can call me Bob."

"Bob, huh? And here you sound more like an Andy to me."

It was a thinly veiled reference to Andrew Bensen. The UNSUB didn't bite.

"I want my money," the caller said. "I get my cash, you get to play a little game. Here's the deal—"

"We have the money," Candi cut in amiably, trying to slow the conversation, exercise her own form of control. "Twenty thousand dollars. In cash. As you requested."

"I don't like to be interrupted," the caller said. "Interrupt me again, and I will kill the kid. Do you want that on your conscience, Miss Candi? The death of a seven-year-old boy?"

Candi's gaze flew to Kincaid. She said evenly, "I'm sorry, Bob. I didn't mean to offend you. Like I said, I'm here to cooperate."

"There is a pay phone on the corner of Fifth and Madison, another at the Wal-Mart on Highway 101, a third at the cheese factory. I assume you know these locations."

Kincaid started furiously scribbling down the instructions. Candi said, "Actually, Bob, I'm from out of town, so I might need a little help with this. You said three pay phones, the first being at the corner of Fifth and Madison. Which corner? North, south, east, west? I don't want to miss it."

"You'll see it."

"Okay, Bob, I'll trust you on that. Now, the second pay phone is at the Wal-Mart. I'm assuming it's a big Wal-Mart. Can you tell me which entrance?"

"To the left," the caller conceded, "as you're facing it."

"All right, and the third phone at the cheese factory?"

"Right out front."

"Thanks, Bob, I appreciate you clarifying things for me. So we're talking three pay phones: one at the intersection of Fifth and Madison, one at the left-side entrance of Wal-Mart, and one right outside the cheese factory. Those are the phones you're talking about?"

"Go."

"Sorry? I didn't catch that."

"You have fifteen minutes."

Candi glanced back and forth. "You want me to be at three different locations in fifteen minutes? I'm sorry, Bob, I'm trying to help you, but I honestly don't understand. And to tell you the truth, before I do anything, you know I'm going to need to talk to Rainie and Dougie—"

Bob didn't care. "You have fifteen minutes," he said again.

Then the connection went dead.

CANDI WHIPPED THE HEADSET from her ears. "Well, fuck! He didn't even give us a chance. No explanation, no proof of life—"

"Time," Quincy interrupted crisply.

"Ten-oh-six." Kincaid was already writing it down, studying his watch. "Those pay phones are on a linear track, Fifth and Madison being only three minutes from here, then shooting north to the farthest point, the cheese factory, which is probably an eight-minute drive."

"Then we have seven minutes for strategy."

Quincy turned to Shelly Atkins. "As Candi put it, we're fucked. We need you to get people in street clothes in unmarked cars to each of those locations right now."

"It's gonna take us longer than that to change—"

"Got any people still at home?"

"Five—"

"Then pull the three closest out of bed and have them drive their personal vehicles to those locations right now."

"What do I say—"

"Now!"

Shelly went wide-eyed, grabbed the walkie-talkie from her utility belt, and headed for the lobby to contact dispatch.

"We're going to need audio on those pay phones." Kincaid was already thinking out loud. "No way we can tap 'em in fifteen minutes. Walkie-talkie. Kimberly can hold it up to the receiver when he calls and air the conversation for the rest of us. Then we can advise her over a second channel set on her earpiece." He shook his head. "I don't get it. Is she supposed to run from phone to phone? It doesn't make any sense."

"He's going to make it impossible," Kimberly murmured. "He's seeking an excuse to kill."

"We send three officers," Quincy said flatly. "One to each pay phone. Whoever gets the call takes it from there."

"We only have one GPS," Lieutenant Mosley protested.

"Then we have a thirty-three percent chance of using it. If not, we do it the old-fashioned way. Follow the contacted officer on the ground and in the air."

"Because he certainly won't notice a chopper," Kincaid commented dryly.

"Then on the ground. But we can't leave a phone uncovered—it's too dangerous."

Kincaid seemed to have reached the same conclusion. "We'll split the money; that gives each officer some hope of negotiating payment. Of course, now we're going to need two more duffel bags."

"Got 'em," Mac declared. "Just give me sixty seconds to dump our clothes and they're yours." He went running for the parking lot.

"I'll take the Fifth and Madison phone," Kincaid said, ticking off the locations on his fingers. "Detective Spector can do Wal-Mart. Kimberly will handle Tillamook Cheese Factory. That leaves Sheriff Atkins to handle the ground crew, and you"—Kincaid nodded toward Quincy—"to coordinate communication strategy here."

"No."

"You're not handling the ransom drop—" Kincaid began.

"And neither are you or Spector." Quincy's gaze went to Detective Grove, then to Kimberly. "The UNSUB's first request still stands—the officers have to be female. Anyone else will simply piss him off."

"I'll go," Candi said, rising to her feet.

Kincaid shot her a look. "Don't be an idiot. You're a negotiator—"

"This is a phone call—"

"Leading to a ransom drop. It's walking, not talking. You get to sit back here, listen to the conversation, and advise the others on what to say."

"You need three women," Candi shot back. "I see only two others sitting here."

"Knew I shoulda gotten that boob job," Shelly Atkins spoke up from the doorway.

"No need on our account," Kincaid told her crisply. "You get Fifth and Madison, Detective Grove handles Wal-Mart, and Kimberly covers the cheese factory."

He checked his watch. "That's our seven minutes, people. Let's roll."

FROM KIMBERLY'S PERSPECTIVE, she'd spent the past two hours twiddling her thumbs, only to now have everything happen at once. Mac was throwing money into duffel bags. A deputy was thrusting a walkie-talkie at her. Then Sheriff Atkins yelled at Mitchell to take over the surveillance van while Candi roared across the room for everyone to remember to remain calm.

Mac hustled Kimberly out the door; she had the farthest to drive, so had the most demands on her time.

Her last glimpse of her father was Quincy leaning over Candi's shoulder, spreading out the Tillamook County maps.

Then Kimberly was in her rental car, Mac slapping her cell phone into her hand.

"We'll be right in front of you. Give me thirty seconds, and I'll call."

He went to slam the door. Stopped. Bent down. Gave her a hard, fierce kiss. Then Mitchell was yelling at him to load up and they all hit the road.

Kimberly had barely made it out of the parking lot when her cell phone rang.

"We got you on the screen, so the GPS is working nicely," Mac announced from inside the unmarked white van.

"Roger." Kimberly was holding the steering wheel too tight. She forced her hands to relax, reminded herself to use the short drive to breathe deep, pull it all together. Quincy had told them it would get complicated. And this was only the start of it.

"You'll need to repeat everything the UNSUB says," Mac was instructing her over the cell phone. "Walkie-talkies can get distorted; the call may be tough for us to follow."

"I know."

"If you get the call, I want you to give us a signal. Put your hand behind your back and show us two fingers. Then we'll know it's a go."

"Two fingers."

"Don't let him fluster you. If he wants his money, he's going to have to cooperate."

"I've sat through the same meetings you have, Mac."

"If he can't provide proof of life, you don't go anywhere, Kimberly. I mean that. There's no guarantee we'll be able to track you, there's no guarantee this guy won't try to grab another hostage. If you can't speak directly to Rainie to know she's okay . . ." Mac let the rest of that thought speak for itself. "Don't put yourself in danger needlessly," he said, more quietly. "Protect what your father has left."

They were at the intersection now. The van put on its turn signal, made a left. Kimberly drove straight through. She would take the back roads, while Mac and Deputy Mitchell looped around to the front. It would allow her to arrive first and without any sign of a police escort.

In case the man was watching. In case the man was waiting.

"The minute we know which phone receives the call," Mac was saying now, "we'll rendezvous at that location. Wal-Mart is only a few minutes from the cheese factory, so there's a good chance we can still get you into play, or even do a quick handoff of the GPS."

"Okay."

"I don't know much about Detective Grove, how much experience she's had. I think it would be better if you could handle things. You know, not just because you have the GPS."

"Understood."

The van was long out of sight. Mac, going down his road. She, going down hers.

"I need to go," she told him.

"Kimberly . . ."

"It's going to be okay, Mac. Everything is going to be okay."

Kimberly clicked off the cell phone. Tucked it in the pocket of her jacket. Took a last steadying breath . . .

The Tillamook Cheese Factory came into view.

Two minutes and counting. Kimberly parked her car, jumped from the driver's seat, and ran for the pay phone.

"Ring," she urged, under her breath. "Please, just *ring*."

*   *   *

SHELLY COULDN'T FIND THE DAMN PAY PHONE. She was driving around the block, craning her neck like a lunatic. She'd only lived in the town for the past few months; she was still learning her way around. And hell, who used pay phones anymore anyway? Seemed the whole world had gone cellular, even nine-year-old schoolkids.

Fuck it. She was burning too much time circling the intersection in her car. She cranked her vehicle up onto Madison Street, parking illegally and too frantic to care. No sign of a backup vehicle, least not that she could tell.

Looked like for the moment at least, she was on her own.

Shelly jogged down to Fifth Street, feeling the weight of her utility belt around her hips, the burden of seven thousand in cash slung over her shoulder. Her palms were sweaty, her breathing harsh. She'd never been in this kind of situation before and sometimes it didn't matter if you were the sheriff, the boss woman, the leader of the pack. Not knowing was not knowing.

If Rainie and Dougie lived through this day, that was it. Shelly was going to Paris.

She arrived at the corner. Still no sign of a damn phone. A trick good ol' Bob had played to pull the task force apart? She hefted the duffel bag back onto her shoulder and considered her options.

Then, just as she was starting to hyperventilate, it came to her. The glass doors leading into the diner.

Shelly wrenched them open and discovered a single phone.

"Please, God," Shelly Atkins murmured under her breath, "don't let it be me."

ALANE GROVE KEPT HER COOL. The Wal-Mart parking lot was crowded and had a lousy layout for a store of its size. She turned in and was promptly blocked by a minivan waiting for a parking space.

She impatiently counted to twenty; the minivan finally pulled in, only for Alane to find herself face-to-face with one harried mother and three milling kids. Each kid took off in a different direction while the mother stood in the middle of the parking lot and screamed for their return.

The kids weren't that impressed with their mother's tantrum. They dodged two cars and a monster pickup truck before finally being corralled in back of a station wagon.

Two more minutes ticked by with agonizing slowness, then Alane found a parking spot.

She got out, trying not to appear too agitated. She was conscious that she might be watched. Aware that as a young, female police officer, she started out with two strikes against her.

She was a good detective, however. Had joined the force after serving four years in the Army Reserve. She could handle the pressure. At least that's what she told herself.

She hefted the duffel bag over her shoulder, checked that she had the walkie-talkie easily accessible in her front jacket pocket, then headed for the store. She found the bank of pay phones outside the main entrance of the big-box retailer. Two phones. A man in a ripped-up flannel shirt was already talking on one.

Alane nearly stopped in front of the available phone, intent on her task. At the last minute, her brain kicked into gear. She passed by the first phone, noting the man's height, lean build, the mud on his work boots. She gazed at his open heavyweight flannel top, perfect for concealing a weapon. She went straight inside the store and radioed in her description.

Kincaid promised her that backup was already on its way. Play it cool, don't give anything away.

Alane walked by the glass doors again, making a big show of looking for a shopping cart. When she glanced outside, however, the man was gone.

She exited, inspecting the parking lot. She didn't see any sign of the man, however, which didn't make much sense. The parking lot was a big open space. No one could simply vanish.

The hairs on the back of her neck stood up. This was it. Something was happening, something was going down.

Seventeen minutes since the first phone call. Detective Alane Grove stood outside the Wal-Mart and readied for action.

She didn't notice the man again until it was much too late.

SILENCE. SILENCE. SILENCE.

Quincy stood in the middle of the conference room, where only Candi, Lieutenant Mosley, and Kincaid remained. The negotiator paced the length of the room. Kincaid filled out paperwork. Lieutenant Mosley finally headed to the lobby, to deal with his hyperactive pager.

Fifteen minutes went by. Twenty minutes. Thirty minutes.

And still there was only silence over the airwaves.

"What the hell is going on!" Quincy demanded at last.

But nobody had an answer.

34

SHE WAS FLOATING. It was a curious sensation. One tinged with both a sense of wonderful weightlessness and a heavier sense of dread. Maybe she wasn't floating. Maybe she was falling, plummeting, racing down a dark abyss.

She felt the wind in her hair, the chill on her face.

She opened her arms.

And she was awake.

Dougie spoke first. "Rainie?"

"Dougie?"

The room was dark. She couldn't get her bearings. Something had changed, but she couldn't figure out what. From across the way, she heard the rustle of clothes, Dougie moving toward her.

"You're not dead," Dougie said.

"No." She licked her lips, trying to find moisture to ease her parched throat. Her tongue felt swollen with thirst, her mouth cracked and painful. She blinked her eyes, but nothing appeared in front of her, not even shades of gray. Maybe she'd gone blind.

"Where?" she managed to ask hoarsely.

"It's a room," Dougie supplied. "I gave you the bed. I thought you needed it more."

"Dark."

"He boarded up the windows. I tried to get the wood off, but I need a tool. Do you have a tool?"

Dougie's tone was wistful. He knew the answer, of course. Sometimes, it was just hard not to ask.

"I got food," Dougie said a bit more brightly. "Crackers. Cheese. I saved you a piece."

"Water," she croaked.

Dougie's voice went low. "I drank the water," he said quietly.

"Oh, Dougie . . ."

She couldn't summon enough moisture for further words. Instead, she reached over and tousled his hair. In response, he pressed his cheek against her leg. It immediately sent a bolt of pain through her body, but she didn't protest. It was unbelievably nice to feel his presence in this unrelenting dark. To know that neither one of them was alone.

"I told him we were cold," Dougie said in a muffled voice. "I told him the cellar was too wet and we wouldn't stay there anymore."

"Brave . . . of you."

"He laughed at me. He said he didn't fucking care if we froze to death—"

"Dougie . . ."

"He said it! I'm only repeating what he said. Didn't fucking care."

Rainie rolled her eyes. Now Dougie was clearly milking the opportunity to swear. But it made her smile. He sounded like a seven-year-old. He sounded, for the moment at least, normal.

"He didn't put us in the cellar," Dougie said now, perplexed. "He led me down the hall. He put me in this room. I didn't like it at first. I yelled at him to let me out. I was . . . I was afraid." He mumbled the last word, making it hard to catch. "But then he came back with you. And gave me some blankets. And I had some cheese and crackers. And water"—another mumbled word. "But only a little bit. I swear it wasn't that much. And I did save a cracker. Don't you want a cracker?"

Rainie felt the boy press the saltine against her fingers. She took his gift, not wanting to offend him. She didn't think she could eat the cracker, however. She didn't have enough moisture left in her mouth.

"How long?" she asked.

"I don't know. I kinda . . . I think maybe I fell asleep."

Rainie nodded, looking around the room, trying to get her bearings. It was unbelievably dark, even darker than the cellar. She would guess that not only had the man boarded up the windows, but he had painted everything black. Why? Sensory deprivation? Another tool for controlling his hostages?

Why this room, if he had the cellar? Unless maybe he'd realized the truth behind Dougie's words. The cellar was too cold and damp, running the risk of hypothermia.

Maybe he couldn't afford for them to be dead just yet.

The thought invigorated her. If he needed them alive, they wielded more power than they thought. They could afford to keep fighting. In fact, they'd better start ramping up their efforts, fight hard now, before that equation changed.

Rainie sat up. Out of nowhere, a white-hot harpoon of pain lanced up her left side and nailed her left temple. She cried out before she could stop herself, falling back, clutching her head with her bound hands. As swiftly as it came, the sharp pain was gone again, except now she was aware of too many things. Strange, tingling currents zooming up and down her limbs. A heavy dull ache swelling her left knee. The sharp sensation of her head being squeezed in an unbearable vise grip.

"Rainie?" Dougie asked fearfully.

"Sorry . . . Moved . . . wrong."

"He zapped you. I saw him do it. He had this thing in his hand, and then he pressed it into your neck and pulled the trigger. Your body went *bzzzzzzt,* just like they do on TV."

"Need . . . a moment. Dougie—"

But before she could say the rest, the door burst open, and the room was flooded with brilliant white light. Rainie flung up her bound hands to protect her eyes. Dougie cowered beside her.

"Heard you were awake," the man announced. "Excellent. Get up. We got work to do."

Rainie tried to move, tried to roll away from the man, find her feet, put up some kind of fight. Her muscles would not respond to her brain. Her legs didn't move, her hips remained motionless, her shoulders refused to rotate. She lay helpless as the dark silhouette stepped into the room and grabbed Dougie by the arm.

"You first. She's not going anywhere."

Dougie cried out in terror, flailing with his feet, thrashing against the bed. Rainie tried to grab his hands, tried to draw him against her, as if that would make a difference. The man wrenched him away, tossing the boy easily over his shoulder.

Dougie screamed again and the sound cut Rainie to the bone. *Goddammit, do something,* she commanded herself. *Get off this fucking bed!*

She strained against the mattress, begging her body to move.

"No, no, no!" Dougie was screaming down the hall.

Rainie remained pinned to the bed, tears pouring down her face. *No, no. Please move. Oh, goddammit. Oh, goddammit, Rainie, you miserable piece of shit. How could you be so weak?*

She heard a door open, a door shut, and then there was no sound at all.

Time elapsed. She didn't know how much. Her left leg twitched uncontrollably. The pressure built behind her temples, pressed against her eyeballs.

Then the man was back. She heard his hard, fast footsteps pound into the room. He grabbed her bound wrists and dragged her out of bed. She flopped like a dead fish onto the floor and lay there, too stunned to move.

"Get up," he commanded her. "Like hell I'm carrying you down the stairs."

"Water." She sounded pathetic, beaten, a wounded animal begging for mercy. How did someone like her ever get to sound this way?

"Oh, trust me, you'll have plenty of water soon enough."

He yanked her to her feet. Her left knee wouldn't take it. The minute he let go, she collapsed again. The man wasn't happy. He kicked her in the ribs, then stood above her, hands on his hips.

"Rainie, I don't have time for this shit."

Hit him, she thought. *Bite his kneecaps.* She remained curled up in the fetal position. She didn't know a head could hurt as much as hers did and still not explode.

"Oh, for crying out loud." He kicked her again. She remained motionless.

He got pissed off and waled on her as if she were a beaten dog.

It didn't do him any good. She couldn't stand up and no amount of physical abuse was going to make a difference. The man finally seemed to reach the same conclusion. He stopped kicking her and, instead, sighed heavily.

"You know, this is getting to be way too much trouble for the money."

He bent down, looping his arm around her bound wrists. "Next time, fuck proof of life. I'm gonna kill up front and get it over with. None of this dragging people around, having to feed them, having to house them, having to put up with their puny attempts at escape. Frankly, you've really annoyed me, Rainie. I can understand why your husband moved out. You're fucking incompetent."

He started dragging her by the arms down the hall. She kept herself still, deadweight. Halfway down the hall, the man's breathing became ragged. He stopped, gasping for breath and cursing her. A human body was cumbersome, not easy to pull. If he was going to kill her, she'd at least make him work for it.

He hooked his hands beneath her armpits, took a deep breath, and resumed his laborious journey down the hall. They entered the kitchen. He yanked her around the corner, down the long row of cabinets. At the last minute, she twisted her leg just enough for her foot to hook the corner unit. In response, he cuffed her on the side of the head.

Then they were off again.

She understood where they were going now. Back to the cellar. The dark. The bone-biting cold. She balked, more desperate now, arching her back, trying to twist out of his arms. She didn't want to go back down into that pit. He would toss her down the stairs. He would bolt the door.

And no one would ever see her or Dougie alive again.

"No, no, no." She didn't know she had started moaning, until her own voice reached her ears.

"Shut up!" the man warned.

They went by the last cabinet. She desperately clawed at the handle.

"You're pissing me off, Lorraine!"

But she wouldn't let go, couldn't let go. She was weak and battered and delirious from the withdrawal of her medication. But she had one lucid thought: He hadn't killed them last night, which could only mean he still needed them. So she had to fight now, make a last stand before their usefulness expired and he abandoned them completely.

"I'll get the Taser," the man roared. "Don't make me do it, Rainie."

"Water, water, water!"

He grabbed her fingers and yanked them from the knob. One of her fingernails ripped off. She yelped with pain, then he had the cellar door flung open and was pushing her onto the top step.

"I'd start walking," he said, "otherwise it's a long fall."

He pushed her hard. She barely caught the wooden railing, using it to slow her momentum as she careened violently down the stairs, landing in a puddle at the bottom.

"Let me out!" Dougie shouted from the shadows. "I don't want to play anymore!"

His voice ended in a high-pitched scream.

"Hey, Rainie," the man taunted from the top of the stairs. "Enjoy your precious water."

The man started to laugh. Then he slammed the door shut and Rainie heard the click of the lock securing the door in place.

Dougie started screaming again, loud, wild, outraged. "No, no, no, no, no!"

Rainie would've joined him, if only she had the strength.

"No, no, no, no, no!"

Moment slid into moment. Dougie finally fell silent. They both absorbed the dark.

And then, for the first time, Rainie became aware of a new sound. Low, constant, vibrating. Hissing in the dark.

Rainie finally got the man's joke. And she realized now the question she should've asked Dougie from the moment she'd woken up—

why had the man given him cheese and crackers? What had Dougie done to earn such a treat?

"Dougie," she called out quietly. "You have to tell me the truth—did the man take your picture?"

"I'm sorry," the boy said immediately, which was answer enough.

Rainie closed her eyes. "Dougie, were you holding a newspaper?"

"It had my picture on the front page! Yours, too," he added belatedly.

"Dougie, you need to get to higher ground. Can you find the workbench? Climb up on that."

"I can't! I'm tied to a pipe! I can't move!"

"Oh no." Rainie tried to stagger to her feet, to find Dougie in the dark. But her legs wouldn't move, her body wouldn't cooperate. She remained sprawled on the cold floor, feeling the water rise against her cheek.

The hissing sound had gained momentum and was now accompanied by a gurgle.

The man had burst a pipe. He was flooding the basement. He had his proof of life.

Now, he'd put them down here to die.

35

LIEUTENANT MOSLEY HAD SPENT TWENTY YEARS of his life in the OSP uniform. Two decades of starting each day with navy blue pants, a gray short-sleeved shirt, and a black patent-leather utility belt.

He drove a state trooper car, updated now with a gold star shooting across a navy blue backdrop. He worked out of the latest incarnation of the Portland field office, actually a former post office located smack-dab in the middle of a strip mall; last time a registering sex offender had decided to make a run for it, they'd gotten to chase him past the Hometown Buffet into the Dollar Tree store. It was the kind of thing that was frightening at the time—a convicted sex offender bolting through a public area filled with little kids—but made for a good story when all was said and done and the felon was safely behind bars.

In his career, Lieutenant Mosley figured he'd worked hundreds of motor vehicle accidents and written thousands of traffic citations. He'd learned firsthand what a speeding car could do to a sixteen-year-old kid as well as to a family of five. Then he'd served three years on a gang task force, right about the same time the L.A. gangs brought their particular brand of violence to the Portland area and taught nine-year-old boys to beat each other to death with baseball bats. Finally, he'd spent five years fighting the war on drugs, watching the growing crack epidemic envelop entire city blocks in a wave of addiction and decay.

When the public information officer position became available two years ago, Mosley figured he was ready for a change. And maybe other officers thought he was coasting, easing his way toward the retirement years, but at this stage of the game, he knew he'd paid his dues. He'd driven the highways; he'd walked the streets. He'd won battles; he'd lost fights. He had a pretty good idea of both how much and how little law enforcement could do.

In colloquial terms, he thought he'd seen it all. And yet he'd never seen anything quite like what he was seeing now.

Mosley finally turned away from the small TV the Fish and Wildlife officers had blaring at the front desk. He poked his head back into the conference room.

"Hey," he said to Kincaid and Quincy, "you got to see this."

Wednesday, 10:45 a.m. PST

ADAM DANICIC WAS HOLDING a press conference. Impeccably dressed in a charcoal gray suit with a pastel pink shirt and darker pink satin tie, Danicic seemed to be channeling Regis Philbin as he stood on the lawn of a small white house, hands clasped in front of him, face painfully sincere.

The yard was filled with an assortment of reporters, cameramen, and awestruck neighbors.

"After much soul-searching," Danicic was declaring to the gathered masses, "I have decided I have an obligation to come forward as a civilian and not as a member of the press, to report what I know about the tragic kidnappings of a woman and child right here in Bakersville. As a newspaper reporter, naturally I was honored and excited to be covering the kidnappings for the *Bakersville Daily Sun* and the ensuing investigation. Indeed, I was up most of last night working on this morning's front-page story for the *Sun*.

"I feel, however, that a journalist has an ethical obligation to be an objective outsider in any story, to be separate from the events unfolding. The longer I worked on my story, the clearer it became to me that I am no longer an objective outsider. In fact, just minutes ago, I received new information that puts me at the heart of this investigation. Thus, I feel I must remove myself as lead reporter for the piece and, instead, fully disclose everything I know, in the hopes that it might lead to the discovery of Lorraine Conner and seven-year-old Douglas Jones."

"What the hell is he talking about?" Kincaid asked Lieutenant Mosley.

"Who knows," the PIO said flatly. "But we are about to get screwed."

"It all began yesterday morning," Danicic continued expansively, waving his arms now, playing to his audience, "when the *Daily Sun* received the most frightening letter addressed to the Opinions Editor. This letter declared that someone among us had kidnapped a woman, but that she would remain unharmed, *as long as we did as the kidnapper said.*"

Danicic went on to describe yesterday's events in detail after painful detail. The deal the *Daily Sun* had struck to cooperate with the law enforcement task force: "Because a local paper is by definition part of the community, and thus must show restraint and compassion when a fellow member of the community is in harm's way."

The attempt at renegotiating the ransom drop: "A desperate move from a desperate task force, racing against the relentless drumbeat of time." The kidnapper's unexpected retaliation against Dougie Jones, and the letter left on the windshield of Danicic's car: "I started to realize then that in the events that were unfolding, I might be called upon to play an unusual and unexpected role."

But it wasn't until this morning, Danicic assured his fellow members of the press, that he realized clearly what that role might be. Upon e-mailing his lead story directly to Owen Van Wie, the *Daily Sun's* owner, he finally caught some badly needed sleep. Only to wake up to the sound of a doorbell and discover an envelope, addressed to him, sitting on his front steps.

"Ah shit," Kincaid groaned.

"We should've locked him up last night," agreed Lieutenant Mosley.

Quincy continued to study the screen.

"This note was typewritten, but similar in tone and content to the other letters, which I have been privileged to see," Danicic reported. "I have no doubt of its validity, and that it came from the kidnapper himself. In this note, the kidnapper reiterated his desire to ransom Lorraine Conner and Douglas Jones for twenty thousand dollars. The writer of the note, however, declared that he no longer trusted the police task force and did not feel that he could work with them. He indicated that if this matter was not resolved shortly, he felt he would have no choice but to kill both his victims. As proof of his claim, he included this."

Danicic held up a photo. The local network camera zoomed in. The picture was dark and distorted. The face of a small boy appeared in the middle, but the flash had bleached out the child's face, making individual features hard to discern. The boy was holding something.

"This photo clearly depicts Dougie Jones. Note the boy's fingers, pointing to the date on the top of the front page of this morning's paper as he poses next to his own photo in the *Daily Sun*. I believe you can just make out the face of a woman, lying behind Dougie. I believe the woman is Rainie Conner, but the police will need to be the judge of that.

"To say the least, I was deeply disturbed to receive this photo and this note. My first impulse, of course, was to call the authorities, as I have done with all communications I have received. This note's tone, however, gave me pause. Needless to say, I'm distressed to hear that the kidnapper feels he can no longer cooperate with law enforcement. Having seen firsthand what that kind of distrust can do—the abduction of an additional victim, a small boy, just yesterday afternoon—I am concerned about what this means for both Dougie and Rainie. Thus, I reached a difficult decision. I have decided I must handle this note in a different manner.

"I am bringing it to you, the public. I am standing here right now, in the hopes that my message will reach the person who is holding Rainie Conner and Dougie Jones. And I am offering my services as a negotiator." Danicic turned slightly to peer directly into the camera lens.

"Mr. Fox," he said solemnly. "Following is my cell phone number.

I encourage you to call it anytime. And I promise to do everything in my power to assure that you receive your twenty thousand dollars. All I ask is that you do not harm Dougie Jones or Rainie Conner. Do not make innocent victims pay for the mistakes of law enforcement."

Danicic rattled off his phone number. A few of his neighbors began to clap.

In the front lobby of Fish and Wildlife, Kincaid shook his head, as if trying to wake himself from a particularly bad dream.

Mosley recovered first. "We need to hold our own press conference immediately. We will issue a statement that we are in contact with the kidnapper and are working with him to meet his demands. We need to say that while we appreciate any help the public has to give, it is crucial to give the task force time and space to handle this delicate case. We should also mention we brought in a professional negotiator; that will increase public confidence."

"Let's pick Danicic up," Kincaid decided. "I want him and that note down at the Tillamook field office ASAP. Call the lab and get a scientist from QD up here to analyze the note, as well as some kind of expert on photos. And I want Danicic cooling his heels in an interrogation room. If the UNSUB does take him up on his cockamamie scheme, I don't want to be hearing the details on CNN."

Mosley nodded. Both men turned toward Quincy, who was still staring at the TV screen.

"You're quiet," Kincaid stated. His eyes narrowed. "You don't really think we should work with him, do you?"

"What? No, no. That's not it. Just trying to see the future."

"Good luck to you."

"He called at ten," Quincy said abruptly. "The UNSUB fulfilled his promise from yesterday's letter, and seemed to be setting up for the ransom drop by ordering three female officers to three separate pay phones. But at the same time he was doing this, he was also leaving a note on Mr. Danicic's front door, claiming that he couldn't work with the assembled task force. Why?"

Kincaid shrugged. "Confuse matters. Rattle our chains. Once more have a good laugh at our expense."

"True. But it's certainly no way to get rich. He hasn't even made contact by pay phone."

"You said it yourself: His primary motivation isn't money."

"He's playing a game."

"Son of a bitch," Kincaid agreed.

"But all games have an end."

"Theoretically speaking."

"Then where is this game headed, Sergeant? What don't we see?"

Kincaid didn't have an answer. He shrugged, just as Candi appeared in the doorway.

"We have activity," she reported.

"The UNSUB's made contact?" Kincaid was already running for the conference room.

"No, but Trooper Blaney just radioed in. He's at the Wal-Mart. He can't find any trace of Detective Grove."

"What?" Kincaid drew up short.

"He's searched inside and outside the store," Candi reported. "Best he can tell, Alane is gone."

36

KIMBERLY WAS PACING IN FRONT of the pay phone when her walkie-talkie crackled to life. It was Mac:

"We got a situation at Wal-Mart. We need to rendezvous there, ASAP."

"Contact with the kidnapper?" Kimberly jerked away from the phone and headed across the parking lot, already ramping up on adrenaline.

"More like Detective Grove appears to be missing."

"Say what?"

"Exactly."

Kimberly found her car, and headed for Wal-Mart.

A CROWD OF CURIOSITY SEEKERS had already gathered outside the Wal-Mart, blocking access. Deputy Mitchell chirped the surveillance van's hidden siren three times, and the throng reluctantly gave way.

Following behind the van, Kimberly counted half a dozen patrol cars and three unmarked detectives' sedans clogging the front of the lot. No reporters on the ground yet, but when she glanced up, she spotted the first network chopper in the air. The situation wasn't about to become a media circus, it was already there.

Deputy Mitchell parked the van in the middle of a lane; Kimberly followed suit. As she climbed out of her car, she could see the deputy craning his neck and pointing up at the chopper.

"Is that what I think it is?" he was asking Mac.

"Yep."

"Ah hell, that's not fair. Most of us haven't even had a chance to shower!"

Mac and Kimberly exchanged glances. They tugged on the tired deputy's arms, navigating him to the front of the store. Sheriff Atkins was already there, in a huddle with Lieutenant Mosley and a heavy woman wearing a red floral-print dress. According to her name tag, Dorothy was the manager.

"Yes, we have cameras all over the store. Of course you can check the tapes. I don't see what could've happened though. I mean, it's midmorning. I didn't get any word of anything or anybody acting strange." Dorothy was rocking from side to side, sending her red dress into billows of distress.

"I understand," Shelly consoled. "But that's the beauty of security cameras. They're always paying attention, even on a routine day." She spotted their approach and beckoned them closer. "Deputy Mitchell, this is Dorothy Watson. Dorothy is going to take you to the back office and show you the security tapes. I want you to check all the film starting at nine forty-five this morning and ending at ten-thirty. In particular, pay attention to the footage of the pay phones. I want to know when Detective Grove arrived on scene, and if we can catch any sign of where she went. Got it?"

Mitchell nodded. He was still eyeing the news chopper, tugging nervously at the collar of his shirt. Clearly, he didn't feel ready to make his film-at-eleven debut. Sometimes, it was tough to be a cop.

As Dorothy and Mitchell disappeared back inside the store, Shelly brought Mac and Kimberly up to date. "We don't know diddly," the sheriff said bluntly. "Detective Grove arrived on time. Radioed Kincaid to provide a description of a man talking on one of the pay phones. Kincaid advised her that backup was on its way. And that's the last we heard from Alane Grove."

"What time did she radio Kincaid?" Kimberly asked.

"He logged it at ten twenty-eight."

"And the backup arrived?"

"Well, that's the bad news. It took Kincaid ten minutes to find an available officer, then another ten minutes for Trooper Blaney to get his butt over here. Upon arrival, Blaney didn't see any sign of Alane or the gentleman outside, so he parked his cruiser and went into the store. It's a big store. He walked it another fifteen minutes, before getting nervous.

"That point, he radioed back in to the task force. Kincaid advised him to initiate full lockdown. Blaney paged the manager, had Dorothy lock up the store. The employees and customers were lined up in the front. Then Blaney and Dorothy did a full-scale search aisle by aisle, including the employees' lounge, rest rooms, stockroom, everywhere. There's no sign of Detective Grove."

"Her car?"

"Still in the lot."

"Shit."

"It's a public relations nightmare," Lieutenant Mosley spoke up. "Danicic just held a news conference reporting that our own ineptitude led to the kidnapping of Dougie Jones. If word gets out that the subject is now snatching members of the task force in broad daylight . . ."

"I'm sure Detective Grove isn't thrilled about things either," Kimberly snapped. "Let's not lose perspective here."

"The media controls perspective; that's all I'm trying to say. Our UNSUB is playing to the media. A *Daily Sun* reporter is playing to the media. We are doing nothin'. How the hell many people have to be kidnapped before I get to do my job?"

Kimberly got a little wide-eyed. The color in her face rose alarmingly.

Mosley, however, refused to be rattled. He had his cell phone out and was working the numbers. "Look, you all set?" he asked Shelly.

"I think we can handle things here."

"Fine, then I'm heading to the county field office. I might as well see if I can talk some sense into Danicic, or get really lucky and issue a formal statement to the press. We gotta start taking control of the situation. This kind of thing"—Mosley pointed up to the hovering chopper—"is bullshit."

Mosley stalked off, cell phone glued to his ear. Kimberly worked on getting her blood pressure back under control.

"Can you believe—" she started.

Mac laid a soothing hand on her arm. "He's doing his job. Just like we gotta do ours. So, first things first: Did any of the pay phones receive a call?"

"Not that we know of," Shelly said.

"So the only person who reported any activity at all was Detective Grove, and now she's vanished."

"That's right."

"I don't like the sound of that."

"Gets the little hairs on the back of my neck standing up, too."

A beep sounded at Shelly's waist. She frowned, checked the digital display of her pager, then unclipped her police radio from her utility belt. "Sheriff Atkins," she said.

The crackling sound of a police dispatch operator came over the airwaves. "We have a male caller, identity unknown, who is demanding to speak with you. He will not give us his name or reason for calling. Just keeps insisting you'll want to have the conversation."

Shelly arched a brow at Kimberly and Mac. "All right, I'll bite. Put him on the line."

Mac and Kimberly huddled closer. There was a moment of silence, then a male voice boomed over the airwaves: "I have information on the missing woman and child. I want to know what the reward is."

"For being a good citizen?"

The man continued talking as if he hadn't heard her: "I read in the paper 'bout a woman who got seventy thousand dollars for helping catch a cop killer. I got information on saving two people's lives. I figure that's worth at least one hundred grand."

"Hal Jenkins, you miserable piece of shit," Shelly said. "Did you honestly think I wouldn't recognize your voice just 'cuz you're calling over the police radio?"

Long silence. Then Shelly's eyes suddenly narrowed.

"Don't suppose you were at the local Wal-Mart this morning, Hal? Perhaps wearing a blue flannel shirt? Think real hard before you answer; we got tapes from the security cameras."

"Ahh shit," Hal said.

"That's what I thought. Let me tell you about reward, Hal. I'm sending a deputy to your house right now. You're gonna get into the back of his cruiser without making a fuss. You're gonna come straight here and tell me face-to-face what you know about those missing people. And you're gonna tell me everything, Hal, or I'm going to rip apart your entire property stove by stove, brick by brick. I told you yesterday we weren't foolin' around, and I meant it."

"I just want some money," Hal retorted sulkily. "Other people get reward money. I don't see what's so wrong with wanting that."

"Get out on your porch, Hal. Deputy will be there anytime."

Shelly clicked off with Hal. Then she was back with police dispatch, ordering a deputy to ferry Hal to the Wal-Mart. After that she requested the county DA's office, where she filled the man in on Hal's extortion attempt and requested a search warrant for his property, due to his obvious involvement in the abduction of a known member of law enforcement.

Kimberly was impressed. "I thought you were going to spare his property," she told the sheriff.

"I lied. By the time the search warrant goes through, Hal will have already told us everything we need to know. Right about then, it'll be nice to have a little surprise for Mr. Jenkins. Besides, I've been wanting to search that farm for weeks now. I hate to look a gift horse in the mouth."

It took nineteen minutes for Hal to arrive at the Wal-Mart. In that time, Deputy Mitchell confirmed that Hal Jenkins had been at the second pay phone when Alane Grove arrived. On the security camera tape, Grove had disappeared inside the store. Shortly thereafter, Hal drifted off-camera in the direction of the parking lot. Grove reappeared briefly by the pay phones, then also disappeared into the parking lot. She never appeared on camera again.

"No camera angles of the parking lot?" Shelly asked grumpily.

"The only exterior cameras monitor the front of the store, plus the entrance to the parking lot," said Mitchell. "In the good-news department, we have clear footage of every vehicle that entered the parking lot this morning, including license plates. In the bad-news department, it's gonna take some time to cross-reference all those vehicles, plus it wouldn't include anyone arriving on foot."

"We'll take what we got. Let's get the footage to Kincaid for delivery to the state crime lab. Someone's gonna work a lot of hours tonight."

Shelly was back on the radio to dispatch. Kimberly took the opportunity to call her father.

"How are you?" she asked quietly, moving away from the squawk of the police radio, the overexcited chaos of chattering onlookers, the constant thrum of the news chopper hovering overhead.

"We're in trouble," Quincy answered bluntly.

"We may have gotten a break. We know who was at the second pay phone. And he says he has information on Rainie and Dougie."

"The subject should be on the phone demanding money," Quincy told her. "He's not even pretending anymore."

"Mac said there was a photo on the news. It proves that Rainie and Dougie were alive this morning."

"It proves Dougie is alive. Rainie is in the background of the photo. Lying down. Eyes closed. I know, I'm looking at the photo right now."

Kimberly pressed the phone closer to her head, her other hand flattened against her ear to block the background noise. Her father's voice was low, not at all like him. She could feel his anxiety in the flat tones, the heaviness of his despair.

A police cruiser arrived, tooting its horn as it muscled its way through the crowd. Kimberly had a glimpse of a man sitting in the back, hunched shoulders, scruffy cheeks, a blue flannel shirt.

"Hal Jenkins is here," she informed Quincy. "Give me fifteen minutes, I'll call you back."

"You're still wearing the GPS transmitter?" her father asked abruptly.

Kimberly frowned. "Yeah. Why?"

"I want you to promise me you won't take it off."

"You're scaring me, Dad."

"I'm trying to. We haven't paid the subject one red cent. But if he did kidnap Detective Grove—"

"He just scored seven grand."

"It's something to think about," her father said.

Then Hal Jenkins was getting out of the police cruiser, Shelly was waving her over, and Kimberly had to shut her phone, feeling even worse about the day ahead.

Wednesday, 11:35 a.m. PST

HAL JENKINS WASN'T A FRIENDLY GUY. And clearly, he had issues with Sheriff Atkins.

"Touch my place, I won't tell you a damn thing," he said by way of greeting.

"Now, Hal, a promise is a promise."

"Bullshit, I want that in writing."

Shelly yawned, gave Hal a droll look, then issued a negligent shrug. "Well, Hal, if that will make you happy . . ." She waved Deputy Mitchell over. He produced a spiral notepad and pen. Shelly made a big show of writing, *I, Sheriff Shelly Atkins, do solemnly promise* not *to search the premises owned by one Hal Jenkins, of Tillamook County, in the understanding that he will cooperate fully in disclosing what he knows about missing persons Lorraine Conner, Douglas Jones, and Detective Alane Grove.* Shelly signed it with great flourish.

Hal scowled at her. "Who's Alane Grove?"

Shelly paused for the first time. "Why don't you first tell me what you know about Rainie Conner and Dougie Jones?" she said.

"Wait a minute. Was that the girl who showed up at the pay phone? The one with the duffel bag? I thought she moved like a cop!" And then, eyes going a little wild, "Well, shit, you're not pinning that on me, are you? I don't know nothing 'bout her. Saw her, thought it was strange to carry a duffel bag into a superstore, and then boom, she was gone and I was on my merry way."

"Why were you at the pay phones, Hal?"

"I like my privacy."

"So you're using a public phone?"

"Hey, we all got our little, what do you call them, fetishes."

Shelly chewed on the inside of her cheek and looked like she was contemplating slugging her informant. "So you were at the phone."

"Yep."

"Made a call?"

"Maybe."

"Remember, Hal, we have grounds to pull the records."

Hal appeared crestfallen again.

"Yeah, these missing people," Shelly said dryly, "they're really fucking with your life."

"Don't swear. You're a lady. Ladies shouldn't swear."

"Why, Hal, you're making me positively googly-eyed. Tell me about your phone call."

"The phone call doesn't matter," Hal said abruptly, seeming to have reached some sort of conclusion with himself. "What matters is that I dropped my quarter."

"You dropped your quarter?"

"Yep. And when I reached down to pick it up, I saw what was taped to the bottom of the phone."

"Talk a little faster, Hal. We don't exactly got all day."

Hal had enough of talking, however. He reached into his back pocket and pulled out a battered white envelope. He held it in front of him, dangling it like a prize. "I'll give you my note if you'll give me yours."

Shelly immediately handed over her signed pledge not to search Hal's farm. Hal handed her the discolored envelope.

"This it?" Shelly asked.

"That's it. Trust me, I didn't mess with it or change anything. Like I said, this whole kidnapping thing is not my cup of tea."

"But you read it?"

"'Course. Still think I should get a reward. Crimestoppers. The Sheriff's Department. I'm doing a good thing here."

"Cuff him," Shelly instructed Deputy Mitchell.

"What?" Hal asked.

"Take him in, get him processed," Shelly ordered Mitchell. "We'll see how his story checks out."

"This is no way to treat a Good Samaritan!" Hal cried.

"Oh, it gets better, Hal. There's some fine folks right now, already arriving to search your farm."

"But you promised!"

"Ah, Hal," Shelly said kindly. "*I'm* not the one searching your property. The DA is."

Hal tried to make a run for it. Deputy Mitchell grabbed his cuffed hands and stuffed him in the backseat of the cruiser.

"You bitch!" Hal was screaming.

"Shhh," Mitchell said, pointing up at the sky. "Smile at the pretty people, Hal. You're on *Candid Camera*."

37

THE WATER WAS COMING FOR HER.

Rainie could feel its steady onslaught, rising from her toes to her ankles, licking languorously at her shins. Originally, progress had seemed slow, the water creeping up quarter inch by quarter inch. Something to worry about, but no cause for immediate panic.

Circumstances, however, were changing. Perhaps the pipe had sprung a second leak, or the force of the gushing water had enlarged the existing hole. The sound had gained force now, changing from a mewling hiss to a charging roar.

Rainie knew about water. She'd worked drowning cases, pulled bloaters out of the engorged rapids of freshly thawed rivers, even retrieved an auto or two that had taken the wrong turn in a sharply curved road. She had seen the torn nails and broken, curled fingers of the people who had fought to the bitter end. In one of the vehicles, the woman had managed to work her arm through a two-inch crack in the passenger window. The image had haunted Rainie for weeks. That pale face plastered against the glass, bloody arm reaching frantically for life.

Water was a force, governed by its own laws, feeding its own needs. It started by saturating Rainie's clothes, weighing down the hem of her jeans. Cold tendrils then wrapped around her ankles, rubbed against her skin, sending the chill deep into her bones.

Soon, the water would be lapping against her chest, squeezing the air from her lungs. Ironically enough, the air would start to feel cold and the water warm. So it would be easier to sink down into its depths. Let the water tickle her lips, slide down her throat.

By the time it rushed into her lungs, triggering a last-minute coughing fit, it would be too late. The water would have closed over the top of her head, suspending her and Dougie in its final, chilly embrace.

Water destroyed. But as part of its seduction, it also revived. She felt its coolness against the angry heat in her knee. She splashed refreshing drops against the pain in her arms, the throbbing in her temples. She drank from the dank, oily depths, and the liquid soothed her parched throat. The water would kill her, most definitely. But at least it made her feel better first.

Slowly but surely, she pulled herself off the basement steps. She rose shakily to her feet. And she reached into her pocket for the only hope they had left.

"Dougie," she called out softly.

"Y-y-yes."

"Have you ever played Marco Polo?"

"Y-y-yes."

"Marco."

"Polo."

"Marco."

"Polo."

She found his huddled body, tied to the pipe in the dark.

"Dougie," she said, "hold very still."

Wednesday, 11:45 a.m. PST

SHE HAD PALMED THE SHARD OF GLASS during their failed attempt at escape. Frantically reaching out with her fingertips, she had hoped for a possible weapon. Maybe a five-inch shank she could slash against their captor's throat or stab into his kidneys. No such luck. All she had found was a slender shard, perhaps half an inch thick. It felt unbelievably fragile between her thick, swollen fingers. It also felt sharp.

She had to work to get the piece positioned between her numb, frozen fingertips. She started rubbing the zip tie binding Dougie's wrists and promptly dropped the shard. She grappled in the water for the delicate piece, only to drop it again. By the time she finally got the glass into place again, the water had hit Dougie's knees and he was shaking uncontrollably.

"You're drunk," Dougie accused.

"No."

"I saw you with that bottle."

"I wasn't looking for booze, Dougie. I was looking for a weapon."

She worked the sharp edge against the plastic band. She thought she felt it give. Right at that moment, of course, she dropped the piece of glass again.

"Liar," Dougie said.

Rainie reached down, sifting through water with her fingers. The shard bumped lazily against the back of her hand, washed away. She frantically fished after it.

"Would you like to know the truth, Dougie? I *am* a liar. Every time my mother beat me, I lied to my teachers and told them I fell off my bike. Every time I took a drink, I lied to myself and told myself it was the last one. I've lied to my husband. I've lied to my friends. And yes, I've lied to you. There are a million lies in the world, Dougie. Lies we tell to protect others, lies we tell to protect ourselves. I'm pretty sure I've told each and every one. And I'm pretty sure, so have you."

Dougie didn't say anything. She'd found the piece of glass, trapped it between her fingertips. The water was past Dougie's knees, approaching his thighs. She could hear more gurgling, old water seeking new ways to burst free.

"A few months ago," she continued evenly, "I started taking some pills. I hoped they would help me stop feeling sad all the time. Maybe they would even help me not want to drink. Unfortunately, it's not the kind of drug you can just stop taking. And when our kidnapper snatched me, he was not kind enough to also grab my meds. What you see now is not me being drunk. You're seeing my withdrawal symptoms. They're going to get worse."

"Oh," Dougie said in a small voice. Then, more curiously, "Does it hurt?"

"I've felt better."

"Do you want a drink?"

Rainie was back at work, sawing on the binding. "You know how you feel about matches, Dougie?"

"I wish I had a match right now!" the boy said immediately.

"Well, that's how I feel about booze. But I don't have to drink, Dougie. Just like you don't have to play with fire."

Her fingers slipped. The shard drove into the palm of her hand. She winced, grateful for once for the lack of sensation in her blood-deprived fingers, then dug the slippery spike of glass out of the meat of her thumb. She was trembling again. Cold, shock, she didn't know. She was very tired. It would be so nice to retreat to the stairs. Sit a while. Rest. She'd get back to Dougie soon enough . . .

"Rainie, do you believe in Heaven?"

Rainie was so startled, she nearly cut herself again. She answered, carefully, "I want to."

"My first second family, they said my mother went to Heaven. They said she's waiting for me. Do you think my mommy watches over me?"

"I think it's a nice idea," she said quietly.

"Stanley said my mother's disappointed in me. Stanley said every time I set a fire, I make Mom cry. Rainie, does my mom hate me?"

"Oh, Dougie." She floundered, honestly at a loss for words. "A mother never stops loving her child."

"I burned her picture."

"A picture is just a picture. I'm sure she understands."

"I burned my first second parents' house and my second second parents' house. If I could get a match, I would burn this house. But it's wet." He frowned. "Wet doesn't burn so well."

Rainie arched a brow, returning to work on the binding. "You know what, Dougie? Mothers *always* love their children; they just don't always love what their children *do*. Think of it this way: Your mother loves you, but I'm sure she doesn't like you setting things on fire."

"I am a bad boy," Dougie said matter-of-factly. "I'm very naughty. Nobody loves a naughty boy."

"You saved a cracker for me. I don't think a naughty boy would save a cracker for his friend."

"I drank all the water."

"You didn't know I was thirsty. You also tried to get us help. You ran when I asked you to run. I don't think a naughty boy would be so brave to help his friend."

Dougie didn't say anything.

"I think, Dougie," Rainie said after a moment, "that you're just like the rest of us. You're a good boy *and* you're a bad boy. Just like I'm a good girl and I'm a bad girl. Every day, we have to make a decision: Which person will we be—good or bad? But it's our choice. Your choice. My choice. Personally, I'm trying to choose better these days."

"Stanley never hit me," Dougie said quietly.

"I know, Dougie, I know."

She heard a snap. The plastic tie split, fell into the water. And Dougie was finally free.

Wednesday, 11:53 a.m. PST

"MY TURN, DOUGIE." Rainie held out the glass shard. Dougie was dancing around, splashing through the water merrily. She was dismayed to realize that the water was already at his waist.

She spoke up more sharply. "Cut the tie around my wrists, Dougie. Then we're gettin' out of here."

The boy stopped dancing, but he didn't take the piece of glass. For a moment, both of them just stood there. Rainie could feel Dougie watching her, but at this distance, she couldn't see the look on his face.

"Dougie," she prompted.

Nothing.

"Dougie, the water is rising very fast. I'm going to climb up the stairs now. I think you should, too."

But even after she was halfway up the stairs, Dougie refused to follow.

"Dougie, what are you doing?"

"I can't," he said quietly.

"Can't what?"

"I can't. I made a promise. Cross my heart, hope to die. I can't."

"Dougie?"

"I didn't know," he said mournfully. "I didn't know."

Rainie came down a step. "Did he threaten you, Dougie? Did the man tell you he would hurt you if we escaped? You don't need to be afraid of him anymore. When we get out of here, I'll make sure you're safe."

"I didn't want to burn my mom's stuff," Dougie said. "But I did. And once a fire starts, you can't go back again. Fire is forever, you know. Fire is real."

"Help me, Dougie." Rainie could hear the urgency in her voice, the growing edge of panic. She tried to swallow it back down, to sound forceful. "Cut the tie around my wrists. I'm going to get us out of here!"

Nothing.

"Dougie?"

Nothing.

"Dougie!"

And then, out of the dark: "I killed her," Dougie whispered. "I didn't mean to. But now she's gone and can't come back again. Because I was a naughty boy. Nobody loves a naughty boy. Except maybe my mommy. I miss my mommy. I just want to see her again."

Rainie heard a splash.

She raced down the stairs. She plunged back into the water. "Dougie? Dougie? *Dougie?*"

But the water remained unbroken. Dougie had sunk beneath the chilly depths. He did not come up again.

38

"It's a map."

"Surprise, surprise."

"Once the twenty grand has been delivered to location X," Kimberly reported by phone, "the UNSUB will contact the media with Rainie and Dougie's location."

"Media? Or Adam Danicic?" Quincy pressed.

"Just says media. Maybe Danicic is implied. The note reminds us that our guy's not a monster. P.S.," Kimberly read out loud, "after one p.m., he cannot be held accountable for what happens to the woman or child. 'Their fate,' and I quote, 'is in your hands.'"

"Son of a bitch," Kincaid swore in the background. "Someone tell me the damn time."

"Eleven forty-two," Kimberly replied, just as her father, standing beside Kincaid in the command center, also rattled off the hour.

"Can you read the map?" Quincy asked.

"Shelly already took a look. She believes it's a lighthouse up the coast. Building's been closed for the past few months, supposedly earmarked for repairs, but she doesn't think the work has started yet. She's making some calls to check on it now."

"How long will it take to get there?"

"Thirty-five, forty minutes."

"Have you searched the other phones? You're sure there's no other communication?"

"Mac's already run to the cheese factory. Nothing there. Trooper Blaney has headed back into town. We should know shortly."

"One note gets the job done," Quincy murmured. "The three pay phones, fifteen-minute deadline, that was all window dressing. A way for him to have a little fun. But we jumped when he said jump. Now, as our reward . . ."

"Another stupid map," Kincaid filled in. He repeated, "Son of a bitch."

The noise was too loud outside. Kimberly ducked inside the Wal-Mart, still deserted with all the employees and customers segregated out front. She discovered Shelly in the book department, cell phone glued to her ear as she ranted at someone over the air waves. Kincaid was speaking again. Kimberly headed for the peace and solitude of feminine hygiene.

"If Shelly thinks she knows where she's going, then she should go. You can join her in the car, we'll get some other officers bringing up the rear. You still have the GPS?"

"Yeah."

"Then we can track you. So, thirty-five-minute drive, say another ten minutes to locate the precise spot . . . You'd better get going."

"We can't."

"You can't?"

Kimberly sighed heavily. "Don't either of you get it yet? Detective Grove's gone—we don't have the twenty thousand dollars anymore."

"Son of a bitch!" Kincaid swore.

Her father said nothing at all.

Wednesday, 11:45 a.m. PST

FOR THE SECOND TIME in one day, Lieutenant Mosley was flabbergasted. In his day, when a trooper picked up a "person of interest," the man was brought straight to the nearest field office. He was set up in an interrogation room. He was offered a beverage of choice.

Then the interrogation room door was shut, and the man was given plenty of time in a small, barren space sitting on a hard metal chair with a rapidly filling bladder to think about things. It's not like everyone suddenly cracked under the pressure. But it certainly softened most of them up.

For starters, Adam Danicic was not shut in the interrogation room. He was not sitting on a hard metal chair. He was not, from what Mosley could tell, suffering from any lack of creature comforts.

In fact, the *Daily Sun* reporter was currently at the sergeant's desk, stretched back in the sergeant's leather office chair and chattering away on the sergeant's phone.

Mosley walked in, took one look at what was happening, then headed straight for the state trooper who'd brought Danicic in.

The officer immediately snapped to attention. "It's not how it looks!" he burst out when Mosley stopped in front of him.

"And how does it look?"

"I mean, I had no choice!"

"Because you're not wearing a pair of handcuffs or a gun?"

"He said he would only come with us if he could make some calls. And then once we got here, he said if we didn't give him a phone, he would use his cell phone, and of course, we wouldn't want him tying up his cell phone."

"Because the kidnapper wouldn't be able to get through."

"Exactly, sir!"

"Tell me, Officer, do you really think a reporter would jeopardize his chance of speaking directly to the man who has abducted two people?"

The officer's eyes darted from side to side, which Mosley took as a no.

"Do you really think he would do anything to risk his airtime on the nightly news, or the number of copy inches he can command on the front page?"

"I was told we needed him to cooperate. And I wasn't given anything to charge him with."

"Then you find something, Officer. Obstruction of justice. Expired license. Broken taillight. You were at the man's home, standing in front of his car, for God's sake. You can always find one little infraction. Even the Pope has committed some sort of misdemeanor in his life."

The officer didn't answer anymore, which was answer enough.

Lieutenant Mosley returned to the front of the small field office, where Danicic was still jabbering away on the phone. Mosley hit the line-one button with his index finger and the phone went dead.

"Hey, that was my lawyer!"

"You feel you need a lawyer?" Mosley asked levelly.

"In the entertainment industry, you bet. I've already gotten called by Larry King, not to mention the *Today* show. But then you also have to figure in the possible book deals. I mean, I tell everything up front, who's gonna be left to buy the hardcover? I need a strategy."

"Sit up," Mosley snapped. "Feet off the desk. Show some respect."

Danicic arched a brow but did as he was told. He uncrossed his ankles. Straightened in the chair. Dusted off his gray jacket, which up close was not as nice a fabric, nor as tailored a cut, as it had looked on TV. His shirt was too big around the neck. His tie a bit too harsh a shade of pink.

The cameras had given him a certain level of mystique. Now he looked exactly like who he was, a small-town reporter trying desperately to make it in the big leagues.

"You ever meet Rainie Conner in person?" Mosley asked.

"No."

"Dougie Jones?"

"Am I a suspect? Because if you're thinking of me as a suspect, then I *am* calling my lawyer."

"I'm trying to think of you as a person. Trust me, every minute it's becoming more difficult."

Danicic scowled, but looked away.

"Those are real people somewhere out there," Mosley said. "A woman and a child fighting for their lives. Have you ever been to a crime scene, Danicic? And I don't mean standing behind a string of yellow tape. I mean up close, personal, where you can see it's not some Hollywood special effects. Ever sat through an autopsy? Ever read a medical examiner's report? Do you really know what a bullet, what a knife, can do to the human body? Get up," Mosley said abruptly. "I have something to show you."

Mosley jerked Danicic to his feet. The reporter was too stunned to react. Mosley marched him to the back, sat him in the interrogation room, which was a former janitor's closet and still looked it.

Back in the front office, Mosley pilfered the first gray filing cabinet he came to. He took only cases marked closed and adjudicated. If the past two years had taught him anything, it was that you could never be too careful with the press.

He stormed into the interrogation room and started slapping the photos down onto the table. "Teenager, hanged. Woman, gutted. Man, hit by a freight train. Body, sex undeterminable, dragged from a river. Hands, covered in marijuana leaves. Eighteen-month-old boy, drowned. Still thinking of book deals, Mr. Danicic? Because there are plenty more where these came from."

Danicic picked up each photo. Studied them. Carefully placed them back down.

He looked up at Mosley. He shrugged.

"The world is filled with bad things, yada yada yada. I'm not an idiot, Lieutenant. I'm not even that different from you. Your job is to give these people justice. My job is to tell their story. Today, we have a story. You can't stop me from telling it."

"And if it puts the victims further at risk?"

"Further at risk?" Danicic snorted. "Tell me how. You people are the ones playing games. I'm at least making an attempt at salvaging a very precarious relationship. Face it, the kidnapper doesn't trust you. And if he gets too nervous, Rainie and Dougie are dead. I'm offering a viable alternative. Kidnapper calls me, everybody wins. And yeah, so maybe that means I get a book deal. As long as they're found alive, I don't think Rainie or Dougie will mind."

"You are messing with the lines of communication in a time-sensitive case. He calls you, we have to wait to get the news. We don't have time to wait. Sometimes, law enforcement is war. And in war, you need a single line of communication."

"On the other hand, every time the kidnapper contacts me, he has to surface. More times he surfaces, better chance you have at catching him."

"More manpower it takes to cover all angles," Mosley countered.

"Then it's a good thing you have so many jurisdictions involved." Danicic leaned forward. "Lorraine Conner is a former FBI profiler's wife. You want quid pro quo? You tell me, is the FBI involved? Is this now officially an FBI case? And I still want to know about the other guy I saw on the fairgrounds, the one wearing the windbreaker from the Georgia Bureau of Investigation. Seems to me, there's a lot going on here you still aren't telling the public. Think how that's gonna play when two people turn up dead."

"*When?* That doesn't sound like positive thinking."

"Current investigative efforts have done nothing to convince me otherwise." Danicic pushed back the chair, stood up. "You arresting me?"

"Not yet."

Danicic arched a brow. "That doesn't sound like positive thinking," he deadpanned. "I'm outta here."

The reporter took a step forward. Mosley grabbed his arm. The look Danicic gave him was harder than Mosley had expected. More calculating. Apparently, once enough was at stake, even a fairly inexperienced journalist learned fast.

"If we find out that you received information and didn't share it with us, that would make you a coconspirator," Mosley said softly. "Which would make you party to the crime. Which would mean you cannot profit from anything related to the crime—no book deals, no paid appearances, nothing. Think about that."

"You know," Danicic said impatiently, "not all journalists are the bad guys. Or—let me guess—you voted for Nixon."

"He's using you, Danicic. Why send a letter to the editor, why leave a ransom note on the windshield of your car? You want to be an objective reporter, then start asking yourself the hard questions. This subject is driven by his lust for celebrity. You can quote me on that. Except we can't make him infamous; only the media can. You can quote me on that, too. The more coverage you give him, the more you're rewarding his efforts. And the more you make him like it . . ."

Danicic jerked his arm free, just as the police radio crackled to life on the sergeant's desk. The trooper picked it up, but in the small space, Danicic was still standing close enough to hear.

Mosley watched the reporter's face, waiting for some kind of reaction. If the guy was an actor, then he was good.

"Ah jeez," Danicic murmured, shoulders coming down, hand raking through his short-cropped hair.

Dispatch was calling for more officers; investigators had found a grave.

39

FOR QUINCY, TIME STOPPED at precisely eleven fifty-two a.m. Wednesday morning. Up until that point, he thought he'd been doing fairly well. Poring over his notes in order to see what they might have missed. Working with Kincaid to analyze the whiteboard listing investigative tasks: They didn't have Detective Grove's official report of Rainie's last twenty-four hours. They needed to press Sheriff Atkins for a completed assessment of local offenders. Then there was still the matter of following up with Laura Carpenter, of tracking down Andrew Bensen. In the past thirty-six hours, many things had gotten started, but too few had been finished. It happened in an investigation moving in this many directions at this kind of speed.

Candi offered her assistance. Apparently, anything was better than sitting around a conference table, twiddling her thumbs. Kincaid sent her off to Laura Carpenter's house. A trained hostage negotiator shouldn't have any problem interviewing a battered wife, and that would earn them at least one check mark on the whiteboard.

Quincy agreed to take over the search for Andrew Bensen, Army's efforts be damned. With the clock still ticking, they didn't have time to wait for official reports. Quincy booted up his laptop and started working his cell phone. Calling Bensen's grandmother. Getting the name of the man's former high school classmates, drinking buddies. What were his hobbies, interests? Did he take any prescription medication? Had he come to Bakersville often? How well might he know the area? Had anyone ever heard him express any particular anger over his father's death, or any interest in contacting Lorraine Conner?

"Well, at least Lucas wasn't shacking up with some whore, raising her bastards all these years," Eleanor Bensen said with a snort, when Quincy asked what she'd thought upon hearing the news that her son Lucas had been shot.

And Andrew?

"Never told him. Boy hadn't asked about his father in fifteen years. Why start now?"

"Did he learn the news from anyone else?"

"How the hell should I know? I'll tell you one thing, though. That boy's a moody S.O.B. Thinks the world owes him something just because he grew up without parents. What does he think I am, chopped liver?"

Quincy was still mulling over that particularly cheerful conversation when Kimberly called about the note taped to the bottom of the Wal-Mart pay phone.

And once more, Quincy and Kincaid shifted gears. No need to worry about coordinating complicated ransom drops. Now it was purely a matter of X marks the spot. Deposit the hidden treasure. Worry about what the subject would do to fuck with them next.

They needed another seven thou. Kincaid ordered Shelly and Kimberly to hit the road. Quincy whipped out the yellow pages. A branch of his bank was located in Garibaldi, on Kimberly and Shelly's way north. He tried demanding money by phone. The bank manager hung up on him. Kincaid called back, rattled off enough legalese to make a lawyer proud, and secured the promise of seven thousand in cash to be handed over to a law enforcement officer in approximately eight minutes.

They were still feeling pleased with themselves, jazzed in the sort of way people who never dealt in matters of life and death would ever understand, when the other call came in.

And Quincy's world stopped. Kincaid talked, but his words had no meaning. Quincy stared at the whiteboard, but couldn't read the writing.

A local farm, owned by a suspected drug dealer. A county investigator, executing a search by poking through a pile of manure. The discovery of a woman's pale white hand.

The ME was on her way. The DA was formally requesting a primary examiner from the Portland lab. All activity at the farm had ceased. Nobody wanted to make a mistake. They had one body. Now the question was: Did they have three?

"I'll call Kimberly," Kincaid said.

"No."

"They might as well come back. Shelly was the one who arranged for the search. She's going to want to be involved in what they found."

"Not until we know for certain."

Kincaid didn't say anything.

"It might not be Rainie; we don't want to blow the drop."

Kincaid didn't say anything.

Quincy finally turned around. "You don't understand," he said quietly. "I'm the one who's supposed to die first."

Kincaid had to go. Quincy sat alone in the conference room, staring at the whiteboard and thinking, for once in his life, of nothing at all.

Wednesday, 11:56 a.m. PST

CANDI'S FIRST IMPRESSION OF the Carpenters' house was there was no way she would ever live here. Not that she'd grown up on Park Avenue, but her Grandma Rosa had prided herself on her home. Every morning she swept the front steps. Afternoons found her polishing her furniture with lemon-scented Pledge. Heaven help you if you came into her kitchen with mud on your shoes. Candi and her cousins would be handed a rag and sentenced to spend the next hour scrubbing floors on their hands and knees.

Rosa's Portland bungalow may have contained seven kids under the age of ten, but for as long as Candi could remember, that little house had glowed. Starched lace curtains on the windows. Strands of green ivy cascading from the window seat, the mantel, even curling around the cross of crucifixion. All the neighborhood kids preferred coming over to Rosa's house to play. They would drink Kool-Aid in a lemon-scented kitchen, then play in the tiny backyard, overgrown with Rosa's carefully cultivated wisteria vines.

The Carpenters' house, on the other hand. Dark, Candi thought. Too many tall trees towering over a tiny house. The giant firs blocked the sun, sucked the moisture from the grass, and left only the moss alive on the dilapidated roof. Definitely no wild cascades of purple flowers here.

Candi parked on the muddy drive. She followed an uneven brick path, picking her way carefully over the heaving stones, interspersed with giant clumps of crabgrass. The front of the house was painted mud brown, with the door to match. She knocked, waited, but no one answered.

Candi thought she heard the sound of voices, however. She cocked her ears, then realized it was the radio, coming from around back. She followed the noise.

She found Laura Carpenter standing on a cement patio that was pretty much in the same state as the brick walk, inhaling a cigarette. Minute she saw Candi, Laura dropped the Marlboro to the ground and stepped on it. The woman shifted her balance forward, as if trying to cover the motion as a random step.

Candi thought she'd seen twelve-year-olds better at disguising their habit.

She held out her hand. "Candi Rodriguez, Oregon State Police."

Laura Carpenter didn't scowl, but she didn't exactly roll out the welcome mat either. She ignored Candi's extended arm, shrugging instead.

"So what d'you want to search now?" the woman asked. She had her arms crossed over her chest. Baggy purple sweatshirt. Stringy brown hair. Hollow brown eyes. She spoke with a voice of practiced indifference.

"Actually, I was wondering if Stanley was home."

"Nope."

"Is he running some errands?"

Laura jerked her head toward the encroaching woods. "He's out there. Still looking for the boy. Stanley," she added derisively, "thinks he's Knute Rockne. Quitters never win. Winners never quit. Just because a bunch of police officers have declared the boy kidnapped doesn't mean Stanley's gonna hang up his hat. Not Stanley."

Laura's hands were trembling. Candi decided to make it easy on both of them. She made a show of patting down her jacket. "Ah shit, I must've left them in the car."

Laura looked at her.

"My cigarettes," Candi explained. "Don't suppose you happen to have one . . ."

The woman finally smiled. She wasn't fooled, just grateful. "Don't suppose I do." She whipped out the red -and-white pack. Banged one out for herself, then handed the pack to Candi. There was a book of matches by the grill. They both lit up, Laura exhaling smoothly, Candi managing not to cough. It'd been years since her last cigarette. Ah man, though, it did taste nice.

"I'm supposed to have quit," Laura volunteered finally, waving away the gathering smoke. "We were trying to have a baby. Can't smoke while you're pregnant. Can't smoke, can't drink, can't eat fish. Kind of funny when you think about it—all the rules they have now. I got a picture of my mom, seven months pregnant with me, with a beer in one hand and cigarette in the other. Then again, some days I look in the mirror and I think I'm a walking advertisement for the surgeon general."

"Take it it didn't work," Candi commented neutrally.

"Five years of in vitro," Laura said. "Gotta love the unions. Give the workers such great insurance, they'd be crazy not to burn it up."

"Five years? That's hard."

Laura didn't say anything, just pursed her lips. Candi thought of her earlier statement about her husband—quitters never win, winners never quit. Maybe that worked on the football field, but when it came to matters of the bedroom . . .

She could understand why Laura Carpenter looked so tired. Like the life had been drained out of her, and now she was just a human shell, hanging out till it all came to an end.

"Is that when you decided to adopt?"

Laura looked at Candi, eyes sharp, not fooled. "Maybe you should ask Stanley."

"It was his idea?"

"A man wants a son. That's what he told me."

"What does a woman want?"

Laura laughed; the sound hurt Candi's ears. "I can get pregnant. That was never the problem; I just can't seem to carry 'em to term. First time, you blame nature. Second time, you blame yourself. Third time, you blame God. Four, five, six times later, I think a smart woman stops blaming anyone and simply takes the hint."

"I'm sorry."

"Ever think of having children? Maybe it doesn't mix well with the career. Then again, you're young, you have plenty of time left."

"I don't know," Candi told her honestly. "I grew up the oldest of seven cousins. Some days, I think I've spent enough time changing diapers. Other days, I'm not so sure."

"Got a husband?"

"Haven't met anyone who could keep up with me yet."

Laura smiled, finished off her cigarette. "Why don't you come inside, Miss Rodriguez. Ask me what you really want to know."

She picked up her cigarette stubs, deposited them in a plastic bag she had in the back pocket of her jeans. The pack of cigarettes went up high, tucked behind the downspout of the gutter. The matches she returned to the grill.

Laura had spent some time perfecting her deceit. Inside, she whipped out the Lysol spray. Then she excused herself.

"These are my smoking clothes," she said by way of explanation before retreating to her bedroom.

Left alone, Candi wandered the small space. Nineteen seventies kitchen with dark stained cabinets and gold Formica countertop. Eat-in kitchen with round pedestal table and four solid wood chairs. An oversized TV, easily the most expensive item in the room, wedged on top of a rickety microwave stand. Surround-sound speakers were plunked in every corner. Candi wasn't sure why anyone needed surround sound in a space this tiny, but she supposed boys wanted their toys.

The walls were covered in dark wood paneling and dotted with pictures of the high school's football teams, spanning ten years. Two mounted shelves displayed the decade's bounty—various trophies in metallic shades of red and green and gold.

Candi ducked her head into one small room, discovered a bathroom. Pushed back a second door to find a tiny office. Third time was the charm: She saw a bare mattress topped by a single white sheet. So this was Dougie's room.

No pictures on the walls, but three impressive holes. No clothes in the closet, but a two-quart bucket. No toys of any kind. The room reminded Candi of a prison cell.

"Got a good enough look?" Laura asked from behind her. She had changed into another pair of jeans and a fresh baggy sweatshirt—this one dark green. She'd done something to her hair—probably splashed it with water—then wrapped it in a turban to disguise the cigarette smell. She really was pretty good, if you didn't consider the nicotine stains on her fingers or the state of her teeth.

"Where's his stuff?"

"Dougie doesn't have any stuff. It's part of the program. Kid starts with nothing, then earns things back bit by bit."

"He doesn't even get clothes?"

"He has clothes. They're in our room. I provide him with one outfit a day, my choosing. If he wants his own clothes, again, he's gotta behave."

Candi arched a brow. Laura merely shrugged.

"With a boy like Dougie, what else are you gonna do?"

"Do you like Dougie, Mrs. Carpenter?"

"Not really."

"Have you ever hit him?"

Laura's gaze remained level. "My mama whacked me most days of my life. I don't feel a need to return that favor."

"And Stanley?"

"I've never seen him raise a hand to the boy."

"What about to you?"

Laura raised a brow. "Stanley has his faults; that's not one of them."

"So what are his faults?"

"He's a man. What are all men's faults? Pigheadedness, self-centeredness. He wants what he wants, no matter what anyone else says."

"Like he wanted Dougie."

"Like he wanted Dougie."

"So you just go along with it?"

Laura cocked her head to the side. She studied Candi for a full minute. "I know what you think, Miss Rodriguez. I know what you all think when you traipse through here. Look at that poor woman, with her face like a hundred miles of bad road. Look at that ugly little house with its ugly gold carpet and cheap Wal-Mart furniture. How can she live like that? How can she keep any man happy?

"You want to know the truth? I don't always keep my man happy, but I always keep him. We're no Catherine Zeta-Jones and Michael Douglas, but we understand each other. We've known each other since we were five. And compared to the trailer park where we grew up, we are living in a fucking mansion and this is our slice of paradise. Maybe no one else wants it, but for us, our life is doing just fine."

"You're taking care of a child you don't even like," Candi said bluntly.

"I'm taking care of my responsibilities."

"He's lost."

"He ran away."

"Or is kidnapped."

Laura snorted. "Honest to God, not the devil himself could make that boy do something he didn't want to do."

"Then why are you raising him?"

"Because my husband asked me to."

"And you always do what your husband wants?"

Laura exhaled sharply. For the first time since Candi had arrived, the woman appeared angry. "You people," she said suddenly. "You keep coming here, searching, searching, searching. I've never seen so many people look so hard for something that's right in front of their faces. Come here!"

Laura marched into the family room. Candi followed in her wake. The woman jerked down a photo album, flipped it open, then stabbed at a photo with her finger.

"That help you any?"

Candi could barely believe what she was seeing. "No way."

"Yes way."

"But . . ."

"Big men don't always start out as big men." Laura gazed down at the photo. She looked like she could use a cigarette again. "He honestly loves that boy," she murmured. "Stupid son of a bitch."

40

FIFTY-EIGHT MINUTES BEFORE DEADLINE, Kimberly and Shelly screeched into the parking lot of the local credit union. Shelly dashed inside, flashed her badge, signed two forms in triplicate, then dumped seven thousand dollars in cash into a brand-new Wal-Mart duffel bag.

The manager stared at her, dumbfounded.

Shelly yelled, "Thanks" over her shoulder and bolted for the door. Abrupt about-face, grabbed two lollipops from the bowl next to the teller, then ran once more.

Back in the SUV, she jerked the vehicle into drive and pulled onto the road. Kimberly watched the rearview mirrors. One car behind them, then another, then the white surveillance van. Entourage was complete.

Shelly passed over a grape lollipop. Kimberly welcomed the sugar rush while cracking open the Tillamook County map.

"Okay, looks like we have five more miles, then we'll come to an access road on the left. Leads out to the cliff and boom, we got a lighthouse."

Kimberly folded up the map and went to work on the money.

Mac had secured the original twenty thousand, dutifully recording each serial number as provided by the bank. Of course, there hadn't been time to record the new deposit, not for the bank or for the officers. Instead, Kimberly mixed in the new twenties with the previously recorded bills. If the subject went to pull out a wad of cash, chances were at least some of the documented bills would wind up in circulation, helping them beat a path to the kidnapper's door.

For the record, twenty thousand dollars in small bills was a fairly impressive sight. Broad. Tall. Heavy. The front cab of the SUV filled with the smell of printer's ink. Kimberly ruffled the stacks with her thumb. They felt cold and silky to the touch.

"Time?" Shelly asked tersely.

"Forty-eight minutes till deadline."

Shelly grunted. "We can do it. Ten-minute drive, five-minute walk, then we're there."

"Assume another ten minutes to find the precise spot for depositing the money . . ."

"We still have twenty-three minutes to spare."

"I want to watch," Kimberly said abruptly. "You don't have to if you don't want to. Might even be better if it's only one of us. But I want to find a hidey-hole. There's gotta be someplace I can take up position."

"You don't trust him?"

"Not for a minute."

"Of course, he might be watching," Shelly mused. "He's had more time to set this up. For all we know, he's in place and if he sees you staying behind . . ."

Kimberly scowled, chewed on the inside of her cheek. "I'll think of something. There's always something."

Radio crackled to life. Dispatch came on, requesting Sheriff Atkins. With a frown, Shelly answered the call.

Neither of them was quite prepared for the news they heard next. Reports of an unidentified female body, located on Hal Jenkins's farm. Signs of blood in the man's vehicle. Immediate request for the ME's office.

Kimberly grabbed the dash. She didn't know why. To support herself as the world took an unexpected turn? To brace herself for the news she'd always feared to hear? To simply hold on to something, because this couldn't be happening? Not after how hard they had tried and all the steps they were taking. And dear God, hadn't her father had enough bad luck in his life? Couldn't he catch a break, just this once?

"We have to go back," she whispered.

"No."

"But my father . . ."

"Wouldn't want us to jump to any assumptions."

"Oh, for heaven's sakes, you're the one who arranged the search of Jenkins's property. You're the one who suspected he might be involved!"

"I'm also the one who interviewed Hal at five p.m. yesterday. Around the same time Dougie Jones went missing."

"Maybe he's working with an accomplice."

"Hal?" Shelly snorted. "He's too greedy to share."

"But if he didn't do the kidnapping . . . He just randomly killed a woman around the same time two people were already missing?"

The expression on Shelly's face grew sad. "I don't think it was random."

And then, Kimberly got it, too. "Detective Grove," she whispered.

"He already knew about the ransom. Imagine him showing up at Wal-Mart, seeing a lone female officer, duffel bag slung over her shoulder. That kind of opportunity . . ."

"Ah, Jesus." Kimberly turned toward the window. She stared at the passing miles of gray asphalt, the impenetrable mist of rain. "You know what's worse than thinking Rainie is dead?" she asked brusquely.

"What?"

"Thinking it might be a fellow officer and feeling grateful."

"Well, we're going to have plenty of time to put bad news into perspective."

"Why?"

"We just passed our access road—it's closed."

Shelly hurtled them into a U-turn, tires squealing on wet pavement. An oncoming car blared its horn. Kimberly had a glimpse of wide, panicked eyes. Then the vehicle rushed past as Shelly cranked their SUV around in the dirt. Minutes later, they were parked in front of a narrow asphalt road, barred shut by a heavy metal gate. The orange construction sign read: *Closed for Repairs, September 1– December 15.*

"Think the Parks Department could've mentioned this by phone," Shelly muttered tightly.

She slid out of the SUV and rattled the gate. The padlock held, and there wasn't enough room to go around. A hundred yards back, Mac and Deputy Mitchell pulled over in the white surveillance van, waiting to see what they would do.

"Looks like three miles," Kimberly reported, eyeing the map.

"We can't drive," Shelly declared.

"And we don't have time to walk."

Which left only one option. Kimberly slid out of the van, hefting the duffel bag around her shoulders like a backpack. She staggered briefly under the weight of twenty grand, then found her footing.

"I got the first mile," she said.

They slid around the steel gate and started to run.

Wednesday, 12:15 p.m. PST

CANDI CALLED THE COMMAND CENTER. With no one else around, Quincy answered the phone.

"You're never gonna believe this," Candi said.

"Try me."

"Stanley Carpenter is Dougie's biological father."

Quincy paused. "You win."

"I got the wife talking. According to Laura, she and Stanley have known each other since they were kids and are a genuine love match. No abuse, just the normal, run-of-the-mill marital discord. He doesn't like her smoking. She's a bit peeved to learn he cheated on her with a high school girl."

"Dougie's mother." Quincy's eyes grew wide. And all of a sudden, he could see the possibilities. "Who knew?"

"Well, Laura found out about it, obviously, though apparently not until after Dougie's mother died. According to her, Stanley brought home Dougie's picture, saying he wanted to adopt this boy, and Laura knew immediately. She showed me Stanley's second-grade photo—honest to God, Dougie could be his twin."

"Obviously Stanley's growth spurt was late in life," Quincy said drolly.

"Apparently. Naturally, Laura wasn't so thrilled to learn that her husband had impregnated someone else. According to her, however, what really had her steamed was that Stanley hadn't faced up to his responsibilities. If he'd fathered the child, then of course they would take care of him. To hear her talk, she was simply angry he hadn't told her sooner."

"How very enlightened of her."

"Not that she's a big fan of Dougie's. Frankly, she thinks the boy is trouble with a capital T. But she swears neither she nor Stanley have ever raised a hand to him. In fact, Stanley is positively guilt-stricken over everything Dougie's been through and desperate to make amends."

"What a noble guy."

"Laura believes he may have supported Dougie financially."

"Willingly or unwillingly?" Quincy murmured.

"That we may never know. But after Laura learned of Dougie's existence, she went through the checkbooks. The year Dougie was born, a lot of cash withdrawals were made. Always small amounts, so she didn't think much of it at the time. But lots of transactions. She figures Stanley's been withdrawing an extra two grand a year, without explanation."

"*Is* withdrawing two thousand a year? Dougie's mother died three years ago."

"Yeah, that's what I thought. Laura didn't have an answer. Maybe he's been paying the foster families or supplying presents on the side. You'd think Laura could just ask about it, but then again, you can't always talk to your love match."

"Dougie has been in the foster system for three years," Quincy considered out loud. "If Stanley is still paying money, then somebody has to be keeping him informed. Which means . . ."

"Someone else had to know of his interest in Dougie."

"Which presumably means that person knows Stanley is the father." Quincy sighed heavily. He could see only one explanation: "I believe Peggy Ann Boyd has been holding out on us."

"Peggy Ann Boyd?"

"Dougie's social worker. Who knew his mother, Gaby, and has taken a great deal of personal interest in his case."

There was a moment of silence. "Call me cynical," Candi said slowly.

"But what if the money wasn't for Dougie?" Quincy provided. "What if it was for Peggy Ann? I believe I'm just as cynical as you."

"Two thousand dollars would sure buy a lot of personal interest. And it's a fairly cheap price to pay for a whole town not to learn that you—the respected football coach—had gotten an underage girl pregnant."

Quincy continued that line of thinking: "The system has lasted for seven years. But now some things have changed. One, Stanley is trying to actually take care of his son, straining his marriage and no doubt his sanity. Two, Dougie has accused Stanley of abuse, inviting in an outside investigator."

"She found out," Candi said quietly. "Oh my God, Rainie figured out that Stanley is Dougie's biological father. Did she mention anything to you?"

"No, but she wouldn't. It would've violated the laws of confidentiality." Quincy's mind was already racing ahead. "But she might've spoken to Stanley. Or followed up directly with Peggy Ann."

"Now they have a liability—someone knows. And it's not just one career, it's two. Stanley's name will get dragged through the mud; Peggy Ann is guilty of corruption. They're both on the hook."

"On the other hand," Quincy said quietly, "if something happened to Rainie . . ."

"Her husband, a former FBI profiler, would no doubt tear the town apart looking for answers," Candi said bluntly. Then filled in the rest of the pieces: "So they gave you one: a stranger, kidnapping people for money. And they inverted things. Rainie isn't kidnapped because of Dougie—Dougie is kidnapped because of Rainie."

"Tying up two loose ends. The incorrigible boy who is proof of the liaison, and the court-appointed representative who made the connection." Quincy closed his eyes, not liking what he was thinking, but thinking it nonetheless. "It would fill in the blanks. Why Rainie was kidnapped. How the subject knows so much about her. The persistent attempt to mislead us by stating the kidnapper isn't local, doesn't know Rainie, just wants money. It's all part of a carefully crafted scenario, engineered to keep me—and everyone else— in the dark."

Quincy glanced at his watch. Forty minutes until one o'clock. "We need to speak to Stanley Carpenter."

"He's not at home. Laura claims he's still looking for Dougie in the woods. For the record, however, his truck's not in the driveway. I looked on my way out."

"We'll pull Stanley's records from the DMV, get an APB out on his license plate. That ought to round him up."

"Hot damn!" Candi said, and Quincy could hear the sound of her hand slapping the steering wheel. "Now we're cooking with gas. Okay, I'm coming in."

"No you're not."

"I'm not?"

"Forty minutes isn't long enough to locate a truck in all of Tillamook County. If Stanley isn't available, then we're going straight to Peggy Ann. Unless, of course, you really want to wait quietly next to the phone."

"Not in a million years."

Quincy pawed through his notes, rattled off an address.

"Ten minutes," he said. "I'll meet you there."

41

RAINIE COULDN'T FIND DOUGIE. She waded frantically into the cold, dark waters, calling his name, churning the depths with her arms. She shivered uncontrollably, shorn wet hair plastered to her skull, T-shirt glued to her body.

"Dougie! Dougie, Dougie, Dougie!"

Her leg bumped something hard. She dove down, discovered the leg of the workbench. She was moving in the wrong direction. He'd been to the left of the bottom of the stairs. At least that's what she'd thought. It was hard to get her bearings down in the endless dark.

She heard a gasp, a gurgle. Dougie burst up from the water, gasping for air.

"No, no, no!" he cried, then sank down again.

"Dammit!" She pushed off from the workbench, water now so deep it was easier to swim. She felt a hand flail against her hip. She dove down, looped her bound arms around the boy's waist, and dragged him to the surface.

"Let me go! I don't want to live! I don't want to live!" Dougie pushed against her shoulders, flailing at her head, scratching her face.

Rainie let him go. Then she drew back her hands, knotted them into a fist, and slugged Dougie across the jaw. The boy went limp. She dragged his unconscious form over to the steps.

She had to climb up seven steps to get out of the steadily growing flood. Then she collapsed next to Dougie, coughing uncontrollably, while chills raced up and down her body.

Her temples screamed with pain. She wanted to clutch her head, beat it against the wooden step. Instead, she staggered to the side of the stairs and vomited violently.

Her left leg wouldn't stop shaking. Red-hot bolts of pain ebbed and flowed. Her leg shook against the steps. She kicked Dougie twice, not meaning to, and his eyes opened.

He looked at her, realized she had dragged him from the water, and scowled.

Rainie took a deep breath. "Dougie Jones," she told him with all the force she could muster, "I have been angry at you, and I have been frustrated with you, but never, ever have I been disappointed in you! You weak, cowardly little boy, don't you ever do that again! You hear me? Never!"

Dougie remained staring at her, jaw set stubbornly. "I got out of bed," he said suddenly. "My mommy told me not to. But I got up. I undid all the locks, I opened the front door, which is a Very Bad Thing. 'Dougie,' my mommy said, 'you can't keep disappearing outside. Someone's going to get hurt.' But I did it. And she died. Now you're trying to be like my mommy and you're going to die, too."

"Oh, Dougie. You did not kill your mother."

"Yes, I did. I opened the front door. I did a Very Bad Thing. I killed her." Dougie's lower lip had started to tremble. His shoulders hunched, his chin folding into his chest, as if, by sheer force of will, he could cease to exist.

Rainie couldn't help herself; she reached out her hands. But at first contact, Dougie flinched.

"You didn't kill your mother, Dougie," she stated firmly. "She went to get milk, which is what mothers do. And you woke up and went looking for her. Sometimes that's what four-year-olds do. But what killed your mother that night was a drunk driver. He hit her shortly after she left the apartment complex, before she ever knew you had gotten out of bed. It wasn't your fault. It wasn't her fault. It was simply a tragedy. I know, sweetheart, I've read the police report."

"I left the room."

"She didn't know, honey. She was still walking to the grocery store."

"I did a Very Bad Thing."

"But that's not what hurt your mommy, sweetheart. It was a drunk driver who killed your mother. Not you, Dougie. Someone else."

A long pause. "Someone else?"

"Yes, Dougie. Someone else."

"Rainie," Dougie said quietly, "I want my mommy back." Then Dougie started to cry.

This time, Rainie curled her arms around him. She pulled his wet, trembling form onto her lap. Dougie sobbed harder, face buried into the crook of her shoulder. He cried angrily. He cried noisily. He cried himself into a series of small, pathetic hiccups that hurt more than real tears.

"Shhhh, Dougie. Shhhh, it's going to be all right. Everything's going to be all right."

But she knew she lied as soon as she said the words. For the water was already at their feet, and they had only seven more steps on the staircase to go.

Wednesday, 12:18 p.m. PST

WHEN THE WORST OF DOUGIE'S SOBBING had stopped, Rainie very carefully pulled away. Her hands were still bound; any chance of cutting the plastic ties had probably disappeared with the glass shard somewhere in the dark churning water. She didn't worry about that anymore.

"Dougie," she said firmly. "We're going to get out of here."

The boy sniffled, wiped his nose with the back of his hand, while staring at her uncertainly.

"You remember the light above the door? The one where you broke the bulb?"

"Yeah."

"We're going to put you on my shoulders again, except this time, you're going to tear down the grille surrounding the light."

"It's metal."

"Yes, but you're strong and you can do this. Then we're going to take that grille and use it to break the basement windows."

"They're too high."

"Not anymore, Dougie. We can swim right over."

The boy turned, seeming to notice for the first time the steady advance of water, now licking at their toes. "It must take a long time to drown," he said with a frown. "Water is more complicated than fire."

"Trust me, honey, if we do things my way, we're never going to have to find out."

Rainie had him climb on her shoulders. It was just as awkward as last time, but in the good-news department, if she dropped him, he'd simply splash into the growing lake. And with both hands free, the boy could get a good grip on the grille.

Unfortunately, the metal refused to budge.

Dougie tried wrenching it three or four times. Then Rainie's leg spasmed and they both went into the water. Dougie emerged gasping and shaking his head. Beside him, Rainie grabbed the railing to keep herself afloat while her hips jerked spasmodically. She felt like a wooden doll being controlled by a very bad puppeteer.

And then, out of nowhere, she thought of Quincy. She wondered what he was doing right now. She wondered what he was feeling. She wondered if she would ever see him again.

Dying wasn't the ultimate cruelty; she understood that now. It was all the unfinished business a person's death left behind. A mother died, and her son spent the rest of his life thinking it was his fault. A wife died, and her husband spent the end of his days never knowing how much she loved him, that she was sorry that her weakness hurt herself, but even sorrier for how much it hurt him.

Dying made a person realize how much she had squandered her life. Unfortunately, that knowledge was too little too late.

Rainie crawled her way back up the stairs. The water had advanced another three inches. They had six stairs left. Dougie sat at the very top, regarding her with solemn eyes.

"Rainie, I'm scared."

And she lost it for a moment. She rushed the stairs, threw herself madly against the top door. The solid wood frame sent her reeling back down into the water, which felt warm and comforting given her sodden state. She tried one more time, really got her shoulder into it. She thought she heard something crack as she connected. Not the door, however, but her ribs.

She careened back into the water, gritting her teeth so that she wouldn't scare Dougie by howling with rage. She didn't want to die like this. Trapped like an animal in a pitch-black cellar, waiting for the water to close over her head. She wanted to run, wanted to fight. Wanted to lash out at the world because that's what she did best.

It wasn't fair, it wasn't fair, it wasn't fair. Goddammit, it just wasn't fair!

She ducked beneath the water. Swam to the right, swam to the left. Her bound hands moved in front of her, searching hopelessly for some mythical weapon that would magically appear.

But as always, the basement remained empty. The man had planned ahead.

She surfaced under the windows, the water high enough now so that she could reach them easily while treading water with her legs. She examined the thick glass, the metal edges around the high, narrow frames. The calking was old, peeling. Ironically enough, when the water got high enough, the windows would leak. Not enough to help them, of course.

She started to go to work on the edges, simply to have something to do. She heard a splash. Dougie swam over to join her.

"Do you have anything in your pockets, Dougie?"

"N-n-no," the boy said through chattering teeth.

She patted briefly at her own, though she knew nothing was there. Her legs were starting to tire. She could feel the cold now, too. Her movements were growing more sluggish, a longer lag time occurring between her brain thinking and her muscles responding.

She returned to the staircase. Crawled up to the top step. Collapsed, coughing, her head against the door. Dougie climbed up beside her. He curled up against her back and the weight of his trust goaded her back into action.

So the metal grille was out. Breaking the windows was out. Smashing down the door was out. What did that leave them with?

Dougie wore jeans, sneakers, and a sweatshirt. She had on nearly the same—jeans, T-shirt, sneakers, bra, and panties. Was there something they could do with shoelaces? What about the underwire from her bra? Finally she had a thought:

"Dougie, are you wearing a belt?"

The boy lifted up his sweatshirt, looked down. "Yep."

"All right, buddy. We got one chance left at this."

Wednesday, 12:23 p.m. PST

KINCAID HAD TO PARK a quarter mile down the road from Hal Jenkins's farm. The line of vehicles was so long—county investigators, crime scene technicians, the ME's office, the sheriff's department—he was amazed he'd gotten that close.

Word had already leaked out. A young officer, probably from the county, was directing traffic as news vans descended like locusts, cutting one another off and blocking law enforcement vehicles while they fought for the best view. Kincaid had to bleep his sirens numerous times, then finally went with the old-fashioned approach of leaning on the horn. He was tempted to throw the finger, but didn't want to have that particular clip airing at eleven.

Finally parked, he trudged up the narrow road, passing a double-wide that had seen better days. A tall, gangly boy stood out in the yard, chain-smoking as he looked toward the activity. His gaze flickered toward Kincaid as the detective walked past. Neither of them said a word.

A light mist still blanketed the county. The wet road unrolled before Kincaid like a shiny black ribbon, disappearing behind soaring fir trees. He couldn't see the mountains on the horizon. Instead, the world had become a small gray space, where headlights seemed to appear out of nowhere, only to disappear back into the gloom.

Kincaid missed his wife. He missed his boy. Hell, he missed his dog.

And he was very sorry for what he was probably going to have to do next.

Arriving at Jenkins's farm, he checked in with the officer standing outside the crime scene tape, formally adding his name to the murder log. Looking over the officer's shoulder, he could see the list of investigators was long and only going to grow longer.

"Any news yet?" he asked the man.

The deputy just shrugged. "I've been standing here for the past twenty minutes. Haven't heard a thing."

Kincaid thanked him, then ducked beneath the tape.

Once on the grounds, the level of activity was astonishing. He saw three technicians meticulously piecing their way through a pile of rubbish, checking each discarded refrigerator and rusted-out stove. Four more investigators worked a trail of auto parts, cast-off engines, and metal shells of abandoned cars. Officers were crawling inside the home, outside the home, swarming the various outbuildings. It would take days to work a scene this involved. It would take months to have any definitive answers.

The DA appeared from around the back of the house. He spotted Kincaid and came over.

"Hoped it would end better," Tom Perkins said by way of greeting. They shook hands.

"You have an ID?"

"Still working. ME just arrived, so we're getting serious now. Come on. I'll give you the grand tour."

Kincaid followed Perkins around the house, past a fenced-in corral that was a sea of muck, into a fair-sized barn with a rusted metal roof that appeared to be sliding to the right. In its heyday, the barn had probably served as milking parlor for twenty or thirty head. Jenkins, however, had obviously never kept it up. Grain bins held nothing but mold. Milking equipment dangled uselessly, emitting a sour, fermented smell. Kincaid already had a handkerchief over his nose, and that was before he ever made it to the back.

There, six people, three of them in hazmat gear, were kneeling around a ten-foot-high pile of hay and cow shit. The smell nearly knocked Kincaid back a step. Not decay, but manure.

"Body was found in a pile of waste," the DA reported. "Not a bad strategy. Would've thrown off the heat sensors, and probably the search dogs. He didn't get it quite covered enough, though. One of the initial officers noticed something white, and on closer investigation, realized it was a hand."

"Any idea of how long?"

"We don't know anything, other than the fingers clearly appear female."

"Rings?" Kincaid asked sharply.

"Not that we've seen."

They made it to the clustered group. Very carefully, one technician was working manure off the pile, depositing small shovelfuls onto a blue tarp. A second person dusted each body part as it emerged. They were being meticulous, preserving as much evidence as possible.

It took fifteen minutes to find a face.

Even knowing what was coming, it hit Kincaid harder than he thought it would.

"Alane Grove," he whispered. "OSP."

The DA looked at him sharply. "You're sure?"

"She's my detective! Of course I'm sure."

Perkins didn't comment on his tone. Instead, the man merely sighed and rubbed his face. "All right," he said at last.

"Any more graves?" Kincaid needed to know.

"Not yet, but give us time. Jenkins owns twenty acres."

"Ahh shit." Kincaid's turn to sigh, rub his forehead. "I gotta make some calls. You'll tell me the moment you know more?"

"We'd never dream of doing it otherwise."

Kincaid left the barn, trying to find one patch of quiet in the middle of all the craziness, then flipping open his cell phone. He started with headquarters, notifying his lieutenant. Then he paged Lieutenant Mosley, who would need to prepare a statement. Then he called the task force center, one call, at least, where he was providing less than bad news.

Quincy, however, was no longer there.

42

KIMBERLY FELT LIKE A LUMBERING RHINO. Running down the closed access road, she hit a pothole, stumbled left, and felt the weight of twenty thousand dollars twist her body dangerously to one side. She righted herself, made it another hundred yards, then slid on the wet pavement and got to do some fancy footwork to keep herself from going splat. Finally, she spotted the dark tower rising out of the gloom. She plunged into the woods and dropped behind a boulder next to Shelly, who'd run ahead to do reconnaissance.

"I ... gotta ... work out ... more," Kimberly gasped.

Shelly looked at the FBI agent's red, sweat-soaked face, then the duffel bag. "Or switch to a credit card."

"Very ... funny."

Shelly gestured forward and Kimberly peered over the boulder to check out their target through the thick coastal mist.

The lighthouse teetered dangerously close to the edge of a rocky cliff, seeming to rise out of a sea of fog. It was a relatively simple structure: white-painted windowless base, forming an octagon that rose up nearly twenty feet to a metal-and-glass-enclosed tower that housed the fifteen-foot-high lens. True to the Parks Department report, however, the whole structure had seen better days. The paint was cracking and peeling on the lower level, while the glass panes appeared shattered in the upper tower. Upon closer study, Kimberly realized the entire structure tilted suspiciously to the left.

"Wood rot," Shelly murmured. "Whole structure is riddled with it. Hence they shut it down."

"Wonderful. A scenic little death trap. Who said kidnappers didn't have a sense of humor?" Kimberly slipped her cell phone out of her pocket, hit Send. "Hear us?" she whispered into the speaker.

"Loud and clear," Mac replied.

"We're at the lighthouse. No sign of activity. You?"

"Got the GPS on screen. Staring patiently, or not so patiently, as the case may be."

"Well, good news is, we only have ten minutes left, so something has to happen soon."

Kimberly returned the phone to her pocket, leaving it on speakerphone so Mac could hear what was happening. She looked at Shelly, who was now studying the UNSUB's map. "Looks like we place the money inside the lighthouse by the bottom of the stairs. I think. Guy really isn't gonna win too many art contests." Shelly turned the map this way and that, then lowered it with a sigh. She returned to staring pensively at the tilted structure. "Seems like he's gotta be watching. If someone was bringing you twenty thousand dollars, wouldn't you be watching?"

"I would. Do you suppose Rainie and Dougie might be in the area?"

Shelly considered it, then shook her head. "Would be risky. They might call out, even escape. Two people are hard to control."

"So we pay the money, he retrieves it, and then what? We get a call?"

"Sounds like a newspaper reporter gets a call," Shelly said drolly. "Or maybe there will be another letter to the editor. With a map."

"Which, for all we know, will lead us straight to their bodies," Kimberly muttered bitterly. "I don't like this. We're following all his orders, with no game plan of our own. It's bad policing."

"Got a better idea?"

"No."

"Well then . . ." Shelly gestured toward the lighthouse.

Kimberly scowled, glanced at her watch, and hefted the duffel bag over her shoulder. But then, at the last minute, she did have an idea.

She threw down the bag, unzipped it, and stuck her GPS monitor into a stack of bills.

"You sure?" Shelly asked sharply, the hidden dangers implicit in her question. Such as the minute Kimberly stepped into the lighthouse, she was vulnerable to abduction herself. Such as without the GPS on her person, they would have no means of finding her. Such as they still had no idea what the kidnapper's true agenda was, therefore hurting another law enforcement officer might be just his thing.

"I want to get him," Kimberly said firmly.

"Then I got you covered," Shelly said solemnly. The sheriff unsnapped her holster. Removed her gun.

Five minutes to one, Kimberly rounded the boulder. She looked left, looked right.

"Here goes nothing," she murmured to no one in particular.

She entered the lighthouse.

Wednesday, 12:52 p.m. PST

"WE KNOW ABOUT THE MONEY," Quincy said.

Peggy Ann Boyd sat on the edge of the bed in her tiny studio apartment, looking at him with a frown on her face. Candi had taken up position next to the door, arms crossed over her chest to make her six-foot frame appear even more imposing.

"I don't know about any money," Peggy Ann said. "Do you have any word on Dougie?"

"When did you figure out that Stanley was Dougie's biological father, that's what I would like to know," Quincy continued. "Did Dougie's mother tell you? Woman confiding to woman? Or did Stanley tell you himself, once he heard that Gaby Jones was dead?"

Peggy Ann's eyes went wide. "I don't know what you're talking about," she said primly. But the young social worker was a terrible liar. Already her gaze was locked upon the carpet, her fingers fidgeting on her lap.

Quincy knelt down until he was eye level with the woman. He regarded her for so long, she had no choice but to meet his stare.

"Once upon a time, you must have cared for Dougie. He was only four years old when his mother died. Such a young, defenseless boy. He needed someone to look out for him, someone to find him a home. He needed you, Peggy Ann. And Gaby needed you. Someone to save her boy."

Very quietly, Peggy Ann started to cry.

"When did you figure out Stanley was Dougie's father?" Quincy repeated firmly.

"I didn't. Not at first. Gaby had implied it was someone at the high school. But I had always assumed a teenage boy. You know, the high school quarterback who knocks up the cheerleader but doesn't want to make good. It wasn't until Stanley attended the funeral, the way he looked at Dougie . . . as if he were a dying man and Dougie represented his last hope to live. I started to wonder. But Stanley never said anything, and I certainly had no evidence. Plus, then the Donaldsons came along and they were such great candidates it seemed best to give the boy to them. I was sure Dougie would have a good home."

"Until he burned it down."

"Until he burned it down. I approached Stanley then. I asked him point-blank if he knew anything about Dougie's father. I even bluffed, said I knew for certain it was someone from the football team. He said he didn't know, but that Gaby used to hang out at the practices so maybe it was true. He couldn't help me though. He didn't know anything more than that. Then he slammed the door in my face.

"So I found Dougie another home, what else could I do? And then I found a home after that. Except now I started visiting the high school, watching the practices. Trying to learn about past players, looking at pictures of boys on the team. Trying to see anybody who might look like Dougie, because it was becoming clear to me that I had to find the boy's father."

Quincy was frowning. This was not quite how he'd expected the story to go. "Then what happened?"

"One evening, I found Coach Carpenter—Stanley—in his office.

I told him Dougie had gotten into trouble again. I told him the boy would most likely be sent to a detention home now. I told him Dougie didn't have any hope left. And I begged him. I begged him for information about Dougie's father and I told him how much Gaby loved that boy and how happy he'd once been. . . . And I started to cry. Blubber like a lunatic. Because I wasn't bluffing, Mr. Quincy." Peggy Ann looked at him earnestly. "Dougie had a documented history of arson. In the world of child services, he was done. Washed up at the age of six. By the next week, he'd be shipped out to a boys' home, where older, more experienced delinquents could teach him new tricks. In between the beatings, of course. And sexual abuse. I've been to those homes. I know what goes on there."

"Stanley caved?"

"Stanley told me he was the boy's father. Just like that. And then he said, very gravely, that he'd been a coward long enough. Dougie was his."

"Say what?" Candi quizzed from the doorway. She'd unfolded her arms. She was looking back and forth between Peggy Ann and Quincy, as if waiting for one of them to say something that made sense. Quincy couldn't blame her. He was waiting for it all to make sense as well.

"I didn't believe Stanley at first," Peggy Ann offered. "I thought he was just trying to do a nice thing. Or maybe get a hysterical female out of his office. I wrung some half-assed promise from him to take Dougie. By the next morning, however, I'd already figured that was it, he'd forget the whole thing. Instead, he showed up at my office bearing a family album. He presented an old grade-school photo, and by God, he was the spitting image of Dougie, no doubt about it. I . . . I never would have guessed."

"So that's when he offered you the money to keep quiet," Quincy tried.

Peggy Ann frowned at him. "What money? He offered to take Dougie. That's what I cared about. He and Laura gave the boy a home."

Candi and Quincy exchanged glances again. "Stanley Carpenter got an underage girl pregnant, and you left it at that?" Quincy pressed.

Peggy Ann shrugged miserably. "Gaby was dead, so it's not like she could press charges. And Stanley was trying to do right by his son. What else could I ask for?"

"Oh, for heaven's sake," declared Candi. "Aren't there procedures you have to follow? Tell me you don't let statutory rapists get by with a shrug and a handshake."

"Of course there are procedures. And normally, I would contact the police. But again, Gaby's dead. And frankly, I'm not trying to save Gaby, I'm trying to save Dougie. I contact the police, and the father I've spent three years trying to find becomes immediately off-limits. Or I say nothing about Gaby's age, and instead just declare that Stanley is Dougie's biological father. In which case, he takes a paternity test, fills out about approximately ten million forms, and waits about another three years for everything to grind through the legal system. Or there's option C. I say nothing at all, about anything, Stanley applies to become a foster father, and Dougie gets placed immediately. Which, frankly, does both Dougie and Stanley a lot more good."

"Which I'm sure Stanley encouraged," Quincy murmured, "as it let him off the hook for everything."

"I wouldn't say his wife let him off the hook," Peggy Ann said drolly. "Laura's a lot tougher than she looks. But sure, I don't think Stanley wanted to air all of his dirty laundry for the community. Frankly, I didn't care. Child services is a system, Mr. Quincy. It's a human system and that's what I tried to navigate."

"Miss Boyd," Quincy said, "Stanley has been paying out two thousand dollars a year since Dougie was born. If he wasn't paying that money to you, then who was receiving the funds?"

"I have no idea."

"He never offered you money in return for silence?"

"I didn't want money! I wanted a home for Dougie, and Stanley stepped up to the plate."

"What about Dougie's allegations of abuse?" Candi asked with a frown.

"I brought in a child advocate immediately. But I have to tell you the truth: I don't think Stanley would hurt Dougie. You had to see his face when he told Dougie he was taking him home. Stanley was weeping. His hands were shaking. He was that moved at finally having his son. Now, Dougie on the other hand . . ."

"Not so excited?"

"I swear to God, he was already searching for matches. Stanley didn't tell Dougie that he was his biological father, for the record—he thought that might be too much. He wanted them to get to know each other first. And I understand that his tough-love approach looks harsh, but he consulted experts for the best way to deal with a boy as angry and troubled as Dougie. From everything I've seen, Stanley is a committed father. Slow to find that commitment, granted, but really, truly there. He wants this to work. His wife can't have children, you know. Dougie is the only son he's ever going to get."

"I have a headache," Quincy said.

Peggy Ann regarded him curiously. "Do you want some aspirin?"

"No, what I want is to know how many people knew Stanley was Dougie's father."

"I know. Rainie knows—"

"She found out?" Quincy asked abruptly.

"She came to me with the news about a month ago. I think she'd been suspecting it for a while. She wondered if I knew. I said yes. She let it go at that."

"Did Stanley know that she knew?"

"I have no idea. You'd have to ask him."

Quincy arched a brow. He'd love to ask Stanley. Unfortunately, the man still hadn't been located, and it was now two minutes before one p.m.

He leaned down again, tone urgent. "Did Rainie say anything else? About the abuse, Dougie, Laura, anything?"

Peggy Ann seemed bewildered. "No. But she played things pretty close to her chest. Though . . . well, of course, there was one other person who knew."

"Tell me!"

"Dougie. Maybe Stanley said something to him or maybe he figured it out on his own. But I think he realized that Stanley was his father, and that by definition, Stanley had abandoned his mother. In my personal opinion," Peggy Ann said carefully, "that's why Dougie came up with the allegations of abuse. Dougie hates Stanley's guts. He'd do anything to hurt him, including put him in jail."

"Or befriend the wrong person," Quincy filled in with a frown. He backed away from Peggy Ann, pinching the bridge of his nose. He could feel the bits of information churning around in his mind, fragmented pieces of one whole. Stanley Carpenter fathered a child out of wedlock. He had kept the secret for seven years, but just as others started to figure it out—his wife, Peggy Ann Boyd, Rainie, Dougie himself—two of those people disappeared. Dougie, because the boy was too much trouble? Rainie, because she was a court-appointed child advocate who was legally bound to tell the truth?

But what about Laura, what about Peggy Ann? It didn't feel quite right. He couldn't believe Rainie's and Dougie's kidnappings weren't related to Stanley Carpenter, and yet the puzzle still refused to come into focus. He was missing something.

The two thousand dollars. If Peggy Ann wasn't blackmailing Stanley, then who was?

"Does Stanley have a 'special place'?" Quincy asked at last. "I don't know, maybe a hunting cabin, or a spot in the woods he likes to go when he needs to think?"

"Why would I know a thing like that?" Peggy Ann said primly.

"Well, Miss Boyd, so far you seem to know more about Stanley than anyone else."

The social worker flushed. Her gaze fell again, her hands fidgeted.

"I don't need to know if you're sleeping with him, Miss Boyd—"

"I would never!"

"I just need to know where he is."

"He has a fishing cabin," she said at last. "In Garibaldi. It's hard to describe. Maybe I could draw a map."

"Yes," Quincy said slowly, "by all means, let's use a map."

Wednesday, 12:59 p.m. PST

QUINCY AND CANDI WERE out the door, climbing into Quincy's car, when Quincy's cell phone rang.

"Where the hell are you?" asked Kincaid.

"Hunting down Stanley Carpenter. You?"

"At Jenkins's place, identifying Alane Grove."

Quincy paused, caught himself, then put his key in the ignition. "I'm sorry," he said quietly.

"Not half as sorry as her parents will be. Why the hell aren't you at the command center?"

"Candi discovered a new lead: Stanley Carpenter is Dougie's biological father. We came to talk to Peggy Ann Boyd." Quincy rattled off a quick summary of events, including a request to issue an APB for Stanley Carpenter. Then he glanced at his watch: 1:02 p.m. Damn.

"I gotta go. Don't want to miss a call from Kimberly."

"Quincy—"

But Quincy had already flipped shut his phone and was putting his car into gear.

"Just out of curiosity," Candi asked, "why are we still pursuing Stanley Carpenter if he wasn't paying off Peggy Ann Boyd? Seems to eliminate his motive."

"One, because he was still paying two grand a year to someone. Two, because by all accounts, he wanted to keep his parenthood secret. And three, because it's the only lead we have."

"That works for me," Candi declared. "Let's go fishing."

They hit the road.

Wednesday, 1:00 p.m. PST

RAINIE'S HANDS WERE SHAKING. She was trying to wield Dougie's belt as a lock pick, the metal tongue wedged between two fingers as she worked the doorknob again.

The belt slipped, gouging the wood door and twisting her elbow. She dropped the leather, swore savagely, and fished around in the depths.

The water, past her knees, reached for her waist.

Rainie shook Dougie's arm one last time.

"Dougie," she said quietly, "get ready to take a deep breath."

43

KIMBERLY HAD WATCHED TOO MANY horror movies. She was keenly aware of the preternatural silence lingering inside the abandoned lighthouse. The way the floor felt soft, almost mushy beneath her feet, while the shadows reached dark tendrils into every corner, sending shivers up her spine.

The front door had swollen with age and moisture. She'd had to put her shoulder into it, until it gave with an unnatural shriek. Once inside the gloom, she hardly felt better about things. The low ceiling seemed to press against the top of her head. With no windows on the lower level, the only light filtered down the outer wall from the staircase twisting up to the glass tower. Kimberly found herself holding her breath, listening for footsteps sneaking down those stairs, or maybe for a dark, hulking figure to materialize out of a shadowed corner.

Shelly was outside watching. Mac was listening over her cell phone. She was not alone. She was not alone.

She had her gun out, pressed against her right thigh. She carried the money over her left shoulder.

The wind gusted through. She heard the moaning creak of the

lighthouse twisting, the tinkle of broken glass falling somewhere upstairs. She came to a halt, ears strained.

Another gusting wind. The door blew shut behind her, the slamming echo making her nearly jump out of her skin.

Kimberly put down the duffel bag. She forced her hand to stop shaking long enough for her to study the crude map. Shelly had been right. The X seemed to be toward the left by the bottom of the stairs.

Then she saw the box.

It was small, wooden. Not to be coy about things, the UNSUB had painted a giant red X on its lid. She gingerly peered in but it was too dark to see the bottom.

She paused one last time, looking around the small, gloomy space. Maybe there were cameras mounted in the corners? Or a man waiting upstairs?

She felt something brush her shoulder. Jumped. Nearly screamed. Just the edge of the rising staircase, which she had drifted back into. She was spooking herself out, no better than a kid getting all goosebumped at the local horror show. Enough was enough.

She returned to the box. Opened the lid. Crossed herself, because imminent danger brought out the religion in anyone. Then tossed the bag in.

Pop. Crack. Blinding flash.

Kimberly flung her arms in front of her face, stumbling back reflexively.

"What the hell . . ."

She felt it before she saw it. The lighthouse had started to burn.

Wednesday, 1:05 p.m. PST

MAC HEARD IT OVER THE CELL PHONE. Sounded like a small explosion, then the telltale crackle of wood.

"Kimberly? What's happening? Are you okay?"

But before he could get a reply, Deputy Mitchell was pointing excitedly at the screen. "We got movement. Due west."

"She can't be going west," Mac countered with a frown. "We're on the edge of a cliff. Due west—"

"Is an ocean. She's in a boat!" Mitchell declared.

Mac was back on his cell phone. "Kimberly—"

"I'm here, I'm here," she suddenly came over the airwaves, then paused in a fit of coughing. "I'm in the lighthouse."

"But the monitor—"

"Shows you the money."

"Kimberly, what did you do?"

"I don't know," she answered in a small voice. "But, Mac, I have a problem. He must have rigged the drop box, because when I deposited the money, it set off a small explosion. Now the lighthouse is on fire. Mac . . . I can't get out."

"I'm coming," Mac said.

"You can't. The road's blocked off."

"Then I'll run."

He was three miles away. They both knew that.

Kimberly was coughing again. "Mac," she said quietly over the phone, "I love you."

Wednesday, 1:05 p.m. PST

SHELLY HEARD A STRANGE POP, followed immediately by a small explosion. She had a moment's bewilderment, followed by the immediate thought to look for a man fleeing from the lighthouse. But she didn't see a person emerge. Instead, flames shot out of the top of the lighthouse.

"Holy crap!" Shelly was on her feet, running for the decaying structure. The radio was crackling on her belt. She heard Mac calling for Kimberly. Kimberly saying she was trapped.

Shelly arrived at the door and threw herself against it. For fifty years she'd lived with the shoulders of a plow horse. By God, it was about time they did her some good. But nothing happened. She threw herself against the swollen wood again and again.

She could feel the door growing hot beneath her touch. She heard a sinister creaking as the fire found fresh air in the top of the structure and raced greedily up the walls. And then she heard coughing, lots and lots of coughing as Kimberly stumbled through the flames.

With no windows on the lower level, and the fire already consuming the top . . .

Shelly stripped off her outer shirt and wrapped it around her face. Then she stepped back and kicked the door as hard as she could. This time, she felt it give. One more kick, and the warped door gave with a shriek.

And the fire responded with a giant *whoosh!*

Shelly staggered back from the ball of heat. She felt the hair on her arms singe. Her eyebrows burn. Then the first wild tendrils of flame recoiled, the fire inhaling like a living beast.

The lighthouse twisted beneath the pressure. Old wood starting to buckle.

Shelly did the only thing she knew how to do.

She ran into the flames.

Wednesday, 1:07 p.m. PST

KINCAID'S CELL PHONE WAS GOING INSANE. He had a frantic call from Deputy Mitchell. The ransom drop had gone bad. Lighthouse on fire. FBI Agent Quincy was trapped inside. He had a triumphant call from Trooper Blaney. License plate matching Stanley Carpenter's had just been found outside the Bakersville Bowling Alley. What should Blaney do?

And he finally had Lieutenant Mosley on the phone, apologizing for his absence—he'd had to "take care of some things."

Kincaid didn't know what those things were, and at the moment, he didn't care. He was too busy being pissed off.

He needed fire-and-rescue. He needed backup. He needed Lieutenant Mosley to get in front of the press *right now,* and he needed to hunt down Quincy once again and notify the man that his daughter was in mortal danger. Oh yes, and he still needed to catch a kidnapper.

One-oh-seven p.m., Kincaid was watching his case disintegrate in front of his eyes. And he was too far away to do a damn thing about it.

He finally retreated to his car outside the Jenkins farm, turned on his scanner, and listened to various reports as Kimberly Quincy fought for her life.

Wednesday, 1:08 p.m. PST

LIEUTENANT MOSLEY WAS ON THE RUN. He had twelve million things to do and approximately ten minutes to get it all done. He didn't bother trying to round up the press; instead he went straight to them.

He found most major networks positioned outside the Hal Jenkins property, having abandoned Danicic's house in favor of a crime scene.

He took up position outside the yellow crime scene tape, always a favorite visual, and hoped no one would notice his sweaty face and labored breath. He held up the hastily prepared statement and began:

"It is with great sadness that the Oregon State Police confirms the loss of one of its own. The body of Detective Alane Grove, a four-year veteran of the force, was discovered this morning on a farm in Tillamook County. We believe she was killed serving above and beyond the call of duty. The owner of the farm has been taken into custody, and we anticipate will soon be charged in this case."

There was a flash of camera bulbs. Several reporters thrust their microphones into the air.

"Can you tell us how she was killed?"

"The investigation is ongoing."

"Was she part of the task force working on the recent ransom case?"

"Detective Grove was working on behalf of the task force."

"So her death is related?"

"Naturally, we are pursuing that possibility."

"What about Rainie Conner and Dougie Jones? Any word?"

"Not at this time."

"But if you have a suspect in custody . . ."

"The investigation is ongoing," Mosley repeated. The gathered reporters groaned.

"Come on," one of the newsmen said up front. "It's after one o'clock. You got a guy in jail. Surely you know something about the woman and boy."

Mosley looked the man in the eye. "I have no comment at this time."

And then, when there was another collective groan, he shrugged. "What do you want me to tell you guys? We have one detective who is confirmed dead. As for the fate of Lorraine Conner and Douglas Jones . . . Pray. That's all I can say. Everyone out there, pray for them."

44

THE WATER HAD SWALLOWED her hands when Rainie suddenly felt the lock give. She twisted the handle and the door burst open, water spilling into the laundry room and taking her with it.

For a moment, she was beached against the far wall, too stunned to react. Then she scrambled to her feet, ducking back into the basement stairwell. Dougie remained curled around the stair's hand railing. She grabbed him awkwardly with her bound hands. The boy was unconscious. His head lolled against her shoulder, lips blue, eyelids fluttering alarmingly against his icy cheeks. She carried him against her chest like an oversized baby, staggering drunkenly as her own limbs shook with cold and fatigue.

The laundry room was dark, shades drawn, lights off. The door connecting to the kitchen was closed. She had no idea if the man already stood right behind it or was maybe running down the hall, alerted by the noise.

She propped Dougie on top of the washing machine, then tried the third door, shaking it savagely, playing with the lock. Just like last time, it refused to budge. She banged her fists against it, weeping in frustration now. So close, so close. *Get me out of this house!*

She ended up backed into a corner, waiting for the inevitable. The man to come crashing in. To lash out at her with his hands, his feet, maybe the Taser. She was cold and exhausted and frightened. Her left leg didn't want to bear her weight. She thought maybe she was losing Dougie.

She cried harder, the feel of her warm tears against her cheeks suddenly pissing her off. They were out of the basement, dammit. By God, she wasn't going to act like a trapped animal now. She'd had enough.

Rainie hefted Dougie back into her arms and stormed for the connecting door. She kicked it open with her right foot, powered by sheer adrenaline into the kitchen. The space was empty, the house dark. She paused for one second, heard nothing, then came to her senses and rattled through a drawer in search of a weapon. She found a paring knife. It would do.

Water was still pouring in, whirling around her feet, making the linoleum slippery. She abandoned the kitchen, whisking down the carpeted hallway, always aware of her back.

She ducked inside the first door she found. A bedroom. Quickly, she dropped Dougie on the bed. Paused. Listened. No sound of footsteps. Moving fast, she positioned the knife between her thick, frozen fingers and went to work on the binding around her wrists. In the bad-news department, her flesh had swollen around the zip tie. In the good-news department, she could barely feel anything anyway. She hacked through the tough strap and some of her own skin. The minute the band ripped free, she didn't care anymore. She could wiggle her fingers. She could rub her numb hands against her thighs. A thousand angry nerve endings screamed to life. She welcomed each and every one of them. Pain is life. Life is good!

Now she had work to do. First, Dougie.

She yanked the boy's unconscious form into a sitting position, jerked his sodden clothes off his body, and rolled him into the thick comforter like a giant burrito.

"Come on, Dougie," she whispered, briskly rubbing his arms, his legs, his damp hair. "Stay with me."

Her own teeth were chattering, her body still hemorrhaging precious heat. She left Dougie long enough to rifle the nearby bureau, then the closet. She found an old flannel man's shirt that smelled like a locker room. Too cold to care, she slid off her soaked T-shirt and drew the flannel around her body. It felt like a warm cup of cocoa, a nap in front of a blazing fire. It was the best shirt she'd ever worn and she found herself weeping again, a mess of emotions and fatigue and fear.

She returned to the bed, rubbing Dougie's form again and again, desperate to get some heat into him. Just as his eyelids fluttered open, the water started snaking into the bedroom.

She looked at the growing deluge. She studied Dougie's pale, dazed face.

She would have to carry him. Heft him over her shoulder and run for it.

It sounded good, but the minute she tried to lift him up, her left leg buckled again. As heat reentered her body, so did searing pain. Her busted knee, her bruised ribs, her endless collection of scrapes, cuts, and contusions. She dropped Dougie back onto the mattress and fell beside him.

And that quickly, she was exhausted beyond belief. She couldn't lift her arms. She couldn't move her legs. She just wanted to sleep. To curl into a tight little ball, close her eyes, and feel the world slip away.

Just for a minute.

She forced her eyes back open. Felt herself once more start to cry. And through the delirium of pain and fear and exhaustion, she willed herself to do just one last thing: *think, Rainie, think.*

And then, she saw the phone.

Wednesday, 1:13 p.m. PST

SHELLY WAS ON FIRE. In an abstract sort of way, she understood. That the stench of burnt meat and seared hair was her own. That the white-hot pain she'd always read about was genuinely true. That the air could be so hot, it literally boiled the water inside her mouth, evaporated the moisture from her lungs.

First time she inhaled, she would bring the fire inside her body and it would kill her.

So she held her breath as she dove through the flames licking up the twisting exterior. As she bent down and grabbed Kimberly's fallen form. As she draped the smaller woman's body around her broad shoulders. As she headed once more for the door.

Shelly thought of her dreams of a Parisian adventure. Oh, if that Left Bank artist could see her now, as she strode through the fire, hair curling, skin blistering, comrade on her shoulders.

I am woman, hear me roar.

Pity, she thought, as she stumbled through the doorway, collapsed onto the wet ground, and started to lose consciousness.

Because no one was ever going to want to paint her now.

Wednesday, 1:17 p.m. PST

QUINCY AND CANDI WERE JUST PULLING onto the dirt road leading to Stanley Carpenter's fishing cabin when Quincy's cell phone rang. It was Abe Sanders from Astoria. He'd sent two men to watch their double-murder suspect, Duncan, as promised. He wanted Quincy to be the first to know that they'd lost him.

"Lost him?" Quincy echoed. "How the hell do you lose someone as slow as Charlie Duncan?"

"Well now, Quincy—"

"Abe, it's fifteen minutes past the deadline for learning that my wife is still alive. Talk faster."

Sanders cut to the chase: Duncan went to a local diner for breakfast. Not a big deal, he did that most days as the man couldn't cook. He walked in the diner. Never walked out. When the detectives finally entered the establishment two hours later, they learned he'd exited through the kitchen. The owner had thought it was odd, but then, Duncan was an odd sort of guy.

"Honest to God," Sanders said, "my officers swear up and down he didn't make the tail."

"Just felt like sneaking out the back door for old times' sake?"

"Maybe." Sanders must have heard how defensive he sounded. "Look, we're tearing apart the town as we speak. Best we can tell, his vehicle is still parked outside the diner, so he's on foot."

"Or he had a friend pick him up, or he helped himself to a car," Quincy argued in exasperation.

"We're considering all options. Give me some time."

"Time? What time? It's one fifteen, Sanders. There's been no word from the kidnapper. Do you know what that means? It means Rainie is probably dead."

Quincy threw down his cell phone, already cursing himself for not having pursued Duncan harder or located Andrew Bensen, or done any of the eight thousand other things they had considered but never developed because they just didn't have the time. From the very beginning, there had never been enough time.

His phone rang again. Kincaid's number. Quincy glanced at his watch. He wondered if this would be it. Kincaid calling with official news from Danicic or some other reporter. They had been late with the ransom drop, and their punishment would be . . .

He had set his shoulders and tightened his gut before he ever took the call. It didn't help him.

It was Kincaid, but he wasn't calling about Rainie.

He was calling about Kimberly.

Wednesday, 1:18 p.m. PST

"IT MAY NOT BE AS BAD AS IT SOUNDS," Kincaid was saying urgently. "Your guy Mac managed to rip through a chained gate with a county surveillance van, which opened up access for fire-and-rescue. They are at the scene now."

"I need to talk to her."

"She is receiving immediate medical attention. The second she is stabilized, I'm sure you can give her a call."

"She's my daughter!"

"Quincy . . ." For a moment, the phone was simply silent, Kincaid searching for words that didn't exist. "She did good today."

Quincy bowed his head, squeezed the bridge of his nose. "She's always done good," he whispered.

"The guy rigged the drop box somehow. Lined the upper level of the lighthouse with explosives maybe—we don't really know yet. The minute the weight of all that money hit the bottom of the box . . . She never really had a chance. If not for Shelly charging into the inferno . . ."

"Shelly? Sheriff Atkins?"

"Yeah, Shelly is who dragged her out—"

"I'm sorry," Quincy said, a little bewildered now. "Somehow I assumed it had been Mac."

"No, he was in the surveillance vehicle. It was Shelly who was backup. From what I understand, she went straight into the lighthouse and dragged Kimberly back out through the flames. Sounds like it was quite a feat."

"Is she okay?" Quincy asked sharply.

Silence.

"Kincaid?"

"They're medevacing her to St. Vincent's in Portland," Kincaid replied quietly. "It . . . it doesn't sound good."

And then it was Quincy's turn to say nothing at all. First Detective Grove, then Sheriff Atkins and his own daughter. And for what?

"Any word from Danicic?" he asked, although he already knew the answer.

Kincaid said, "None at all."

Wednesday, 1:20 p.m. PST

IN THE SPACE OF FIFTEEN MINUTES, Mac felt as if he'd aged fifty years. Kimberly's throat had been seared by the fire, swelling shut and blocking her airway. The medics had had to tube her at the scene, not something Mac ever wanted to see again.

At least the medics seemed pleased with her progress once they got her intubated. Her color improved; her chest rose and fell rhythmically. She appeared to be merely sleeping, if not for the singed ends of her hair, the black, sooty look of her clothes, the scent of seared meat.

She looked a lot better than Shelly Atkins.

The sheriff's reddened flesh had already started to blister by the time the EMTs had arrived, her arms and legs swelling up grotesquely. Shelly had had the foresight to tie her shirt around her face. Her shoulders and arms, however. . . .

Mac had only read of such things. Never seen them firsthand. The smell alone roiled the stomach, made him want to turn and retch. Mitchell had turned green immediately. But the deputy had held his own.

As they scrambled with the first-aid kit. As they tried to cover the most severe burns with pathetically few patches of sterile gauze. As Shelly went into shock from the pain and stress, right about the same time Mac had realized Kimberly had stopped breathing.

He had never been so happy to see an emergency vehicle in his life. Grateful to the point of humbleness. Desperate to the point of tears leaking from the corners of his eyes as he tried to report what happened, what Kimberly needed, what Shelly needed, until the EMTs simply shouldered him and Mitchell aside and went to work with ten times the competence and ten times the gear, and Mac and Mitchell stood there, dazed and confused, as they tried to tell each other it would be all right.

Kimberly disappeared into the ambulance just as the chopper arrived for Shelly. Mac and Mitchell helped load the sheriff into the chopper. Then it was gone and Kimberly was gone and they were both reporting in the best they could.

All in all, it probably took twenty minutes. The longest twenty minutes of Mac's life. And he didn't even get to go with Kimberly. He wasn't family. Just the man who loved her.

Which left him standing outside the battered surveillance vehicle, thinking of the ring. He wished she was wearing it now, maybe on a chain around her neck. If not for her, then for him, so he could see it, and know that she had said yes and told him that she loved him. That they had been happy, right before this.

He finally climbed into the van. Mitchell got in behind him. With nothing left to do, Mac crawled into the driver's seat, started putting the vehicle into gear.

And Mitchell said, "Holy shit! Look at this!"

45

RAINIE DIALED QUINCY'S CELL PHONE. She clutched the receiver against her cheek. She held her breath when she heard his phone ring, a strange fluttering in her stomach, like a schoolgirl calling for a date. Wondering if he would answer. Wondering what she would say.

"Quincy," he said, and for a moment, she was so overwhelmed, she couldn't speak.

"Who is this?" he asked sharply.

Rainie started to cry.

"Rainie? Oh my God, Rainie!" There was the sound of squealing. Then cursing. She had caught him driving. Now he was obviously wrestling his car to the side of the road.

"Don't hang up," he was yelling. "Don't hang up, just tell me where you are. I'm coming, I'm coming, I'm coming," and in his voice, she heard all the desperation she'd felt for the past few days.

She cried harder, huge, hoarse sobs that pounded against her ribs and exacerbated the pain in her head. The emotion felt as if it would tear her body apart, become the final blow to her battered frame. But she couldn't stop sobbing. She rocked back and forth, clutching the phone against her mouth and frantically gasping out the only words that mattered: "I . . . love . . . you."

"I love you, too. And I'm sorry, Rainie. I'm sorry for . . . everything." And then, even more urgently, "Rainie, where are you?"

"I don't know."

"Rainie . . ."

"I don't know! It's a house. With a basement. And it's flooded and we're cold and Dougie's not doing so well and I'm not doing so well. I need my medication. My head hurts so bad and I know I should've told you—"

"The Paxil. We found out. We'll bring it. Help me, Rainie. Help me find you."

"It's dark," she whispered. "So dark. The windows, the walls. I think he painted everything black."

"How long did it take you to get there? Do you remember the drive?"

"I don't know. I think he drugged me. A dirt road, I would guess. But I smelled the ocean. Maybe someplace near the water?"

"Do you know who took you, Rainie?"

"White light."

"He blinded you?"

"Yes. And now we live in the dark."

"Do you know where the man is right now?" Quincy asked crisply.

"I have no idea."

"All right. Stay on the line, Rainie. Don't you dare hang up. I'm going to find a way to trace this call."

But just then Rainie did hear a noise. The scrape of a key in a lock. Then the sound of a front door crashing open.

"Honey," the man called out cheerfully. "I'm home! And boy, did I bring home the bacon today!"

"Uh-oh," Rainie whispered.

And Quincy said, "Danicic?"

*   *   *

"I GOTTA GO," Rainie whispered to Quincy, and without waiting for a reply, tucked the phone under the bed, receiver lying next to it. She would have to trust Quincy to trace the call. She would have to trust herself to keep her and Dougie alive until he got there.

She heard sloshing, wet footsteps as the kidnapper splashed through the family room, headed for the kitchen. He was still whistling tunelessly, oblivious to their escape.

In the good-news department, Rainie had a knife and the element of surprise. In the bad-news department, he had a Taser and was much more physically fit. She had taken him on twice now and lost. Given her deteriorated condition, she saw no reason to expect that equation to change.

It would be a matter of wits then, not brute strength.

She crossed to Dougie, moving as quietly as she could. The boy remained unconscious but was no longer shivering so hard. She didn't know if that was a good sign or bad.

She got an awkward grip on his cocooned body. Staggered over to the closet. Deposited him inside.

Just in time to hear a cry of rage from the laundry room.

Not much time left.

Rainie closed the closet door and crossed immediately to the window. Please let her be lucky. Please, just this once, let God give her a break.

She found the old metal latch. She flipped it open. She grabbed the top of the wooden-framed window, and with all her might, she pushed up.

Nothing.

She tried again.

More splashing. Furious footsteps running through the kitchen.

"Come on," she begged in the darkened room. "Come on!"

But the old window wouldn't budge. After all these years, it was either swollen or painted shut.

Footsteps in the hall.

Rainie ducked behind the door. Got a grip on the knife.
Time was up.

Wednesday, 1:27 p.m. PST

MAC THREW THE VAN into gear and they went charging down the access road before either of them had their seat belts on. Mitchell had the radio and was furiously trying to raise Kincaid.

"We got a location. GPS has stabilized on a single set of coordinates. We're running them through the program now and should have an address in a matter of minutes."

Kincaid squawked on the other end in delight and surprise. He wanted the address the moment they got it. He was calling for SWAT, he was calling for backup, by God . . .

Then there was a short interruption as he took a call from his cell phone. Quincy. He had Rainie on the line. She was trapped in a house and the kidnapper had just returned home. Quincy would swear to God the man's voice had sounded just like Danicic's.

"We got an address," Mitchell yelled.

"Danicic's house?" Kincaid pressed.

No, it was Stanley's fishing cabin in Garibaldi.

"We're ten minutes away," Mac reported, and hit the gas.

"I'm already there," Quincy said as he went tearing back onto the dirt road and Candi grabbed the dash.

Wednesday, 1:29 p.m. PST

"COME OUT, COME OUT, wherever you are," the man called softly down the hall. "Whoo-hooo. Come on, Dougie. Say hi to your old friend."

Rainie held her breath, remaining in position with her back pressed against the wall. She could see a small sliver of hallway through the crack in the spine of the door. A foot came into view.

"I know you're still in here. The doors are locked from the outside, the windows screwed shut. It pays to be prepared when kidnapping a law enforcement officer and her little felonious friend."

Another step. She had a view of black jogging pants, now splotched with water.

"You're not getting out of this house, Rainie. Dougie and I have a deal. If you escape, I will have no choice but to fulfill my end of the bargain and burn Peggy Ann alive. You don't want Peggy Ann to suffer, do you, Dougie? You wouldn't want to kill her the way you killed your own mom?"

The man's whole profile appeared. Rainie inched back, feeling his eyes go to the gap between the back of the door and the wall.

"Come on, Dougie," he said impatiently. "Enough of this foolishness. Step forward, confess what you've done, and I'll forgive you. It's Rainie who's hurt you, remember? She lied to you. Pretended to be your friend." And then, as a new thought struck him, "Hey, Rainie, let's make this real simple: You come forward, and I'll pour you a drink."

The man stepped into the doorway, and Rainie slammed the door on his face. She heard a crack, followed by a sharp cry. "My nose, my nose, my nose! You bitch, you broke my nose! Do you know how that'll look on TV?"

Rainie fumbled with the knob, tried to find some sort of lock. Nothing. She dug her heels in, pressing her weight against the door as her eyes searched the room. She needed a chair to jam beneath the knob. Or a heavy piece of equipment.

She spied the bureau, but it was too cumbersome and distant. Then her whole body thudded as the man threw himself against the door, howling in outrage.

"You are not getting out of this house. Do you hear me? You are dead."

He slammed against the door a second time, and Rainie rocked back on her heels. She got her weight forward just in time for the third blow. Then, slowly but surely, he went to work, twisting the slippery knob beneath her hand.

She tried to get a better grip. Fumbled with the knife so that she could use two hands.

He was too strong. He'd eaten and slept and not spent two days trapped down in a frigid basement. He had more muscle. Less fatigue. He was going to win.

She started the countdown in her mind. When she got to ten, she sprang away from the door.

The man burst in, stumbling forward and promptly falling onto the bed.

And Rainie bolted out the door.

She was aware of many things at once. The weight of water, now nearly at her ankles, as she splashed down the hall. The sight of the front door, looming nearly fifty feet away as she struggled through the kitchen, into the living room, reaching, reaching, reaching.

The sound, maybe in her mind, of car doors slamming shut. The voice, maybe in her head, of Quincy saying *I love you.*

Then the louder, closer scream of outrage as the man came barreling after her.

She turned at the last minute. She saw a large black figure bearing down on her. Lucas Bensen appearing on the deck when she was only sixteen. Richard Mann waiting for her with a shotgun a decade after that. All the nightmares she had ever had, careening down the hall, racing toward her.

Rainie planted her feet. She brought up her knife. She prepared for her last stand.

The front door burst open. "Stop, police! Put down your weapon."

Rainie dropped to the floor.

Danicic lunged forward.

Quincy and Candi Rodriguez opened fire.

46

IN THE HOURS THAT FOLLOWED, things moved slower, evened out, tried to make sense.

Medics arrived. Pronounced Danicic dead. Found Dougie still alive, slowly warming back to consciousness within his cotton cocoon. They took the boy to the hospital. Tried to take Rainie, too. She refused to go. Just sat in the back of Quincy's car. She had his coat around her shoulders, four blankets on her lap, and a steaming cup of coffee in her hands.

She wanted to feel the warmth seeping back into her bones. She wanted to inhale the scent of Quincy's cologne in the collar of his coat. She wanted to realize herself, inch by inch, as she ventured back to the land of the living.

Quincy sat in the car with her as more investigators arrived and started to work the scene. The house, Rainie learned, belonged to Stanley Carpenter, his grandfather's old home that he kept for periodic rental income. He had been pleasantly surprised to receive an inquiry in August to rent the property for the entire winter. The renter claimed to be a writer from out of town, looking for someplace quiet to work on his next novel. Stanley had received a cashier's check for the entire winter's rent up front and hadn't thought about the house much since.

The house sat on a heavily wooded property, just a mile from the ocean. The nearest neighbor was five miles away to the west. Rainie and Dougie could've run all night and still never found a single person to help them.

A Sergeant Detective Kincaid appeared. He stared at Rainie so hard and so somberly, Rainie didn't know what to say. Then he nodded once to Quincy and walked away.

Next came a gorgeous Hispanic officer named Candi. She had been one of the first officers at the scene, arriving with Quincy. Now she took a seat on the gravel drive beside the open door on Rainie's side of the car and, with a surprising gentleness, drew out Rainie's account of the past few days. How Rainie had pulled her car over in the middle of the night. Been surprised by a blinding white light. Woken later to discover herself drugged and bound in the back of a vehicle. She'd done the best she could, working hard to protect herself and Dougie.

She had no idea who had taken her. When Candi used the name Danicic, Rainie was genuinely startled. "Isn't he a reporter for the *Sun?*"

No one had that answer for her. Candi disappeared and Lieutenant Mosley took her place. He wanted to personally make sure she was okay. Then he was off to make a statement to the press.

"It's about time we had some good news today," the officer said, which left Rainie, in the back of the car, staring at Quincy.

Alone at last, he started to speak. He told her of the ransom notes, of the task force team. He told her of Mac and Kimberly flying immediately from Atlanta to help.

And he told her, expressionlessly, for that was the tone he used for things that mattered most, how a detective, Alane Grove, had been murdered while working the case. Best they could tell, a local had spotted her with the ransom money and, unable to resist the temptation, had snatched her into the back of his truck and strangled her for the cash.

Then had come the disastrous ransom drop. Danicic had rigged the scene with explosives, resulting in serious injuries to the Bakersville sheriff, Shelly Atkins, as well as to Kimberly. Kimberly was now listed in stable condition, but would probably be in the hospital for days while they monitored her lungs and treated her burns. For Sheriff Atkins, the prognosis did not look so good.

"We should go to the hospital," Rainie said immediately.

"No."

Rainie frowned at him. "But Kimberly . . ."

"Is finally getting to see her fiancé. If we interrupt them now, they both will kill us."

"They're engaged?"

"That's what I'm told."

"Why didn't you say so in the beginning? Men!"

Quincy took her hand. "Yes, men. We like time alone with our women. Mac has his. Now I have mine. And you're not going anywhere."

Which made her both smile and cry, but also proved not to be entirely true. She went to get out of the car, passed out cold, and Quincy got to yell once more for the paramedics.

She woke up hours later, screaming hoarsely in the dark. The room was pitch black, the water closing over her head. She banged her hand against the metal bars of the hospital bed, searching desperately for leverage. Monitors screamed. The IV wires became tangled. Then Quincy was there, grabbing her hand, telling her she would be all right.

She drifted back off, only to wake up screaming once again.

"I don't think I'm quite sane," she told him.

"None of us are," he said, and climbed into the bed beside her.

In the morning, Rainie was discharged with orders to rest, eat, and drink. Her cracked ribs were tightly wrapped. Her left knee, with a torn ACL, was secured in a metal brace. She would need surgery to repair the injury, but not until she got her strength back. With Quincy by her side, she limped gamely to Kimberly's room.

The young agent had been moved from the intensive care unit to the general-population ward. She was on oxygen, fluids, and antibiotics to protect her damaged throat from infection; the doctors did not expect to release her for many more days.

But she seemed in good spirits, giving Rainie a fierce hug, flashing her engagement ring. She couldn't speak a word, and Mac was already saying that he preferred her this way.

He speculated out loud about a huge, four-hundred-person wedding, held out at his parents' orchard. They'd roast a pig, hire a country-western band, have a hoedown. Kimberly mimed strangling him with her bare hands. He expanded his vision to include a barefoot bride wearing petticoats and carrying a bouquet of peach blossoms.

Kimberly stopped trying to kill him and started nodding instead. That scared him back into silence, and Quincy and Rainie left the two lovebirds holding hands.

Dougie's room next. The boy was still asleep, Stanley and Laura Carpenter standing next to his bed. Stanley looked terrible, as if he hadn't slept in a month. Laura Carpenter looked just like Rainie remembered—as if she'd been trampled on all her life and didn't expect things to get any better soon.

"He's going to be okay," Stanley said hoarsely the minute Rainie walked into the room. "Doctors say he's in surprisingly good shape. Just needs to rest."

"Has he woken up?"

"A few times. He asked for you. We told him you were doing all right; he could see you soon. I mean, that is, if you don't mind. I would understand . . ."

"I'd appreciate that."

"A policewoman came," Laura volunteered. "That Rodriguez woman. Asked Dougie a few questions. He did okay. Didn't get too upset."

"He knew Danicic, didn't he?" Quincy asked gently. "He thought the man was his friend."

"Our fault," Stanley said immediately. "He approached us soon after we became foster parents for Dougie. Said he was doing an article on kids in the system. Wanted to profile Dougie as a happily-ever-after piece. You know, the kid who's been around but finally has a good home. He stopped by regularly for a bit. We didn't think much of it. We never saw the story appear, of course, but every time we asked, Mr. Danicic said his editor had held it back—it wasn't timely, just a general-interest piece, that kind of thing. He used to be a foster kid, too, you know."

"Danicic?"

"That's what he said. Parents died young, something like that." Stanley shrugged, looking abashed. "I kind of liked that he'd taken such an interest in Dougie. Thought he might be a good role model. He seemed . . . Well, guess you can't see 'em all coming. God knows we honestly believed him."

"Danicic used Dougie, didn't he?" Quincy prodded. "Found out information on you, on Rainie? Is that when you started paying him money?"

Stanley looked at Quincy in confusion. "I never paid anyone any money."

"Not even two thousand dollars a year?"

"Oh, that." Stanley flushed, darted a look at his wife, who scowled back at him. "When Dougie was born . . . Look, I didn't know how to handle the situation that well. But I was proud of Dougie. I wanted to do something for him. So I started a college fund."

Laura rolled her eyes. "A boy needs more than college, Stanley. A boy needs a father, someone who will take responsibility for him."

"I am."

"We are," she corrected him. Stanley flushed again, and in that moment, Rainie could see how a young high school girl would seem so attractive to him. Someone who looked up to the big, strong football coach. Hung on every word he said.

"Has he ever talked to you about the night his mother died?" she asked Stanley.

The man shook his head.

"He needs to talk about that more. On his own terms, in his own time. But he believes it's his fault that she's dead. And that guilt fuels a great deal of his rage. Toward himself and you."

"Why would he think it's his fault his mom got hit by a car?" Laura asked with a frown.

"Because apparently he left the apartment that night. He went looking for her, and in his own mind, she was killed chasing after him."

Stanley's eyes widened. "Was she?"

"Of course not," Rainie said impatiently. "She was killed by a drunk driver before Dougie ever left the apartment. Just check the police report."

"Poor kid," Stanley murmured, and for a change, his wife didn't argue.

"There's one thing I don't understand," Laura said at last. "Why'd the reporter do all this? Befriend Dougie. Kidnap you, kidnap him. I mean, what was the point?"

"Fame, fortune, and a finely baked apple pie," Quincy murmured, then he and Rainie left the room.

Quincy waited until they had checked out of the hospital, had gotten into his car. "How would a police report include the detail that Dougie's mother was killed *before* he left the apartment? From what you're saying, no one even knew that the boy had left the room."

Rainie shrugged. "You know that and I know that. But they don't know that."

He reached across the front seat, squeezed her hand. "You're a very nice woman, Rainie Conner."

"For a liar?" she asked lightly.

But he heard the catch in her voice as she turned away from him and started to cry.

Home was harder than Rainie thought it would be. She took her medication, roamed rooms that were supposed to make her feel comfortable, and waited to magically get on with her life. While she cycled back to a refrigerator that had been cleared of all booze. While she woke up in the middle of the night, sweat soaked and bursting with fear. While Quincy stared at her and told her he loved her, and she remembered again what it was like to be so loved and still feel all alone.

Kimberly was given a clean bill of health. She and Mac stayed the night, and for twenty-four hours the house was filled with talking and laughter once more. They played cards, talked shop.

Mac and Quincy stayed up late after the women had gone to bed. Mac had an idea for the Astoria case. Quincy thought it wasn't half bad.

And then, before Mac went to bed: "How is she doing?" he asked, head nodding toward the master bedroom.

"Terrible," Quincy said bluntly.

"Do you want us to stay?"

"It's not the kind of thing where another person can make a difference."

"That must really suck for you," Mac said quietly.

And Quincy said the first words that came to mind: "Thank you."

Quincy waited until the next morning, when Rainie had gone for a run, to give Abe Sanders a call. They had touched base briefly after Rainie had been recovered. Sanders's suspect, Duncan, had magically reappeared later that night, only to disappear twice more since then. They had stepped up surveillance but were still hampered by lack of evidence. They had no basis for a warrant, no plausible reason to even stop the man for a search. But Duncan was up to something. Sanders felt fairly strongly the man had a new target.

Quincy passed along Mac's idea. Sanders considered it. "Well, we've tried dumber tactics."

"Let me know."

Sanders hung up, Rainie returned from her run, and Quincy searched her things while she took her shower, looking for any sign of recently purchased beer.

This was what it meant to live with an alcoholic.

Then he went into his study and sat for a long time simply staring at the photo of his daughter.

He drove to Portland several times, visited Shelly in the hospital. She was the belle of the burn ward, entertaining nurses and patients alike with dirty jokes and stories of incompetent criminals. She seemed to look forward to Quincy's visits, particularly as he always brought her chamomile tea.

She'd show off her most recent skin grafts. He'd nod somberly and try not to turn too many shades of green.

Shelly's policing days were done. She was looking at one year at least of various surgeries and rehabilitative therapies. Her left foot was twisted. Her hip ruined. She was still one of the best-spirited people Quincy knew, and he often thought he felt more comfortable with her in the burn ward than with Rainie at home.

The fourth visit, she had good news.

"I'm going to Paris!" she announced.

"You're going to Paris?"

"Yep. It's always been a dream of mine. I mentioned it a few weeks ago when I did that crazy interview. Guess it twisted some soft sap's heart. The sheriff's department received an anonymous donation of an all-expense-paid trip to Paris for me. Soon as they get my burned ass out of this wheelchair, I'm on a plane."

"The Left Bank will never be the same," Quincy assured her.

"Sure you don't know anything about the donation?" she quizzed. "Absolutely not."

She'd always been the smart one. "Thanks," she said quietly. "I owe you one."

Which, Quincy thought, looking at the long ropes of scar tissue twisting down her arms, was the saddest thing he'd ever heard.

Kincaid stopped by later in the day. Forensic experts had been going through Danicic's computer. The reporter had truly enjoyed the written word. In addition to crafting long, rambling e-mails to himself, he had already started his autobiography, *Life of a Hero*.

From what they could piece together, Danicic had concocted his plan not for the ten grand, but to cast himself as the hero in a real-world drama that would catapult him to instant fame. Through his selfless efforts, he would single-handedly help police officers negotiate the rescue of two innocents. Tragically, the victims would already be dead by the time investigators arrived at the scene, cruelly locked up in the basement and left to drown. This would allow Danicic to

appear mournful as he embarked on his nationwide media tour, culti-
vating a new personality as an expert on violent crime who would
soon become a permanent fixture on the cable news channel of your
choice. Basically, Danicic hadn't been motivated by quick money.
He'd been looking for a whole new lifestyle.

In the attic of his house, they found box after box of books. Case
studies of violent offenders. Textbooks on police procedure and the
latest forensic techniques. Printout after printout cataloguing famous kidnappers and where they had gone wrong. In many ways, the
kidnappings had been his life's work.

As for why Rainie and Dougie, Kincaid still wasn't sure. Maybe
they were back to Quincy's point: A woman and small child seemed
less threatening targets. Maybe it was opportunity, because Danicic
had struck up a friendship with Dougie and quickly realized how
easily the troubled boy could be manipulated. Maybe because Rainie's
spouse and occupation would lend the case that much more media
interest.

They could only guess; Danicic wasn't alive to tell them.

One week later, Quincy had a phone call out of the blue. Special
Agent Glenda Rodman wanted to let him know that Andrew Bensen
had been located in Canada, where he was seeking special status as a
conscientious objector of the war. She thought Quincy would like to
know.

And two days after that, Quincy finally got the call he'd been
waiting for.

Afterward, he found Rainie outside, staring at the mountains,
sipping a cup of tea with hands that still had a tendency to tremble.

"Let's go," he said, and headed for the car without another word.

Quincy was the one known for his silence. But in all the years he had
spent with Rainie, he'd come to understand her quietness as well.
The way she could sink deep within herself, shoulders hunched, chin
down. The way she would stop making eye contact, her gaze going
more and more to the grand outdoors, as if she would like to disap-

pear into that towering bank of firs, as if she could will herself to cease to exist.

By the time they had arrived in Astoria, she was curled up in a ball, knees by her chin, arms around her legs for support. Her eyes had taken on a bruised, haunted look.

He wondered sometimes if this was how she had looked when her mother struck her. And sometimes, the image was too sharp in his head. A younger, more defenseless version of Rainie curled up on the floor. And an older, drunken version of Rainie, pounding away. Two sides of his wife. A past she was seeking to escape. A future she was desperate to avoid.

They arrived at the cemetery. Rainie knew where they were. She'd come here before with Quincy and, he would guess, many more times on her own.

She walked straight to the grave. Looked down at the stone angel. And then, as if unable to help herself, stroked the granite cheek with her fingers.

"Charles Duncan was arrested today," Quincy said. "I wanted you—and them—to hear the news from me. Duncan confessed to killing Aurora and Jennifer Johnson. Sanders has a signed statement, as well as a confession on tape."

"He confessed?" Rainie asked, sounding bewildered.

"It was Mac's idea. With all the forensic reports now done, Sanders and the experts have a fairly clear idea what happened that night. Order of events, details of the rampage. So Sanders picked Duncan up. Told him they had a new development: They'd found a receipt in Jennifer's papers for a nanny cam. Turns out there was a camera stuffed in a bear in Aurora's room."

"Really?"

"No. This was Mac's gambit. I believe it's called blindman's bluff. It's not the easiest thing in the world to pull off, but again, this is where the evidence reports made the difference. Sanders dangled a few details. Duncan cracked. Good thing, too. Sanders found a Peeping Tom report filed away—Duncan's taken to following and spying on a checkout girl who works at his neighborhood Safeway."

"Oh, thank God." Rainie's hand went over her mouth. "It's over. He did it. It's done."

"Yes," Quincy said, and in spite of himself, his own voice grew hoarse. "It's over, Rainie. It's done."

"I don't want to have nightmares anymore." Rainie started to cry. "I don't want to keep reaching out for a little girl I can't save. The world is cruel. Our jobs are hopeless. I don't even know how to love anymore. I just need to hate."

She collapsed in his arms, still weeping, still talking. Half of it made sense. Half of it didn't. He held her, let her get it all out. And then he stroked her back, playing with the short, feathery wisps of her hair. He willed his strength into her, as if one man's love could heal his wife. And he wasn't surprised when she stepped away from him and wiped her eyes.

They went back to the car in silence. They drove home in silence.

And later that night, when she said she was going to see Dougie, Quincy let her go, and prayed for his own sake, as much as anyone's, that she wasn't actually going to a bar.

Dougie's room had a new decoration: the yearbook photo of his mother, blown up to an eight-by-ten and nicely framed. Laura of all people had had it done. In return, Dougie had started using words such as "please" and "thank you" when the older woman was around. It gave Rainie a surreal feeling every time she came to the house.

He must have had a good day, because he was playing in his room with a new toy car when she drove up. Outside, it was pitch black with the threat of freezing rain, so even Dougie was in for the night.

Rainie sat cross-legged on the floor, while Dougie drove the car all over his mattress. "Vroooooom. Vroom. Vroom. Vroom."

"So, what did you think of Dr. Brown?" she asked.

The boy shrugged. "He's all right."

"Good toys?"

"Too many Spider-Men," Dougie said seriously. "What's so great about Spider-Man? Now Beetle-Man, that would be a hero. Vrooooom."

"Maybe you can help him see the light. When do you see him again?"

Dougie stopped driving his car, looked at her perplexed. "See him again? But I went!"

Rainie had to laugh. "It's therapy, Dougie. It takes more than one session to figure things out. You have to give it time."

"But it's *talking*."

"Well, maybe you'll come to like Spider-Man."

Dougie gave her a skeptical look and resumed racing his car around the mattress.

Driving home, Rainie thought of Dougie and smiled. The boy was doing okay in his own way. He still antagonized Stanley. He still talked longingly of fire. But he was now more and more inside the house, playing, relaxed, part of the family, whether he realized it or not. She liked that he had the picture of his mother back. She liked that from time to time, he would tell a story from when he was a baby. Some of his tales sounded like fantasy to her, but in his own way, Dougie was reclaiming his past. It seemed to settle him, give him a first glimpse of the future.

He had hope. Unlike so many other children. Unlike Aurora Johnson.

The thought bruised her, hurt her all over again even after all these months. And she could feel the darkness rear up in the back of her mind, feel the telltale heaviness settle in her shoulders. And her thoughts, of course, fed on the darkness from there.

All the children out there who never had a chance. The child predators on the prowl right now. What eight-year-old was being tucked into bed right now who would never live to see the morning? What young girl was about to be snatched from her own home while her parents slept unaware down the hall?

And Rainie was left hurting, aching, reeling from the sheer hopelessness of it all.

Think happy thoughts, she told herself, almost inanely. Yellow-flowered fields, smooth-flowing streams. Of course, none of it worked.

So she thought of Dougie again. She reminded herself of the satisfied look on his face as he raced his car around the room. And she thought of all the other children out there who were bruised and battered, but somehow—somehow—found a way to survive.

She wanted so much for those children. Fiercely. Passionately. For them to grow up. For them to be free. For them to break the cycle of abuse, to find the unconditional love every person was entitled to. For them to be happy.

And she wondered how she could want so much for them, yet so little for herself. She was one of those children, too. She was a survivor.

And then, for the first time in a long time, she knew what she had to do.

She drove up the gravel driveway. She strode through the stinging rain into her house. She found Quincy sitting in front of the fire, a tight look around his mouth.

"Dougie says hi," she volunteered loudly. "He earned himself a new toy car."

And that quickly Quincy's shoulders came down, the tension eased in his face. She knew what he'd been thinking, what he'd been worrying, and it brought tears to her eyes.

She stood there for the longest time. Minutes. Hours. She didn't know. She looked at her husband and she knew she was seeing him again for the very first time. The gray that was now more visible than the jet in his hair. The fresh lines creasing the corners of his mouth. The way he sat so stiffly in his own home before his own wife, as if he were steeling himself for what she'd do next.

She strode forward before the momentum left her. She dropped to her knees in front of him. She reached out her hand. She said the words that needed to be said: "My name is Rainie Conner, and I am an alcoholic."

The look on his face was so grave, it nearly broke her heart all over again. He took her hand. "My name is Pierce Quincy, and I'm the man who still loves you. Get off your knees, Rainie. You never have to bow before me."

"I'm so sorry—"

"Shhh."

"I want our life back."

"Me too."

"I don't know where to start."

"Tell me you still love me."

"Oh, Quincy, I love you."

"Tell me you won't drink again."

"I'll join a program. I'll do what needs to be done. I won't ever drink again."

He drew her up onto his lap, buried his face against the soft wisps of her newly grown hair. "Congratulations, Rainie. You've just taken the first step."

"It's a very long road," she whispered softly.

"I know, sweetheart. That's why I'm going to hold your hand all the way."

ACKNOWLEDGMENTS

My favorite part of writing any novel is easily the chance to pester a bunch of fine folks who have the misfortune to answer their phones, or in this case, their e-mail. Each book brings me a bunch of new research topics. And each research topic brings me a bunch of new experts to harass.

This time around, I'm deeply indebted to the patient men and women of the Oregon State Police. In particular, Lieutenant Gregg Hastings, for helping me understand the inner workings of the department, as well as life as a public information officer; Lieutenant Jason Bledsoe, who has a mind even more devious than my own and challenged my fictional crime over and over again until I finally got it right; and Lieutenant Beth Carpenter, Portland Crime Lab, who graciously permitted my husband and myself to tour the new, state-of-the-art facility, which at the time was decorated with the wackiest decorations I've ever seen (shotgun-shell Christmas tree lights, anyone? Or how about the latent-prints Christmas tree, which was decorated with fake thumbs?).

Of course, I also harassed my pharmacist of choice, Margaret Charpentier, for her yearly contribution to my fictional murder and mayhem. And I pressed my dear friend Dr. Greg Moffatt, whose brilliant insights into troubled minds allow my characters to reach new levels of twistedness.

As always, these people shared with me accurate and precise information. I, of course, abused, corrupted, and heavily fictionalized everything from there.

Finally, on a personal note, I never could have completed this novel without proper care and feeding from others: my husband, who once more provided his fine engineer's eye for detail and who volunteered to ply his wife with chocolate only to be thwarted by her decision to start the South Beach diet two weeks before deadline (what was I thinking?); Sarah Clemons, who takes such enormously good care of all of us; Brandi Ennis, for easing a working mom's guilt by loving my daughter nearly as much as I do; my daughter, who is addicted to the Care Bears soundtrack and thus taught her mother the valuable lesson of how to craft a crime novel with *Journey to Joke-a-Lot* running through her brain; and my two adorable dogs, who bark so much it is a miracle I can think anyway.

Last but not least, my heartiest congratulations to Alane Grove, winner of the second annual Kill a Friend, Maim a Buddy Sweepstakes at www.LisaGardner.com. Alane won the honor of naming the person of her choice to die in this novel. Alane nominated herself and more power to her. Hope you enjoy your role as a lucky stiff, Alane.

And to all those out there still waiting for their shot at literary immortality, never fear. I'm already working on the next novel, which means I need more experts to harass, and more contest winners to kill.

Happy reading, everyone.

Lisa Gardner

0'0L